SALVATION IN DEATH

J. D. ROBB

PIATKUS

PIATKUS

First published in Great Britain in 2008 by Piatkus Books
First published in the United States in 2008 by G.P. Putnam's Sons,
a division of Penguin Group (USA) Inc.

A CIP catalogue record for this book
is available from the British Library.

Hardback ISBN 978-0-7499-0888-1
Trade Paperback ISBN 978-0-7499-0890-4

Printed in the UK by CPI Mackays, Chatham ME5 8TD

Papers used by Piatkus Books are natural, renewable and recyclable
products made from wood grown in sustainable forests and certified
in accordance with the rules of the Forest Stewardship Council.

Mixed Sources
Product group from well-managed
forests and other controlled sources
www.fsc.org Cert no. SGS-COC-004081
© 1996 Forest Stewardship Council
FSC

Piatkus Books
An imprint of
Little, Brown Book Group
100 Victoria Embankment
London EC4Y 0DY

An Hachette Livre UK Company
www.hachettelivre.co.uk

www.littlebrown.co.uk

SALVATION IN DEATH

Titles by J. D. Robb

Beware of false prophets,
which come to you in sheep's clothing,
but inwardly they are ravening wolves.

—MATTHEW 7:15

The faith that looks through death.

—WILLIAM WORDSWORTH

 AT THE MASS OF THE DEAD, THE PRIEST PLACED
the wafer of unleavened bread and the cheap red wine
on the linen corporal draping the altar. Both paten and
chalice were silver. They had been gifts from the man inside the
flower-blanketed coffin resting at the foot of the two worn steps that
separated priest from congregation.

The dead had lived a hundred and sixteen years. Every day of those
years he'd lived as a faithful Catholic. His wife had predeceased him
by a mere ten months, and every day of those ten months he'd grieved
for her.

Now his children, grandchildren, great- and great-great-grandchil-
dren filled the pews of the old church in Spanish Harlem. Many lived
in the parish, and many more returned to it to mourn, and to pay their
respects. Both his surviving brothers attended the rite, as did cousins,
nieces, nephews, friends, and neighbors, so the living packed those
pews, the aisles, the vestibule to honor the dead with the ancient rite.

Hector Ortiz had been a good man, who'd led a good life. He'd died
peacefully in his bed, surrounded by photographs of his family and
the many images of Jesus, Mary, and his favorite saint, Lawrence. St.

Lawrence had been grilled to death for his faith and in the way of irony became the patron saint of restaurateurs.

Hector Ortiz would be missed; he would be mourned. But the long, good life and easy death lent a flavor of peace and acceptance to the Requiem Mass—and those who wept shed the tears more for themselves than for the departed. Their faith assured them, the priest thought, of Hector Ortiz's salvation. And as the priest performed the ritual, so familiar, he scanned the faces of the mourners. They looked to him to lead them in this final tribute.

Flowers and incense and the smoking wax of candles mixed and merged their scents in the air. A mystical fragrance. The smell of power and presence.

The priest solemnly bowed his head over the symbols of flesh and blood before washing his hands.

He'd known Hector, and in fact had heard his confession—his last, as it came to be—only a week before. So, Father Flores mused as the congregation rose, the penance had been the last Hector had been given.

Flores spoke to the congregation, and they to him, the familiar words of the Eucharistic Prayer, and through to the Sanctus.

"Holy, Holy, Holy Lord, God of power and might."

The words and those following were sung, as Hector had loved the music of the Mass. Those mixed voices rose up, tangling in the magically scented air. The congregation knelt—a baby's fretful wail, a dry cough, rustles, whispers—for the Consecration.

The priest waited for them to quiet, for the silence. For the moment.

Flores implored the power of the Holy Spirit to take the gifts of wafer and wine and transform them into the body and blood of Christ. And moved, according to the rite, as representative of the Son of God.

Power. Presence.

And while the crucified Christ looked down from behind the altar, Flores knew he himself held the power now. Held that presence.

"Take this, all of you, and eat it. For this is my body," Flores said, holding up the host, "which will be given up for you."

The bells rang; heads bowed.

"Take this and drink it. This is the cup of my blood." He raised the chalice. "The blood of a new and everlasting covenant. It will be shed for you and for others for the forgiveness of sin. Do this in memory of me."

"Christ has died, Christ has risen, Christ will come again."

They prayed, and the priest wished them peace. They wished peace to each other. And again, raising voices, they sang—*Lamb of God who takes away the sins of the world, have mercy on us*—while the priest broke the host, placed a piece of it in the chalice. The ministers moved forward, stopping short of the altar as the priest lifted the chalice to his lips.

He was dead the moment he drank the blood.

St. Cristóbal's Church in Spanish Harlem knelt quietly between a bodega and a pawnshop. It boasted a small gray steeple and was innocent of the graffiti that tagged its near-neighbors. Inside, it smelled of candles, flowers, and furniture polish. Like a nice, suburban home might smell.

At least it struck Lieutenant Eve Dallas that way as she strode down the aisle formed by rows of pews. In the front, a man in black shirt, black pants, and white collar sat with his head bowed and his hands folded.

She wasn't sure if he was praying or just waiting, but he wasn't her priority. She skirted around the glossy casket all but buried in red and white carnations. The dead guy inside wasn't her priority either.

She engaged her lapel recorder, but when she started to climb the two short steps to the platform that held the altar—and her priority—her partner plucked at Eve's arm.

"Um, I think we're supposed to, like, genuflect."

"I never genuflect in public."

"No, seriously." Peabody's dark eyes scanned the altar, the statues. "It's like holy ground up there or something."

"Funny, it looks like a dead guy up there to me."

Eve walked up. Behind her, Peabody gave a one-legged bounce before following.

"Victim has been identified as Miguel Flores, age thirty-five, Catholic priest," Eve began. "The body's been moved." She flicked a glance up to one of the uniforms securing the scene.

"Yes, sir. The victim collapsed during Mass, and there was an attempt to revive him while the nine-one-ones were placed. A couple of cops were on scene attending the funeral. That guy's funeral," he added with a chin point at the casket. "They moved people back, secured. They're waiting to talk to you."

Since she'd sealed her hands and feet before coming in, Eve crouched. "Get prints, TOD, and so on, for the record, Peabody. And for the record, the victim's cheeks are bright pink. Facial injuries, left temple and cheekbone, most likely incurred when he fell."

She glanced up, noted the silver chalice on the stained white linen. She rose, walked to the altar, sniffed at the cup. "He drink from this? What was he doing when he collapsed?"

"Taking Communion," the man in the front row answered before the uniform could speak.

Eve stepped to the other side of the altar. "Do you work here?"

"Yes. This is my church."

"Yours?"

"I'm the pastor." He rose, a compact and muscular man with sad, dark eyes. "Father López. Miguel was officiating the funeral mass, and was taking Communion. He drank, and he seemed, almost immediately, to seize. His body shook, and he gasped for air. And he collapsed." López spoke with the faintest of accents, an exotic sheen over rough wood. "There were doctors and other medicals here, and they tried to revive him, but it was too late. One said, one thought, it was poison. But I don't believe that could be."

"Why?"

López merely lifted his hands. "Who would poison a priest in such a way, and at such a time?"

"Where did the wine come from? In the cup?"

"We keep Communion wine locked in the tabernacle, in the ante-room."

"Who has access?"

"I do. Miguel, Martin—that is, Father Freeman—the Eucharistic ministers serving the Mass."

A lot of hands, Eve thought. Why bother with a lock? "Where are they?"

"Father Freeman is visiting family in Chicago, and expected back tomorrow. We have—had—three ministers today due to the large attendance at the Requiem Mass."

"I'll need their names."

"Surely you can't believe—"

"And this?"

He actually paled when Eve lifted the silver disk holding the wafer. "Please. Please. It's been consecrated."

"I'm sorry, now it's evidence. There's a piece missing. Did he eat it?"

"A small piece is broken off, put in the wine for the rite of fraction and commingling. He would have consumed it with the wine."

"Who put the wine in the cup and the . . ." What the hell did she call it? Cookie? Cracker?

"Host," López supplied. "He did. But I poured the wine into the receptacle and placed the host for Miguel before the Consecration. I did it personally as a sign of respect for Mr. Ortiz. Miguel officiated, at the family's request."

Eve cocked her head. "They didn't want the head guy? Didn't you say you were the head guy?"

"I'm pastor, yes. But I'm new. I've only had this parish for eight months, since Monsignor Cruz retired. Miguel's been here for more than five years, and married two of Mr. Ortiz's great-grandchildren, officiated at the Requiem for Mrs. Ortiz about a year ago. Baptized—"

"Just one minute, please."

Eve turned back to Peabody.

"Sorry to interrupt, Father. ID match," Peabody told Eve. "TOD jibes. Drink, seize, collapse, die, red cheeks. Cyanide?"

"Educated guess. We'll let Morris confirm. Bag the cup, the cookie. Pick one of the cop witnesses and get a statement. I'll take the other after I have López show me the source of the wine and the other thing."

"Should we release the other dead guy?"

Eve frowned at the casket. "He's waited this long. He can wait a little longer." She turned back to López. "I need to see where you keep the . . ." Refreshments? "The wine and the hosts."

With a nod, López gestured. He walked up, turned away from the altar to lead Eve through a doorway. Inside cabinets lined one wall, and on a table stood a tall box, deeply carved with a cross. López took keys from the pocket of his pants and unlocked the door of the box.

"This is the tabernacle," he explained. "It holds unconsecrated hosts and wine. We keep a larger supply in the first cabinet there, also locked."

The wood gleamed with polish, she noted, and would hold prints. The lock was a simple key into a slot. "This decanter here is where you took the wine for the cup?"

"Yes. I poured it from here to the vessel, and took the host. I brought them to Miguel at the beginning of the Eucharistic Liturgy."

Purplish liquid filled the clear decanter to about the halfway point. "Did the substances leave your hands at any time before that, or were they unattended?"

"No. I prepared them, kept them with me at all times. To do otherwise would be disrespectful."

"I have to take this into evidence."

"I understand. But the tabernacle can't leave the church. Please, if you need to examine it, can it be done here? I'm sorry," he added, "I never asked your name."

"Lieutenant Dallas."

"You're not Catholic."

"What gave you the first clue?"

He smiled a little, but the misery never left his eyes. "I understand you're unfamiliar with the traditions and rites of the church, and some may seem strange to you. You believe someone tampered with the wine or the host."

Eve kept both her face and her voice neutral. "I don't believe anything yet."

"If this is so, then someone used the blood and body of Christ to kill. And I delivered them to Miguel. I put them in his hands." Beneath the misery in his eyes, Eve saw the banked embers of anger. "God will judge them, Lieutenant. But I believe in earthly laws as well as God's laws. I'll do whatever I can to help you in your work."

"What kind of priest was Flores?"

"A good one. Compassionate, dedicated, ah, energetic, I'd say. He enjoyed working with young people, and was particularly good at it."

"Any trouble recently? Depression, stress?"

"No. No. I would have known, I would have seen it. We live together, the three of us, in the rectory behind the church." He gestured vaguely, as if his mind was crowded with a dozen other thoughts. "We eat together almost daily, talk, argue, pray. I would've seen if he'd been troubled. If you think he might have taken his own life, he wouldn't. And he would never do so in such a way."

"Any trouble with anyone? Someone with a grudge, or a problem with him—professionally or otherwise?"

"Not that he mentioned, and as I said, we talked daily."

"Who knew he'd be doing the funeral today?"

"Everyone. Hector Ortiz was a fixture in the parish. A well-loved and well-respected man. Everyone knew about the funeral mass, and that Miguel was officiating."

As she spoke, she crossed to a door, opened it. The May sunlight beamed through the exit. The door had a lock, she noted, nearly as simple as the one on the wooden box.

Easy in, easy out.

"Were there any masses earlier today?" she asked López.

"The six o'clock weekday Mass. I officiated."

"And the wine, the host came from the same supply as the funeral mass?"

"Yes."

"Who got it for you?"

"Miguel. It's a small service, usually no more than a dozen people, maybe two. Today, we expected less as the funeral would be so well attended."

Come in, Eve mused, attend Mass. Go back, poison the wine. Walk away. "About how many did you bring in this morning?"

"At morning Mass? Ah . . . Eight or nine." He paused a moment, and Eve imagined him going back, counting heads. "Yes, nine."

"I'll need that list, too. Any unfamiliar faces in that one?"

"No. I knew everyone who attended. A small group, as I said."

"And just you and Flores. Nobody assisting."

"Not for the six o'clock. We don't generally use a minister for the morning weekday service, except during Lent."

"Okay. I'd like you to write down, as best you can remember, the vic's—Flores's movements and activities this morning, and the times."

"I'll do that right away."

"I'm going to need to secure this room as part of the crime scene."

"Oh." Distress covered his face. "Do you know how long?"

"I don't." She knew she was brusque, but something about all the . . . holiness made her twitchy. "If you'd give me your keys it would be simpler. How many sets are there?"

"These, and a set at the rectory. I'll need my key to the rectory." He took a single key off the chain, gave Eve the rest.

"Thanks. Who was Ortiz and how did he die?"

"Mr. Ortiz?" A smile, warmer, moved into his eyes. "A fixture of the community, and this parish, as I said. He owned a family restaurant a few blocks from here. Abuelo's. Ran it, I'm told, with his wife up until about ten years ago, when one of his sons and his granddaughter took over. He was a hundred and sixteen, and died quietly—and I hope painlessly—in his sleep. He was a good man, and well loved. I believe he's already in God's hands."

He touched the cross he wore, a light brush of fingers. "His family is understandably distressed by what happened this morning. If I could contact them, and we could complete the Requiem Mass and hold the Commitment. Not here," López said before Eve could speak. "I'd make arrangements, but they need to bury their father, grandfather, their friend. They need to complete the ritual. And Mr. Ortiz should be respected."

She understood duty to the dead. "I need to speak to someone else now. I'll try to move this along. And I'll need you to wait for me at the rectory."

"I'm a suspect." The idea didn't appear to shake him or surprise him. "I gave Miguel the weapon that may have killed him."

"That's right. And right at the moment, pretty much anyone who walked into the church and gained access to this room is a suspect. Hector Ortiz gets a pass, but that's about it."

He smiled again at that, just a little. "You can probably eliminate the infants and toddlers, of which there were scores."

"I don't know. Toddlers are pretty suspicious. We'll need to take a look at Flores's room at the rectory. As soon as I can, I'll see about moving Mr. Ortiz from the scene."

"Thank you. I'll wait at home."

Eve led him out, locked the door, then told the closest uniform to bring in the second police witness.

While she waited, she circled Flores again. Good-looking guy, she mused. About six feet—hard to tell body type with the funny robes, but she'd scanned his official ID. That had him weighing in at a trim one-sixty.

He had even features, a lot of dark hair with a few glints of silver running through it. Smoother, she thought, than López. Leaner, younger.

She supposed priests came in all types and sizes, just like regular people.

Priests weren't supposed to have sex. She'd have to ask somebody the root of that rule, if she found it could apply. Some priests also ignored the rule, and got their jollies, just like regular people. Maybe Flores didn't care for celibacy.

Who would?

Maybe he'd diddled the wrong person. Angry lover or angry spouse of lover. Worked particularly well with young people, she mused. Maybe he liked to poke into the underage well. Vengeful parent.

Or—

"Lieutenant Dallas?"

Eve turned to see a hot number in sedate black. Petite would be the word, Eve supposed, as the woman hit maybe five-five in her black dress heels. Her hair was jet black as well, sleeked back into a quiet knot. She had huge, almond-shaped eyes in a kind of simmering green.

"Graciela Ortiz. Officer Ortiz," she added, almost as an afterthought.

"Officer." Eve came down from the altar. "You're related to Mr. Ortiz."

"Poppy. My great-grandfather."

"I'm sorry for your loss."

"Thank you. He lived so well, and long. Now he's with the angels. But Father Flores . . ."

"You don't think he's with the angels?"

"I hope he is. But he didn't live long, or die peacefully in his bed. I've never seen death like that." She took a breath, and there was a shudder in it. "I should have acted more quickly, to preserve the scene. My cousin and I—Matthew is with Illegals—should have acted sooner. But I was closer. Matt was in the back of the church. I thought—we all thought—Father had had some sort of attack. Dr. Pasquale and my uncle, who is also a doctor, tried to help him. It happened very quickly. In minutes. Three, four, no more than that. So the body was moved, and the scene compromised. I'm sorry."

"Tell me what happened."

Graciela relayed the events, set the scene as López had.

"Did you know Flores?"

"Yes, a little. He married my brother. I mean to say he officiated at the marriage of my brother. Father Flores also gave time to the youth center. I do the same, when I can, so I knew him from there."

"Impressions?"

"Outgoing, interested. He seemed to relate to the street kids. I thought he'd probably been there and done that in his time."

"Did he show any interest in any particular kid or kids?"

"Not that I noticed. But I didn't run into him there often."

"He ever move on you?"

"Move . . . No." Graciela seemed shocked, then thoughtful. "No, no moves, no sense he considered it. And I never heard of him breaking that particular vow."

"Would you have?"

"I don't know, but my family—and there are a lot of them—is very involved in the church and this is our home parish. If he was going to move on someone, odds are the someone would've been related or connected to the Ortiz family. And family gossip runs pretty hot and strong. My aunt Rosa housekeeps for the rectory and not much gets by her."

"Rosa Ortiz."

"O'Donnell." Graciela smiled. "We diversify. Is it homicide, Lieutenant?"

"Right now it's suspicious death. You might talk to family members, get their impressions."

"Nobody's going to be talking about much else for days," Graciela commented. "I'll see what I can find out from those who knew him better than I did."

"Okay. I'm going to have your great-grandfather released from the scene. You and your cousin should take that detail as soon as we're clear."

"We appreciate that."

"Where's your house?"

"I'm with the two-two-three, here in East Harlem."

"How long on the job?"

"Almost two years. I thought I wanted to be a lawyer, changed my mind."

Probably change it again, Eve thought. She just didn't see a cop in those sizzling green eyes. "I'm going to get my partner, and we'll clear the casket. If anything regarding Flores occurs to you, you can reach me at—"

"Cop Central," Graciela finished. "I know."

As Graciela clicked out on her funeral heels, Eve took one more scan of the crime scene. A lot of death for one small church, she mused. One in the coffin, one at the altar, and the one looking down on both from the really big cross.

One dies in his sleep after a long life, one dies fast—and the other gets spikes hammered through his hands and feet so they can hang him on a cross of wood.

God, priest, and the faithful, she thought. To her way of thinking, God got the worst deal of the three.

I can't decide," Peabody said as they walked around to the rectory, "if the statues and candles and colored glass are really pretty or really creepy."

"Statues are too much like dolls, and dolls are creepy. You keep expecting them to blink. And the ones that smile, like this?" Eve kept her lips tight together as she curved them up. "You know they've got teeth in there. Big, sharp, shiny teeth."

"I didn't. But now I've got to worry about it."

The small, unimposing building that housed the rectory had flowers in a pair of window boxes—and, Eve noted, minimum security. A standard lock, those flower-decked windows open to the spring air, and no palm plate, no security cameras.

She knocked, then stood on long legs in simple trousers, on feet planted in worn boots. The pale gray blazer she'd shrugged on that morning covered her weapon harness. The frisky May breeze fluttered through her short, brown hair. Like her legs, her eyes were long, a whiskey brown. They didn't sizzle like Graciela's—and were all cop.

The woman who answered had an explosion of dark curls tipped with gold around a pretty face. Her red-rimmed eyes scanned Eve, then Peabody. "I'm sorry, Father López is unable to take visitors today."

"Lieutenant Dallas, NYPSD." Eve drew out her badge. "And Detective Peabody."

"Yes, of course. Forgive me. Father said to expect you. Please come in."

She stepped back. She wore a red carnation on the lapel of her black mourning suit—and both over a beautifully curved body. "It's a terrible day for the parish, for my family. I'm Rosa O'Donnell. My grandfather . . . It was his funeral mass, you see. Father is in his office. He gave me this for you." She held out an envelope. "You asked him to write out what Father Flores did today."

"Yeah, thanks."

"I'm to let Father know if you need to see him."

"No need at this time. You can tell him that we've released Mr. Ortiz. My partner and I need to see Father Flores's room."

"I'll show you upstairs."

"You cook for the rectory," Eve began as they moved from the tiny foyer to the stairs.

"Yes, and clean. Some of this, some of that. Three men, even priests, need someone to pick up after them."

The stairs rose straight to a narrow hallway. The walls were white and adorned here and there with crucifixes or pictures of people in robes looking benign or—to Eve's eye—sorrowful. Occasionally annoyed.

"You knew Father Flores," Eve prompted.

"Very well, I think. You cook and clean for a man, you come to know who he is."

"Who was he?"

Rosa paused outside a door, sighed. "A man of faith, and humor. He enjoyed sports, watching them, playing them. He had . . . energy," she decided. "And put much of that into the youth center."

"How did he get along with his housemates? The other priests," Eve explained when Rosa looked blank.

"Very well. There was respect between him and Father López, and I'd say they were friendly. Easy with each other, if you understand."

"Yeah."

"He was friendlier, well, closer, you know, with Father Freeman— they had more in common, I'd say, outside the church. Sports. He and Father Freeman would argue about sports, as men do. Go to games together. They ran together most mornings, and often played ball at the center."

Rosa sighed again. "Father López is contacting Father Freeman now, to tell him. It's very hard."

"And Flores's family?"

"He had none. He would say the church was his family. I believe his parents died when he was a boy." She opened the door. "He never had calls or letters from family, as Fathers López and Freeman often do."

"What about other calls, other letters?"

"I'm sorry?"

"Who was he connected to? Friends, teachers, old schoolmates."

"I . . . I don't know." Her brows drew together. "He had many friends in the parish, of course, but if you mean from outside, or from before, I don't know."

"Did you notice anything off—in his mood, his routine, recently?"

"No, nothing." Rosa shook her head. "I came in to fix breakfast for him and Father López this morning, before the funeral. He was very kind."

"What time did you get here?"

"Ah . . . about six-thirty, a few minutes later than that."

"Was anyone else here?"

"No. I let myself in. I have a key, though. As usual, Father López forgot to lock up. The fathers came back from Mass shortly after, and I gave them breakfast. We all talked about the service, then Father Flores went into the office to work on his sermon."

She pressed her fingertips to her lips. "How could this have happened?"

"We'll find out. Thank you," Eve said by way of dismissal, then stepped into the room.

It held a narrow bed, a small dresser and mirror, a night table, a desk. No house 'link, she noted, no computer. The bed looked to be neatly made, and over its head a picture of Christ on the cross hung next to a crucifix. Seemed like overkill to Eve.

There were no personal photographs in evidence, no loose credits scattered over the dresser. She saw a Bible, a rosary of black and silver and a lamp on the bedside table, a comb and a pocket 'link on the dresser.

"That explains why he didn't have a 'link on him," Peabody commented. "I guess they don't take them when they do a service." As she turned, the sassy little flip at the ends of her dark hair bounced. "Well, I guess this won't take long, considering he didn't have a whole lot."

"Take a look in the other rooms. Just a scan from the doorway. See if they're the same as this."

As Peabody went out, Eve opened a dresser drawer with her sealed hand. White boxers, white undershirts, white socks, black socks. She pawed through, found nothing else. Another drawer held T-shirts. White, black, gray—some with team logos emblazoned on the front.

"They've got more stuff," Peabody announced. "Photographs, man junk."

"Define 'man junk,'" Eve said as she drew out the bottom drawer.

"Golf ball on a display tee, pile of discs, a pair of boxing gloves, that kind of thing."

"Check the closet here." Eve drew the bottom drawer all the way out, checked the bottom, the back.

"Priest's suits, two sets with pants, and one of those dresses. A pair of black shoes that look worn, two pairs of high-tops, one pair looks shot. Shelf . . ." Peabody paused as she rummaged. "Cooler-weather gear. Two sweaters, two sweatshirts, one hooded sweat jacket—Knicks."

After checking all the drawers, backs, bottoms, sides, Eve pulled the small dresser out from the wall, checked the back of the mirror.

With Peabody, she moved to the desk. It held a date book, a few memo cubes, a short stack of brochures on the youth center, the Yankees' schedule, and another for the Knicks.

Eve checked the last entries in the date book. "Vigil for Ortiz at the funeral home last night. Yankees game Wednesday. Let's see if anyone went with him. He's scheduled for FHC—need to find out what that is—for a week from this coming Sunday at two. Got a few games and sessions at the youth center on here. Pre-C counseling. Need to get the meaning of that. Two of those—last Monday and Tuesday. Names of whoever he was counseling in here. We'll run them down. The funeral's on here. A teaching gig at St. Cristóbal's Friday, a baptism a week from Saturday. All priestly, except for the Yankees."

She bagged the date book. "Take a look at the 'link," she told Peabody, then began on the little night table.

She flipped through the Bible, found a few small pictures of saints. In Hebrews, she read an underscored line: <u>And thus, having had long patience, he got the promise.</u> And in Proverbs: <u>With me are riches and honor, enduring wealth and prosperity.</u>

Interesting. She bagged the Bible for evidence. Inside the drawer were a couple more community flyers, and a mini-game player. She found a silver medal taped behind the drawer. "Well, well. Why does a priest tape a religious medal behind a drawer?"

Peabody stopped her own search. "What kind of medal?"

"It's a woman, with the robe thing, hands folded, and it looks like she's standing on a pillow or something with a little kid holding her up."

"It's probably the Virgin Mary, and the Baby Jesus. And, yeah, weird place for a medal."

Carefully, Eve peeled the tape away, turned the freed medal over. *"Lino, May La Virgen de Guadalupe watch over you—Mama.* Dated May 12, 2031."

"Rosa said she thought his parents died when he was a boy—and he'd have been about six at this date," Peabody commented. "Maybe Lino's a nickname, a term of affection in Spanish?"

"Maybe. Why tape it to the back of a drawer instead of wearing it, or keeping it *in* a drawer? Are priests allowed to wear jewelry?" Eve wondered.

"Probably not big honking rings or chains, but I've seen them wearing crosses and medals and stuff." To get a closer look, Peabody squatted down. "Like that sort of thing."

"Yeah. Yeah. So why is this hidden? You hide something so nobody sees it, and you hide it close when you want to look at it in private now and then. This mattered to him, whether it was his, a friend's or relative's, or he picked it up in a secondhand store, it mattered. It looks like silver," she murmured, "but it's not tarnished. You have to polish silver to keep it shiny."

After another study, she bagged it. "Maybe we can trace it. What about the 'link?"

"Logged transmissions, in and out from Roberto Ortiz—that would be the late Mr. Ortiz's oldest surviving son. A couple to and from the youth center, and the oldest last week to Father Freeman."

"Okay, we'll have a look and listen. Let's call the sweepers in for a pass, then I want this room sealed."

She thought of the two underlined passages, and wondered what riches and honor Flores waited for.

2 IT WAS A LONG WAY FROM SPANISH HARLEM TO the Lower West Side and Cop Central. Long enough to have Peabody do the initial run on Miguel Flores and recite the salients while Eve maneuvered through traffic for a large chunk of Manhattan's length and breadth.

"Miguel Ernesto Flores," Peabody read from her PPC. "Born February six, 2025 in Taos, New Mexico. Parents, Anna Santiago Flores and Constantine Flores, were both killed when their bodega was robbed, summer of 2027. The mother was seven months pregnant."

"They get them?"

"They got them. Two guys, barely eighteen, and both serving life sentences. No parole. Flores was put in the system."

"The inscription was dated '31—and his mother had been dead four years by then. So who's Mama?"

"Maybe foster mother?"

"Maybe."

"Early education, State, but private Catholic high school and college."

"Private?" Eve interrupted, and snarled when a Rapid Cab cut her off. "Takes dough."

"Yeah. Maybe a scholarship? I'll check on that. He entered the seminary straight out of college, spent several years working and living in Mexico. Held dual citizenship. Transferred to St. Cristóbal's November of 2054. Huh, there's a lag here, though. His last position was at a mission in Jarez until 2053, June."

"So where was Flores for over a year, and what was he doing? He had to have a boss—like López. A pastor or whatever. Let's find out. Any youthful high jinks of the criminal variety?"

"Nothing here, and no flag indicating a sealed record."

"Private Catholic education's gotta be pricey. Unless there was a scholarship, and it covered most of the ground, how did he afford it? Where'd the money come from? We're going to need to peel some layers."

Eve frowned as she skirted around a maxibus. "The vic had a wrist unit on him—cheap one—and just under forty dollars in his wallet. Who pays these guys? Do they get paid? He had a standard ID, no credit or debit cards, no driver's license. A silver cross."

"Maybe the Pope pays them." Peabody's square face turned thoughtful. "Not directly, but he's the head guy, so maybe it comes from him. I mean they must get paid something. They've got to live—buy food, clothes, pay for transportation."

"Under forty on him, no money in his room. We'll check bank accounts." Eve tapped her fingers on the wheel. "Let's go by the morgue, see if Morris has established COD."

"If it was poison, it doesn't feel like self-termination. Plus," Peabody added, "I know Catholics are way against that, so it doesn't skew right for a priest to off himself."

"Pretty harsh to do it in front of a church full of people at a funeral service," Eve commented. "Or . . . ironic. But no, it doesn't play. Wit statements are that he was moving right through the service, SOP. If you're going to knock back some wine laced with poison, even if you're dead—ha-ha—set on it, you'd show some nerves, some hesitation. A little moment of: *Okay, here goes nothing.* Whatever."

"Maybe it wasn't target specific. Maybe whoever laced the wine just wanted to kill a priest. Like a religious vendetta."

"It wasn't in the wine for the morning service, and it was in—if it was—for the funeral. Maybe somebody snuck in, broke into the box-thing, laced the wine without knowing who'd be taking the first drink. But my vote is Flores was the target."

But she'd hold her report in reserve until she talked to Morris.

Into the chilly, artificial air, death slipped and snuck—the god of all thieves. No amount of filtering, sealing or cleaning could quite banish the insidiously sweet and human smell. Used to it, Eve wound through the white, harshly lit corridors of the morgue—thought fleetingly about hitting Vending for a tube of Pepsi to kick up the caffeine level—and pushed open one of the doors of an autopsy room.

It surprised her to be immediately assaulted with the romantic perfume of roses. They stood, red as fresh blood, on one of the rolling tables used to hold the nasty tools of the trade performed there. Eve studied the small forest of them, and wondered if the naked corpse behind them appreciated their elegance.

Elegant, too, was the man who hummed along with the choral music drifting through the rose- and death-scented air. Chief Medical Examiner Morris wore black today, but there was nothing ghoulish or funereal in the sharply tailored suit. The lightning-bolt blue T-shirt—probably silk—kicked it up a notch, Eve supposed. He'd pinned one of the red rosebuds to his lapel, and wound red and blue cords through his long black ponytail.

The clear, protective cloak didn't diminish the style, and when he turned his exotic eyes to her and smiled, Eve had to admit that kicked it up another notch.

"Nice flowers," she commented.

"Aren't they? A token from a friend. I decided to bring them in. They class up the place, don't you think?"

"They're mag." Peabody walked over, took a sniff. "Man, there are like two dozen easy. Some token."

It was an obvious ploy for more information, but Morris only continued to smile. "She's a very good friend. It occurred to me I should have had flowers in here before. It's traditional, after all, to bring them to the dead."

"Why is that?" Eve wondered.

"I believe they're symbolic of a resurrection, a kind of rebirth. Which," Morris continued, "your current interest should appreciate. Along with, I hope, the music. Mozart's 'Requiem.'"

"Okay." Eve looked over at Flores and doubted he appreciated much of anything, being dead, on a slab, and currently opened by one of Morris's delicate and effective Y cuts. "How'd he get here?"

"The road is long and winding. But his ended with a dose of poison with his wine and wafer."

"Cyanide."

Morris inclined his head. "Potassium cyanide to be precise. It dissolves easily in liquid, and the dose was lethal. Enough, in fact, to have felled a rhino. I haven't finished with him yet, but other than being dead, he appears to be a very healthy corpse. Fit as a fiddle, if not ready for love."

"Sorry?"

"A play on an old song. The injuries were a result of his fall. He had bran cereal, rehydrated bananas, yogurt, and soy coffee about three hours before death. Sometime around puberty he suffered a broken radius, left arm—it healed well. I'm assuming he trained—let's say religiously, because we can—and played sports."

"That fits."

"And may explain some of the wear on the joints, but doesn't satisfy me regarding the scarring."

"What scarring?"

Morris crooked his finger, then offered Eve a pair of microgoggles. "Let's start here." He adjusted his scope so Peabody could observe on the comp screen, then bent over Flores with Eve. "Here, between the fourth and fifth ribs. Very faint, and I believe someone made an attempt with Nu Skin or something similar to reduce the scarring. Nu Skin won't help on the rib itself, which still carries its own scar. See here."

Peabody made a gurgling sound behind them as Morris exposed the rib cage.

Eve studied the rib through the goggles. "Knife wound."

"Yes, indeed. And a second one here." He indicated the faint scar on the right upper pectoral. "I'll run tests, but my extremely expert opinion puts the first wound at no less than five, no more than ten years old, the second between ten and fifteen. And here, on the left forearm. Again, this would be barely visible to the naked eye. A good job."

"That's not a wound," Eve muttered as she scanned the faint pattern on the skin. "Tat removal."

"My prize student." Morris gave her a quick pat on the back. "I'll send a copy of the enhanced visual to the lab. They should be able to re-create the image your priest had on his arm. Now for something really interesting. He's had face work."

Eve's head came up, her magnified eyes meeting Morris's. "What kind?"

"A full compliment, I think. But again, I haven't finished. I can tell you it was a first-class job, and first-class face work is very pricey. One would think out of the range of a servant of God."

"Yeah, you would." Slowly, she pulled off the goggles. "How long ago did he have the work?"

"I'll need to work my magic to refine that, but again, about the same time he had the tattoo removed."

"A priest with tats who gets into knife fights." Eve set the goggles under a forest of red roses. "Who comes here going on six years ago with a new face. Yeah, it's pretty interesting."

"Who has jobs like us, Dallas?" Morris grinned at her. "Aren't we the lucky ones?"

"Well, we're a hell of a lot luckier than Father Dead here."

You gotta wonder who," Peabody said the minute they walked back down the white tunnel.

"Of course I wonder who. I get paid to wonder who."

"No, well, yeah. But I meant about the roses. Who'd send Morris all those roses, and why?"

"Jesus, Peabody, the why's obvious. I can't believe I made you detective. The why is: Thanks for banging me into another plane of existence."

"It doesn't have to be that," Peabody countered, just a little miffed. "It could be a thank-you for helping her move into a new apartment."

"If you get a token for lifting furniture, it's going to be a six-pack of brew. A big-ass bunch of red roses is for sex. Really good sex and lots of it."

"I give McNab really good sex, and lots of it, and *I* don't get big-ass bunches of red roses."

"You cohab. Puts sex on the to-do list."

"I bet Roarke buys you flowers," Peabody muttered.

Did he? There were always flowers all over the place in the house. Were they for her? Was she supposed to acknowledge them? Reciprocate? Jesus, why was she thinking about this?

"And the who is probably the Southern belle cop with the big rack he's been hitting on for the last while. Now, since that mystery's solved, maybe we could spend a couple minutes contemplating the dead guy we just left."

"Detective Coltraine? She hasn't even been in New York a year. How come she gets Morris?"

"Peabody."

"I'm just saying, it seems to me if somebody's going to get Morris, it should be one of us. Not *us* us, because, taken." Peabody's brown eyes sizzled with the insult. "But one of us that's been around more than five damn minutes."

"If you can't bang him, why do you care who does?"

"You do, too," Peabody muttered as she dropped into the passenger seat. "You know you do."

Maybe a little, but she didn't have to admit it. "Could I interest you in a dead priest?"

"Okay, okay." Peabody heaved a huge and sorrowful sigh. "Okay. The tattoo thing isn't necessarily a big deal. People get tats then change their mind all the time. Which is why temps are smarter. He could've gotten it when he was younger, then decided it wasn't, I don't know, dignified enough for his job."

"Knife wounds."

"Sometimes priests and religious types go into dicey areas, and sticky situations. He could've been stabbed trying to help someone. And the older one could've happened when he was a teenager, before the holiness."

"I'll give you both of those," Eve said as she drove to Cop Central. "Face work."

"That's tougher. But maybe he was injured. A vehicular accident, say, and his face got messed up. Maybe the church or a member thereof paid for the reconstruction."

"We'll check the medicals and see."

"But you don't buy it."

"Peabody, I wouldn't take it for free."

In her office at Cop Central, Eve wrote up her initial report, opened the murder book. She set up a board, then fixed a copy of Flores's ID photo in the center. And spent the next few minutes just staring at it.

No family. No criminal. No valuable earthly possessions.

Public poisoning, she mused, could be seen as a kind of execution. The religious symbolism couldn't be overlooked. Too obviously deliberate. A religious execution?

She sat again, started a time line from witness statements and López's memo.

0500—gets up. Morning prayer and meditation. (In room.)

0515—showers, dresses.

0540 (approx.)—leaves rectory with López for church.

0600–0635—assists López in morning service. Accesses Communion wine and crackers—strike—hosts.

0630 (approx.)—Rosa O'Donnell arrives at—unlocked—rectory.

0645 (approx.)—leaves church for rectory with López.

0700 to 0800—has breakfast with López, prepared by Rosa O'Donnell.

0800–0830—retreats to communal office to review readings, etc., for funeral.

0830—Roberto and Madda Ortiz arrive at church with funeral staff and body of Ortiz.

0840—returns to church with López to greet family and assist in floral placements.

0900—retreats to anteroom (where tabernacle is kept) to dress for service.

0930—begins service.

1015—drinks poisoned wine.

Which gave the killer from five-forty to six-thirty to walk into the rectory, take the keys to the box, and from seven to nine hundred to doctor the wine. Anytime from seven to nine hundred to walk back into the rectory and replace the keys.

Pretty big windows, Eve mused, especially if the killer was a member of the church, and others were accustomed to seeing him or her coming and going.

Even without the keys, bypassing the lock on the box would have been ridiculously simple if the killer possessed bare minimum skills. Accessing the keys almost as ridiculously simple, particularly if the killer had knowledge of their location, and the basic routines of the church and rectory.

The how wasn't the deal, though the how would certainly help lock up the killer. The why was the point. And the why was wrapped around Miguel Flores.

She picked up the photos of the medal, front and back.

This was important to him. Important enough to hide, and to keep close so he could take it out, touch it, look at it. Fresh tape, Eve mused, but with traces of older adhesive on the drawer back. Had it awhile, but took it out very recently.

She read the inscription again.

Who was Lino?

A Spanish given name, she discovered after a quick search, for Linus. It also meant linen or flax, but she doubted that applied.

According to the bio, Flores's mother had died in 2027, so the *mama* on the medal couldn't be Anna Flores. A Spanish name, a Spanish phrase for the image, but the rest in English. It said mixed culture to Eve. Latino roots, American soil? That fit Flores as well.

Had Lino been a friend, another priest, a lover? Flores would have been six when the inscription was made. An orphan, spinning through the system.

She knew all about that.

Maybe she didn't know about making close and lasting ties while spinning through that system, but others did. Flores might have done so, and kept the medal as a connection to a friend.

Then why hide it?

Never adopted, but educated through the church. Had Lino been the one to take an interest in him, help educate him?

She turned back to her comp and began digging down through the layers of Miguel Flores.

Peabody came in, opened her mouth to speak.

"Pretty good timing," Eve said without looking up. "I see my coffee cup is empty."

With a roll of her eyes, Peabody took the cup, walked to the Auto-Chef to program another. "It's a challenge getting medicals from Mexico. No record of treatment for a knife wound, or any cosmetic work

here. After much and heroic persistence—which is why I'm also getting coffee—I've accessed his medicals from his years in Mexico. No
record of either treatment there either."

Eve leaned back, took the coffee. "What *is* on the record in Mexico?"

"Pretty much standards. Annual physicals, vision corrections, semi-
annual dental, treatment for a stomach virus and a cut on his hand. No
majors."

"Uh-huh. And during his five years in New York?"

"Not much different. The annuals, blah blah, a couple of treatments
for sprains, one for a dislocated index finger, another for an injured
knee."

"What were likely sports-related injuries." Drumming her fingers
on the desk, Eve contemplated. "Funny, he didn't have any of those
types of injuries or treatments while in Mexico. Get me the dental
records from Mexico."

"Jeez! Do you know how much red tape I'm going to choke on to
get those? Plus, he moved around a couple of times, so that means
more than one dentist, and it's *Catholic* stuff, and they weigh in, let me
tell you. Why do you . . ."

It took her a while, Eve thought, but Peabody usually got there.

"You don't think the dead guy is Miguel Flores."

"I think the dead guy's name was Lino."

"But . . . that means maybe he wasn't even a priest, and he was up
there doing the Mass thing, and marrying people, burying people."

"Maybe God struck him down for it. Case closed. We'll arrest God
before end of shift. I want those dental records, and the dental records
from New York."

"I'm pretty sure that arrest God stuff is blasphemy." Thoughtfully,
Peabody took another swig of coffee. "Why would anyone pretend to
be a priest? You can't have *stuff* or sex. And you have to know all the
rules. I think there are a shitload of rules."

"Maybe he was a quick study. Maybe he thought it was worth it.
Maybe he *is* Miguel Flores. Let's get the dentals and find out."

When Peabody hustled out, Eve swiveled around to study the photo on her board. "But you're not, are you, Lino?"

She engaged her 'link and made her own calls to Mexico.

It took twenty minutes, and brought on the beginning of an annoyance headache, but she finally reached someone who not only spoke excellent English, but who'd known Miguel Flores personally.

The old man was ancient, with two thin roads of white hair riding down the sides of his bald, sun-freckled head. Eyes of bleary brown squinted out at her. His white collar hung loosely on his thin, grooved neck.

"Father Rodriguez," Eve began.

"What? What?"

"Father Rodriguez," she repeated, bumping up the volume on the 'link.

"Yes, yes, I hear you. No need to shout!"

"Sorry. I'm Lieutenant Dallas, with the New York City Police and Security Department."

"How can I help you, Lieutenant Ballast?"

"Dallas." She spoke each syllable clearly. "You knew a priest named Miguel Flores?"

"Who? Speak up!"

Sweet, sweaty Jesus. "Miguel Flores? Did you know him?"

"Yes, I know Miguel. He served here at San Sabastian Mission while I was pastor. Before they retired me. Let me ask you, Sister Ballast, how can a priest retire? We're called to serve God. Am I not still capable of serving God?"

Eve felt a muscle begin to twitch just under her eye. "It's Lieutenant. I'm a police officer in New York City. Can you tell me when you last saw Miguel Flores?"

"When he took it into his head he needed a year, or more, to travel, to explore his faith, to determine if his calling was a true one. Nonsense!" Rodriguez slapped his bony hand against the arm of what looked like a wheelchair. "The boy was born a priest. But the bishop gave him leave, and he took it."

"That would have been about seven years ago?"

Rodriguez stared off into the distance. "The years come and go."

Wasting my time, Eve thought, but persisted. "I'm going to transmit a photograph."

"Why would I want your photograph."

"No, not *my* photo." She wondered if there was a particular saint she could hit up for enough patience to get through this interview without screaming. "I'm going to transmit a photograph. It's going to come up on-screen. Can you tell me if this is Miguel Flores?"

She ordered the transmission, watched Rodriguez squint his eyes into crepey slits as he leaned forward until his nose nearly touched his screen. "It may be. It's not a clear picture."

Only clear as glass, Eve thought. "Is there anyone else available who knew Flores?"

"Didn't I tell you I know him?"

"Yes, you did." Eve cancelled the photo, took a deep breath. "Have you heard from him, from Flores, since he left on his travels?"

"Sabbatical." Rodriguez sniffed at the word. "They sent Father Albano to replace him. Always late, that one. Punctuality is a sign of respect, isn't it?"

"Flores. Have you heard from Miguel Flores since he left?"

"Didn't come back, did he?" Rodriguez said with considerable bitterness. "He wrote me once or twice. Maybe more. From New Mexico—he came from there. From Texas, or Nevada, I think. And somewhere else. There was a letter from the bishop. Miguel requested and was given a transfer to a parish in New York."

"Can you give me the name of the bishop who granted the transfer?"

"The who?"

Eve repeated, slowly easing up the volume again.

"Bishop Sanchez. Or it might have been Bishop Valdez."

"Do you have the letters? The letters Flores wrote you?"

"No." Rodriguez frowned, or Eve thought he did. It was hard to tell. "There was a postcard. Did I keep the postcard? Of the Alamo. Or . . . that might have been from Father Silvia."

One day, Eve reminded herself, one day she would be as old and irritating as Rodriguez. Then she would just eat her weapon and get it over with.

"If you find it and it is from Flores, I'd appreciate you sending it to me. I'll return it to you. I'm going to text you my contact information."

"Why would I send you a postcard?"

"I'm investigating the death of a priest identified as Miguel Flores."

Some of the blurriness cleared from the black eyes. "Miguel? Miguel is dead?"

"A man identified as Miguel Flores died this morning."

The old man bowed his head, and murmured in Spanish what Eve took to be a prayer.

"I'm sorry for your loss."

"He was young, eager. An intelligent man who questioned himself often. Perhaps too often. How did he die?"

"He was murdered."

Rodriguez crossed himself, then closed his hand over the crucifix around his neck. "Then he is with God now."

"Father Rodriguez, did Flores have a silver medal, one of the Virgin of Guadalupe?"

"I don't remember. But I remember he carried, always, a small medallion of Saint Anna to honor his mother who was killed when he was a boy."

"Did Flores know, have business or dealings with someone named Lino?"

"Lino? It's not an uncommon name here. He may have."

"Thank you, Father." Chasing your own tail now, Eve warned herself. "I appreciate the time."

"Young Miguel has gone to God," he murmured. "I must write Monsignor Quilby."

"Who is that?"

"Miguel's sponsor. His mentor, you could say. He would want to know that . . . Oh, but he's dead. Yes, long dead now. So there is no one to tell."

"Where did Miguel meet Monsignor Quilby?"

"In New Mexico, when he was a boy. Monsignor saw to it that Miguel had a good education, and mentored him into the priesthood. He was Miguel's spiritual father. Miguel spoke of him often, and hoped to visit him during his travels."

"Was he alive when Flores took his sabbatical?"

"Yes, but dying. It was part of Miguel's purpose in leaving, and part of his crisis in faith. I must go pray for their souls."

Rodriguez ended the transmission so abruptly, Eve only blinked.

Letter from New Mexico, spiritual father dying in New Mexico. It was a sure bet Flores had paid Quilby a visit during his sabbatical.

So, Eve wondered, where do priests go to die?

EVE HAD A MORE STRAIGHTFORWARD CONVERSA-
tion with Sister Patricia, Alexander Quilby's attending
physician during his last days at the Good Shepherd
Retirement Home.

While she mulled it, added it to her notes, Peabody staggered in, and
held up her hands.

"I'm cut to pieces by red tape. The loss of blood is making me
weak."

"Soldier up. Where's the dental?"

"Tied in the bloody tape. I got the dentist, but the dentist is also a
deacon, and a dick. He hits the three Ds. He won't release the records
unless his bishop approves."

"Get a court order."

"I'm working on that." She shot out both hands. "Can't you see the
scars? The dentistry is affiliated with the church, and judges and stuff
get all wishy-washy when religion weighs in. Our subject is dead, has
been officially ID'd. Nobody wants to push on dental records until this
bishop guy gives his blessing or whatever. Pretty much the same deal
for the New York records."

"Well, talk to the bishop and have him sign off."

"Do you see the blood pooling at my feet?" Peabody demanded, pointing at her red-hot airskids. "I got as far as the bishop's assistant, which was a vicious battle with many casualties. And the upshot is I had to put in a request, in writing and in triplicate, and send that in. The bishop will consider the request, and give us his decision within ten days."

"That's bullshit."

"I want an alcoholic beverage, and a nap."

"Get him on the 'link. From here."

"As long as I get to watch."

Peabody put through the transmission, then dropped into Eve's single, rickety visitor's chair.

The assistant, Father Stiles, came on-screen. Eve decided he looked pious and smarmy at the same time.

"Lieutenant Dallas, NYPSD."

"Yes, Lieutenant, I spoke with your assistant."

"Partner," Eve said and got a weary double thumbs-up from Peabody.

"Partner, excuse me. And I explained the protocol for your request."

"And now I'm going to explain something to you. There's a dead guy in the morgue who may or may not be Miguel Flores. The longer you run around with me on this, the longer he's going to be lying on a slab. And the longer he's lying on that slab, the easier it is for information—such as some New Mexican guy in a pointy hat obstructing a murder investigation—to leak."

Pure shock, and it seemed sincere, widened Stiles's eyes. "Young woman, your lack of respect won't—"

"Lieutenant. Lieutenant Eve Dallas, Homicide, New York Police and Security Department. I don't respect you. I don't know you. I don't know your bishop, so, hey, no respect there either. I don't give a rat's ass if you respect me, but you will respect the law."

She gave him half a second to sputter, before she continued the pounding. "And you'd be smart to respect the power of the press, pal, unless you want this all over the media. Screw with me, you better believe I'll screw with you. So you better get your bishop New York talking to your bishop Mexico, and have both of them tell the respective dentists to have those records on my desk by noon tomorrow, New York time, or there will be hell to pay. Savvy?"

"Threats will hardly—"

"You got it wrong. No threats. Facts. Hell. To. Pay."

"There are reasonable channels within the church, and this is a dual request, and international. Such matters take—"

"Priest poisoned with sacramental wine at funeral service. Catholic hierarchy blocks police investigation. There's a headline. There'll be more. Oh, how about this one?" she continued, gleefully now. "Priest's body rots in morgue while bishops block official identification. It's dental records. It's freaking teeth. I have them by noon, or I'm coming to see you personally, and I'll have a warrant for obstruction with your name on it."

"I will, of course, speak to the bishop."

"Good. Do that now."

She cut transmission, sat back.

"I am your slave," Peabody stated. "I wipe tears of awe from my cheeks."

"Okay, that was fun. I just had a more mellow, if less entertaining conversation with a nun—a doctor—a doctor nun," Eve supposed, "at a priest's retirement home in—"

"They have those? Retirement homes?"

"Apparently. The priest who sponsored and mentored Flores, saw to his education and so on, was her patient. Flores took a sabbatical seven years ago from his job in Mexico. Supposed to be for a year or so. This old priest, Quilby, was ill. Dying. Flores visited him. Sister M.D. remembered him, as Quilby had spoken of him often, and they'd corresponded."

"Could she ID him from the photo?"

"Unsure. Close to seven years ago when he paid his call. Looks like him, she says, but she remembers, thinks she remembers, him being a little fuller in the face, having less hair. Both of which can and do fluctuate, so that's no help either way. Flores left her his 'link and e-contact information, asking her to contact him when Quilby died. She contacted him about five months later, at Quilby's death. He didn't respond, nor did he attend the funeral. And it had been Quilby's wish, to which Flores agreed, that Flores personally perform the funeral mass. He hasn't contacted the home since he said good-bye to Quilby in July of '53."

"Guy who educated you, who you make a point to visit shortly after leaving your job, dies and you don't acknowledge it? Not very priestly. Not very human, either." Peabody studied the photo on Eve's board. "We need to find more people who knew Flores before he came to New York."

"Working on it. And I've got another couple angles to play. Flores's DNA isn't on file, but I've got Morris sending a sample of the vic's to the lab. Could get lucky. Meanwhile, whether he's Flores or Jack Shit, he's still dead. Let's go talk to Roberto Ortiz."

She'd assumed the funeral and its aftermath would be done. Eve found out differently when she tracked down Roberto Ortiz, and a couple hundred close friends and family, at Abuelo's, the family restaurant.

He was a tall, striking man who carried his eighty-plus years well on a sturdy frame. At Eve's request to speak to him and his wife, he escorted them up to the third floor, where the noise level dropped significantly, and into a tidy parlor with colorful sofas and bold poster art.

One of the posters sported Eve's oldest friend and current music vid queen, Mavis, wearing what seemed to be a rainbow hue of hair extensions artfully twined over nipples and crotch, and a big smile.

In sharp contrast, the mood screen was set on a quiet meadow under a candy blue sky.

"We keep this apartment for family. My cousin's granddaughter has it now. She's in college, and helps out in the restaurant. Please sit." When they had, he lowered himself to a chair with a long, soft sigh.

"It's a difficult day for you," Eve began.

"My father had a life. Every moment of every day, he lived. Full. He opened this restaurant when he was twenty-five years old, and named it for his grandfather. Then he became a father, and his children had children, then theirs. Family, community, church. These were his strongest loves, and strongest beliefs. The order varied," Roberto said with a smile. "For every moment of every day for the rest of my life, I'll miss him."

He sighed again. "But it's not my father you're here to speak of. Father Flores. May God keep him."

"You knew him personally?"

"Oh, yes. He was active in the parish, in the community. He gave much of his time and energies to the youth center. My family is active there—contributes monetarily and, those who can, in time and energy as well. For this to happen, and in the church, it's unspeakable."

"You and your wife were the first to arrive, with the funeral staff."

"Yes." He looked over as two women and a young man came in carrying trays of food and drink. "You'll eat," Roberto said as plates, glasses, food were set down.

"I brought iced tea." The older woman, a golden blonde with hazel eyes, poured two glasses. "I'm Madda Ortiz. I'm sorry to interrupt." She waved the other two away with an absent smile, then sat on the arm of her husband's chair. "Please, go on."

"Can I just say first, this looks amazing."

Madda smiled at Peabody. "Enjoy."

"We're sorry to intrude, Mrs. Ortiz. You and your husband were the first to arrive at the church this morning."

"We went to the funeral home, and then to the church with Hector. Father Flores—" She crossed herself. "And Father López met us."

"That would have been about eight-forty."

"More or less," Roberto agreed. "We'd only just arrived and begun to transfer the flowers into the church."

"Did you see anyone else at that time?"

"Some began to arrive soon after—to help. My uncles as well, with my cousins to help them."

"Did you notice anyone go into the anteroom?"

"Fathers Flores and López, of course, to put on their vestments for the service. Ah, my granddaughter, my nephew, Madda's cousin. They were serving as Eucharistic ministers."

"I think Vonnie went back," Madda said. "To speak to Father Flores about her reading."

"Anyone before either of the priests went in?"

"Not that I noticed," Roberto told them. "We were in the vestibule for some time, and many of us were in the church proper. We've heard you believe Father Flores was poisoned, so you're asking if we saw anyone who might have done that. There's no one." Roberto spread his hands. "I'm sorry."

"It was a big service. You couldn't have known everyone who attended."

"No." Roberto frowned for a moment. "I think between Madda and me we knew most. Family, of course. And others we know well, or know by name, by face. But no, not all."

"It wouldn't have been family," Madda insisted. "Even if someone could do such a terrible thing, family would never have disrespected Hector in such a way."

Regardless, Eve spoke to all three who'd participated in the service. She didn't get anything new, but Peabody got her fill of Mexican food, and an enormous take-away bag.

"My God, that was the best enchilada I've ever had in my *life*. And the chilies rellenos?" She cast her eyes upward, as if giving thanks. "Why is this place on the other side of the world from my apartment? On the other hand, I'd gain five pounds just sniffing the air in there."

"Now you can walk it off. Take the subway and go home. I'm going to tug at those other angles, and I'm not driving back down to the other side of the world. I'll work at home."

"Mag. I can probably get home from here only about an hour past end of shift. I'm practically early. Dallas, will you really leak that stuff if we don't get the dental by noon?"

"Don't make threats unless you intend to follow through. Start running the names of known attendants from this morning. Take the first twenty-five. That ought to keep you busy on the ride home."

For herself, Eve drove back to the church. People walked in and out of the bodega—seemed to slink in and out of the pawnshop. Groups of young toughs hung out in doorways, on the sidewalk.

She walked to the church door, broke the seal, used her master.

She walked down the center aisle, and had to admit it was just a little weird hearing her own footsteps echo while she strode to the altar and the suffering Jesus over it. At the anteroom door, she broke the second seal, unlocked it.

Came in just like this, she imagined. Maybe through the back or the side, but just as easily. Bottle of cyanide in a pocket or a purse.

Had the keys, that's what I think. Had the keys to the box. Just had to slip into the rectory, take them, walk over, walk in. Unlock the box, take out the little decanter. Sealed or gloved hands. Pour in the cyanide, replace, relock, walk out. Return keys to the rectory.

Five minutes, tops. Ten maybe if you wanted to gloat.

Did you attend the morning Mass? Maybe, maybe, but why stand out? Why stand out in so small a group when later you'd be covered by a crowd?

You know what time the service starts every day, what time it usually ends. You just have to wait for the priests to leave the rectory, go in, take the keys. You could step into the vestibule, listen outside the door if you wanted. Wait until they leave, do the job, go wait—stay close. Priests return, Rosa comes over to the church to help her family. Keys go back to the rectory, you circle around, join the mourners.

You had to watch it happen. You'd need to watch him go down.

Because it's revenge. Public poisoning. Execution. That's vengeance. That's punishment.

For what?

She stepped back out, replaced the seal, locked the door.

Then looked up at the cross. "Didn't worry about you, or didn't care. Hell, maybe he thought you were on the same team. Eye for an eye? Isn't that one of yours?"

"That's from the Old Testament." López stood just inside the front doors. "Christ taught forgiveness, and love."

Eve gave the cross another scan. "Somebody didn't listen."

"This was His purpose. He came to us to die for us."

"We all come here to die." She waved that off. "Do you lock the rectory when you come over to do Mass?"

"Yes. No." López shook his head. "Rarely."

"This morning?"

"No. No, I don't think I did." He closed his eyes, rubbed the bridge of his nose. "I understand, Lieutenant, all too well, that our faith in our neighbors may have helped cause Miguel's death. The church is never locked. The anteroom yes, because of the tabernacle, but the church is always open to anyone in need. I know someone used that to murder my brother."

"Will you lock it now?"

"No. This is God's house, and it won't be closed to His children. At least not once you allow it to reopen."

"The scene should be cleared sometime tomorrow. The next day latest."

"And Miguel? When will we be able to wake and bury him?"

"That may take longer."

She gestured for López to walk out ahead of her, then resealed the door, locked it. Overhead, an air blimp blatted out a stream of Spanish that all seemed to revolve around the words *Sky Mall!*

A sale, Eve supposed, was a sale, in any language.

"Does anybody ever actually listen to those damn things?" she wondered.

"What things?"

"Exactly." She turned, looked into those deep, sad eyes. "Let me ask you this, which is more to the point. Is killing ever permitted in your religion?"

"In war, in self-defense or to defend the life of another. You've killed."

"I have."

"But not for your own gain."

She thought of her blood-slicked hands after she'd stabbed the little knife into her father. Again and again. "That might be a matter of degrees."

"You protect, and you bring those who prey on others to justice. God knows his children, Lieutenant, and what's in their hearts and minds."

She slid her master back into her pocket, left her hand in there with it. "He probably doesn't like what's in mine a lot of the time."

On the sidewalk, people bustled by. On the street, traffic chugged. The air buzzed with the sound of them, of business, of busy, of life, while López stood quietly studying Eve's face.

"Why do you do what you do? Every day. It must take you places most can't look. Why do you? Why are you a cop?"

"It's what I am." Weird, she realized, that she could stand with a man she barely knew, one she couldn't yet eliminate as a suspect, and tell him. "It's not just that someone has to look, even though that's just the way it is. It's that I have to look."

"A calling." López smiled. "Not so different from mine."

She let out a short laugh. "Well."

"We both serve, Lieutenant. And to serve we each have to believe in what some would call the abstract. You in justice and in order. In law. Me, in a higher power and the laws of the church."

"You probably don't have to kick as many asses in your line."

Now he laughed, an easy and appealing sound. "I've kicked my share."

"You box?"

"How—ah, you saw my gloves." With that, the sadness dropped away. Eve saw through the priest to the man. Just a man standing on the sidewalk on a spring evening.

"My own father taught me. A way to channel youthful aggression and to prevent your own ass from being kicked."

"You any good?"

"As a matter of fact, we have a ring at the youth center. I work with some of the kids." Humor danced over his face. "And when I can talk one of the adults into it, I grab a few rounds."

"Did Flores ever spar?"

"Rarely. Dropped his left. Always. He had an undisciplined style, more a street style, I'd say. But on the basketball court? He was a genius. Smooth, fast, ah . . . elastic. He coached both our intramural and seniors. They'll miss him."

"I was going to go by the youth center before heading home."

"It's closed tonight, out of respect. I've just come from counseling a number of the kids. Miguel's death hits hard, his murder harder yet." He breathed out a sigh. "We wanted the kids to be home, or with each other tonight, with family. I'm holding a service there tomorrow morning, and continuing the counseling where it's needed."

"I'll be by tomorrow then. Before I take off, can you tell me what FHC might stand for? Flores had that in his appointment book."

"First Holy Communion. We'll be holding First Holy Communion for our seven-year-olds in a couple of weeks, where they'll receive the sacrament of the Eucharist for the first time. It's an important event."

"Okay. And Pre-C counseling?"

"Pre-Cana. Counseling the engaged couple before the sacrament of marriage. The wedding at Cana was Christ's first miracle. Changing the water into wine."

She nearly said, "Nice trick," before she caught herself. "Okay, thanks. Ah, do you need a lift anywhere?"

"No, thanks." He angled to scan the street, the sidewalk, the people. "I can't talk myself into going home, even though I have work. It's so empty there. Martin—Father Freeman—will be in later tonight. He changed his shuttle flight when I contacted him about Miguel."

"I heard they were tight."

"Yes, good friends. They enjoyed each other a great deal, and this is hard, very hard on Martin. We'll talk when he gets in, and that may help us both. Until then . . . I think I'll walk awhile. It's a nice evening. Good night, Lieutenant."

"Good night."

She watched him walk away, saw him stop and speak to the toughs in doorways and in clusters. Then walk on, oddly dignified, and very solitary.

It wasn't the other side of the world, as Peabody had put it, from Spanish Harlem to home. But it was another world. Roarke's world, with its graceful iron gates, its green lawns, shady trees, with its huge stone house as distant as a castle from the bodegas and street vendors.

All that stood behind those iron gates was another world from everything she'd known until she'd met him. Until he'd changed so much, and accepted all the rest.

She left her car out front, then strode to the door, and into what had become hers.

She expected Summerset—Roarke's man of everything and resident pain in her ass—to be standing like some black plague in the wide sweeping foyer. She expected the fat cat, Galahad, poised to greet her. But she hadn't expected Roarke to be with them, the perfectly cut stone gray suit over his tall, rangy body, his miracle-of-the-gods face relaxed, and his briefcase still in his hand.

"Well, hello, Lieutenant." Those brilliantly blue eyes warmed—instant welcome. "Aren't we a timely pair?"

He walked toward her and *wham!* there it was. There it always was, that immediate, staggering lift of her heart. He cupped her chin, skimmed his thumb down its shallow dent, and brushed that gorgeous mouth over hers.

So simple, so *married*. So miraculous.

"Hi. How about a walk." Without taking her eyes off his, she tugged his briefcase from his hand, held it out toward Summerset. "It's nice out."

"All right." He took her hand.

When she got to the door, Eve looked down at the cat who'd followed and continued to rub against her legs. "Want to go?" she asked him, opening the door. He scrambled back to Summerset as if she'd asked him to jump off a cliff into a fiery inferno.

"Outside means the possibility of a trip to the vet," Roarke said in that voice that hinted of the misted hills and green fields of Ireland. "A trip to the vet means the possibility of a pressure syringe."

Outside, she chose a direction, wandered aimlessly. "I thought you were somewhere else today. Like Mongolia."

"Minnesota."

"What's the difference?"

"A continent or so." His thumb rubbed absently over her wedding ring. "I was, and was able to finish earlier than scheduled. And now I can take a walk with my wife on a pretty evening in May."

She angled her head to watch him while they walked. "Did you buy Mongolia?"

"Minnesota."

"Either."

"No. Did you want it?"

She laughed. "I can't think why I would." Content, she tipped her head to his shoulder for a moment, drew in his scent while they wound through a small grove of trees. "I caught a new case today. Vic was doing this Catholic funeral mass and bought it with poisoned Communion wine."

"That's yours?"

She watched the evening breeze dance through the black silk of his hair. "You heard about it?"

"I pay attention to New York crime, even in the wilds of Mongolia."

"Minnesota."

"You were listening. That was East Harlem. Spanish Harlem. I'd think they'd assign a murder cop from that sector, with some ties to the parish perhaps."

"Probably didn't to ensure more objectivity. In any case, it's mine." They came out of the trees, strolled across a long roll of green. "And it's a mess. It's also prime media bait, or will be if I'm right."

Roarke cocked a brow. "You know who killed him?"

"No. But I'm pretty damn sure the dead guy in Morris's house isn't a priest. Isn't Miguel Flores. And a whole bunch of people are going to be really pissed off about that."

"Your victim was posing as a priest? Why?"

"Don't know. Yet."

Roarke stopped, turned to face her. "If you don't know why, how do you know it was a pose?"

"He had a tat removed, and a couple of old knife wounds."

He shot her a look caught between amusement and disbelief. "Well now, Eve, some of the priests I've bumped into over the years could drink both of us under the table and take on a roomful of brawlers, at the same time."

"There's more," she said, and began to walk again as she told him.

When she got to the part with the bishop's assistant, Roarke stopped dead in his tracks. "You swore at a priest?"

"I guess. It's hard to be pissed off and lob threats without swearing. And he was being a dick."

"You went up against the Holy Mother Church?"

Eve narrowed her eyes. "Why is it a mother?" When he cocked his head, smiled, she sneered. "Not that kind of mother. I mean, if the church is she, how come all the priests are men?"

"Excellent question." He gave her a playful poke. "Don't look at me."

"Aren't you kind of Catholic?"

The faintest hint of unease shifted into his eyes. "I don't know that I am."

"But your family is. Your mother was. She probably did the water sprinkling thing. The baptizing."

"I don't know that . . ." It seemed to strike him, and not comfortably. He dragged a hand through all that dark hair. "Well, Christ, is that something I have to worry about now? In any case, after today, if you get to hell first, be sure to be saving me a seat."

"Sure. Anyway, if I browbeat him into getting the records, I'll know for certain if I'm dealing with Flores or an imposter. And if it's an imposter . . ."

"Odds are Flores has been dead for around six years." Roarke skimmed a finger down her cheek. "And you'll make him yours, by proxy."

"He'd be connected, so . . . yes," Eve admitted, "he'd be mine. The ID on Flores looks solid. So, let me ask you this. If you wanted to hide—yourself and maybe something else—why not a priest?"

"There'd be the whole going to hell thing, as well as the duties if you meant to solidify that pose. The rites and the rules and the, well, God knows all."

"Yeah, but the advantages are pretty sweet. We're talking about a priest with no family, whose spiritual family, we'll say, was dead or dying. One who had a year or more leeway from his job to kick around, and no solid connections. Kill him—or he dies conveniently. You take his ID, his possessions. You have some good face work to make you look like him, enough like him to pass. No big to get a new ID photo."

"Did you look up the older ones?"

"Yeah. It's the dead guy, at least ten years back. Then, maybe." She eyed Roarke thoughtfully. "You'd need some serious skills or money to hire somebody with serious skills to go in and doctor an old ID that passes scanners."

"You do, yes."

"And you need someone with serious skills who might be able to go in and see if whoever doctored those IDs left any trace of the switch."

"You do." He tapped her chin with his finger. "And, aren't you lucky to be so well acquainted with someone with skills?"

She leaned in, kissed him. "I'll program dinner first. How about Mexican?"

"*Olé,*" he said.

They ate on the terrace, washing down *mole pablano* with cold Mexican beer. It was, she thought, somehow indulgent—the easy meal, the evening air, the flicker of candles on the table. And, again, *married.*

Nice.

"We haven't been to the house in Mexico for a while," Roarke commented. "We should take the time."

Eve cocked her head. "Have we been everywhere you've got a house?"

Obviously amused, he tipped back his beer. "Not yet."

She'd figured. "Maybe we should make the complete circuit before we repeat any one place too often." She dug into the nachos again, piling on salsa that carried the bite of an angry Doberman. "Why don't you have one in Ireland?"

"I have places there."

The salsa turned her mouth into a war zone. She scooped up more. "Hotels, businesses, interests. Not a house."

He considered a moment, then found himself mildly surprised by his own answer. "When I left, I promised myself I'd only go back when I had everything. Power, money, and though I likely didn't admit it, even to myself, a certain respectability."

"You've hit those notes."

"And I did go back—do. But a house, well, that's a statement, isn't it? A commitment. Even if you've a home elsewhere, having a house creates a solid and tangible link. I'm not ready."

She nodded, understanding.

"Would you want one there?" he asked her.

She didn't have to consider, and she wasn't surprised by her answer. Not when she looked at him. "I've got what I want."

4 AFTER THE MEAL, EVE DUMPED THE FLORES data on Roarke so they could separate into their connecting offices. In her little kitchen she programmed coffee, then took it back to her desk. She stripped off her jacket, shoved up her sleeves.

Curled in her sleep chair, Galahad stared across at her with annoyed bicolored eyes.

"Not my fault you're too spooked to go outside." She sipped her coffee, stared back. Time passed in silence. Then she stabbed a finger into the air when the cat blinked.

"Hah. I won."

Galahad simply turned his pudgy body around, shot up his leg and began to wash.

"Okay, enough of this cozy evening at home stuff. Computer," she began, and ordered it to open the Flores file, then do a second-level run on the list of people with confirmed access to the tabernacle.

Chale López, the boxing priest, born in Rio Poco, Mexico, interested her. She didn't get a suspect vibe from him, but something about him gave her a little buzz. He'd had the easiest access to the wine—and as a priest, wouldn't he be more likely to recognize a fake than a—what was it—layman?

But she didn't get the vibe.

Nor could she poke her way through to motive.

A sexual thing? Three guys sharing a house, a job, meals, leisure time. Could get cozy. And that couldn't be discounted.

Priests weren't supposed to get cozy—with each other or anyone else—but they did, and had throughout the ages.

Flores hadn't been a priest. Five, nearly six years, vow of chastity? Would he, a good-looking, healthy man, have no interest in sexual gratification or have self-serviced for that length of time to keep his cover?

Unlikely.

So . . . López catches him banging a parishioner, or hiring an LC, whatever. Anger and righteousness ensue.

Just didn't play through for her.

López was forty-eight, and had gone into the seminary at the age of thirty. Wasn't that kind of late in the day for a priest?

Flores—wherever he was—had gone in at twenty-two, and the third guy—Freeman, at twenty-four.

But López—sad, sincere-eyed Chale López—had boxed for a few years professionally. Welterweight, she noted, with a solid twenty-two wins, six of them knockouts. No marriages (were they allowed that before the collar thing?), no official cohabs on record.

There was a short gap in his employment records. About three years between dropping out of the boxing game and entering the seminary. Something to fill in.

She started with Rosa O'Donnell, then picked her way through her portion of the Ortiz family attending the funeral. A few pops, but nothing unexpected, Eve thought, when dealing with an enormous family.

What did people do with enormous families? All those cousins, aunts, uncles, nieces, nephews. How did they keep them straight?

How did they breathe at any sort of family function?

A couple of assaults—no time served—for the Family Ortiz, she noted. One Grand Theft Auto, short time. A few slaps for illegals and other minor bumps. A handful of sealed juvies. She'd get those open, if and when.

Some had been victims along the way. Robbery, assault, two rapes, and a scatter of domestic disturbances. Some divorces, some deaths, lots of births.

She kicked back for a moment, propped her feet on her desk.

No connection to Flores except as the parish priest. But, she mused, Flores wasn't the connection. *Lino* or whoever took Flores's identity was.

Better when the dentals confirmed it, she thought, but she didn't have a doubt. According to the records, Flores requested assignment at that parish, that specific parish, in November 2053.

Coming home, Lino, or running away? That was a question that needed an answer. Did someone recognize you? Someone who lived here, or was visiting here? Someone who felt strongly enough, passionately enough to execute you in church?

What did you do? Who'd you piss off, betray, hurt?

And thus, having had long patience, he got the promise.

What were you waiting for? What was the promise at the end of the wait?

"It's fake," Roarke announced from the adjoining doorway.

"Huh?"

"The ID, it's fake. Which you already knew so I don't see why you had me spend all this time on it."

"Confirmation's nice."

He gave her a cool look, then came over to sit on the corner of her desk. "Then you have it. It was good work, costly. Not the best, by far, but not a patch job either. A bit more than six years back. Flores reports his ID lost, applies for a new one."

"When, exactly?"

"October of '53."

"The month before he requests a transfer to St. Cristóbal's." She punched a fist against Roarke's leg. "I *knew* it."

"As I said. A new photo was provided by the applicant, along with copies of all necessary data. It's a common way to make the switch."

"Prints?"

"Well then, that's where the cost comes in. You'll need to grease the right palms or have a skill with hacking, and an unregistered. So you'd be switching the fingerprints all the way back, replacing with your own. And that means transferring them from childhood on, if you want to be thorough—and he did. It's the first change where the hitch is most easily tripped. After that, it's you, isn't it? In your new skin."

She frowned up at him. "How many forged IDs have you provided and/or used in your shady career?"

He smiled. "It's a good living for a young lad with certain skills and considerable discretion, but was hardly my life's work."

"Hmm. Yeah, I ran the prints. They come up Flores, so he went deeper and hacked, or paid someone to hack, into the database to change them. The rest is pretty standard identity theft."

"To do otherwise, to save a few pennies, would be foolish."

"Having the face work though, that adds coin, time, trouble. That's long haul." She pushed away from her desk, to think on her feet, to move through it. "That's major commitment."

"To go to those lengths, and for that amount of time, means you'd be giving up yourself, wouldn't it? Your name, your face, the connections. You'd have to strip off your own skin to slip on someone else's. A commitment, yes. Maybe your victim wanted a fresh start. A new life."

"He wanted more than that. I think he came back here, to New York, to that neighborhood specifically. He picked this place, so he knew this place. He was hiding, and needed to change the face—and he was patient." She thought back, murmured, "'And thus, having had long patience, he got the promise.'"

"Is that so?"

"I figure the patient get run over in Promiseland more than half the time, but the Bible says no. He had that passage highlighted in his. And this other one . . ." She had to walk back to her desk to look it up. "'With me are riches and honor, enduring wealth and propriety.'"

"A promise of money, respect, stature," Roarke speculated. "Yeah, all of that fits, and for some all of that's worth killing for, and waiting for. It's nice to have familiar surroundings while you wait—and maybe you even get a charge out of seeing people you know, and knowing they don't recognize you."

She narrowed her eyes. "People tell priests stuff, right? Intimate, personal stuff. That would be a kick, wouldn't it?"

"I had an acquaintance once who sometimes posed as a priest."

"Because?"

"Cons. As you say, sins are confessed, which is handy for blackmail, and collection plates are passed regularly. I didn't like the gambit myself."

"Because?"

"Well, it's rude, isn't it?"

She only shook her head. She knew the things he'd done, and yet understood he was the kind of man who'd find bilking sinners rude.

"Maybe that's part of it. Maybe he blackmailed one of the sinners, and he or she sent him to hell. It's got a nice rhythm to it. Fake priest using collar to con marks, mark uses priest ritual to off fake priest."

She turned away from the desk, wandered around the room. "But I'm not going to get it, not going to get the *thing,* until I get him. Who was he? I need the tat. I need the lab to push through the reconstruct of the tattoo. That's something. Figuring he had it removed and the face work done around six years ago, and getting a bead on where the actual Flores was last alive and well will give me an area to focus on."

She looked back at Roarke, who simply sat where he was, watching her. "There's always echoes, right, always shadows? That's what you e-geeks say about the hacking, the layering, the wiping data. And there's always a way to get down to those echoes and shadows."

"Almost always," Roarke replied.

They wouldn't find yours, Eve thought. But how many had Roarke's resources or skill? "If he was as good as you, or could pay someone as good as you, he wouldn't have been playing priest in Spanish Harlem. He'd have been hiding out and waiting for whatever it was on some balmy beach."

"I can't fault your logic."

"It's all speculation. It's all projection. I don't like working that way. I'll get Feeny and EDD digging into this tomorrow."

"And you? What will you do tomorrow?"

"I'm going back to church."

He rose, moved to her. "Well then, let's go sin first."

"Even I know it's not a sin if you're married."

He leaned down, nipped her bottom lip. "What I have in mind might be."

"I'm still working here."

He flipped open the top button of her shirt as he backed her toward the elevator. "Me, too." And the next as he nudged her inside the car. "I love my job," he said, then brought his mouth down to hers.

And he was good at it, she thought, as his hands got busy and her pulse jumped to gallop. She let the kiss take her under, and was already sunk deep when the elevator doors reopened and her shirt hit the floor.

The cool air whisked over her bare skin; her eyes blinked open.

He backed her toward the roof terrace where the open glass dome let in the night. "What—" Then his mouth took hers again, and she could all but feel her brain dissolving.

"We had a walk outside, dined al fresco." He pressed her back into the stone rail. "We'll consider this a hat trick."

She slid her own hands down, found him hard. "Well, I see you brought your hockey stick."

With a laugh he flipped open her bra—the simple white cotton she preferred and that never failed to allure him—and toyed first with the fat diamond she wore on a chain. "Now I feel I should come up with something clever to say about your puck, but everything that occurs sounds crude."

He skimmed his hands over her breasts. Small and firm, with the diamond he'd given her gleaming between them. He felt the trip of her heart under smooth skin, and the warmth of her spread under his hands. However clear her eyes, however much humor in them, he knew she was already as aroused as he.

He turned her, eased her down on the edge of a wide, padded chaise. "Boots," he said, and lifted one of her feet. She leaned back on her elbows, watching as he stood in front of her pulling off one boot, then the other.

Naked to the waist, her skin glowing a little in the pale light of the urban moon, the faint smirk on her face—irresistible. He sat beside her to take off his own shoes, shifting to meet her mouth again when she went to work on the buttons of his shirt. And she angled, straddled him, pressed herself to him.

She dived now rather than sank. Into the heat, the need, the wonder they brought to each other. Now, as ever, it was a shock to the system, a stunning, breathless *rightness* she'd never expected to know. Here. Him. Hers. That gorgeous mouth seduced and demanded at the same time, and those hands—so skilled—possessed. Just the feel of him against her—skin to skin—so familiar now could still dazzle her senses.

He loved her, wanted her, needed her, just as impossibly as she loved, wanted, needed him. Miraculous.

He murmured to her, first her name. Just Eve. Only Eve. Then in Irish. *A grha.* My love. His love. And the rest was lost as his hands guided her, as in a dance, and she bowed back for him.

Those lips skimmed up her torso, a warm, gentle line, then his mouth took her breast with a quick, stunning hunger. Her sigh became a gasp that shuddered to a moan.

Everything and all things. That was Eve for him. Nothing he'd ever dreamed of, even in secret in the dirty alleys of Dublin, approached the reality of her. Nothing he possessed could ever be as precious. The taste of her in the cool night, in the pale light, stirred a craving he understood would never be fully sated.

He rose, lifting her with him, feeling that craving spike and tear when her mouth went wild on his. Once again he pressed her back to the stone, now dropping her to her feet as he yanked her trousers down. As she dragged at his.

"Mine," he said, clamping her hips, thrust into her.

Yes, God, yes. The first orgasm burst through her, a reeling blow that left her dizzy, drunk, then desperate for more. She hooked a leg around him, opening so he would fill, and her hips pistoned, matching him stroke for frantic stroke.

The cool stone at her back, the heat of him against her, in her, drove her up again as he took and took.

When the need built again, when she felt herself about to fall into those wild blue eyes, she clamped around him. "Come with me, come with me, come with me."

The pleasure flashed, bright as that sizzling diamond, as they took the fall together.

She didn't know if she'd sinned, but she woke up the next morning pretty damn relaxed.

It might have been the calm, uncluttered mind that had a fresh thought popping in as she showered. She chewed over it as she stepped into the drying tube, turned the angles while the warm air swirled. Distracted, she ignored the robe on the back of the door and walked back into the bedroom naked.

"Darling." Roarke smiled at her as he sat drinking coffee with the cat sprawled beside him. "You're wearing my favorite outfit."

"Ha-ha. Question." She moved to the dresser to hunt up underwear. Her hand stopped dead, then lifted a red bra with sparkling, and sharply abbreviated, cups. "Where did this come from?"

"Hmm. The goddess of lingerie?" he suggested.

"I can't wear a tit-sling like this to work. Jesus, what if I had to strip off?"

"You're right, that bra would make you appear undignified when you're standing half-naked on the job."

"Well, it would." Since she didn't wear one half the time, she pulled out one of her favored support tanks instead.

He watched her drag on the unadorned, practical white. "Question?"

"What? Oh, yeah. Question." She stepped into equally unadorned, equally practical white panties.

And he wondered why the look of her in the simple, the basic, stirred him as much as red lace or black satin.

"If you had to go under awhile, potentially a number of years, would you tell a trusted friend?"

"How much do I trust this friend?"

"That's a factor, but let's say enough."

"For me, it would depend on the risks, and the consequences if someone drove me to the surface before I was ready."

She considered that as she strode to the closet. "Five years is a long time—a hell of a long time to be someone you're not—and the highlighted stuff in the Bible makes me think it was something he intended to shed when the time was right. In five years, it would take a lot of willpower not to contact a friend, a relative, someone to dump some of the frustration on, or share the joke with. If New York was home for Fake Father Flores, odds are he had a friend or relation handy."

Absently, Roarke scratched Galahad between the ears and set the cat to purring like a jet engine. "On the other hand, he might have chosen New York because it was a good distance from anyone who knew him, and/or closer to what he was waiting for."

"Yeah, yeah." She scowled as she dragged on pants. "Yeah." Then she shook her head. "No. He could have requested a position in the East, in New York or Jersey, say. But he specified *that* church. If all you want to do is get distance, you wouldn't narrow options. But, on the yeah side again, it could be the place is connected to the what he was waiting for."

She thought of the youth center.

"Maybe, maybe. I'll check it out."

As she finished dressing, Roarke walked over to the AutoChef. Galahad unsprawled himself in ever-hopeful anticipation of another meal. Eve strapped on her weapon holster and eyed the plates Roarke carried back to the sitting area.

"Pancakes?"

"I want to have breakfast with my wife, and they're a particular weakness of hers." Roarke set the plates down, then pointed a finger at the cat as Galahad gathered himself to spring. The cat flopped down again, sneered, and turned his head away.

"I think he just cursed you," Eve commented.

"That may be, but he's not getting my pancakes."

To save time, Eve had Peabody meet her at the youth center. The five-story concrete building boasted a fenced, asphalt playground with the far end set up for half-court basketball. A handful of youths had a pickup game going, complete with trash rock, trash talk, and regular fouling. As she crossed the asphalt, several eyes slanted toward her, and in them she saw both nerves and sneers. Typical reaction, she thought, toward a cop.

She homed in on the tallest of the bunch, a skinny, mixed-race kid of about thirteen wearing black baggies, ancient high-tops, and a red watch cap.

"School holiday?"

He snagged the ball, dribbled it in place. "Got twenty before bell. What? You a truant badge?"

"Do I look like a truant badge?"

"Nope." He turned, executed a decent hook shot that kissed the rim. "Look like badge. Big, bad badge." His singsong opinion elicited snorts and guffaws from his audience.

"You'd be right. Did you know Father Flores?"

"Everybody knows Father Miguel. He's chill. Was."

"He show you that hook shot?"

"He show me some moves. I show him some. So?"

"You got a name?"

"Everybody does." He dismissed her by signaling for the ball. Eve pivoted, intercepted. After a couple of testing dribbles, she pivoted again. And her hook shot caught nothing but net.

The boy's eyebrows rose up under his cap as he gave her a cool-eyed stare. "Kiz."

"Okay, Kiz, did anybody have a hard-on for Flores?"

Kiz shrugged. "Must be somebody did, 'cause he's dead."

"You got me there. Do you know anybody who had a hard-on for him?"

One of the others passed Kiz the ball. He dribbled it back a few feet, bagged a three-pointer. He curled a finger, received the ball again, passed it to Eve. "You do that?"

Why not? She gauged her ground, set shot. Scored. Kiz nodded in approval, then sized her up. "Got any moves, Big Bad Badge?"

She smiled, coolly. "Got an answer to my question?"

"People liked Father Miguel. Like I say, he had the frost. Don't go preaching every five, you know? Gets what it's like in the world."

"What's it like in the world?"

Kiz retrieved the ball again, twirled it stylishly on the top of his index finger. "Lotta shit."

"Yeah, lotta shit. Who'd he hang with?"

"Got moves?" Kiz repeated, shot the ball to her on a sharp one-bounce.

"Got plenty, but not in these boots. Which are the boots I wear to find killers." Eve bounced the ball back to him. "Who'd he hang with?"

"Other priests, I guess. Us 'round here, Marc and Magda." He jerked his head toward the building. "They run the place, mostly. Some of the old guys who come 'round, pretending they can shoot the hoop."

"Did he argue with anyone recently?"

"Don't know. Didn't see. Gotta make my bell."

"Okay."

Kiz shot her the ball one last time. "You get yourself some shoes, Badge, I'll take you on."

"We'll see about that."

When Eve tucked the ball in the crook of her arm, Peabody shook her head. "I didn't know you could do that. Shoot baskets and stuff."

"I have a wide range of hidden skills. Let's go find Marc and Magda."

The place smelled like school, or any place groups of kids regularly gathered. Young sweat, candy, and something she could only define as kid that translated to a dusky, foresty scent to her—and was just a little creepy.

A lot of babies and toddlers were being transported in and passed over by men and women who looked either harried, relieved, or unhappy. Drawings showing various degrees of skill along with scores of flyers and posters covered the industrial beige walls like some mad collage. In the midst of it, a pretty blonde stood behind a reception desk greeting both kids and what Eve assumed were their parents as the transfers were made.

The sound of squeals, screams, crying, and high, piping voices zipped through the air like laser fire.

The blonde had deep brown eyes, and a smile that appeared sincere and amused as the assault raged around her. Those brown eyes seemed clear, as did the cheerful voice. But Eve wasn't ruling out chemical aides.

The blonde spoke in Spanish to some, in English to others, then turned that warm welcome onto Eve and Peabody. "Good morning. How can I help you?"

"Lieutenant Dallas, Detective Peabody." Eve drew out her badge. "We're looking for Marc and Magda."

The warmth dropped instantly into sorrow. "This is about Father Miguel. I'm Magda. Could you give me just a few minutes? We run a day care and a preschool. You've hit a high-traffic zone just now. You could wait in the office. Just down that hall, first door on the left. I'll get someone to cover for me as soon as I can."

Eve avoided the next wave of toddlers being carried, dragged, chased, or led, and escaped into an office with two desks pushed together so their occupants could face each other. She scanned bulletin boards holding more flyers, memos. A mini AutoChef and small Friggie crowded a shelf while piles of athletic equipment, stacks of discs, actual books, writing materials jammed others.

Eve crossed to the window, noted it afforded a view of the playground, where even now some of those toddlers were being released to run and shriek like hyenas.

"Why do they make that sound?" Eve wondered. "That puncture-the-eardrums sound?"

"It's a release of energy, I guess." Because they were there and so was she, Peabody poked at some of the papers on the desks. "Same reason

most kids run instead of walk, climb instead of sit. It's all balled up inside, and they have to get it out."

Eve turned back, pointed her finger at Peabody. "I get that. I actually get that. They can't have sex or alcohol, so they scream, run, punch
each other as a kind of orgasmic or tranquilizing replacement."

"Ummm" was all Peabody could think of, and she glanced over
with some relief as Magda hurried in.

"Sorry about that. A lot of parents get here at the last minute, then
it's chaos. Please, have a seat. Ah, I can get you coffee, tea, something
cold?"

"Just your full name, thanks."

"Oh, of course. Magda Laws. I'm the codirector." She fingered a
small silver cross at her throat. "This is about Father Miguel."

"Yes. How long did you know him?"

"Since he came to the parish. Five years? A little longer."

"And your relationship?"

"We were friends. Friendly. He was very involved with the center,
very energetic about his participation. I honestly don't know what
we'll do without him. That sounds so selfish." She drew a chair from
behind one of the desks, rolled it toward the visitors' chairs. "I can't
quite take it in. I guess I keep expecting him to pop his head in here and
say hello."

"How long have you worked here?"

"Nearly eight years now. Marc—I'm sorry, he's not in this morning.
He's taking a course, a psychology course, and doesn't come in until the
afternoon. For another few weeks, anyway. That's Marc Tuluz."

"And he and Flores were also friendly?"

"Yes, very. In the last few years, I'd say the three of us considered
ourselves a team. We have lots of good people here—counselors, instructors, care providers. But, well, the three of us were—are—I don't
know . . ." She lifted her hands as if she didn't know quite what to do
with them. ". . . the core. Miguel was very proactive. Not just with the

kids, but with fund-raisers, and raising community awareness, drafting sponsors and guest instructors."

Her eyes filled as she spoke; her voice thickened. "It's hard. This is very hard. We had a short memorial this morning, for the school-aged kids, and we're having another at the end of the day. It helps, I guess, but . . . We're going to miss him so much, in so many ways. Marc and I were just talking last night about naming the gym after him."

"Last night?"

"Marc and I live together. We're getting married in September. Miguel was going to marry us." She looked away briefly, struggling against those tears. "Can I ask? Do you have any idea what happened, or how, or why?"

"We're pursuing some avenues. Since you were friendly, and worked closely, did Flores ever talk about what he did before he came here?"

"Before?" She pushed at her sunny hair, as if aligning her thoughts. "Ah, he worked in Mexico, and out West. He was born out there, out West. Is that what you mean?"

"Did he talk about his work out West—specifically."

"God. He must have, now and then, but we were always so involved with now, and tomorrow. I do know he worked with kids out there, too. Sports, getting them involved. Teams. He liked teaching them to value being part of a team. He, ah, he was orphaned at a young age, and didn't like to talk about it. But he would say his own experiences were a key reason why he wanted to devote so much time to kids. He was great with them."

"Any kid or kids in particular?" Peabody wondered.

"Oh, over the years, any number. It depends, you know, on what a child needs from us—needed from him."

"Are you from this area?" Eve asked her.

"I went to college here, and stayed. I knew it was exactly where I wanted to be."

"How about Marc?"

"He moved here with his family when he was a teenager. Actually, his sister is married to one of the Ortiz cousins. She was at the funeral yesterday when . . . She's the one who came down to tell us."

"Do you know anyone who had trouble with Flores? Who disliked him? Argued with him?"

"There are lots of degrees in that. Certainly there were times Miguel had to sit on a kid. Or a parent, for that matter. Arguments happen during sports. But if you mean something serious, something that could have lead to this, I have to say no. Except . . ."

"Except."

"There was Barbara Solas—she's fifteen. She came in one day a few months ago with her face bruised. To condense, her father often hit her mother, and—we learned—had sexually molested Barbara."

On her lap, Magda's hands balled into fists. "She resisted, and he beat her. And the day she came to us, she said she'd gone at him. Lost it, and gone at him. He'd beaten her and tossed her out. So she came to us for help, finally came to us, told us what was happening at home. We helped. We notified the authorities, the police, child protection."

"This Solas blamed Flores?"

"I'm sure he did, and us. Barbara told us, and it was confirmed later, that her father had started on her little sister. Her twelve-year-old sister—and that's when Barbara went at him. I convinced the mother to go to a shelter, to take Barbara and her other children. But before I went to see her, before the police came and arrested Solas, Marc and Miguel went to see Solas on their own."

"They confronted him?"

"Yes. It's not policy, not the way we're supposed to handle something like this, but Miguel . . . We couldn't stop him, so Marc went with him. I know things got heated, though neither Marc nor Miguel would give me the details. I know they got heated because Miguel's knuckles were torn and bloody."

"How long ago was this?"

"In February."

"Did they attend church?"

"Mrs. Solas, and some of the children. Not him, not Solas."

"And now? Are they still in the area?"

"Yes. They stayed at the shelter about a month, then we—Marc, Miguel, and I—were able to help her get a new place, and another job. Lieutenant, she wouldn't have hurt Miguel. She's grateful."

"All the same, I need an address."

As Peabody noted down the address Magda gave them, Eve tried another tack. "You said you knew this was where you wanted to be. Would you say Flores seemed as at home here, as quickly?"

"I'd have to say yes. Of course, I didn't know him before, but it struck me he'd found his place." She smiled then, obviously comforted by the idea. "Yes, very much so. He loved the neighborhood. He often took walks or jogged around here. He and Father Martin—Father Freeman—jogged most mornings. Miguel routinely stopped into shops, restaurants, just to chat."

"He ever put a move on you?"

"What?" Once again, Magda clutched at her cross.

"You're a very attractive woman, and you worked together closely."

"He was a priest."

"He was a man first."

"No, he did not make a move on me."

Eve angled her head. "But?"

"I didn't say 'but.'"

"You thought it. Magda, he's dead. Anything you tell me may help us find the who, and the why. I'm not asking to get my rocks off."

Magda heaved out a breath. "Maybe I felt there was something, that he might have thought about it, or wondered. It feels wrong to say this."

"You got the vibe," Eve prompted.

"Yes, all right, I got the vibe. He might have looked at me now and then more like a man does, who's interested, than a priest should. But that's all. He never suggested, or touched me inappropriately. Ever."

"Could there have been someone else?"

"I never got that impression."

"Okay. Other than you and Marc, who did he spend time with?"

"Fathers López and Freeman, of course. Father Freeman especially. They were both into sports—playing and watching—and Father Freeman often helps us out here, too. And he, Miguel, made time for the kids, for his parishioners, even just people in the neighborhood. He was outgoing."

 EVE AND PEABODY WENT BACK TO THE CHURCH.
"Are you thinking the Solas woman changed her
mind about being grateful?" Peabody wondered.

"Wouldn't be the first time. Poison skews female. She went to
church here, would've known the setup, or could have found out. She's
not on the list for the funeral, but it wouldn't have been hard to get in
and out. Not my favorite theory, but we'll check it out."

"Solas himself could have arranged for it. Maybe we should check
his communication from prison."

"We'll do that."

"But you don't like that theory either."

"Not top of my hit parade. A guy gets his ass kicked, he wants physical, violent payback. A bigger ass-kicking." Eve crossed the vestibule
and walked into the church proper. She watched the tall man with
dark skin genuflect, then turn.

"Good morning," he said in a rich baritone that echoed theatrically.

He wore black sweats and a short-sleeved sweatshirt. Eve wondered,
if she hadn't studied his ID photo already, if she'd have made him for a
priest, the way the kids playing ball had made her for a cop.

She wasn't entirely sure.

"Father Freeman, I'm Lieutenant Dallas. My partner, Detective Peabody."

He was compelling in his photo, but more so in person, to Eve's mind. Tall, muscular, strikingly handsome, with large, liquid brown eyes, and an athletic way of moving. He met them in the center of the aisle, held out a big hand. "It's a lousy way to meet anyone, Lieutenant. Detective. Chale—Father López—said you'd probably come by to talk to me. Would you like to go to the rectory?"

"Here's fine, unless you're expecting some business."

He smiled, went from handsome to hot. "Things are usually quiet in here this time of morning. I thought I'd go for a run after early Mass, but I . . . I didn't have it in me. I ended up coming here. A little alone time to think about Miguel, to say a few prayers."

"You used to run with him in the mornings."

"Yes. Most days we'd take a run together, around the neighborhood. I guess that's why I came here, instead of taking our loop. It just . . ."

"Yeah. You were close."

"We were. We hit it off, enjoyed debating, long discussions—about everything under the sun. Church law, politics, why the Yankees traded Alf Nader."

"Yeah." Eve jabbed a finger at Freeman. "What were they smoking?"

"Idiot weed, if you ask me, but Miguel thought it was the right move. We argued that one for hours the night before I left for Chicago."

It struck him, showed on his face, that he remembered it was the last he'd seen or spoken to Flores. "We watched the Yankee game on-screen in the parlor, the three of us. Chale went up during the seventh-inning stretch. But Miguel and I sat and watched, argued the trade and the calls, everything else, and killed six brews."

"You can do that? Drink brew."

The faintest smile played around Freeman's mouth. "Yes. It's a good memory. It's a good one to remember. How we watched the game and argued about Alf Nader."

Freeman turned to look back at the altar. "It's better than trying to imagine what it was like, what it must've been like when he died up there. The world's full of terrible things, but this? To kill a man, and to use faith, his calling as the weapon." Freeman shook his head.

"It's hard to lose a friend," Eve said after a moment.

"Yes, it is. Hard, too, not to question God's will."

Eve thought God took a lot of blame, when to her mind it came down to one human being choosing to slaughter another. "You said 'loop.' You had a usual jogging route?"

"In the mornings? Yes. Why?"

"You never know. Where did you habitually run?"

"We'd head east to First, then go north to East 122nd. Turn back west, to Third Avenue, south from there to finish the loop. He often— or sometimes both of us—might stop at the youth center before coming home. Toss a few baskets with the kids."

"When's the last time you ran together?"

"About a week ago. The day before I left for Chicago. I had an early shuttle, so I didn't run that morning."

"Did he meet anyone along the way, have words with? Or mention anyone he'd had trouble with?"

"Nothing like that. Well, we might see people we know leaving for work, or coming home after a night shift. People who might call out hello, or some comment. People who live or work along the route. Mr. Ortiz, for instance. We passed his house every day, and in good weather, Mr. Ortiz walked in the mornings, so he might be out."

"Mr. Ortiz. The one who died."

"Yes. He'll be missed. I'll miss seeing him on my run, just as I'll miss having Miguel running with me."

"Did Flores talk to you about anyone, or anything, that troubled him?"

"We all wrestle with faith, and our purpose. We would, when we felt the need, discuss in general terms the problems of someone who'd come to us. How we could best help."

When Eve's 'link signaled, she nodded to Peabody to take over, and stepped away.

"Father, what about Mr. Solas? We're told they had an altercation."

Freeman let out a sigh. "Yes, Miguel was incensed, furious when we learned Barbara had been abused. We're told to hate the sin, not the sinner, but there are times that's very hard. He did have an altercation with Mr. Solas, and that altercation was physical. The fact is, Miguel knocked Solas out, and might have done more if Marc Tuluz hadn't stopped it. But Solas is in prison."

"And Mrs. Solas?"

"She's in counseling, as are her children. She's making progress."

Eve stepped back. "We may want to take this to the rectory after all. Is Father López in?"

Obviously puzzled, Freeman checked his wrist unit. "Yes, he should be. He has neighborhood calls shortly."

"Then we'll meet you there."

Peabody waited until they stepped out. "What's up?"

"Dental records are in. We can stop pussyfooting around."

R osa escorted them into López's office, where he sat at his desk and Freeman stood by the small window.

"You've learned something," López said immediately.

"Confirmed something. The man who died yesterday wasn't Father Miguel Flores."

"I don't understand what you mean." Placing his hands on the desk, López pushed out of his chair. "I was there. I saw him."

"The man you knew as Flores assumed that identity. We believe he assumed it sometime between June and October of 2053, and had some facial surgery to enhance the facade. As the actual Miguel Flores hasn't been seen or heard from in that time, we speculate he's dead."

"But . . . He was sent here."

"At his request, and with the use of that falsified identification."

"Lieutenant, he performed Mass, the sacraments. There must be a mistake."

"You said you confirmed it," Freeman interrupted. "How?"

"Dental records. The body in our possession has had facial surgery. Cosmetic surgery. A tattoo removal. There were scars from knife wounds."

"I saw those," Freeman stated. "The wounds. He explained them. He lied." Now Freeman sat. "He lied. Why?"

"There's a question. He went to some trouble to be assigned here, specifically. That's another why. Did he ever speak to you about anyone named Lino?"

"No. Yes. Wait." Freeman massaged his temples, and his fingers trembled. "We were debating absolution, restitution, penance, forgiveness. How sins may be outweighed by good deeds. We had different philosophies. He used Lino as an example. As in, let's take this man— call him Lino."

"Okay. And?"

Freeman pushed up, those dark eyes rested on his fellow priest. "This is like another death. Worse, I think. We were brothers here, and servants, and shepherds. But he was none of that. He died in sin. The man I just prayed for died in sin, performing an act he had no right to perform. I confessed to him, and he to me."

"He'll answer to God now, Martin. There's no mistake?" López asked Eve.

"No, there's no mistake. What did he say about Lino?"

"It was an example, as I said." Freeman sat again as if his legs were weary. "That if this young man, this Lino, had sinned, even grievous sins, but that he then devoted a portion of this life to good works, to helping others, to counseling them, and leading them away from sin, it would be restitution, and he could continue his life. As if a slate had been wiped clean."

"You disagreed."

"It's more than good deeds. It's intent. Are the good deeds done to balance the scales, or for their own sake? Did the man truly repent? Miguel debated that the deeds themselves were enough."

"You think he was Lino?" López put in. "And this debate was about himself, about using the time here to . . . balance out something he did in the past?"

"It's a theory. How did he handle your take on this discussion?" Eve asked Freeman.

"He was frustrated. We often frustrated each other, which is only one of the reasons we enjoyed debating. All the people he deceived. Performing marriages, tending the souls of the dying, baptisms, hearing confessions. What's to be done?"

"I'll contact the Archbishop. We'll protect the flock, Martin. It was Miguel . . . It was this man who acted in bad faith, not those he served."

"Baptism," Eve said, considering. "That's for babies, right?"

"Most usually, but—"

"Let stick with babies, for now. I'm going to want the records of baptisms, here at this church, let's say from 2020 to 2030."

López looked down at his folded hands, nodded. "I'll request them."

P eabody sat thoughtfully as they drove away from the rectory. "It has to be really hard on them. The priests."

"Getting snookered's always a pisser."

"Not just that. It's the friendship and brotherhood, finding out that was all bullshit. It's like, say you go down in the line."

"You go down in the line."

"No, this is my scenario. You go down—heroically—"

"Damn straight."

"And I'm devastated by the loss. I'm beating my breasts with grief."

Eve glanced over, deliberately, at Peabody's very nice rack. "That'll take a while."

"I'm not even thinking, 'Hey, after a decent interval I can jump Roarke,' because I'm so shattered."

"Better stay shattered, pal, or I'll come back from wherever and kick your ass."

"A given. Anyway, then the next day it comes out that you weren't Eve Dallas. You'd killed the actual Eve Dallas a few years before, dismembered her and fed the pieces into a human-waste recycler."

"Go back to beating your tits."

"Breasts, otherwise it's not the same thing. So anyway, now I'm shattered *again* because the person I thought was my friend, my partner, and blah de blah, was in reality a lying bitch."

Eve turned to stare, narrow-eyed, at Peabody's profile.

"Keep that up and you'll be dismembered and fed into a human-waste recycler."

"I'm just saying. Anyway, back to Flores, who we'll now call Lino."

"We get the records, check out all the Linos, narrow it down."

"Unless he wasn't baptized there, because his family moved there when he was, like, ten. Or he was never baptized, or he stuck a pin in a map to pick this parish for his hidey-hole."

"Which is why EDD will be working on the fake ID, and why we'll be running his prints and his DNA through IRCCA, Global, and so on. Something's going to pop out."

"I think it's pretty damn low," Peabody added, "faking the priesthood thing. If you wanted to fake something, you could fake something else. Like something you did before, something you were. Hey! Hey! Maybe he was a priest. I mean not Flores, but another priest. Or he tried to be one and washed out."

"That's not bad. The washing out. We get the records, you crosscheck with guys who washed out of the priesthood. Then do another check on the seminary where Flores trained. Maybe the vic knew him, trained with him."

"Got that. I'll kick it back a little more, do a search on men of the right age span who went to the private schools with Flores, might have connected with him there."

It was an angle, Eve thought, and they'd work it through. "The guy had to figure he had the ultimate cover. Nobody's going to run a priest, at least not like we're going to. Not when he keeps out of trouble. And the only time we've learned he came close to the line was with this So-las. And we'll be checking that, too."

As she spoke, Eve pulled over to the curb in front of the Trinidad, a small business hotel on East 98th. She flipped on her On Duty sign.

It didn't run to a doorman—which was a shame only because she enjoyed snarling at them—but the lobby was bright and clean. A sultry-looking brunette manned check-in. Eve headed for the distinguished silver-haired guy standing as concierge.

"We need a few moments with Elena Solas."

"I see." He skimmed the badges. "Is there a problem?"

"Not as long as we get a few moments with Elena Solas."

"Yes."

"Excuse me." He moved to the far end of his station and began speaking to someone on his headset. When he came back, he kept his neutral smile in place. "We have a small employee lounge on the fifth floor. I'll escort you, if meeting her there will suit."

"That's good."

He walked them down to a staff elevator. "Mrs. Solas has only worked here for a short time, but has proven to be an excellent em-ployee."

"That's good, too."

Eve said nothing else, simply followed him as he stepped off the el-evator, turned down a hallway, then used his key card to open a pair of double doors.

It was more of a locker room than a lounge, but as with the lobby, clean and bright. The woman who sat on one of the padded benches had her hands clutched in her lap, fingers threaded as if in prayer. She wore a gray dress under a simple white apron, and thick-soled white shoes. Her dark, glossy hair rolled into a thick, tight bun at her nape. When she lifted her head, her eyes were dull with terror.

"He got out, he got out, he got out."

Even before Eve could move, Peabody hurried over. "No, Mrs. Solas. He's still in prison." She sat, laid her hands over the knot of Elena's. "He can't hurt you or your children."

"Thank God." A tear slid down her cheek as she crossed herself, and rocked. "Oh, thank God. I thought . . . My babies." She launched off the bench. "Something happened to one of my kids."

"No." This time Eve spoke, and spoke sharply to cut off the rising hysteria. "It's about the man you knew as Father Flores."

"Father . . ." Her body visibly shook as she lowered again. "Father Flores. God forgive me. I'm so selfish, so stupid, so—"

"Stop." Eve whipped the word out, and color flooded Elena's face. "We're investigating a homicide, we have a few questions, and you need to pull yourself together." She turned to the concierge. "You need to go."

"Mrs. Solas is obviously upset. I don't see—"

"She's going to be a lot more upset if I have to take her downtown because you won't leave the room. If you're not her lawyer or legal representative, don't let the door hit you on the way out."

"It's all right, Mr. Alonzo. Thank you. I'm all right."

"You've only to call if you're not." He sent Eve a frigid look as he turned to go.

"I never thought of Father Flores," Elena murmured. "When they said the police were here, I thought of Tito, and what he said he'd do to me, and our three girls. I have three girls."

"And he used to tune you up."

"Yes. He used to hit me. He would drink and beat me, or not drink and beat me."

"And he molested your daughter."

Her face tightened, a flash of pain. "Yes. Yes, my Barbara. I didn't know. How did I not know? She never told me, until . . . She never told me because I did nothing when he hit me. Why should I protect her when I didn't protect myself?"

"There's a question." Eve caught herself, ordered herself to stick to the point. "But not the one we're here for. You're aware that Flores confronted your husband about the minor child Barbara."

"Yes. He and Marc and Magda called the police. But he and Marc came first. And that's how I found out what he'd done to my baby. And had started to do to my little Donita."

"How did you feel about that?"

"About what Tito had done?"

"About what Flores did about it?"

Elena straightened her shoulders. "I thank God for him every day. I say a rosary for him every night. He saved us, when I was too scared and stupid to save us, he did. I know he's with God now, and still I'll thank God for him every day, and say a rosary for him every night."

"Has your husband contacted you from Rikers?"

"He doesn't know where we are. Magda took us to a shelter, one downtown from here. Duchas."

Eve shot Peabody a warning glance as her partner started to speak.

"We stayed there for three weeks. Tito took a plea. Ten years. It's not enough, but it's ten years of peace. We've moved, and I have a new job. When I have enough, we'll move again. Out of the city. Far away. He'll never find us. Father Flores promised."

"Did he? Did he tell you how he could be so sure?"

She sighed. "He said there were ways, if need be, and that there were people who could help if we had to hide. But that I shouldn't worry. He had faith that Tito would never trouble us again. I don't have such strong faith."

When they were in the car headed downtown, Peabody cleared her throat. "I wasn't actually going to mention your connection to Duchas back there."

"It's not my deal. It's Roarke's."

Hence the connection, Peabody thought. "Well, it's a good thing. It really helps women and kids in trouble. You were a little hard on her. Elena Solas."

"Really?"

The ice in the single word froze the air, and had Peabody pulling out her PPC. "Anyway, I'll check with Rikers, see if Solas contacted anyone interesting in the last couple months."

"You do that."

Silence hung, a frosty curtain, for ten blocks. "She deserved it," Eve snapped out. "That and more, for leaving it to her kid to get them out. For taking the slaps and punches and sniffling in the corner while her daughter's getting raped. She deserved it for doing nothing."

"Maybe she did." Dangerous ground, Peabody thought. "But she didn't know . . ." She trailed off, slapped back by a single and ferocious look from her partner. "She should have known. I guess that's what she has to live with now."

"The kid lives with worse." And that was that. "No way that punching bag had a part in poisoning Lino. This one's going to be a dead end. Contact Marc Tuluz, see if we can get him to come to us."

Eve needed to get back to her office. She needed five minutes alone to get rid of this burning rage in her gut, one she had no right feeling. She needed decent coffee so she could clear her head and take another look at the facts. Realign them.

She needed to check in with EDD and their progress, maybe set up a consult with Mira. No, she decided immediately. The profiler saw too much, too easily. Until that rage was banked, she'd steer clear of Mira.

She didn't need someone telling her she was projecting herself on a kid she'd never met. She already knew it.

What she needed was her murder book, her murder board. Lab reports, EDD. What she needed was the job.

They were a good ten feet from the Homicide bullpen when Peabody's nose went up like a hound on the hunt. "I smell doughnuts." When Peabody increased her pace, Eve started to roll her eyes, but then she smelled them, too.

Which meant her men would all be in various stages of sugar highs. And she wasn't.

She saw Baxter first, tall and slick in one of his stylish suits. And a mouthful of chocolate-iced, cream-filled. Then Jenkinson kicked back at his desk, scratching his belly while he shoveled in a cruller. And Carnegie, looking busy on her 'link while breaking tiny pieces off a glazed with rainbow sprinkles.

Peabody pounced on the glossy white bakery box. And her face when she lifted it was a study in grief and disgust. "Gone. Every crumb. You vultures."

"Damn good doughnuts." Baxter smiled around the last mouthful. "Too bad you missed them."

Eve gave him a sour look. "This has bribe by Nadine all over it."

"She's in your office."

"Does she have more?" Peabody turned to make the rush, and stopped short when Eve slapped a hand on her shoulder.

"Desk. Work. Here."

"Oh. But. Doughnuts."

"Oh. But. Murder." With that, Eve turned and headed into her office to see what her friend, and the city's top on-air reporter and news personality thought was bribe-worthy today.

Nadine Furst, her fashionably sassy, sun-tipped hair perfectly groomed, sat in the single, saggy visitor's chair in Eve's tiny, unfashionable office. Her excellent legs were crossed, and the skirt of her suit—

the color of arctic ice—showed them off. Her eyes, crafty as a feline's, smiled casually at Eve as she continued to talk animatedly on her mini 'link. She gestured toward Eve's desk, and the second bakery box.

Then she went back to admiring her shoes, the same murderously sexy red as the hint of lace slyly kissing her cleavage. "Yes, I'll be there. And there. Don't worry. Just make sure I have that research on my desk by two. I have to go, my next appointment's here." She clicked off, tucked the 'link into one of the outside pockets on a bag that looked as though it could swallow Cleveland.

"We had an appointment?"

"We have doughnuts," Nadine responded. She gestured to the murder board. "A lot of buzz on that. Priest poisoned with sacramental wine. It's good copy. Anything new you want to share?"

"Maybe." Eve flipped open the bakery box, and was immediately assaulted with the scent of fried fat and sugar. "Maybe."

Eve went directly to the AutoChef to program coffee. After the briefest of hesitations, she programmed a second cup for Nadine.

"Thanks. One minute for personal business before we go back to our natural forms. Charles and Louise. Wedding."

"Oh crap."

"Oh stop." With a laugh, Nadine lifted the coffee, sipped. "The doctor and the retired licensed companion. It's completely adorable and desperately romantic and you know it."

Eve only scowled. "I hate adorable and romantic."

"Bull. You're married to Roarke. In any case, I think it's wonderful you're hosting the wedding, and standing up for her. I just wanted to tell you I'd be happy to help with the shower."

"Louise can take her own shower. She's a big girl."

"Bridal shower."

"Oh crap."

Nadine fluttered her lashes. "You're just too sentimental for your own good. So. Do you think a big-girl party at your place? You could rent a ballroom—or hell, a planet—but Peabody and I thought something more fun and informal at your house."

"Peabody." Eve uttered the word like it was a betrayal.

"We've chatted about it a couple times."

"Why don't you chat about it lots more, then I'll show up when and where."

Nadine beamed, flicked a hand in the air as if tapping a magic wand. "Presto and perfect. Just what we hoped. Now, next order of business." Nadine reached in her city-swallowing bag and came out with a disc. "This is it. The book."

"Uh-huh."

"*My* book, Dallas. *Deadly Perfection: The Icove Agenda.* Or it will be the book when I turn it in. I want you to read it first."

"Why? I was there, so I already know how it ends."

"Exactly why. You were there, and you stopped it. Risked your life to stop it. I want you to tell me *if* I went off and where. This is important, Dallas, not just to me. Though, oh boy, it really is. It's important information. It's an important story, and it wouldn't be a story, it wouldn't be *my* story, without you."

"Yeah, yeah, but—"

"Please read it. Please."

Eve couldn't even work up a scowl. "Oh balls."

"And be honest, be brutal. I'm a big girl, too. I want it to be right. I want it to matter."

"Okay, okay." Eve took the disc, laid it on her desk. To compensate, she picked up a doughnut. "I've got work, Nadine. Bye."

"You said 'maybe.'" Nadine gestured back toward the murder board.

She had, and not just because of the doughnuts. Nadine might sink her teeth into a story like a terrier, but she never forgot there were people inside it. And she kept her word. "The NYPSD has confirmed through medical records that the man poisoned in St. Cristóbal's was not Miguel Flores, but an as of yet unidentified individual who posed as same."

"Holy shit."

"Yeah, that sums it."

"Where's Miguel Flores? What medical records?" Nadine dug her recorder out of her bag. "Do you have any lines on the victim's real identity, and is the motive tied to that?"

"Down, girl. Police are pursuing all leads."

"Don't hand me the departmental line, Dallas."

"The departmental line works. We are pursuing all leads. We don't know the whereabouts of Miguel Flores, but are actively pursuing. At this time, we're also pursuing the theory that the victim's real identity may have gone to motive."

"So someone recognized him."

"It's a theory, not a fact in evidence. The victim had some facial surgery, which leads us to believe he had it done to more closely resemble Flores."

"He posed as a priest for five years—close to six, right?"

"Maybe longer. We've got to confirm various details."

"And nobody suspected? The other priests he worked with, the people who attended his church?"

"Apparently, he was good at it."

"Why do you think—"

"I'm not going to tell you what or why I think. You've got what you've got, and with a couple hours' jump on the rest of the media."

"Then I'd better get it on the air." Nadine rose. "Thanks." She paused at the door while Eve licked sugar off her thumb. "Off the record. Why do you think he posed as a priest all this time?"

"Off the record, he needed a mask and Flores was handy. He was waiting for something or someone and wanted to wait at home."

"Home?"

"Off the record, yeah, I think he came home."

"If you confirm that and pass it on, there're more doughnuts in it for you."

Eve had to laugh. "Beat it."

When Nadine beat it, clicking briskly down the hall on her sky-scraper red heels, Eve turned back to the murder board. "Something or someone," she murmured. "Must've been pretty damn important to you, Lino."

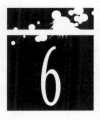

6

EVE TAGGED FEENEY AT HIS DESK. HER FORMER
partner, now captain of the Electronic Detectives Division, sat munching on candied almonds and looking
comfortably rumpled.

"Any progress on my ID?"

"I've got two of my boys on it. McNab and Callendar."

The fact that Callendar had breasts and no Y chromosome didn't
make her any less one of Feeney's boys. "And?"

"They're working on it. I took a quick pass. It's damn good, and it's
dug in deep. It's not going to take five minutes." His droopy eyes narrowed in his saggy face. "What's that? What have you got?"

"What? Where?"

"Doughnuts?"

"What is this, some new EDD toy? Smell-a-'link?"

"I can see the corner of the box. I know a bakery box when I see
one." Feeney shifted right and left as if to get a better angle. "Cookies?
Danishes?"

"You hit it the first time."

"So you tag me instead of coming up and sharing?"

"I got work here. I'm waiting for the lab to reconstruct the vic's tattoo, and I've got to get these baptism records, and run the vic's prints and DNA, and . . . I don't have to share my doughnuts. They're my bribe."

"Then you shouldn't flaunt them in front of my face."

"I—" Damn, she thought, and gave the box a shove to take it out of screen range. "Listen, aren't you Catholic or something?"

"Mostly."

"Okay, so if you're Catholic, is it like a bigger sin to kill a priest rather than a regular guy?"

"Jesus, no. Well, maybe. Wait." Pausing, Feeney scratched his head through the wire brush of silvered ginger hair. "No. He wasn't a priest anyway, right?"

"Right. I'm just trying to cover bases here. It goes two ways. Either they were killing the priest, or they were killing the guy. Or three ways, they were killing the guy who just happened to be a priest. I think it's two."

"I forgot what two is."

"The guy. I think they knew the guy, but since he'd been there for years, why so long a wait?"

Feeney exhaled through his nose, then popped more almonds. "Maybe they weren't around until now."

"Maybe. Maybe. Or he slipped. Five years, you could get careless, say something, do something. Shit. I don't know. Gotta think. Let me know when you've got something."

"You got any jelly-filled?"

"Probably." She smiled, cut him off.

She organized her notes, added the Solas family photos to her board—though she considered them periphery. She was debating calling the lab and pushing for her tattoo when Peabody poked her head in.

"We got— Hey, doughnuts."

"You'll get yours. What have we got?"

"Marc Tuluz. Want him in here or the lounge?"

"Here's a puzzler," Eve began. "If we're in the lounge interviewing him, how many doughnuts will be in this box upon our return?"

"I'll bring him in here."

The man had the long, streamlined build Eve associated with runners, and skin the color of coffee with a liberal dose of creamer. His eyes, a hazy blue, looked weary, but met hers levelly. "Lieutenant Dallas."

"Mr. Tuluz, thanks for coming in. Have a seat."

"Magda said I missed you this morning. We're still not working at full power. Miguel . . . Well, I guess Magda told you we considered ourselves a team. And friends."

"Sometimes friends of the same gender share more openly than they do with friends of the opposite sex."

"Yeah, I guess they do."

"So, tell me about your friend and teammate."

"Okay." Marc took a couple breaths. "It's hard to think about him in the past tense. Miguel was smart and interesting. Competitive. He played to win. He put a lot of himself into the center, into getting the kids involved and excited about being part of something. A team. About contributing to that team. He didn't preach at them, so, well, they listened instead of tuning out half of what he was talking about. They related to him, and he to them. Hell, half the time they didn't think of him as the priest. Just as one of us."

"That's interesting," Eve said, her eyes sharp on Marc's face, "because he wasn't. A priest, that is. He wasn't Miguel Flores."

And the face Eve studied went utterly blank. "Sorry, what?"

Eve glanced at Peabody and motioned to her to take over.

"We've confirmed through dental records that the man you knew as Miguel Flores had assumed that identity approximately six years ago. We haven't yet identified the man who assumed that name." Peabody paused, watched Marc try to take it in. "At this time, we're trying to identify him, and by doing so ascertain why he assumed another identity. By doing that, we may step closer to who killed him. Regardless of who he was, Mr. Tuluz, you were friends for several years. Good friends. Anything you can tell us may help us, and lead us to his killer."

"Give me a minute, okay? This is, like . . . This is so way out of orbit. You just told me that Miguel wasn't a priest?"

"Not only wasn't a priest," Eve put in, "wasn't Miguel Flores."

"Then who— You just said you didn't know." Marc pushed the heels of his hands to his temples, squeezed. "I can't quite get it. I just can't get it. Not a priest. Not Miguel. Not . . ."

"You're absolutely sure of this? Which is a stupid question because why would you tell me if you weren't? All that time. It's surreal. It's . . . thanks," he said when Peabody offered him a bottle of water.

He drank, three long, slow sips. "My mind's blank. It's gone off. I can't remember your name."

"Lieutenant Dallas."

"Right. Right. Lieutenant Dallas, he counseled those kids as a priest, took confessions. He gave some of them their First Holy Communion. They listened to him, believed in him. That's a terrible betrayal. And even saying that, I'm more upset knowing he lied to me every day.

"I loved him," Marc said with a quiet kind of grief. "Like you would a brother. And I thought . . . if he was in trouble, hiding from something, someone, he could've told me. I would've kept his confidence. I'd have found a way to help him."

Eve sat back, digested that. "What happened the day you confronted Solas?"

"Hell." Marc blew out a breath. "We shouldn't have. We were both so pissed. Miguel . . . I don't know what else to call him. He had a temper. He kept it on a leash, worked at it, but now and then, you'd see it flash. Flashed big-time with Solas. Barbara was desperate when she came to us. Her face was all bruised up, and she could hardly talk for crying. It wasn't for herself, that was the kicker, I guess. It came out that the bastard had been abusing her for years. And she took it, too afraid to do anything else. But he moved on her younger sister, and that she wouldn't take. Miguel kept his cool with her. He was really good with her, calm, kind. And he told Magda to take her to the clinic, to have them call the police. As soon as they left, he said we were going to pay Solas a visit."

Marc rubbed the back of his neck. "I didn't argue. It wouldn't have stopped him, and frankly, I didn't want to. When we got there, Miguel whaled right in."

"He attacked Solas," Eve prompted when Marc fell silent.

"He jumped him, pounded him. Not like sparring in the ring, which we'd done. Street moves. He had Solas on his knees and retching in under ten seconds. They went at each other in Spanish. I'm pretty fluent, in formal and in street Spanish, but I couldn't completely keep up."

Marc drank more water, shook his head. "But for damn sure, Miguel wasn't worried about taking the Lord's name in vain. Mrs. Solas had the other two girls, and they were cowering in the corner, crying. Miguel kicked Solas in the face, knocked him out, and he didn't stop—wouldn't stop. I had to pull him off. For a minute, I wasn't sure I'd be able to—and if I couldn't, I think he might have killed the man. He was that over the edge.

"I'd never seen him like that, before or since. You run a place like we do, you see some bad things. Young girls pregnant or on their third abortion. Boyfriends who slap them around, parents on the junk. Illegals, gang fights, parental neglect. You know how it is."

"Yeah, I know how it is."

"He handled that. He might get mad, or impatient, but he never lost it. Until Solas.

"Still, when he got himself under control again, he was good with the woman, the kids. Gentle, kind. It was . . . it was almost like it was someone else who'd beaten down on Solas."

"Maybe it was," Eve said. "Did he ever talk to you about old friends, old enemies?"

"He talked about running a little wild for a couple of years when he was a kid, the rebellion deal most of us get through. He never mentioned any names, or nothing that stood out for me."

"Besides you and Magda, the priests, who did he spend free time with? Hang out with?"

"I have to say he was friendly, the outgoing type. He knew the kids, most of their parents, older sibs, cousins, whatever. If they were around, he'd hang, or join in a pickup game."

"Try this. Did you ever notice him avoiding anyone?"

"No," Marc said slowly. "I can't say I did. Sorry."

"We appreciate the time. If you think of anything, please contact me."

"I will." He pushed to his feet. "I feel . . . it's like when I was in college and did too much zoner. I feel fuzzy-headed and a little sick."

After Peabody escorted him out, Eve sat, swiveled in her chair. When Peabody returned, looked hopefully at the bakery box, Eve waved a hand toward it. Peabody pounced.

"Ohhh, cream-filled. Look out, ass, here it comes!"

"Lino's going to have a sister—or another close friend or relative—who was sexually abused as a child."

"Mmmffh?" Peabody managed.

"He sees all the other shit, hears it in confession, but the one time we can confirm he broke out of his collar—the one time he may have shown his true face—is over a kid being sexually abused."

Peabody swallowed heroically. "Sexual predators of minors are meat in prison. Even stone killers want and do go after them."

"He had more control than that. Five years? He had the control, or an outlet nobody knew about. But he lost it over Barbara Solas. It has to be more personal, more intimate."

"We're going to check the files for sexual molestation of a minor in that sector, for a couple of damn decades, aren't we?"

"Yeah, we are. No guarantee the abuse was reported, but that's what we're going to do. Pull them, copy me."

Eve swiveled again. She'd need to consult Mira, she concluded, but it could wait a day, wait until she had more. For now, she decided to simply send Mira the files, the data, and ask for a profile and/or consult. Once done, she started to contact the lab and find someone to verbally bitch slap.

And her comp signaled an incoming.

"About damn time," she muttered as she noted the sender. She read the text with interest, then studied the reconstruction.

The tattoo was a block cross, with a heart at its intersection. The heart dripped blood—three drops—from the tip of the knife stabbed through it.

"No, I don't guess that's suitable body decor for a priest. Computer, search for significance of current file image. Its usage, meaning, commonality. Is there a regional or cultural significance? Is it a gang-related symbol, a religious symbol, a counter-religion symbol? Secondary task: Search and display names and addresses for tattoo parlors and/or artists within Spanish Harlem between 2020 and 2052."

Acknowledged. Working . . .

While the searches progressed, Eve rose to boost her system with more coffee.

So the guy lost his grip over child rape. Hadn't she done the same, more or less? Hadn't she been a little hard on Elena Solas? And didn't she feel, even now, even calm, that the woman had deserved that, and more?

He'd beaten Tito Solas, cursed at him in street Spanish. And continued to beat him when the man was down and out. It was personal, goddamn it. A trigger.

She knew all about them. She had her own.

But gentle with women, she remembered. Kind, compassionate, protective. Not their fault, that was the line. Mother, sister, young lover. She'd bet the rest of the damn doughnuts it would turn out to be one of those connections.

One connection, she mused, would lead to the next. And they would lead to a name.

Initial task complete. Data displayed. Continuing secondary task.

"Good for you." Eve moved over, sat, and began to scroll and read.

Satisfied, she copied the data as an addendum to Mira, added it to her report, then printed out the image and its usage in duplicate. She took one out to drop on Peabody's desk. "Gang tat."

"The Soldados."

"Soldiers. A badass gang forming just before the Urbans, and holding together until about a dozen years ago—though they'd lost a lot of steam power before that. That was their tat, and what Lino had removed before he came back here. There were some offshoots of Soldados in New Jersey, and in Boston, but primarily, this was a New York gang, turfed in Spanish Harlem. Their biggest rivals, internally, were the Lobos, though they supposedly had a truce during the Urbans, and absorbed the Lobos thereafter. Externally, they went to war regularly with the Skulls, for territory, product, and general pissiness. If you had the tat and weren't a member, you'd be dragged before their council, beat to shit, and they'd remove the tat for you. With acid."

"Big ouch. Odds are our vic was a Soldado."

"Safe bet. And he died on his home turf. Gang initiation could start as early as the age of eight."

"Eight?" Peabody puffed out her cheeks. "Jesus."

"For full membership—which included the tat—ten was the cutoff. And full membership required combat. For the three drops of blood and the knife to be on the tat, blood had to be spilled in that combat. See the black X at the bottom of the cross?"

"Yeah."

"Symbolizes a kill. Only members with the X could serve on the council. He wasn't just a member, he was brass. And a killer."

"So why isn't he in the system?"

"That's a damn good question. We need to find out."

Eve went to her commander. Whitney rode his desk like a general. With power, prestige, and combat experience. He knew the streets because he'd worked them. He knew politics because they were necessary—evil or not. He had a dark, wide, and weathered face, topped by a short-cropped swatch of hair liberally salted with gray.

He didn't gesture for Eve to sit. He knew she preferred to stand.

"Lieutenant."

"The St. Cristóbal's case, sir."

"So I assumed. I've been speaking with the Archbishop. The Church isn't pleased with the publicity, and are put off by the disrespectful manner the primary investigator on the case had employed to gain information."

"A man poses as a priest for several years, and is killed while performing Mass, it's going to alert the media. As for disrespectful manner, I requested dental records. When the red tape starting winding, I cut through it. Those records confirmed that the man in the morgue is not Miguel Flores."

"So I understand. The Catholic Church is a powerful force. Tact can and does grease wheels almost as often as threats."

"It may, Commander, but tact wouldn't have gotten me those dental records in an expedient manner. The Archbishop may be red-faced that some imposter played priest under his nose. Exposing that deception doesn't add to the embarrassment."

Whitney sat back. "That, of course, depends on your point of view."

Eve felt her back go up, but maintained. "If you feel my actions and methods have been improper—"

"Did I say that? Off the high horse, Dallas, and report."

"The unidentified victim was, as reported previously, killed by potassium cyanide, which had been added to the wine used during the funeral mass for Hector Ortiz. This wine was contained in a locked box, but was easily accessed by any number of people. To refine that number, identifying the subject is key. To that end, my partner and I have interviewed the vic's associates and close friends.

"During autopsy, Morris detected the signs of a professionally removed tattoo, as well as old combat wounds and reconstructive facial surgery. The lab has just reconstructed the tattoo."

She put a copy on Whitney's desk. "It's a gang tat," she began.

"The Soldados. I remember this. I remember them. I scraped up what was left of a few in my time, locked up a few others. They haven't been around in a decade. More. Before your time, Lieutenant."

"Then you know what the tattoo symbolizes."

"A full member, with at least one kill. The victim would have been very at home in Spanish Harlem."

"Yes, sir. The medal I found was inscribed to Lino. We're working on getting baptism records from the church. I also believe he may have had a close female friend or relative who was abused sexually as a child."

"Why?"

She told him, quickly, concisely. "These factors indicate this individual would have been in the system at some point. As a gang member, it's hard to believe he wasn't brought in at some time, that his prints and/or DNA aren't on record. But we took both from the body, and we haven't hit a match."

Whitney puffed out a breath. "Any minors who were members, and who were not convicted of any crime that entailed sentencing, had their records expunged. Clemency Order, 2045. An order that was overturned in 2046."

"Even so, sir, the records should still show prints and DNA, even if the record was cleared."

"Not cleared, Lieutenant. Wiped. There is no record for minors who didn't do time. Those who did, those records are sealed, that would be flagged. I'd say your vic was a minor who benefited from the Clemency Order. If he dodged the system after that, you won't find his prints or DNA through our records, or IRCCA."

W ell, that was a pisser, Eve thought as she stalked her way back to Homicide. Some bleeding hearts worry about the city's street rats, and their solution is to pat all the good little murdering, illegals-pushing, gang-raping gangsters on the head and say, "Go sin no more?"

Now she had to dig through reams of *possibly* relevant data to find information that should have been at her fingertips.

Lino had a name, and she was damn sure his killer knew it. Until she did, he'd be John Doeing it at the morgue.

Then there was the real Miguel Flores. She had to ID the vic to have any real hope of finding Flores, dead or alive. He was dead, of course, every instinct told her. That didn't mean he didn't matter.

The more she found out about the victim, the more Miguel Flores mattered.

She stopped at a vending machine, scowled at it. "Give me grief, I dare you." She jammed in her code. "Tube of Pepsi, and stuff your damn contents and nutrition value."

It coughed out the tube, then a tinkle of music. She continued to stalk away as the machine sang out the current Pepsi jingle.

"It's enough to make you go thirsty," she muttered, and turning, nearly ran over Father López. "Sorry."

"My fault. I wasn't sure where I was going, so wasn't watching where I was going. I've never been here. It's . . . big."

"And loud and full of very bad people. What can I do for you?"

"I have the records you asked for."

"Oh. Thanks. I could've come up to get them." Or you could have e'd them, she thought.

"I . . . Actually, I wanted to get out for a bit. Do you have a few moments?"

"Sure. My office is around the corner. Ah, do you want something?" She held up the tube and nearly prayed he'd say no. She didn't want to risk the machine again.

"I wouldn't mind some coffee. I'll just—"

"I have some in my office," she told him as he stepped toward a machine.

She led him down the hall, into the bullpen where Jenkinson snarled into a 'link, "Look, you fucking shit-weasel asshole, I get the intel, you get paid. Do I look like some fuckhead sitting here jerking off? You don't fucking want me coming down there, cocksucker."

"Ah," Eve said. "Office. Sorry."

López's face remained serene. "You neglected to add 'colorful' to your 'loud and full of very bad people.'"

"I guess. How do you take the coffee?"

"Just black's fine. Lieutenant . . . I brought the baptismal records."

"So you said."

"And I intend to give them to you before I go."

Eve nodded. "That would make sense."

"I'm doing so without authorization. My superiors," he continued when she turned with the coffee, "while wishing to cooperate with the investigation, of course, are also cautious about the . . . backlash. And the publicity. They informed me they'd take the request under advisement. Advisement often means . . ."

"Just this side of never?"

"Close. I accessed the records myself."

She handed him the mug. "That makes you a weasel. Coffee payment enough?"

He managed a soft laugh. "Yes, thank you. I liked—Lino. Very much. I respected his work, and his energy. He was my responsibility. I feel I can't understand this, or know what to do until I know who he was, and why he did what he did. I have to counsel my parishioners. Answer them when they come to me upset and worried. Are we married? Has my baby been baptized? Have my sins been forgiven? All because this man pretended to be a priest."

He sat, sipped. He lowered the mug, stared. Then sipped again, slowly. A flush rose to his cheeks. "I've never tasted coffee like this."

"Probably because you've never had actual coffee. It's not soy or veg or man-made. It's the deal. I've got a source."

"Bless you," he said and drank again.

"Have you seen this before?" She took the print out of the tattoo, offered it.

"Oh yes. It's a gang tattoo; the gang's long disbanded. Some of my parishioners were members and still have the tattoo. Some wear it with pride, some with shame."

"Lino had one. He had it removed before he came here."

Understanding darkened López's eyes. "So. This was his place. His home."

"I could use the names of the people you know who have this tattoo." When he closed his eyes, Eve said lightly, "There could be more coffee."

"No, but thank you. Lieutenant, those who lived through those times and aren't in prison are now older, and have work, and families, have built lives."

"I'm not looking to change that. Unless one of them killed Lino."

"I'll get you the names, the ones I know or can learn. I'd like to have until tomorrow. It's difficult to go against the authority I believe in."

"Tomorrow's fine."

"You think he was a bad man. Lino. You believe he may have killed Flores to put on his collar—taken his name, his life. And yet you work like this to find the one who took Lino's life. I understand that. I believe in that. So I'll do what I can."

As he started to rise, Eve spoke. "What did you do before you became a priest?"

"I worked in my father's cantina, and boxed. I boxed for a time, professionally."

"Yeah, I looked that up. You won your share."

"I loved the sport, the training, the discipline. The feeling I'd get when I stepped into the ring. I dreamed of seeing big cities and fame and fortune."

"What changed your mind?"

"There was a woman. A girl. I loved her, and she loved me. She was beautiful, and so unspoiled. We were to be married. I was saving money, nearly every penny I could from the matches I won. So we could marry and have a place of our own. One day, when I was training, she walked from her parents' home toward town, to see me, to bring me lunch. Men—three men—saw her, and they took her. We searched for two days before we found her. They left her by the river. Strangled her. They'd raped her first, and beaten her, and left her naked by the river."

"I'm very sorry."

"I'd never known hate like that. Even bigger than the grief, was the hate, the rage, the thirst to avenge her. Or myself. How can we be sure? I lived on that hate for two years—that and drink and drugs, and whatever dulled the grief so the hate could stay ripe.

"I lost myself in it. Then they found them, after they had done the same to another young girl. I planned to kill them. I planned it, plotted it, dreamed of it. I had the knife—though I doubt I could have gotten near enough to them to use it, I believed I could. I would. Then she came to me. My Annamaria. Do you believe in such things, Lieutenant? In visitations, in miracles, in faith?"

"I don't know. But I believe in the power of believing in them."

"She told me I had to let her go, that it was a sin to lose myself for what was already gone. She asked that I go, alone, on a pilgrimage, to the shrine of Our Lady of San Juan de los Lagos. To draw—I had some little talent—a picture of the Blessed Mother as an offering. And there I would find the rest of my life."

"Did you?"

"I did. I loved her, so I did what she asked. I walked, a long, long way. Over many months. Stopping along the way to find work, to eat, to sleep, I think to heal, and to find faith again. I drew the portrait, though it had Annamaria's face. And I understood as I knelt at the shrine, as I wept, that my life was now for God. I traveled home—many months, and worked to save money to enter the seminary. I found my life. And still there are some nights when I dream she's beside me, and our children are sleeping safe in their beds. I often wonder if that's God's blessing for accepting His will, or penance for testing it."

"What happened to the men?"

"They were tried, convicted, and were executed. There were still executions in Mexico at that time. Their deaths didn't bring Annamaria back, or the other girl, or the one it was found had come before my Annamaria."

"No. But no more girls were raped, terrorized, beaten, and strangled by their hands. Maybe that's God's will, too."

"I can't say, but their deaths didn't bring me pleasure." He rose, put the empty mug neatly beside her AutoChef. "You've killed."

"Yes."

"It didn't bring you pleasure."

"No."

He nodded. "I'll get you the names. Maybe together we can find justice and God's will, on the same path."

Maybe, she thought when she was alone. But as long as she wore a badge, justice had to take priority.

7

SHE FELT PISSY. EVE COULDN'T QUITE FIGURE
out why, but the pissiness stayed full-blown through the
drive home. The floods of tourists cavorting in New
York's spring like a bunch of chickens before the plucking couldn't
shift the mood into mildly irritated or cynically amused. Even the
animated billboards announcing everything from summer fashions—
shoes this summer would apparently be clear to show off pedicured
feet—to butt enhancers didn't make a dent. She tried to imagine the
city full of invisible shoes, painted toes, and padded asses, but it didn't
cheer her up.

The ad blimps cruising overhead and tying up air traffic didn't cut
through the cloud of irritation as they blasted their litany of Sale! Sale!
Sale! (in English this time) at the Sky Mall.

She couldn't find her appreciation for the chaos, the cacophony, the
innate craziness of the city she loved, and so when she finally turned
into the gates, couldn't find her pleasure in being out of it. In being
home.

What the hell was she doing here? She should've stayed at work
where she could turn a pissy mood to her advantage. Should've locked

her office door, programmed a pot of black coffee, and dug in. To the evidence, the facts, the *tangibles*.

Why the hell had she asked López what he'd done before wrapping that collar around his neck?

It wasn't relevant. It didn't *matter*. What difference did it make to the *case* that some bastards had beaten, raped, and strangled the love of his life? It wasn't connected.

Identifying the victim was connected. Finding the killer mattered. The job didn't include imagining some girl in Mexico left naked and dead by a river. She had enough blood and death crowded in her brain without adding more—more that didn't apply to her or the work.

She slammed out of her vehicle, strode into the house. And with that pissiness tangled with a depression she hadn't acknowledged, barely spared a snarl for Summerset.

"Kiss my unenhanced ass," she said before he could speak, and kept walking. "Or I'll plant my visibly shod foot up yours." She stormed straight into the elevator, ordered the gym. What she needed, she thought, was a good, sweaty workout.

In the foyer, Summerset merely cocked an eyebrow at the pensive Galahad, then stepped to the house 'link to contact Roarke up in his office.

"Something's disturbing the lieutenant—more than usual. She's gone down to the gym."

"I'll take care of it. Thanks."

He gave her an hour, though he checked on her by house screen once or twice. She'd hit the virtual run first, and it was telling, Roarke supposed, that she'd chosen New York's streets rather than her usual beach canvas. Then she hit the weights, worked up a solid sweat. Roarke found it mildly disappointing when she didn't activate the sparring droid and beat it senseless.

When she'd moved into the pool house and dived in, he shut down his work. By the time he got down, she was out of the pool and drying off. Not a good sign, he decided. Swimming generally relaxed her, and she tended to draw out her laps.

Still, he smiled. "And how are you?"

"Okay. Didn't know you were home." She pulled on a robe. "I wanted a workout before I went up."

"Then it must be time to go up." He took her hand, brushed her lips with his. Summerset's barometer was, as usual, accurate, Roarke thought. Something was disturbing the lieutenant.

"I've got to put a couple hours in."

He nodded, led the way to the elevator.

"The case is a bitch."

"They're rarely otherwise." He watched her as they rode to the bedroom.

"I don't even know who the vic was."

"It's not your first John Doe."

"No. It's not my first anything."

He said nothing, only moved to the wall panel to open it and select a wine while she grabbed pants and a shirt from her drawer.

"I'm going to stick with coffee."

Roarke set her wine down, sipped his own.

"And I'm just going to grab a sandwich or something. I need to do a search on the records I just got, do some cross-references."

"That's fine. You can have your coffee, your sandwich, your records. As soon as you tell me what's wrong."

"I just told you the case is a bitch."

"You've had worse. Much worse. Do you think I can't see you've got something knotted inside you? What happened today?"

"Nothing. Nothing." She scooped her fingers through the messy cap of hair she hadn't bothered to dry. "We've confirmed the vic isn't Flores, followed a lead that didn't pan, have a couple of others that may." She picked up the wine she'd said she didn't want, and drank as she paced the bedroom. "Spent a lot of time talking to people who worked with or knew the vic, and watched the various degrees of meltdown when I informed them he wasn't Flores, or a priest."

"That's not it. What else?"

"There is no *it*."

"There is, yes." Casually, he leaned back on the dresser, took another sip of his wine. "But I've time to wait until you stop being a martyr and let it out."

"Can't you ever mind your own business? Do you always have to stick your fingers in mine?"

Pissing her off, he knew, was a shortcut to getting to the core. His lips curved, very deliberately. "My wife is my business."

If her eyes had been weapons, he'd be dead. "You can stick that 'my wife' crap. I'm a cop; I've got a case. One to which, for a change, you have no connection. So butt out."

"How's this? No."

She slammed down her wine, started to storm for the door. When he simply stepped into her path, her fists bunched. "Go ahead," he invited, as if amused. "Take a shot."

"I ought to. You're obstructing justice, pal."

In challenge, he leaned in a little more. "Arrest me."

"This isn't about *you*, goddamn it, so just move and let me work."

"And again, no." He caught her chin in his hand, kissed her with more force. Drew back. "I love you."

She spun away from him, but not before he saw both the fury and frustration on her face. "Low blow. Fucking low blow."

"It was, yes. Sod me, I'm a bastard."

She rubbed her hands over her face, raked them back through her damp hair. Kicked the dresser. Coming around now, he thought. He picked up her wine, crossed over to hand it back to her.

"It doesn't have anything to do with the case, okay? I'm just pissed off it has a hook in me."

"Then take the hook out. Otherwise, aren't you the one obstructing justice?"

She took a slow sip, watching him over the rim. "You may be a bastard, but you're a cagey one. Okay. Okay. We followed through on some information," she began, and told him about Solas.

"So I find myself thinking, this Lino or whoever the hell he is, he may have killed Flores. Murdered him in cold blood for all I know. He was a killer."

"You established that?"

"He was Soldados. Badasses in El Barrio. He had the gang tat, had it removed before the ID. They were a New York gang back in the day, and his tat indicates he was high up the chain. He had the Soldados kill mark on the tattoo, so he killed, at least once."

"Harder, isn't it, when your victim had made victims?"

"Maybe it is. Maybe. But at least he did something about this, about this kid. He beat the shit out of Solas, protected the kid, when nobody else did, would. He got her out, got her away."

No one got you out, Roarke thought. *No one got you away. Until you did it yourself.*

"So we go to see the mother, get a gauge on whether she or the kid-fucker might've done Lino." Eve dug her hands into her pockets as she wandered the bedroom. "No chance on her, no way in hell. I can see it as soon as I see her, shaking and shuddering at the thought the husband got out of Rikers. I wanted to slap her." Eve stopped, closed her eyes. "A slap's more humiliating than a punch. I wanted to slap her—and I guess I did, verbally."

He said nothing, waited for her to finish digging it out.

"She was *there,* goddamn it." Her voice rang with it, with the anger, the misery, the bitterness. "She was right there when that son of a bitch was raping the kid, over and over. She let him beat her, and that's her business, but she did *nothing* to help her own kid. Not a damn thing. Didn't know, didn't see, oh my poor baby. And I don't *get* it. How can you not see, how can you not know?"

"I don't know. Maybe some don't see, refuse to know what they can't stand."

"It's no excuse."

"It's not, no."

"And I know it's not like me, it's not the same. My mother hated me, hated the fact of me. That's something I remember, one of the few things I remember about her. If she'd been there when he raped me, I don't think she'd have cared one way or the other. It's not the same, but . . ." She stopped, pressed her fingers to her eyes.

"It pushed it back into your face," Roarke finished. "It made it now again, instead of then."

"I guess."

"And wasn't it worse, isn't that what you think? Worse for this girl because there was someone there who should have seen, should have known, should have stopped it?"

"Yes, yes." She dropped her hands. "And I found myself detesting this pitiful, sad, terrified woman and giving props to a dead man I strongly suspect—hell, I know—was a murderer."

"Giving him props for doing the right thing for a child isn't excusing the rest, Eve."

Calmer, she picked up her wine again. "It got a hook in me," she repeated. "Later, the priest came back to see me. The real one. López. There's something about him."

"Suspicious?"

"No, no. Interesting. King of . . . compelling. He . . ." It struck her, shot out of far left and beaned her with insight. "He reminds me of you."

If she'd fielded the ball and winged it straight into his face, he'd have been no less shocked. *"Me?"*

"He knows exactly who and what he is, and accepts it. He's tough and he gets your measure pretty damn quick. Lino slipped by him, and that's in his craw. He takes responsibility, and he blurred the lines to do what he saw was right."

"All that?" Roarke asked.

"Yeah. He brought me information I needed, even though his superiors wanted to debate and stall on it. He went around them, followed his own code. Then I asked him—it didn't apply, I don't know why I asked him—what he did before he became a priest."

She sat now, had to sit now, and told him about López and Annamaria.

"You thought of yourself again, of being trapped and defenseless all those years when your father beat you, raped you. And more, you thought of Marlena," Roarke added, speaking of Summerset's daughter.

"God." Her eye swam with the memories, the nightmares. "When he was telling me, I could see it. And I could see myself, that last time, in the room when he broke my arm, and was raping me, when I went crazy and killed him. I could see Marlena, and how it must have been when those men took her to get at you, when they tortured and raped and killed her."

She rubbed away tears, but couldn't stop them. "And he's talking about visitations and miracles, and I'm thinking: *But what about before?* What about the terror and the pain and the horrible helplessness? What about that? Because I'm not dead, and I can still feel it. Do you have to be dead not to feel it anymore?"

Her voice broke. Roarke felt the crack in his own heart.

"And he asks me if I've killed, and he knows the answer is yes because he asked me before. But then, he asks if I got pleasure from it. I said no, automatically. I've never taken a life in the line, I've never used my weapon as a cop for pleasure. But I wondered, for a minute, I had to wonder, did I feel it that night? That night when I was eight and I put the knife in him, when I kept putting it in him, did I get pleasure from that?"

"No." He sat beside her now, took her face in his hands. "You know better. You killed to live. No more, no less." He touched his lips to her forehead. "You know better. What you're wondering, what you need to know, is did I find pleasure in killing the men who murdered Marlena."

"There'd have been no justice for her. They killed her—brutalized and killed her to strike at you—and they were powerful men in a corrupt time. No one stood for her. No one but you."

"That's not the point."

She laid her hands over his, joined them. "The cop can't condone vigilantism, can't condone going outside the law to hunt down and execute murderers. But the victim inside the cop, the person inside the cop understands, and more, believes it was the only justice an innocent girl would ever get."

"And still you won't ask what you need to know. Are you afraid you won't be able to stand the answer, and would rather not see? Rather not know?"

Her breath shuddered out. "Nothing you could say will change the way I feel about you. Nothing. So okay, I'm asking. Did you get pleasure from killing them?"

His eyes stayed level on hers, so clear, so desperately blue. "I wanted to feel it, more than anything, I wanted to revel in it. I wanted to fucking celebrate their deaths—their pain, their end. For every second of pain and fear she'd had. For every second of life they'd taken from her, I wanted it. And I didn't. It was duty, when it came to it. Not revenge, but duty, if you can understand that."

"I guess I can."

"I felt the anger, the rage, and maybe at the end of it, that lessened a bit. I can kill with less pain than you—for you feel it, even for the worst of them. We don't stand in the same precise spot on moral ground, on everything. And because I don't believe we must to be what we are to each other, I wouldn't lie to spare your feelings. So if I'd felt pleasure from it, I'd say it. Neither did I feel, nor do I now feel, a single drop of regret."

She closed her eyes, resting her brow to his as another tear slid down her cheek. "Okay. All right."

He stroked her hair as they sat, as she calmed. As she came back. "I don't know why I let myself get twisted up this way."

"It's what makes you who you are. A good cop, a complicated woman, and a pain in the ass."

She managed a laugh. "I guess that's about right. Oh, and about what you said before? I love you, too."

"Then you'll take a blocker for the headache, and have a decent meal."

"How about I have a decent meal first, and see if that takes care of the headache, which isn't so bad anymore, anyway?"

"Fair enough."

They ate where they'd shared breakfast, in the bedroom sitting area. Because she'd dumped on him, Eve thought it only fair to bring him up to date on the case. For a civilian, he had a sharp interest—and sharp sense—of cop work.

Besides, she knew he'd programmed cheeseburgers for the same reason some people offered an unhappy kid a cookie. To comfort her.

"Don't Irish gangs go for tats?" she asked.

"Sure. At least back when I was running the streets."

She cocked her head. "I know your skin intimately. No tats on you."

"No, indeed. Then again, I wouldn't consider my old street mates and associates a gang. Too many rules and regs with gangs, to my way of thinking, and that constant cry to defend the home turf as if it's holy ground. They could've taken my square of Dublin back then and burned it to ashes for all I cared. And tattoos—as you've so recently proven—are an identifying mark, even when removed. And the last thing a young, enterprising businessman, with brains, wants is an identifying mark."

"You got that, which is why Lino had it taken off. The marks it leaves are so faint, it's not going to pop to the naked eye so much—and not at all to the casual glance. Even if it's noticed, it can be explained away—and was—as a youthful folly."

"But it gives you another point of reference toward his identity." He took a thoughtful bite of his burger. "What sort of burke marks himself with an X to announce he's killed? And what sort of killer values ego above his own freedom?"

She gestured with a fry. "That's gang mentality. But still, can't take an X to court. What I need to know is why he left his beloved turf—for how long—and why he needed to assume another identity to come back. It tells me he did something—and something major—after the Clemency Order was revoked, or after he reached legal age."

"You believe he killed Flores."

"Had to be before that. As far as we can track, Flores was out West. Why was Lino out West? And since I'm not going to buy Lino decided to spend the rest of his life pretending to be a priest, there's a reason he came back under that cover, and an endgame. Patience."

"I'd say there's a score involved."

She nodded. "Money, jewels, illegals—which translate back to money. Enough so this gangbanger from Spanish Harlem could afford expensive face work, top-grade ID. Enough that he's got to go under for a solid stretch of time, either because it's too hot, or because he's going to take that stretch of time to get the whole pie." She narrowed her eyes. "I need to do a search for major heists, robberies, burglaries, illegal deals between six and eight years ago. Maybe six and nine, but that's the cap. And run the baptism records. Then I need to find a cop who worked that sector back when Lino would have been an active member of the Soldados. Somebody who'd remember him, give me a picture."

"Why don't I take the first search? I so enjoy heists, robberies, and burglaries. And I did deal with dinner, so deserve a reward."

"I guess you did, and do." She sat back. "How big a bitch was I when I got home?"

"Oh, darling, you've been bigger."

She laughed, held out a hand. "Thanks."

Backstage at the recently reopened Madison Square Garden, Jimmy Jay Jenkins, founder of the Church of Eternal Light, prepared to greet his flock. He prepared with a short shot of vodka, followed by two breath strips, while the voices of the Eternal Light Singers poured in faith and four-part harmony through his dressing room speakers.

He was a big man who enjoyed good food; white suits—of which he had twenty-six and wore with various colorful bow ties and matching suspenders—tailored for his girth; his loving wife of thirty-eight years, Jolene; their three children and five grandchildren; those occasional sly swigs of vodka; his current mistress, Ulla; and preaching God's holy word.

Not necessarily in that order.

He'd founded his church nearly thirty-five years before, laying those bricks with sweat, charisma, a talent for showmanship, and the utter and unshakable faith that he was right. From the tent revivals and country fields of his beginnings, he'd erected a multibillion-dollar-a-year business.

He lived like a king, and he preached like the fiery tongue of God.

At the knock on the door, Jimmy Jay adjusted his tie in the mirror, gave his shock of white hair—of which he was not-so-secretly vain—a quick smooth, then called out a cheerful, basso, "Y'all come!"

"Five minutes, Jimmy Jay."

Jimmy Jay beamed his wide, wide smile. "Just checking the package. What's the gate, Billy?"

His manager, a thin man with hair as dark as Jimmy Jay's was white, stepped in. "Sold clean out. We're going to take in over five million, and that's before the live-feed fees or donations."

"That's a godly amount." Grinning, Jimmy Jay shot a finger at his manager. "Let's make it worth it, Billy. Let's get out there and save us some souls."

He meant it. He believed he could—and had—saved scores of souls since he'd first taken the road, out of Little Yazoo, Mississippi, as a preacher. And he believed his lifestyle, like the diamond rings on each of his hands, was reward for his good works.

He accepted he was a sinner—the vodka, his sexual peccadillos—but he also believed only God could claim perfection.

He smiled as the Eternal Light Singers finished to thunderous applause, and winked at his wife, who waited in the wings, stage left. She would enter as he did, meet him center stage as the back curtain rose and the towering screen flashed their images to the back rows of the upper balconies.

His Jolene would take some of that spotlight, and just glitter and glow in it like an angel. After they'd greeted the crowd together, after she'd done her signature solo, "Walking by His Light," he would kiss her hand—the crowd loved that. And she would return to the wings while he went to work, saving those souls.

That would be the time to get down to the serious business of the Lord.

His Jolene looked a picture to Jimmy Jay's loving eyes. As they began the routine they'd made their own over decades, her pink dress sparkled in the stage lights as her eyes sparkled into his. Her hair was a mountain of gold, as bright and shining as the trio of necklaces she wore. He thought her voice when she broke into song as rich and pure as the forest of gems along that gold.

As always, her song brought them both to tears, and brought down the house. Her perfume drenched him, saturating his senses as he kissed her hand with great tenderness, watched her walk offstage through the mist of moisture. Then he turned, waiting until the last clap had died to hushed silence.

Behind him, the screen blasted with light. God's spear through the gilt-edged clouds. And as one, the crowd gasped.

"We are all sinners."

He began softly, a quiet voice in a silent cathedral. A prayer. He built, in volume, in tone, in energy, pausing with his showman's timing for the cheers, the applause, the hallelujahs and amens.

He worked up a sweat so it glistened on his face, dampened his collar. He wiped at it with the handkerchief that matched his tie. And when he stripped off the white jacket, went down to shirtsleeves and suspenders, the crowd roared.

Souls, he thought. He could feel their light building. Rising, spreading, shining souls. While the air thundered with them, he lifted the third of the seven bottles of water (with just a whisper of vodka in each) he would consume during the evening.

Still mopping sweat, he drank with gusto, draining nearly half the bottle in one go.

"'Reap,' the Good Book says. 'You will reap what you sow!' Tell me, tell God Almighty: Will you sow sin or will you sow—"

He coughed, waved a hand as he pulled at his tie. He choked, sucking for air as his big body convulsed, as he tumbled. With a piping squeak, Jolene rushed across the stage on her pink glittery heels.

She shouted, "Jimmy Jay! Oh, Jimmy Jay," while the roars of the crowd turned to a wall of wails and screams and lamentations.

Seeing her husband's staring eyes, she swooned. She fell across her dead husband, so their bodies made a white and pink cross on the stage floor.

At her desk, Eve had narrowed her list down to twelve male babies, baptized at St. Cristóbal's in the years that jibed with the age range of her victim who had Lino as a first or middle name. She had five more that skirted the outside boundaries of those years in reserve.

"Computer, standard run on the names on the displayed list. Search and—hold," she added, muttering a curse under her breath when her 'link signaled.

"Dallas."

Dispatch, Dallas, Lieutenant Eve. Report to Madison Square Garden,
Clinton Theater. Suspected homicide by poisoning.

"Acknowledge. Has the victim been identified?"

Affirmative. The victim has been identified as Jenkins, James Jay.
Report immediately as primary. Peabody, Detective Delia, will be
notified.

"On my way. How do I know that name?"

"Leader of the Church of Perpetual Light. Or no, Eternal Light.
That's it," Roarke said from the doorway.

Eve's eyes sharpened, narrowed. "Another priest."

"Well, not precisely, but in the ballpark."

"Shit. Shit." She looked at her work, at her lists, at her files. Had she
gone completely off, taken the wrong turn? "I've got to go."

"Why don't I go with you?"

She started to say no, to ask him to stay, continue his search. No
point, she thought, if she was after a man-of-God killer. "Why don't
you? Computer, continue assigned run, store data."

Acknowledged. Working . . . it announced as she headed for the door.

"You're thinking dead priest, dead preacher, and you took the
wrong line of investigation."

"I'm thinking if it turns out this guy drank potassium cyanide, it's
no damn coincidence. Doesn't make sense, doesn't make any sense."

But she shook her head, shut it down. She'd need to walk onto the
scene objectively. She detoured into the bedroom, changed into street
clothes, strapped on her weapon.

"It'll have cooled off out there." Roarke passed her a short leather
jacket. "I'll have to tell you that so far I haven't found any major heists,
nothing that fits your bill. Not with the take outstanding or the doers

at large. At least," he added, "none that I don't know the particulars of, personally."

She simply stared at him.

"Well now, you did ask me to go back a number of years. And a number of years back, I might have had my hand in a few interesting pies." He smiled. "So to speak."

"Let's not," she decided, "speak about those particular pies. Crap. Crap. Do me a favor and drive, okay? I want to get some background on the victim before we get there."

As they walked out of the house, Eve pulled out her PPC and started a background run on the recently deceased Jimmy Jay.

 A PLATOON OF UNIFORMS HELD A GOOD-SIZED
army of gawkers behind police barricades at Madison
Square Garden. The winter before last, the terrorist
group Cassandra had blown a good chunk out of the building. Wreaking bloody havoc.

Apparently, the death of an evangelist elicited nearly as much hysteria and chaos.

Eve held up her badge as she muscled her way through. "He's with me," she told one of the uniforms, and cleared the path for Roarke.

"Let me lead you in, Lieutenant."

Eve nodded at the uniform, a fit female with a crop of curly red hair under her cap. "What do you know?"

"First on scene's inside, but the word is the vic was preaching up a storm to a sold-out house. Downed some water—already onstage with him—and fell down dead."

The uniform cut through the lobby, jerked her head toward one of the posters of a portly man with a shock of hair as white as his suit. "Jimmy Jay, big-time evangelist. Scene got secured pretty quick, Lieutenant. One of the vic's bodyguards used to be on the job. Word is he handled it. Main arena," she added, leading Eve past two more uniforms flanking the doors. "I'll go back to my post, if you don't need anything."

"I'm set."

The houselights were on, and the stage lights burned. Despite them, the temperature was like an arctic blast and made her grateful for her jacket.

"Why is it so freaking cold in here?"

The uniform shrugged. "Packed house. Guess they had the temp bottomed out to compensate. Want me to see about getting it regulated?"

"Yeah."

She could smell the remnants of the packed house—sweat and perfume, sweetened drinks and treats that had spilled in the rows. More uniforms and the first of the sweepers milled around those rows, the stage, the aisles.

But the body lay center stage, with an enormous screen behind him where an image of a hellacious, wrath-of-God storm was frozen in mid-lightning strike.

She hooked her badge on her waistband, took the field kit Roarke carried.

"Full house. Like Ortiz's funeral. Smaller scale, but same idea. Priest, preacher—taken out in front of the faithful."

"Same killer, or copycat."

She nodded as she scanned. "There's a question. But I won't ask it until we determine COD. Maybe he had a stroke or a heart deal. Overweight," she continued as they walked toward the stage. "Probably worked up, playing for a crowd this size. People still die of natural causes."

But not Jimmy Jay Jenkins, Eve thought when she got closer to the body. She mounted the stage. "First on scene?"

"Sir." Two uniforms stepped forward.

She held up a finger, scanned over to the grizzled-haired man in a dark suit. Once a cop, she thought. "You're the bodyguard?"

"That's right. Clyde Attkins."

"You were on the job."

"Thirty years, Atlanta."

"Rank?"

"DS when I put my papers in."

He had the eyes for it. "Mind giving me the roundup?"

"Nope. Jimmy Jay had the stage, heading toward halftime."

"Halftime?"

"Well, that's loose, but Jimmy Jay'd preach for 'round an hour, after the singing, then the singers would come back onstage, and Jimmy Jay, he'd change his shirt—'cause he'd've sweat right through the one he started with. Then after that break, he'd come back and fire it up again. He had maybe ten minutes to go when he went down."

Attkins's jaw tightened visibly. "He drank some water, and went down."

"From one of those bottles on the table there?"

"The one that's still open. He drank, set the bottle down, said a couple more words. Coughed, then he choked, grabbed at his collar, his tie—and down he went. His wife—Jolene—she ran out even before I could—and when she saw him, she fainted. I secured the scene as quick and solid as I could, but there was pandemonium for a few minutes."

He looked back at the body, away again. "Some people tried to get up onstage, and we had to work some to keep them back. Others were running for the exits, or fainting."

"Pandemonium," Eve repeated.

"It surely was. Fact is, nobody really knew what had happened. And their daughters—Jimmy Jay and Jolene's—came running, grabbed at their mama, their daddy. Body's been moved some, and one of the daughters—that'd be Josie—she tried to revive him with mouth-to-mouth before I stopped her."

"Okay. Have those water bottles been touched or moved?"

"No, sir, I made sure of that. Security had a hell of a time with the crowd, and with the crew, but I closed things off here in a hurry."

"Appreciate that, Mr. Attkins. Can you stand by?"

"I sure can." He looked down at the body again. "This is a terrible night. I can stand by as long as you need."

Taking out a can of Seal-It, Eve coated her hands, her boots. Then she moved to the glossy white table and picked up the open bottle of water. Sniffed.

She frowned, sniffed again.

"There's more in here than water. I can't place it, but there's something in here."

"Mind?" Roarke stepped over. With a shrug, Eve held out the bottle so he could lean over. "I think it's vodka."

"Vodka?" Eve glanced back toward Clyde, and saw from his expression Roarke was right. "Can you confirm that?"

"Yes, sir, I can. Jimmy Jay liked a shot of vodka in his water bottles. Said it kept him smooth through the preaching. He was a good man, Lieutenant, and a true man of God. I'd sure hate for this to come out in a way that smeared his name."

"If it's not relevant, it won't. Who spiked his bottles?"

"One of his girls, usually. His daughters. Or I would if things got busy. Or Billy, his manager."

"Which is why all these bottles are unsealed. Where's the vodka bottle?"

"That would be in his dressing room. One of your men locked that up."

She went back to the body, crouched. The cheeks were deep pink, the eyes bloodshot. There were bloody grooves at the throat where he'd clawed for air. She could smell the vodka as she leaned close to his face, and the sweat. And yes, just the faintest whiff of almonds.

As she opened her kit, she turned to see Peabody and her partner's skinny, blond heartthrob hustling toward the stage.

"I didn't call EDD."

"We were out with Callendar and her latest hunk," Peabody said. "That is *the* Jimmy Jay, right?"

"Apparently. Take prints to confirm, get TOD for the record." Eve eyed McNab and the red and orange starburst on his purple tee. He wore slick green airskids to match the slick green belt that kept his seeringly orange pants from sliding off his bony hips.

Despite the fashion statement, and the half-dozen colorful rings weighing down his left earlobe, he was a good cop. And since he was here, she might as well put him to work.

"Got a recorder, Detective?"

"Don't leave home without it."

"Mr. Attkins, I'd like you to take a seat out there—" Eve gestured vaguely to the audience. "And give your statement to Detective Mc-Nab. Thanks for your help."

She turned to first on scene. "Officer, where's the vic's wife?"

"In her dressing room, sir. I'll escort you."

"In a minute. Peabody, when you're done, have the body bagged and tagged and flag Morris. I want COD asap. Cap and bag that open bottle separate from the rest. They're all for the lab and they're priority. The vic had three daughters, all here. You take them. I'm on the wife, the manager. McNab can take Security."

"On that."

Eve turned to Roarke. "Want to go home?"

"Whatever for?"

"Then find someplace quiet and comfortable. Dig into the vic." She offered her PPC. "I've got the initial run on here."

"I'll use my own."

"I've got the run started on mine."

He sighed, took hers, tapped a couple buttons. "Now it's on mine, too. Anything in particular you'd like me to find?"

"It'd be really keen if you found Jimmy Jay Jenkins had ties to some guy named Lino from Spanish Harlem. Otherwise . . ." She looked around the arena. "God's a big business, right?"

"Biblical."

"Ha. Find out how much in Jimmy Jay's pockets, and who gets what. Thanks. Officer?"

They exited the stage, moved through the wings. "Where's the vic's dressing room?" she asked.

"Other side." The cop jerked a thumb.

"Really?"

He shrugged. "Mrs. Dead Guy got the hysterics. Had to carry her off, call the MTs in for her. We got a female officer in with her. MT gave her a mild soother, but . . ."

He trailed off as wailing and sobs echoed off the walls.

"Didn't help much," he added.

"Great." Eve stepped to the door where the wails and sobs battered the metal. She rolled her shoulders, opened it.

She might have staggered, not just from the sounds, but from all the *pink*. It was like a truckload of cotton candy exploded, and it immediately gave her a phantom toothache.

The woman herself wore a pink dress with an enormous skirt that poofed up as she sprawled on a chaise like a candy mountain. Her hair, a bright, eye-dazzling gold, tumbled in disarray around a face where several pounds of enhancers had melted and washed down in black, red, pink, and blue streaks.

For a moment, Eve thought Jolene had torn some of her hair out in her mad grief, then realized the hunks of it scattered on the floor and chaise were extensions and enhancers.

The cop on the door gave Eve a look that managed to be weary, cynical, relieved, and amused all at once. "Sir? Officer McKlinton. I've been standing with Mrs. Jenkins."

Please was the underlying message. *Please set me free.*

"Take a break, Officer. I'll speak with Mrs. Jenkins now."

"Yes, sir." McKlinton moved to the door, and mumbled, "Good luck," under her breath.

"Mrs. Jenkins," Eve began, and in response Jolene shrieked and threw her arm over her eyes. And not for the first time, Eve decided, as the arm was covered with smears of the facial enhancers like a kind of weird wound.

"I'm Lieutenant Dallas," Eve said over the shrieks and sobs. "I know this is a difficult time, and I'm very sorry for your loss, but—"

"Where is my Jimmy Jay! Where is my *husband*? Where are my babies? Where are our girls?"

"I need you to stop." Eve walked over, leaned down, took Jolene by the quaking shoulders. "I need you to *stop* this, or I'm walking out. If you want me to help you, help your family, then you'll stop. Now."

"How can you help? My husband is *dead*. Only God can help now." Her voice, thick with tears and the South, shrill with hysteria, sawed through the top of Eve's head. "Oh why, why did God take him from me? I don't have enough faith to understand. I don't have the strength to go on!"

"Fine. Sit here and wallow then."

She turned away, and got halfway across the room when Jolene called out, "Wait! Wait! Don't leave me alone. My husband, my partner in life and in the light eternal, has been taken from me. Have pity."

"I've got plenty of pity, but I also have a job to do. Do you want me to find out how, why, and who took him from you?"

Jolene covered her face with her hands, smearing enhancements like fingerpaint. "I want you to make it not happen."

"I can't. Do you want to help me find out who did this?"

"Only God can take a life, or give one."

"Tell that to all the people, just in this city, who are murdered by another human being every week. You believe what you want, Mrs. Jenkins, but it wasn't God who put poison in that bottle of water."

"Poison. Poison." Jolene slapped a hand to her heart, held the other up.

"We need the medical examiner to confirm, but yes, I believe your husband was poisoned. Do you want me to find out who did that, or just pray about it?"

"Don't be sacrilegious, not at such a time." Shuddering, shuddering, Jolene squeezed her eyes shut. "I want you to find out. If someone hurt my Jimmy, I want to know. Are you a Christian, miss?"

"Lieutenant. I'm a cop, and that's what matters here. Now tell me what happened, what you saw."

Between hiccups and quavers, Jolene relayed what was essentially Attkins's statement of events. "I ran onstage. I thought: 'Oh sweet Jesus, help my Jimmy,' and I saw, when I looked down, I saw . . . His eyes—he didn't see me, they were staring, but he didn't see me, and there was blood on his throat. They said I fainted, but I don't remember. I remember being sick or dizzy, and someone was trying to pick me up, and I guess I went a little crazy. They—it was one of the police and, Billy, I think, who brought me in here, and someone came and gave me something to calm me down. But it didn't help. What would?"

"Did your husband have any enemies?"

"Any powerful man does. And a man like Jimmy Jay, one who speaks the word of God—not everyone wants to hear it. He has a bodyguard, he has Clyde."

"Any particular enemies?"

"I don't know. I don't know."

"A man in his position accumulates considerable wealth."

"He built the church, and ministers to it. He gives back more, so much more than he ever gathered for himself. Yes," she said, stiffly now, "we have a comfortable life."

"What happens to the church and its assets now?"

"I . . . I—" She pressed a hand to her lips. "He took steps to be sure the church would continue after his passing. That if he met God first, I would be taken care of, and our children, our grandchildren. I don't know all the particulars. I try not to think about it."

"Who set the water out for him tonight?"

"One of the girls, I suppose." Her ravaged eyes closed. Eve calculated the tranq had finally cut through the hysteria. "Or Billy. Maybe Clyde."

"Were you aware your husband routinely had vodka added to his water?"

Her ravaged eyes popped open. Then she huffed out a matronly breath and shook her head. "Oh, Jimmy Jay! He knew I disapproved. An occasional glass of wine, that's all right. But did our Lord and Savior have vodka at the Last Supper? Did He change water into vodka at Cana?"

"I'm guessing no."

Jolene smiled a little. "He had a taste for it, my Jimmy. Didn't overdo. I wouldn't have stood for it. But I didn't know he was still having the girls tip a little into his stage water. It's a small indulgence, isn't it? A small thing." Fresh tears spilled as she plucked at the voluminous poofs of her skirt. "I wish I hadn't scolded him about it now."

"How about his other indulgences?"

"His daughters, his grandbabies. He spoiled them to bits and pieces. And me." She sighed, her voice slurring now with the drug. "He spoiled me, too, and I let him. Children. He had a soft spot for children. That's why he built the school back down home. He believed in feeding a child's mind, body, soul, and their imagination. Officer—I'm sorry. I've forgotten."

"Lieutenant Dallas."

"Lieutenant Dallas. My husband was a good man. He wasn't perfect, but he was a good man. Maybe even great. He was a loving husband and father, and a devoted shepherd to his flock. He served the Lord, every day. Please, I want my children now. I want my daughters. Can't I have my daughters now?"

"I'll check on that."

With the oldest daughter's statement on record, Eve cleared putting the two women together. And she moved on to the manager.

Billy Crocker sat in a smaller dressing room on what Eve thought of as Jimmy Jay's side of the stage. His eyes were raw and red, his face gray.

"He's really dead."

"Yes, he is." Eve chose to start at a different point. "When's the last time you spoke with Mr. Jenkins?"

"Just a few minutes before he went on. I gave him his cue. I went to his dressing room to give him the five-minute cue."

"What else did you talk about?"

"I told him what the gate was, that we were sold out. He liked hearing it, pepped him up, knowing there were so many souls to be saved. That's what he said."

"Was he alone?"

"Yes. He always took the last thirty minutes—twenty if we were pressed—alone."

"How long did you work for him?"

Billy took a choked breath. "Twenty-three years."

"What was your relationship?"

"I'm his manager—was his manager—and his friend. He was my spiritual adviser. We were family." With his lips trembling, Billy wiped at his eyes. "Jimmy Jay made everyone feel like family."

"Why is his wife stationed at the other side of the stage?"

"Just a practicality. They come in on opposite sides, meet at the center. It's tradition. Jolene, oh good Jesus, poor Jolene."

"What was their relationship like?"

"Devoted. Absolutely devoted. They adore each other."

"No straying into other pastures—on either side."

He looked down at his hands. "That's an unkind thing to say."

"Am I going to dig a little, Billy, and find out you and Jolene have been breaking any commandments?"

His head snapped up. "You will not. Jolene would never betray Jimmy Jay in that way. In any way. She's a lady, and a good Christian woman."

"Who spiked Jenkins's stage water with vodka?"

Billy sighed. "Josie took care of it tonight. There's no need to bring that out, and embarrass Jolene. It was a small thing."

"The church is big business. A lot of money. Who gets what?"

"It's very complicated, Lieutenant."

"Simplify it."

"Church assets remain church assets. Some of those assets are used by the Jenkins family. The plane used for transportation in the work of the church, for instance. His daughters' homes, which are also used for church business. Several vehicles and other assets. Jimmy Jay and Jolene have—over more than thirty-five years of time and effort—accumulated considerable wealth in their own right. I know, as I was consulted, that Jimmy Jay arranged, should . . . should he go to God, that Jolene and his family are provided for. And that the church itself can and will continue. It was his life's work."

"Did he leave anything to you, Billy?"

"Yes. I'll inherit some of his personal effects, one million dollars, and the responsibility of managing the church in the manner he wished."

"Who'd he cheat on Jolene with?"

"I won't dignify that with an answer."

Something there, Eve decided. "If you're taking that stand to protect him, you may also be protecting his killer."

"Jimmy Jay is beyond my protection. He's in God's hands."

"Eventually, his killer will be in mine." She rose. "Where are you staying in New York?"

"At the Mark. The family was given use of the home of one of our flock. They're at a town house on Park Avenue. The rest of us are at the Mark."

"You're free to go there, but don't leave the city."

"None of us will leave until we take Jimmy Jay's earthly remains back home."

Eve tracked down Peabody, pulled her out of yet another dressing room. "This place is a damn maze. Status."

"I've finished the first two daughters, and I'm on number three. My take is they're in shock, and they want their mother, which is where the first two are now. They're worried about their kids, who are with the nanny who travels with them. The youngest one's in there and about five months pregnant."

"Crap."

"She's holding up, holding on."

"Which one's Josie?"

"Inside. Jackie, Jaime, and Josie." Peabody's face creased with a frown. "What's with all the J's?"

"Who knows. I need to ask this J a couple of questions."

"Okay. Listen, I told McNab to take the husbands since he'd finished with Security."

"That's fine. Maybe we'll get out of here before morning." Eve stepped in.

The woman inside wore white. Her hair was a softer shade of blond than her mother's and worn loose around her shoulders. If she'd indulged in facial enhancers like her mother, she'd cleaned them off. Her face was pale and bare, her eyes red-rimmed with tears shining out of the blue.

After the sugary pink of Jolene's dressing room, the reds and golds of this one came as a relief. Under a lighted mirror stood a tidy grove of stage enhancers, grooming tools, framed photographs.

In one the recently deceased held a chubby baby.

"Josie."

"Yes."

"I'm Lieutenant Dallas. I'm sorry for your loss."

"I'm trying to tell myself he's with God. But I want him to be with me." As she spoke, she rubbed circles over the lump of her belly. "I was just thinking how busy we all were today, getting ready for tonight, and how little time I had with him. How I was doing something or other this afternoon, and I thought: 'Oh, I have to talk to Daddy, and tell him how Jilly—my little girl—how she printed her name today, and got all the letters right.' But I didn't get the chance. Now I won't."

"Josie, did you put the water bottles onstage?"

"Yes. Seven of them. Three for each half, and one extra. He usually only went through the six, but we always put out seven, in case. On the table behind the drop."

"The drop?"

"Curtain. See, the singers open, upstage, then when Mama and Daddy come in, they lift the curtain. The table's there, behind it."

"When did you put them out?"

"Ah, about fifteen minutes before his cue, I think. Not much before that."

"When did you put the vodka in?"

She flushed, pink as her mother's dress. "Maybe an hour or so before. Please don't tell Mama."

"She knows. She understands."

"You got the bottle in his dressing room?"

"That's right."

She wiped at fresh tears with her fingers. "He wasn't in—sometimes he is, and we'd talk a little while I fixed his bottles. If I was doing it. And we'd joke. He liked a good joke. Then I'd take them back to my dressing room. My sisters and I sing, too. We'd perform in the second half with Mama, and at the end, with the Eternal Lights, Mama, and Daddy."

"Did you see anyone around your father's dressing room?"

"Oh, I don't know. There are so many of us. I saw some of the crew going here and there, and the wardrobe mistress—Kammi—she came in with Daddy's suit as I was leaving, and some of the tech crew were here and there. I wasn't paying attention, Miss Dallas. I was thinking how I wanted to get back to the dressing room with my sisters, and stretch out for a few minutes." Her hands moved over her belly again. "I get tired easy these days."

"Okay, let's try this. Did you see anything or anyone out of place?"

"No. I'm sorry."

Eve pushed to her feet. "Detective Peabody's going to finish up, then she'll take you to your mother." Eve started to the door, stopped, turned back. "You said how busy you all were today. Did your father spend the day here, rehearsing?"

"Oh, no. We all had breakfast this morning, at the home where we're staying. And morning prayer. Then the kids have school. My sister Jackie and Merna—that's who helps out with the kids—taught today. Mama came down first, to meet with Kammi, and with Foster, who does our hair. Mama is very hands-on with the wardrobe, the hair, and makeup. Daddy went out for his walk and meditation."

"When?"

"Oh . . . around noon, I guess. No, closer to eleven."

"With his bodyguard?"

Josie bit her lip. "I forgot, that's one of those things like the vodka. Daddy sometimes gives Clyde an hour or two off, and he sort of lets Clyde think he'll be staying in, working. But he just wants to get outside and walk and think, on his own."

"So your father was out on his own, walking and thinking, from around eleven to . . ."

"I'm not sure, because most of us went on before one, to rehearse, and to check with Mama on the wardrobe and so on."

"Everyone was here at one?"

"Well, I don't know. Everyone on the girls' side would've been by around one-thirty anyway. I know that sounds silly, but the singers are all girls, and we're all on stage left, so we call it the girls' side."

"Anyone missing, or late?"

"I just don't know. My sisters and I went straight out to rehearse, and I can't recall anyone not being there when we switched off so the Eternal Lights could rehearse."

"And your father?"

"I heard him doing sound checks. He had such a big voice. Then we all rehearsed the final song, and the encore. I went to spend some time with Walt and Jilly—my husband and my daughter."

"Okay. What's the address where you're staying?"

Eve noted it down, nodded. "Thank you, Josie."

"I know God has a plan. And I know whoever did this will answer to God. But I hope you'll see that whoever did this answers here on Earth before that day."

"Well, that's my plan."

Eve went back out, wound around to Roarke, who sat front row center, happily playing with his pocket PPC. "Status?"

"God is a very big, and very lucrative business. Want a report?"

"Not just yet. You should go home."

"Why do you always want to spoil my fun?"

She leaned down until they were eye to eye. "His wife loved him. That's no bullshit. I love you."

"That's no bullshit."

"If I found out you were screwing around on me, could I off you?"

He inclined his head. "I believe I've already been informed you'd be doing the rhumba—after appropriate lessons—on my cold, dead body."

"Yeah. Yeah." It cheered her up. "Just not sure pink Jolene has the stones for that."

"Jimmy Jay was in violation of the . . . which commandment is it that deals with adultery?"

"How the hell would I know, especially since I wouldn't wait for you to face your eternal punishment, should you be in said violation, before I rhumba'd my ass off."

"Such is true love."

"Bet your excellent ass. I got the vibe he might've been screwing around, but maybe I'm just a cynical so-and-so."

Pleased with her, Roarke tapped a finger over the dent in her chin. "You are, but you're my cynical so-and-so."

"Awww. Money's another good one. What kind of—round figure—lucrative are we talking?"

"If we put church assets, personal assets, assets neatly tipped into his children's and grandchildren's names, his wife's personal assets into the same hat, upward of six billion."

"That's pretty fucking round. I'll get back to you."

She hunted down Clyde, found him in a small backstage canteen, sitting over what smelled like a miserable cup of coffee. He smiled weakly.

"Coffee here's as bad as cop coffee ever was."

"I'll take your word." She sat and looked him in the eye. "Did Jimmy Jay have a sidepiece?"

He puffed out his cheeks. "I never saw him, not once in the eight years I've been with him, behave inappropriately with another woman."

"That's not an answer, Clyde."

He shifted in his seat, and she knew her vibe rang true.

"I've been divorced twice. Drank too much, saw too much, brought it all home too much and lost two wives to the job. Lost my faith, lost myself. I found them again when I heard Jimmy Jay preach. I went to him, and he gave me a job. He gave me a second chance to be a good man."

"That's still not an answer. He's dead. Somebody put something besides a little shot of vodka in his water. So I'm going to ask you one more time, Detective Sergeant: Did he have a sidepiece?"

"I figure it's likely. I never saw him, like I said. But I had a sidepiece or two in my time, and I know the signs."

"Did his wife know?"

"If you asked me to swear to it, I might hesitate, but I'd still say no."

"Why?"

"I'd've seen it, felt it. It's a good bet I'd have heard it. I think she'd have stood by him if she found out, but I think—hell, I *know*—she'd have put the stops to it. She's a soft-hearted woman, Lieutenant, and she loved him to distraction. But she's got a spine in there. She wouldn't put up with it. Fact is, he loved her the same way.

"I know," he said when she stared through him. "We always say we love the wife when we're screwing around on her. But he did. The man was crazy about Jolene. He just lit up when she was around. If she'd found out and put it to him, if he'd seen it hurt her, he'd have stopped."

"He didn't stop the vodka."

Clyde puffed out his cheeks again. "No. No, I guess he didn't."

EVE TOOK TIME OUT TO WATCH A REPLAY OF the live feed. To watch the last minutes of Jimmy Jay Jenkins's life, and study his death. The witness reports fell into the accurate range. But now she was more interested in the reaction than the action.

Jolene, rushing to her fallen husband. Shock, horror, faint. And if that wasn't a genuine faint, Eve would personally nominate her for the evangelical equivalent of an Oscar.

Clyde next, sprinting from the opposite end of the stage while he shouted orders to the security team to keep people back. The daughters, their husbands, crew running, tumbling, screaming, shoving.

Pandemonium.

Clyde holding them back, sharp words—cop's words. And, hmm, she mused, a group of women in sparkly, flouncy blue dresses. All blondes, all clinging together like one entity.

Eternal Light Singers, by her guess. One took a step forward, choked out the victim's name—Eve could see her candy pink lips form the words—before she went to her knees to weep into her hands.

Interesting. Snapping off the replay, she turned to head back. Mc-Nab crossed paths with Eve as she snaked her way toward the dressing areas.

"I got the sons-in-law and the security team. She-Body's finished with the daughters and most of the live-feed crew. We got a snag. One of the sons-in-law's a lawyer."

"Shit."

"Ain't that always the way?" McNab took a strip of gum from one of the pockets of his fluorescent pants, offered it. At Eve's head shake, he folded it into his own mouth. "So. He's making lawyer noises. It's after two A.M., and people have been held here for over four hours, yaddah-blah-blah."

"Did you get anything from any of the interviews?"

"Nothing that buzzed and popped. Lawyer Guy's puffing a bit, but it feels like mostly he just wants to get his family out of here."

Eve considered a moment. She could cut the immediate family loose, for now. Or . . . "Let's let them all go. Nobody's going to cut and run. Maybe we'll give the killer a few hours to think he or she got away with it. Give some of the others time to mull, maybe come up with more on re-interview. I got something I want to check out anyway."

"I'll open the gates."

"I'll want your full report, and Peabody's, by eight hundred, and Peabody at my home office that same hour."

"Ouch." He shrugged good-naturedly.

Eve went back to Roarke. "I'm letting them go. Whoever we didn't get to this round, we'll interview in the morning."

"Aren't you being uncharacteristically considerate?"

"One of the vic's sons-in-law is a lawyer."

"There's one in every crowd."

"And, not only is it not worth dicking with the lawyer, but it may work to my advantage. The sweepers will be a while," she added with a glance back toward the stage. "And I want to check something out on the way home anyway."

SALVATION IN DEATH 131

"All right." He pocketed his PPC and rose.

"Anything in those financials you've been playing with hinky?"

He smiled at the term. "Most financials—if they're worth anything—contain small portions of hink. But no, nothing over the line. Skirting it, in several areas. Your victim had very smart, very creative, and very lucrative advice. He was generous with his good works, but the cynical part of me says he could well afford to be. And those good works played to his advantage tax-wise and publicity-wise. He wasn't shy about tooting his own horn."

"I figure, if you've got a horn, why wouldn't you toot it, so that one never makes sense to me."

"His horn-tooting helped bring in more donations, which translated to a very, very nice lifestyle for Jenkins and family. Multiple homes," he continued, "luxury vehicles, considerable staff, art, jewelry. In addition, they're all—including the minor children—on the church payroll. Perfectly legal as they perform or have specific duties and job descriptions. And the church pays very well."

"So no recent downswings."

"On the contrary, this tour has sold out in every venue, and has generated a solid increase in donations."

"Money's not the motive. Doesn't play out. Sure, they might get a big spike due to the publicity around his death, the nature thereof. The fact that—sweet, leap-frogging Christ—that death was on air live on a gazillion screens on and off planet. But he's the image."

She gestured toward the life-sized billboard as they walked to the car. "He's the draw. He's the guy. Why kill the guy who's providing that really nice lifestyle? Could be the sex, could be professional or personal jealousy. Could be I've got a killer who has a boner against religion and wants to kill preachers."

"I like the sex," Roarke said, silkily. "For so many reasons."

"I'm betting Jimmy Jay shared your view." She gave him the address of the home where the Jenkins family was staying. "Drive by, will you? Then head to the Mark."

"Where do you suspect he was having that sex?"

"If a guy's going to diddle on the side, with the least risk factor, he hires an LC. But if the guy preaches against legalized prostitution, he's not going to take a chance of getting caught paying for a bj or a bang. So, for the extra serving, you'd go to someone you can keep close and trust—and that nobody would blink about you spending time with."

"Still risky. But the risk might have been part of the appeal."

Eve shook her head. "Doesn't strike me as being a risk-taker. More, I think, that he considered himself shielded. Like with the financials. He took steps, he took care. His daughter, most usually, spiked his stage water. Keep it in the family—or close enough with his decades-long manager, his trusted bodyguard. That was his habit—that vodka—but his wife didn't know. She wasn't pretending not to know, she didn't. He gets away with that, why not a little magic on the side?"

"I'm sure Mira would have more lofty terms," Roarke said after a moment. "But the pathology you outline is clear enough, and logical. There's your address."

She studied the town house on Park. "Nice. Roomy. Posh. Private digs for the family, top-drawer security. He took a walk today. A habitual thing, according to the youngest daughter. Ditch the bodyguard, go out for a walk. To meditate, get the energy up. I'm betting he walked as far as the corner here, hailed a cab."

"And rode to the Mark." Roarke made the turn to take them to Madison. "Not much traffic this time of night. There'd have been more during the day."

"Maybe take him twice as long as it'll take us now. He could've walked it in nearly the same amount of time as driving through afternoon traffic. But the six or seven blocks? Too much exposure. Too many people might recognize him. New Yorkers are used to seeing famous faces, and most would rather eat cat shit than react. But see, we're passing a lot of shops now, restaurants."

"Where the tourists would flock."

"And they're not generally so blasé. So, grab a cab and you're there in . . ." Eve glanced at her wrist unit when Roarke slid to the curb in front of the Mark. "Double the time, make it ten minutes. Probably more like eight." She held her badge up as the doorman whisked over to the car. "I need to leave the vehicle here."

The doorman hissed through his teeth. "Well, ya mind pulling down some? We get a lot of pickups, drop-offs for another couple hours."

"Sure." When Roarke pulled down a length or two, she got out on the sidewalk and studied the hotel as she waited for him. "You don't own this, do you?"

"I don't, no, but I can arrange that. If it would help."

"I think I can muddle through without that. Why don't you own it?"

"Despite your routine claims, I don't actually own everything. And this?"

He tucked his hands in his pockets, studied the building as she did. "The location's good, but the architecture doesn't appeal to me. That Post–Urban War utility feel combined with the dignified to the point of boring. It's not nearly old enough to warrant the sort of face-lift I'd want to give it. And there's the interior, which I'd need to rehab and re-configure to suit my own vision. Generally, it runs at only fifty-percent capacity. It's overpriced for its ambiance and its service, and lacks a restaurant of any note."

She rocked back on her heels. "And here I just thought the building was kind of ugly."

"Well, that's the short answer."

"You thought about buying it."

"No. I looked into it. I look into things, darling, which is one of the many things we have in common. I assume you're here to look into something and we're not just standing on the sidewalk at half-two in the morning to take in the air and study unattractive architecture."

"They'll be coming along pretty soon. They'll come straight back af-ter the night they've had, go to their rooms. Or to each other's rooms for comfort, for a rehash. But she won't. She'll want to be alone."

"The side dish."

"Yeah. My money's on the blond singer."

"They were all blondes."

"Yeah, they were. The blond singer with the biggest rack."

"As not all men go for large breasts—as I can attest—I'll also assume you're basing your money on the replay, and the large-breasted blonde who fell to her knees to weep."

She poked a finger at his shoulder. "You watched the replay."

"Looking into things."

"And your take?"

He lifted her hand to his lips. "I wouldn't bet against you."

Eve turned as a limo glided to the curb behind her police issue. She watched people come out. A man, a woman, another couple, another man, then the singing quartet. They clumped together like a puffy blue ball, and rolled into the hotel.

"We'll give them a couple minutes, let them get to their rooms. Could wait to do this in the morning," she said, half to herself, "but she might be easier to open now, and in her room. Away from the venue, from everyone else."

"And if she admits to being his lover, what does it tell you?"

"I don't know. It depends. One angle leads to another. It could be motive. She wanted more; he wouldn't give it. Or there's a jealous boyfriend, or former lover. Or . . . I've got some others cooking. Okay. Let's go intimidate the night clerk. No bribing," she added. "It takes the fun out of it."

She went in, strode across the lobby with its boring gray floors and unfortunate floral upholstery. She had her swagger on, Roarke noted. It never failed to entertain him.

She slapped her badge on the counter where a droid in a severe black suit manned the front desk.

"Good evening," he said, and Roarke wondered whose idea it had been to program the droid with such a pussified Brit accent. "Welcome to the Mark."

"Ulla Pintz. I need her room number."

"I'm sorry. I'm not at liberty to divulge the room numbers of our guests. Ordinarily, I'd be happy to ring the guest room for you, and obtain that permission, but Ms. Pintz just came in, and requested a Do Not Disturb. There's been a terrible tragedy."

"Yeah. Dead guy. I'm a cop." She lifted her badge, wagged it in front of his face. "Guess why I'm here."

He only stared blankly, which Eve admitted was the trouble with service droids. They didn't usually get sarcasm or subtlety.

"Let's put this in short sentences," Eve decided. "Ms. Pintz is a witness to said terrible tragedy. I'm the primary investigator of same. Give me her room number, or I haul all your circuits down to Central, where we'll get a warrant to shut you down due to obstruction of justice."

"Here at the Mark, our guests' wishes are sacrosanct."

"Try this: How are you going to serve your guests' wishes when you're down at Central and the jokers in EDD are playing with you?"

He seemed to consider that, as far as droids considered anything. "I have to verify your identification."

"Go ahead." A thin red beam shot out of his eyes as he scanned the badge on the counter. "Everything appears to be in order, Lieutenant Dallas. Ms. Pintz's room number is 1203."

"Does she have a roommate?"

"No. The other members of the Eternal Lights share a suite, but Ms. Pintz prefers her own quarters."

"I bet."

Satisfied, she walked with Roarke to the elevator. "It's not as much fun to intimidate droids."

"We have to take our small disappointments. Think of how you'll enjoy interrogating Ulla."

"Yeah." She stepped on the elevator. "Maybe that'll make up for it. I also could be chasing my tail by looking at this as essentially unconnected to my first murder, instead of going with the overt and obvious."

"Trusting your instincts instead of the hard facts?"

"If I were to run a probability right now, I'm pretty damn sure I'd get high eighties that we've got the same killer on both."

"And you think not."

"I think not. I think I know who killed Jenkins. Not sure why yet."

Eve got off the elevator, walked down to 1203. The Do Not Disturb light beamed from the door. She ignored it and knocked.

"Ulla Pintz, this is the police. Open the door."

After several seconds of silence, Eve knocked again, gave the same command.

"Hello?" A high, quavery voice spoke through the speaker. "I'm, ah, indisposed. They said I wouldn't have to talk to anyone until tomorrow."

"They were wrong. You need to open the door, Ulla, or I'll secure authorization to use my master."

"I don't understand." Sniffles accompanied the words now as locks clicked off. "Samuel said we could come back, and not talk to anyone." The door opened. "He's a lawyer and everything."

"I'm a cop and everything. Lieutenant Dallas," Eve added, and deliberately said nothing about Roarke as they stepped in. "Rough night, huh, Ulla?"

"It's so horrible." Ulla wiped at her eyes. She'd taken off the poofy dress and wore the hotel's white robe. She'd had enough time to remove several layers of stage makeup so her face was naked, pale, splotchy. And very young. "He *died*. Right in front of us. I don't know how."

Recognizing one who didn't play damsel but simply was one, Roarke took her arm. "Why don't you sit down?"

The room was small, but managed to cram in a tiny sitting area in addition to the bed. Roarke led her to a chair.

"Thank you. We're all so upset. Jimmy Jay was so big and healthy and, and larger than life, so full of the energy of the Lord." She made what Eve could only describe as a blubbery sound, then buried her face in a tissue. "I don't know how he could be *gone*!"

"I'm working on finding out. Why don't you tell me about your relationship with Jimmy Jay?"

As she lifted her head again, Ulla's eyes popped wide, actually jittered. "Why do you say that? I sing. We sing. Me and Patsy and Carmella and Wanda, we're the Eternal Lights. We make a joyful noise."

It was late, Eve thought, and there wasn't any point in screwing around. She sat on the foot of the bed so that her eyes were level with Ulla's swimming ones. "We know, Ulla."

Ulla's gaze shot up, rolled away. Like a kid's might when he denies snitching cookies even when his hand is stuck in the jar. "I don't know what you mean."

"Ulla."

When Roarke spoke before she could, Eve scowled at him. But his attention was focused on Ulla.

"Jimmy Jay would want you to tell us the truth. He needs your help. Someone killed him."

"Oh my goodness. Oh gosh."

"He needs you to tell us the truth so that we can find out who did this, so we can find the answers for those who loved him, who followed him. Who believed in him."

Ulla clasped her hands together, pressed them in the deep valley between her very impressive breasts. "We all did. I think we'll be lost without him, I really *do*. I don't know how we'll find the path to Enlightenment again."

"The truth is the first step on the path."

She blinked, her watery brown eyes fixed on Roarke. "Really?"

"You're carrying a burden now, the burden of a secret. He wants you to lay it down and take that first step on the path. I'm sure of it."

"Oh." Her eyes stayed riveted on Roarke's. "If I could! But I don't want to do anything that would hurt him, or Jolene, or the girls. I'd just never forgive myself."

"Telling us will help them, not hurt them. If they don't need to know this answer, it won't leave this room."

She closed her eyes a moment while her lips moved in silent prayer. "I'm so confused. So sick in my heart. I want to help. I want to stay on the path." Ulla spoke to Roarke. It was, Eve realized, as if she herself had poofed like smoke.

"I guess you could say that Jimmy Jay and I had a special bond. A relationship that transcended earthy barriers."

"You loved each other," Roarke prompted.

"We did. We did." Gratitude poured through her voice at his understanding. "In a different way from the way he loved Jolene, and his girls, and how I love my almost fiancé, Earl, back in Tupelo."

Ulla glanced at the photo beside her bed of a skinny man with a big, gummy grin.

"We created light with each other. And I helped him, with my body, gain the strength to preach the Word. It wasn't just physical, you see. It wasn't like, well, sex."

Eve resisted, by a thin, thin thread, asking what the hell it was like if it wasn't like sex.

"Though we gave each other pleasure, I don't deny it." Eyes leaking, and pleading for understanding, Ulla caught her bottom lip between her teeth. "But through the pleasure, we gained a deeper understanding. Not everyone understands the understanding, so we had to keep it just between the two of us."

"Can I ask how long you had this special bond?" Eve put in.

"Four months, two weeks, and five days." Ulla smiled sweetly. "We both prayed on it first, and that power—the spiritual power—was so strong, we knew it was right."

"And how often did you . . . create light with each other?"

"Oh, two or three times a week."

"Including this afternoon."

"Yes. Tonight was a very big night, for all of us. It was so important that Jimmy Jay have all the light and energy we could make."

She took another tissue, blew her nose delicately. "He came here this afternoon. I stayed in when the girls went out to do a little sightseeing before going to rehearsal. It took almost an hour. It was a special, special night, so we had to create a lot of light."

"Did he ever give you anything?" Eve asked. "Money, presents."

"Oh no, oh goodness. That would be wrong."

"Uh-huh. Did you ever go out together? Travel together, a holiday, out to dinner?"

"No, oh no. We just came together in my room wherever we were. For the light. Or maybe, once or twice, backstage somewhere if he needed a little extra closer to preaching."

"And you didn't worry that you might be found out by someone who didn't understand the understanding."

"Well, I was, a little. But Jimmy Jay felt that we were shielded by our higher purpose, and our pure intentions."

"No one ever confronted you about your relationship?"

Her lips moved into a soft, sad pout. "Not until now."

"You never told, or hinted, to your friends? The other singers, your, ah, almost fiancé."

"No, I didn't. I was bound by my word. Jimmy Jay and I both swore right on the Bible that we'd never tell anyone. I hope it's all right I've told you. You said—"

"It's different now," Roarke assured her.

"Because he's gone to the angels. I'm so tired. I just want to say my prayers and go to bed now. Is that all right?"

B ack on the sidewalk, Eve leaned back against the side of her vehicle. "No way that was an act. She really is that gullible. She really is dumb as a sack of moondust."

"Yet very sweet."

Eve rolled her eyes toward him. "I think you have to have a penis to get that impression."

"I do, and did."

"Despite that—or probably because of it—you pushed the right buttons up there. You handled her very well, and got her to tell us without me having to threaten to haul her silly tits downtown." She couldn't stop the grin. "Set down the burden of the secret and step onto the path of righteousness."

"Well, it was a theme. In any case, she's the type who looks to the penis, in a manner of speaking, to tell her what to do, what to think. Jenkins used that. Or maybe he actually believed what he told her."

"Either way, it's an angle." She opened the car door. When they were inside, she glanced at Roarke. "Could they both be dim enough to believe nobody suspected, got the sex vibe? Nothing? Two or three times a week for months, and the occasional booster backstage. Backstage, as we've seen, that's swarming with people."

"Someone found them out, as you put it," Roarke said as he drove them home, "and killed Jenkins because of it?"

"It's an angle. What would have happened to the church—its rep, its mission, its coffers—if this *understanding* got out, was made public."

"Sex has toppled countries, and buried leaders. I imagine it would have done considerable damage."

"Yeah, I'm thinking more, lots more than the death of the founder and figurehead. The murder of that figurehead by what could be taken as a killer targeting men of God. You could get play out of that, if you spin it right. You could take a few hits, but more, you could drum up more business. The outraged, the sympathetic. You could hold the line until a new figurehead stepped in."

Oh yeah, she thought. It played. It played a marching tune. "Meanwhile, you've got the widow, the family, grieving and steadfast. You'll have media coverage out your ass, that will charge right through the memorial. Hell, if you know what you're doing, you can make this a big plus."

"Who knows what they're doing?"

"Oh. It's his manager. Billy Crocker."

Roarke let out a quick laugh. "And you know this from one interview with him—I assume—and a few hours on the investigation."

She rolled her shoulders, rubbed her eyes. "I should've said I like the manager for it. I'm tired, starting to feel punchy. I like the manager for it if it's a separate killing. If I'm wrong and it's connected to Flores/Lino, I'm fucked if I know."

She yawned, hugely. "Not enough coffee," she muttered. "I think I need a couple hours down, let my brain play with it while I'm out." She checked the time, cursed. "Okay two hours max, since I've got to get my report in order before Peabody comes on. And I need time to do a couple runs, and plug in your financials summary. If I do a probability, even with Ulla's statement, it's going to slap me back. I need some more."

Roarke drove through the gates. "I take it you and I won't be creating light together this morning?"

She gave a sleepy laugh. "Pal, I'm looking for the dark."

"Fair enough. Two hours down and an energy shake in the morning."

"They're revolting."

"We have a new flavor. Peachy Keen."

"Revolting and silly. Yum."

But since that was two hours away, she wasn't going to worry about it. She concentrated on getting upstairs, stripping down, and falling into the bed where Galahad already curled, looking annoyed at the interruption.

By the time the cat relocated to her feet, and she'd snuggled herself against Roarke, she was out.

And out, she walked onto the stage in the great arena of Madison Square Garden. The altar stood under a white wash of light. Both Lino, in his priest robes, and Jenkins, in his white suit, stood behind it.

The black and the white, under the brilliance of light.

"We're all sinners here," Jenkins said, beaming at her. "Just takes the price of a ticket. SRO, and every one a sinner."

"Sins aren't my jurisdiction," Eve told him. "Crimes are. Murder is my religion."

"You got an early start." Lino picked up a silver chalice, toasted her, drank. "Why is it the blood of Christ has to be transfigured out of cheap wine. Want a shot?" he asked Jenkins.

"Got my own, *padre*." Jenkins lifted his water bottle. "Every man to his own poison. Brothers and sisters!" He raised his voice, spread his arms. "Let us pray for this fellow sinner, that she will find her path, find the light. That she repents!"

"I'm not here about my sins."

"Sins are the weight holding us down, keeping us from reaching up for the hand of God!"

"Want some absolution?" Lino offered. "I give it out daily, twice on Saturday. Can't buy that ticket into heaven without paying for salvation."

"Neither of you are who you pretend to be."

"Are any of us?" Jenkins demanded. "Let's see the playback."

The screen behind them flashed on. Dull red light blinking, blinking. Through the small window, SEX! LIVE SEX! beat that red light into the room where Eve, the child she'd been, shivered with the cold as she cut a tiny slice of a molding piece of cheese.

In the dream her heart began to thud. Her throat began to burn.

He was coming.

"I've seen this before." Eve forced herself to keep her eyes on the screen, willed herself not to turn and run from what was coming.

He was coming.

"I know what he did. I know what I did. It doesn't apply."

"Judge not," Lino advised as he shoved up the sleeve of his robes. As the tattoo on his arm began to bleed. "Lest you be judged."

On-screen, her father—drunk but not drunk enough—struck her. And he fell on her. And he snapped the bone in her arm as he raped her. On the screen, she screamed, and on the stage, she felt it all. The pain, the shock, the fear, and at last, she felt the hilt of the knife in her hand.

She killed him, driving that knife into him, again and again, feeling the blood coat her hands, splatter on her face while her broken arm wept in agony. She stood on the stage and watched. Her stomach turned, but she watched until the child she'd been crawled into a corner, huddled like a wild animal.

"Confess," Lino ordered her.

"Repent your sins," Jenkins shouted.

"If that was a sin, I'll take my lumps with God—if and when."

"Penance," Lino demanded.

"Rebirth," Jenkins preached.

Together they shoved at the table of the altar so that it crashed to the stage, broke into jagged pieces of stone. From the coffin beneath, the bloody ghost of her father rose. And smiled.

"Hell's waiting, little girl. It's time you joined me there."

Without hesitation, Eve drew her weapon, flipped it to full. And killed him again.

Wake up now, wake up, Eve. That's enough now. You need to come back."

She felt the warmth, the arms strong around her, the heart beating quick against hers. "Okay. Okay." She could breathe here. She could rest here. "It's done."

"You're cold. You get so cold." Roarke pressed his lips to her temples, to her cheeks even as he rubbed the frigid skin of her arms, her back.

"She wasn't there."

"Who?"

"My mother. I thought, if I dreamed of any of it, if I went back or it came, she'd be there. Because of Solas, because of that. But it wasn't about that. It wasn't about her. I'm okay."

"Let me get you some water."

"No." She tightened her arms around him. "Just stay."

"Then tell me what it was about."

He held her as she did, and the chill left her skin, left her bones, left her heart. "I killed him again. I didn't feel all that fear or the rage or the desperation. I didn't feel pleasure. It was just what I had to do. I could stand there, and I could watch it all happen on the screen, even feel it happening. Like I was in both places. But . . ."

"But?"

"It didn't hurt as much, or scare me as much. I could watch and think: That's over. It's going to be all right. However long it takes, it's going to be all right, because I'm going to do what I have to do. However many times I have to do it, he'll still be dead. And I'm okay."

"Lights on," he ordered, "fifteen percent." He needed to see, to see her clearly enough to be sure. And when he did, he cupped her face in his hands, kissed her brow. "Can you sleep again?"

"I don't know. What time is it?"

"Nearly six now."

She shook her head. "It's nearly time anyway. I'll get up, get started."

"All right then, I'll get that energy shake."

She winced. "I knew you were going to say that."

"And because you're the love of my bloody life, I'll drink one, too."

 SHE'D HAVE PREFERRED COFFEE, BUT SHE DOWNED
the shake, which wasn't as disgusting as it should've
been.

"It tastes like a fruit bowl," she decided. "On Zeus."

"That's rather the idea." He studied what remained in his own glass,
sighed just a little, then drank it. "Well then, that chore's down."

"Why don't they make coffee-flavored ones?"

"There are all manner of coffee-flavored drinks, aren't there? The
point of a protein shake is drinking something healthy. Something
good for you, easily and quickly done."

"Maybe more people would drink it if it tasted like something that
wasn't healthy that they actually liked. Then people who only drink
them under duress might start going, mmm-mmm, I love me those
fudgy, whipped protein shakes."

He started to speak, then angled his head. "Hmm."

"Just saying. Anyway. I've got to grab a shower before I get started."
"So do I."

She narrowed her eyes. "Is that grabbing a shower, or grabbing me?"
"Let's find out."

Eve stripped off her nightshirt as she walked from bedroom to bathroom. She stepped into the shower first. "All jets on full, one-oh-one degrees."

"Christ, it's like being boiled for breakfast."

The crisscrossing streams shot on, a shock to the skin that took the heat straight down to the bones. As they soaked her, she turned. And grabbed him.

"I feel energized." She took his mouth in a hard, hungry kiss, with just a hint of bite, then laughed when her back hit the drenched glass wall. And his body pinned hers. "Hey, you too. What a coincidence."

He ran his hands down her first, wet against wet, so that every inch of her body craved.

"Fast," she said and wrapped herself around him. She bit him again, and those golden brown eyes lit with challenge. "Fast, hard, hot. Now."

He gripped her hips, jerking her up to her toes, and gave her what she wanted.

Pleasure was dark, and had teeth. His eyes, a wild and burning blue, trapped her even as his body plunged and pumped, to propel her over that first barbed peak.

She cried out from the thrill, from the knowledge that here, here, here, she understood the power of finding, accepting, merging with a mate. Here she knew the fire that forged them, and with him—only him—the absolute trust that tempered strength into love.

Whatever had come before, whatever dreams came haunting, she knew who she was, and reveled in the world she'd made with her lover.

She wrapped tighter, only tighter while her system shuddered. Her mouth raced, all speed, all greed, over his hot, wet skin while her heart quaked.

"More. More."

Steam curled; water thundered on glass. Her nails bit into his shoulders as she erupted around him. But she didn't let go. She wouldn't, he knew. She would hold, they'd found that. They would hold, whatever came.

Through the consuming, outrageous lust she incited in him, wove the consuming, outrageous love until they knotted together so truly there was no end or beginning to either.

He drove her up again, drove them both. When he felt her flying over, saw that dazzled shock glaze in her eyes, he went with her.

Still she held. As her body went limp with release, her arms stayed around him. Dazzled, he nuzzled her—the curve of cheek, the line of throat. Then his mouth met hers in a kiss, long and sweet.

"God," she managed. "Jesus. Wow."

"A personal holy trinity?" He tapped a glass block, cupping his hand for the creamy liquid it dispensed. "I feel an urge to stock a lifetime supply of that energy drink."

She smiled as he stroked the fragrant soap over her shoulders, her back, her breasts. "I don't think we need it."

Whether it was the energy boost, the good, strong sex, or coming out of a nightmare, Eve sat down to write her report on the Jenkins investigation with a clear head.

She went back through witness statements, started a time line. And because it was routine, ran a probability on her two active cases.

As she'd suspected, the computer determined both victims had fallen to the same killer at 86.3 percent.

Though she didn't buy it, she rearranged her murder board into two sections, one for Flores/Lino, one for Jenkins.

Sipping coffee, she studied the results.

"On the surface, sure. On the surface," she muttered. But it didn't go deep enough; it ignored the subtleties.

The simple priest—who wasn't a priest—in a predominantly Latino parish, and the big-time, wealthy, media-savvy evangelist. Different faiths, different cultures, different doctrines.

Considering, she circled the board. If the computer was right, and she was wrong, the media itself might be part of the motive. The first murder got plenty of coverage, and with this one, that was going to explode. Both murders had been executed in front of witnesses, both during what could be termed a well-staged, rehearsed performance, and both weapons had been planted backstage. Where, even with the security for Jenkins, people could and did move fairly freely.

Both victims had secrets, and neither was as good and pure as he professed. Or his image professed.

She turned as Roarke came in. "Probability hits mid-eighties I've got one killer, two vics."

"So you predicted."

"Here's a thought: If it's one killer, could that killer have discovered the duplicity of each vic? Flores's fakery, Jenkins with his liquor and his sidepiece."

"Killed for hypocrisy?" Roarke studied her revised murder board. "Then many thousands of religious leaders best mind what they drink."

"Yeah, and more than that. Why these two, in this city? Because, the killer lives here. Jenkins didn't. Multiple homes, but none in New York. Plus he traveled extensively, so he could have been killed pretty much anywhere. Anytime."

"But was killed here, and now. Only a couple of days after Flores."

"Yeah. After. Fanatic psycho-killer? Then why start with the obscure priest, and not the biggest target? And where's the killer's claim for credit?"

Eve shook her head as she circled the board. "Sure, a lot of serials and signatures manage to keep their mouths shut, at least for a while. But it follows, for me, that if you're going to target religious leaders, you're the fanatic. You *believe*. And when you're a fanatical believer, you, by God, just have to spread the word."

"Or what's the fun of being a fanatic?" Roarke agreed.

"Oh yeah. But there's no word. And you kill the fake priest hoping, trusting the cops will discover he's not who he says he is? You, the fanatic, don't make damn sure he's exposed? I don't think so. You leave a sign, or you rent a goddamn ad blimp to denounce him."

Roarke held up a finger, then moved to her kitchen to get his own coffee. "We've substantiated you don't agree with your computer."

"I think the computer's full of shit." She sent it an annoyed glance. "There was ritual in the first killing. It felt personal as well as hinging on the ceremony. The second? It feels . . ."

"Expedient," Roarke suggested, and Eve shot a finger at him.

"Exactly. An opportunity seized. I sent the report to Mira, asked to be scheduled in for a consult."

"Want to hear my opinion?"

"Yes, I do."

"The probability doesn't hold for me, not once you scrape away the thinnest top layer. Both victims were, ostensibly, men of God. But, with the first, there's no gain—nothing known, in any case."

Roarke tapped a finger to Lino's photo. "As Flores," he continued, "while he was liked by those he worked with, and popular among the members of the church, a parish priest can and will be replaced. With the second, there's considerable gain—monetarily, and the potential for some loss. At least potential for some loss in the short run. A replacement there will need to be cultivated. But, Jenkins ran what was, under it all, a business. Moves will be made to protect that business. If steps aren't already being taken to do so, I'd be very surprised. In both cases, I'd say the murders were personal, in that they were target specific. The killer, or killers, accomplished precisely what they'd set out to do."

"To eliminate the targets. But not, necessarily, to expose them." She drank more coffee, her eyes narrowed on the board. "In fact, to expose Jenkins puts the business at considerable risk. No one with an interest in that business would want that."

"There you are."

"Let's hope that's the right track, or we're going to be looking at some rabbi or monk or whatever in the morgue before much longer. Here comes Peabody, and she's brought McNab."

"You've got ears like a cat."

Eve glanced at her sleep chair where Galahad sprawled for his post-breakfast, pre-lunch nap. "Depends on the cat. Reports," Eve said the minute Peabody and McNab came in.

"Right here." Her dark eyes still blurry with sleep, Peabody held up discs. "Please, can there be coffee, and food, and maybe a direct transfusion of massive vitamins?"

Eve jerked a thumb toward the kitchen as she crossed over to plug the discs into her machine. She sent copies to Mira and Whitney unread. She'd have to catch up.

"While your associates are scavenging, I have some work of my own." Roarke tipped her head up with a finger under her chin, touched his lips to hers. "Good hunting, Lieutenant."

"Thanks. Hey, you've got a lot of businesses to protect."

He turned in his doorway. "One or two."

"Zillion," she finished. "The point being, you've got fail-safes and contingencies and whatever. Various people who'd do various things when in the dim, distant future, you die at two hundred and six after we have hot shower sex."

"I'd hoped for two hundred and twelve, but yes."

"And my guess is that you'd have Summerset in charge—coordinating. The one person you know you can trust to juggle all the balls, keep them in the air."

"You realize that would mean he'd have to live to be about two hundred and forty, but yes. While I could trust you, I wouldn't expect you to set aside your own . . . balls to juggle mine. Especially when you're comatose with grief and contemplating the bleakness of your remaining years without me."

"Right."

"You're still liking the manager."

"We'll see."

She went back to her desk, ordered a full run on Billy Crocker. Both Peabody and McNab stepped back in with plates of waffles.

"Carbs," Peabody said between forkfuls. "Energy."

"Yeah, it's a big day for energy. Billy Crocker's a widower. His wife—only marriage—died in a vehicular accident six years ago. He has two grown offspring. One's a professional mother, living in Alabama with her husband and two minor daughters. The other is on the EL payroll, and is married to a woman employed as a publicist for EL. He's sitting more than reasonably pretty financially, even while pumping a full twenty percent of his income back into the EL coffers annually. His home back in Mississippi is virtually next door to Jenkins, while he maintains a smaller second home near the married daughter."

Eve sat back. "He's in charge of booking appearances, clearing the venues, scheduling all Jenkins's appointments, securing his transportation—or working with the transportation head. To get to Jimmy Jay, you've got to go through Billy."

"Second in command," Peabody offered.

"Absolutely. Schedules his appointments," Eve repeated. "I can all but guarantee that both Caro and Summerset know where Roarke is pretty much any given time of the day or night. If not precisely, they know how to reach him, anywhere, anytime. If he was ever stupid enough to cheat on me—"

"I heard that," Roarke called out.

"They'd know. One or both would know."

"So Billy knew Jenkins was . . . preaching to the choir?" McNab suggested.

"According to Ulla, the side dish, she and Jenkins had been saying hallelujah for nearly five months. Regularly. I'm betting Billy knew, just as I'm betting Ulla wasn't Jenkins's first conversion."

"So we pin Billy on how much he knew and see what else we get," Peabody added. "And we see if we can find previous converts."

"Meanwhile, we're running the Flores investigation on parallel but potentially intersecting lines. I've got the results of a run I started last night before the second homicide. I've got about a half-dozen Linos baptized at St. Cristóbal's during the appropriate time frame, who have not lived in that parish during the last six years. On this first pass,

I eliminated those who do, or those who are currently listed as having a spouse, legal cohab, or are incarcerated. If we don't hit on this pass, we'll do another with those eliminated. It may be he created a trapdoor cover ID that's as bogus as he was."

"A lot more work." McNab polished off his waffles. "A lot more complicated. Just adding in the tax filing shit wouldn't make that real practical."

"So we hope we hit first pass. Can Feeney spare you if I want you on this?"

"I don't know how he runs EDD without me, but if you ask, he nods, I'm yours. What about the ID search?"

"Can Callendar handle it?"

"She's almost as good as I am." He grinned. "And I've pointed her in the right direction anyway."

"I'll tag Feeney. Meanwhile, get down to Central and start contacting and interviewing these Linos." She tossed him a disc. "If Feeney can't live without you, just hang onto it for now. I have a copy. Peabody, with me. And if the two of you have to lock lips before parting ways, make it fast."

Eve headed out so she didn't have to watch.

But the rosy flush riding her partner's cheeks when Peabody caught up told Eve there'd been more than a quick lip bump.

"Where first?"

"Morgue."

"Waffles, corpses, and slabs. The cop's trifecta. Did you get any sleep?"

"A couple hours."

"I wish I could bounce on a couple like you do."

"I don't bounce. McNab bounces."

"Yeah." Peabody stifled a yawn as they walked out the front door. "I guess you plow, and I'm down to a crawl." She flopped down in the passenger seat of the vehicle parked at the base of the stairs. "So, the side dish isn't on your suspect list?"

"Dumb as a cornstalk. Roarke says sweet, and I guess I see that, too.

Loyal, I'd say. She may be part of the motive, but she wasn't part of the execution."

"You said how we may intersect lines with the Flores case. But I don't see it."

"Why?"

"Well, I know it looks like they should cross, or merge. Same method, same basic victim type. Except they're not basically the same victim type. And if it's a killer on a mission, why is he keeping the mission to himself? Maybe the vics are connected in another way, but I can't find it. I spent some time doing background on Jenkins. I just can't see where he'd have run into the guy posing as Flores, where they'd have common ground."

"You may not bounce or plow, but you're crawling pretty well on a couple hours." She made it nearly five blocks before she hit the first hideous traffic snarl. "Crap. Crap. Why do they call it rush hour when it lasts days and nobody can rush anywhere?"

She engaged her dash 'link to tag Feeney.

She'd barely finished securing McNab to the team when her 'link signaled an incoming.

"Dallas."

"Lieutenant." Mira's admin sniffed on-screen. "Dr. Mira's schedule is fully booked today."

"I just need—"

"However, the doctor would be happy to discuss your current cases over her lunch break. Twelve o'clock. Ernest's."

"I'll be there."

"Be on time. The doctor doesn't have time to wait."

Before Eve could work up a scowl, the screen went blank. "Like I sit around and play mahjong all frigging day."

"What is mahjong, exactly?"

"How the hell do I know? Am I playing it? Screw this." If nothing else, Mira's dragon's attitude annoyed Eve enough to have her slapping on the sirens and going vertical.

Peabody gritted her teeth and gripped the chicken stick as Eve skimmed over the roofs of honking Rapid Cabs and compact commuters, as she veered around the hulk of a maxibus, veered back around the dingy wedge of a delivery van.

"He's still going to be dead when we get there," Peabody pointed out in a squeak. Then huffed out a breath of relief when Eve landed the vehicle in a short span of clear road.

"Look at that." Eve pointed a finger at one of the animated billboards running news headlines.

There, looming over the circus of Times Square, was Jimmy Jay Jenkins, choking out his last breaths, falling like a huge white pine under the ax.

"They'll be running that clip for days," Peabody predicted. "And any time they do a story on him for the next forever, they'll run it. Whoever had the rights to that feed is now a really rich bastard."

"Stupid!" Eve rapped her fist on the wheel, hit vertical again to zip over another, smaller jam. "Moron. Idiot."

"Who? What?"

"Me. Who owns the fucking feed? Who gets the juice? Find out. Now."

"Hold on. Hold on." Concentrating on her PPC, Peabody stopped visualizing her own mangled body trapped in the police issue after a violent midair collision.

"If it's not the church, I'm even a bigger moron. Why pass that revenue on to someone else? Even if it's a different arm, it's going to be the same body. It has to be the same damn body."

"I get Good Shepherd Productions."

"That's a church thing. Good Shepherd. They aren't talking sheep. Tag Roarke. He can get it faster." Eve's eyes stayed hot and hard on the road as she maneuvered. "Tag Roarke, ask if he can find out if Good Shepherd Productions is an arm of the Church of the Eternal Light."

"One second. Hi, sorry," Peabody said when Roarke's face came on, and she thought, "Gosh, pretty." "Um, Dallas wonders if you could find out if Good Shepherd Productions is part of Jenkins's church. She's currently trying to keep from killing us both in morning traffic, so she's kind of tied up."

"If the lieutenant had managed to read the data I added to her case file, she'd find a complete list of the various arms of the Church of EL, which include Good Shepherd Productions."

"I *knew* it. Thanks. Later."

"Okay. Me, too." Peabody added a smile. "Have a good one."

"The church is going to make a mint from that feed alone. If we need an estimate, Nadine could give it round numbers." Eve threaded through traffic, pushing south. "So you lose your figurehead, and the main source of revenue. But you lose it in such a way that brings you an instant spike in that revenue—there is no downswing, no potential loss. But there is the potential, if you're smart enough, to capitalize on that for years. For, what was it, the next forever."

"Hey. I said that!" Peabody took a moment to preen—then another to exchange shocked stares with the glide-cart operator they skimmed by with the skin of a soy dog to spare.

"You've still got the family, and you're damn straight you've got a replacement already in mind. Plus, your figurehead's drinking and screwing around. That gets out, the money train's going to take a long, unscheduled stop. But this? It's win-win more."

She rode on that, turning the different angles in her mind until she reached the morgue. Striding down the white tunnel, Eve pulled out her 'link to check one of those angles. Then stopped when she saw Morris standing in front of a vending machine. With Detective Magnolia Blossom.

The detective spotted Eve and Peabody first, and brushed back a silky lock of melted butter hair. "Lieutenant, Detective."

"Detective," Eve said with a nod. "You got one in?"

"No, actually, I was just on my way out. Thanks for the coffee," she said to Morris, with a gleam in her deep summer blue eyes that made it clear she was thanking Morris for a lot more than a crappy soy product.

"I'll walk you out. One minute," he said to Eve, then moved with Detective Coltraine side-by-side down the echoing tunnel. His hand reached out, skimmed lightly down her back.

"Wow. They're, like, touching. Oh, and look. She's doing the head-tilt thing. That's a definite invite. I bet they're going to share a big sloppy one at the door," Peabody predicted.

"Gee, you think?" The idea of the big sloppy one made Eve want to do a quick check of Detective Amaryllis Coltraine's on-the-job record. Because the urge annoyed her, Eve put it out of her mind. "He's a big boy."

"That's what I hear." Peabody grinned at Eve's cool stare. "I can't help hearing things. Yeah, big sloppy one was had," she muttered under her breath as Morris strolled back. "He sure looks happy."

He did, Eve realized. And that would be enough. "Sorry to interrupt."

"Now, or when you red-flagged me?"

"Either or both."

"Not to worry. Let's go say good morning to Reverend Jenkins."

"Were you able to start on him?"

"Yes, indeed. Some tests still pending," Morris added as they moved down, then into an autopsy room. "COD was what I assume you'd expected. Cyanide poisoning. He'd also ingested a tad over eight ounces of vodka and approximately thirty ounces of spring water in the last hours of his life. He'd had fried chicken, mashed potatoes and gravy, fried onions, collard greens, biscuits, and peach pie with vanilla ice cream about six P.M. And, if that wasn't enough, about ten ounces of deep fried pork rinds with sour cream dip at around eight."

"I'm surprised he had room for the cyanide," Eve mumbled.

"I'm going to guess he ate that way with some regularity as he was about thirty pounds overweight. Carried most of it in his belly, as you see."

It was hard not to as Jimmy Jay was currently splayed out naked on a slab.

"Unlike your previous entry, I'd say this one didn't believe in regular exercise, and liked to eat, preferring his food fried, starchy, and/or full of refined sugar. Take away the cyanide, and it's still unlikely your soul saver would have made his given one-twenty."

"How much cyanide?"

"Nearly half again as was used for your priest."

"Take him down, quick and hard. If he'd ingested it slowly, over the course of, say, an hour? If he'd had some laced in to his water bottles— multiple?"

"He'd have felt ill—weak, confused, short of breath."

"So not that way. All at once. The first two bottles onstage were most likely clean. It's about timing. Third bottle is consumed right around break time. Everything, everyone's revved up, he's in his groove. Sweating, preaching, pulls off his jacket. That's routine—the audience loves it. Can't risk it happening after the break," Eve said half to herself. "Can't risk even the slight possibility someone else might drink from that bottle, or that bottle is replaced. So it has to be before the break, when he's still by himself onstage. But for the biggest impact, at the end of that period."

"The daughter put them onstage," Peabody pointed out.

"Yeah. Yeah. What does it take?" Eve paced away from the body. "All you have to do is cross that stage. Everyone's used to seeing you, handling details, being around. Who's going to say: 'Yo, what are you doing?' Nobody. You just check the water, that's all. Making sure the lids are loose for good old Jimmy Jay. And you tip in the cyanide."

She paced back. "The water's on the table, behind the drop," she remembered. "Smarter to do it when the singers are already out there— what do you call it—upstage. In front of the drop. Vic's in his dressing room, most everyone is except the ones onstage. It takes a minute, if that. Sealed hands, maybe thin gloves, like a doctor's. I bet there's a medical on staff. Smart, pretty smart. Still, maybe stupid enough to toss the sealant or gloves, the empty poison container in one of the arena's recyclers. Why wouldn't you? It's just going to prove what you want us to find out anyway. Somebody poisoned him."

Morris smiled at her. "As Reverend Jenkins and I are now so intimately acquainted, and you appear to know who somebody is, share."

"His name's Billy Crocker. And it's time we had another chat."

11   THEY TRACKED BILLY DOWN AT THE TOWN HOUSE on Park. The attractive brunette who opened the door looked pale and wrung out—and surprised. "Detective Peabody. Is there—do you have news?"

"No, ma'am. Lieutenant Dallas, this is Merna Baker, the nanny."

"Oh, hello. I'm sorry, when I saw you on the security screen, I thought . . . Please, come in."

The foyer was short and wide, narrowing to a hallway Eve noted bisected the house. Merna stood, puffy-eyed, in her calf-skimming dark skirt and blue blouse. Her short hair curled around a face that showed no signs of enhancements.

Wouldn't have been Jenkins's type, Eve thought.

"We were told Mr. Crocker was here," Eve began. "We'd like to speak with him."

"Oh. Yes, he's here. He's back with Jolene and some of the family. We're . . . It's such a hard day."

"We'll try not to make it any harder."

"Yes, of course. If you'd just wait here a moment."

She walked down the hall, knocked on a door. When it opened, she spoke in a voice so quiet it didn't carry. But Eve heard Jolene's voice spike up inside the room.

"The police? Do they know what happened to my Jimmy? Do they—"

She came out fast, pushing her way through. She wore a long pink robe, and her hair bounced like tangled springs on her shoulders. Both her feet and face were bare, and Eve had a moment to think how much prettier she was without the layers of glop she painted on.

"Jimmy Jay." She gripped Eve's arms, long, pink nails biting in, as several people poured out of the room, into the hall. "You're here about Jimmy Jay. You found out what happened."

"Yes, ma'am, we did."

"It was his heart, wasn't it?" The words hitched on sobs. "That's what I've been telling everybody. His heart, it was just so big, so big and so full. It just gave out, that's all. It gave out, and God called him home."

There was a plea on her face, a terrible need in her eyes.

What was worse than telling someone their loved one was dead? Eve thought. Telling them their loved one was murdered.

"No, I'm sorry. Mr. Jenkins died of cyanide poisoning."

Her eyes rolled back. Even as the small army of people rushed forward, Eve caught her, held her upright. And Jolene's eyes blinked, went clear. Went cold. She slapped back at the hands reaching for her, kept those cold, clear eyes on Eve.

She went from zero to sixty, Eve thought. From fragile matron to avenger.

"You stand here, and you look me in the face, and tell me you know—absolutely, without a single doubt—that someone poisoned my husband. You look me in the eye and tell me that's God's own truth. Can you do that?"

"Yes. Someone poisoned your husband."

Around them, family broke into sobs, into calls for Mama, or Mama Jo. When they pressed in, reached for her, Jolene spun around.

"Y'all *hush!* You hush now, every one of you."

The noise shut off as if she'd slapped a switch. When she turned back to Eve and her lips trembled, she firmed them. When her eyes filled, she blinked back the tears. "How do you know, without a single doubt."

"It's my job to know. I've just spoken to the medical examiner—the Chief Medical Examiner of this city, ma'am—and the cause of death is confirmed. Lab results will confirm that the cyanide was added to his stage water. Unless you can stand here, look me in the face, and tell me you have any reason to believe your husband killed himself by cyanide poisoning, then I'm telling you he was murdered."

"He would never have taken his own life. Life is a gift from God. He would never have left me, his family, his church by his own hand."

She stepped back, drew herself up. All trace of the cotton candy fluff vanished. "You find who did this. You find who took that gift from God away from my husband, from the father of my children. You do your job."

"I will."

"Luke."

"Mama Jo." One of the men came forward, put his arm around her, gently.

"You're head of the family now. I expect you to do whatever needs to be done."

"You know I will. Let Jackie take you upstairs now, Mama Jo. You go on upstairs and get a little rest. We'll make sure everything's done the way Jimmy Jay would have wanted. The way you want. I promise you."

She nodded, rubbed his shoulder. "Thank you for coming to tell me, Lieutenant. I want to go upstairs now."

"Come on with me, Mama." The daughter, Jackie, enfolded her mother, led her to the stairs. Jolene stopped, looked back.

"Billy, you help guide them now, like you guided their daddy."

"I will. Don't worry, Jolene. I don't want you to worry." His face was a study of misery as he watched her climb the stairs.

"Lieutenant, I'm Luke Goodwin—Jackie's husband." Though he offered a firm handshake, his eyes showed a dragging fatigue. "I wonder if you could tell me, ah, when we might be able to take my father-in-law home. We're making arrangements for his lying-in-state and memorial, his burial. We want to get the family home as soon as we can."

"I hope it won't be much longer. I'll have someone contact you directly when we're cleared."

"Excuse me." Another man nudged forward. Not quite as tall as the first, he had sharp cheekbones and a mouth set in hard lines. "Unless my mother-in-law is a suspect, I'm going to insist she be allowed to return home. She's given her statement, and you have no legal reason to detain her."

"And you are?"

"Samuel Wright, Jimmy Jay's son-in-law. I'm a lawyer."

"Really? I wouldn't have guessed. I'm not detaining Mrs. Jenkins, but am requesting she, and anyone involved in last night's production, remain in New York and available while this investigation is ongoing. And I didn't hear Mrs. Jenkins request permission to return to her home residence."

"We're making arrangements for that. She needs to—"

"Then she can talk to me about it herself. In the meantime, I have some follow-up questions. I'd like to speak with you, Mr. Crocker."

"Yes, of course. Could we make an appointment?" He actually reached for his memo book. "We still have so much to do—arrangements, and cancellations."

"It won't take long. And it should be now."

"But—"

"Unless Billy's a suspect," the lawyer began.

"Let's make this easy then. You're all suspects. As far as I can ascertain, every one of you, along with the other members onstage, and behind it, had the opportunity to lace the water with cyanide. Means? Cyanide's not something you pick up at the local pharmacy, but it's easy to obtain through black and gray markets. Motive—lots and lots of money."

"That's both insulting and inappropriate."

"Sue me. Meanwhile, I can follow up with Mr. Crocker here, or we can go downtown."

"That's not necessary, of course that's not necessary. Sam." Billy tapped a calming hand on Sam's arm. "We all want to do whatever we can to help the police."

"You're not talking to her without me being present as your representative."

"Works for me," Eve said cheerfully. "Want to do this here in the hall?"

"Let's just take a moment." Luke lifted his hands. Though his voice was soft, Eve recognized the command under it. "We're all on edge. Lieutenant, would you and the other officer like to use the parlor? Could we get you anything? Tea? Water?" He stopped, shut his eyes a moment. "Will I ever be able to pour a glass of water again and not think of it?"

"The parlor's fine," Peabody told him. "We don't need anything, thanks."

"There's an office on the second floor. I'll be working there, if you need me for anything. Billy, Sam, I'll continue with the arrangements until you're done. Lieutenant." Luke offered his hand again. "Mama Jo has put her faith in you. So will I."

Not just head of the family, Eve thought as he left them. She'd lay odds she'd just shaken hands with the new head of the Church of Eternal Light.

Furniture, statuary, memorabilia, and photographs fought for position in a parlor of deep colors. Privacy screens shielded the window that afforded twin shafts of morning light.

A number of cups, glasses, and memo cubes scattered over tables.

"Please excuse the mess," Billy began. "We'd been making plans and arrangements, discussing the memorial when you arrived." He cleared his throat. "The media hasn't as yet learned the address or the direct number for this house. We hope to keep it that way."

"They won't get it from me, or any member of my investigative team."

"Reporters have managed to unearth my 'link number. I haven't given any comments. I thought that best, for now. But I will have to make a statement. Or rather, Luke will. Very soon. As soon as possible."

"If Mr. Goodwin wants or requires any cleared data from my department for a statement, I'll be happy to discuss it with him. Meanwhile." Eve took out her recorder. "Since your representative wants to keep this formal, I'm informing you that I'm recording this interview. You have the right to remain silent."

As she recited the Revised Miranda, Billy lost another two tones of color.

"Is that necessary?"

"It's for your protection, as your representative will tell you."

"It's best, Billy. It's best if we keep everything to the letter of the law."

"Do you understand your rights and obligations in this matter, Mr. Crocker?"

His hand fussed with the knot of his tie. "Yes, of course."

"And you have chosen Samuel Wright, also present, as your representative during this interview?"

"Yes."

"Very well. Dallas, Lieutenant Eve, Peabody, Detective Delia, in interview with Crocker, Billy, regarding the investigation into the murder of one Jimmy Jay Jenkins. Mr. Crocker, we have the statement you gave to me last night, at the scene, on record. Is there anything you wish to change regarding same at this time?"

"No. Nothing I can think of."

"You stated that you saw the victim approximately five minutes before his stage entrance, in his dressing room."

"Yes. I gave him his five-minute cue, then we spoke for a moment. I walked with him to the wings, stage right."

"What was his mood?"

"He was very energized."

Eve smiled at the term. "At the time you walked with him to the wings, the table and the bottles of water were already onstage?"

"Yes. As always. Behind the drop. At the cue, the curtain comes up, the singers exit—stage right, and Jimmy Jay and Jolene enter from stage right and left, respectively."

"Josie Jenkins Carter has confirmed that she placed the water bottles onstage. That she opened them, and replaced about an ounce of spring water in each with vodka."

"That has nothing to do with this interview," Samuel interrupted, with some heat. "And if you think you can insinuate that Josie had anything to do with what happened—"

"Are you also legal rep for your sister-in-law?"

His jaw tightened. "If need be."

"Fine, I'll let you know if need be and if I require a follow-up with Mrs. Carter. You were aware, were you not, Mr. Crocker, that alcoholic additives were routinely used in the victim's stage water?"

"Yes." Billy sighed. "Lieutenant, as that isn't what killed him, I don't want to see that made public."

"You also stated you were busy during the opening performance by the singers, checking details. You'd have been traveling behind that drop, from one wing to the other, correct?"

"At various points in time, yes."

"And did you see anyone approach the water bottles, see anyone out of place, see anyone behaving in a nervous or suspicious manner?"

"I'm sorry, no. The singers and musicians were onstage. Others were in their dressing rooms, some in the little canteen. I do think I saw Merna there, briefly, with some of the children. Techs would have been moving about, but for the most part, at least in those last few min-

utes, everyone should have been in place. No one should have been behind the drop. I didn't see anyone there."

"Okay. As manager, did you keep Mr. Jenkins's schedule? Arrange
his appointments."

"Yes, those were my duties."

"You'd have his 'link numbers, be able to reach him at any time."

"Absolutely."

"And would, as his manager, know his whereabouts? Particularly
when touring like this."

"That would be essential," Billy agreed. "If something came up,
Jimmy Jay wanted to know. He wasn't just a figurehead, Lieutenant.
He was the head of the church. He worked very hard, and was in-
volved in every aspect, every area."

"And it was your job that he was where he needed to be when he
needed to be there."

"Exactly."

"You also had a long, close relationship with the victim."

"Yes. Yes, I did."

"Did you spend time together—free time, I mean. Leisure time."

"Oh yes. Quite often." His shoulders relaxed, but the hand that had
moved from his tie to his leg plucked, plucked, plucked at his pants at
the knee. "Our families sometimes vacationed together, and we enjoyed
having barbecues. When my wife was alive . . . You remember, Sam."

"I do. She made the best potato salad in Mississippi. Rest her soul."

"And did you and the victim—just the two of you—ever spend
leisure time together?"

"We fished. Often with the boys, or other friends. But, yes, sometimes just the two of us."

"You spent a lot of time—between the work of the church and free
time—in each other's company."

"It was rare for a day to go by we didn't spend time."

"So you know he was engaged in an extramarital affair."

The air went out of Billy, as if Eve had pulled a plug. But Samuel came up out of his chair, quivering with outrage. "How *dare* you! How dare you slander a man like Jimmy Jay! If you speak one word of that indefensible lie outside this room, I can promise we *will* sue you, and the New York City Police and Security Department."

"The affair has been confirmed, and documented on record," Eve said coolly.

"Then I insist on seeing that confirmation, that documentation. If you think I'll take your word, or allow you to go to the media with—"

"Cut your jets, Wright. First, you have no legal right to that access at this time."

"We'll just see about that."

"Yeah, you do that. Meanwhile, I'm not interested in gossip, I'm interested in murder. And motive. For the last four and a half months, the victim engaged in a sexual affair outside of his marriage. He, in fact, engaged in same on the afternoon of his death."

Eve cut her eyes from Samuel to Billy. "But you know that already, don't you, Billy?"

He jolted, as if she'd given him a nudge with her stunner. "I don't know what you're talking about."

"You fished, you barbecued, you vacationed together. You managed his work, his time, and a great deal of his life. You knew where he was and where he needed to be nearly every minute of every day. But you want me to believe you didn't know he was spending an hour or two, two, sometimes three times a week in hotel rooms with another woman? That he often got himself a boost from that woman backstage before he went on to preach?"

"That's enough!" Samuel snapped it out. "You're trying to enhance yourself by besmirching the reputation of a good, Christian man. Neither my client nor I have any more to say to you."

"Nothing more to say, Billy?" Eve shrugged. "Then I guess we'll have to talk to other people who may have known. And I can't control it if those people decide to talk to other people. Including the media."

"That sort of threat—" Samuel began.

"I've got a job to do," Eve shot back. "That's not a threat."

"Please don't." Billy spoke quietly. "Sam, please sit down. I'm sorry. I'm so very sorry." He cleared his throat—a tic, Eve determined, used to give him time to collect his thoughts. "Only God is perfect, Sam."

"No." Outrage quavered into disbelief. "No, Billy."

"Jimmy Jay was a great leader. A visionary, and a humble child of God. But he was also a man, and a man with weaknesses. He did fall victim to lust. I counseled him as a friend, and as a deacon of the church. He struggled against this weakness, and he succumbed to it. You mustn't think less of him. You mustn't cast the first stone."

"How many times?" Samuel demanded.

"Once is too many, so it doesn't matter."

"It may matter to the investigation," Eve corrected.

"I believe he succumbed with six women over the years. He struggled, Sam. This was his demon. We have to believe, if he'd lived, he would have beaten it. Our job now is to shield Jolene and the church from this. To preserve Jimmy Jay's image, so that Luke can take his place and continue the work."

"Killing him before he got careless enough to let it get out," Eve suggested, "that would be a good way to preserve the image."

"This interview is over." Sam strode to the door. Tears as much as anger glittered in his eyes. "Don't come back here without a warrant, or I'll cite you for harassment, and for prejudicial treatment of a sanctioned church."

Eve leaned over to retrieve her recorder, and switching it off spoke quietly to Billy. "I know what you did. I know why you did it. I'll take you down. It'll be up to you whether I take the rest down with you."

She straightened. "I hear confession's good for the soul. Peabody."

They walked out, leaving Billy slumped on the couch, and Samuel nearly weeping at the door.

In the car, Peabody sat silent as Eve began the weave and dodge through traffic. Then she shook her head. "How did you know he did it?"

"He's not cuffed and heading downtown with us, is he?"

"Maybe we can't arrest him, yet. But you know. You knew. How?"

"Besides the guilt-stink rolling off him?"

"Seriously?"

"Okay, stink's too harsh a word. There was a distinctive whiff. He's the one who spoke to the vic last. He's the one who schedules everything and sees to the details. He's the one who has to know pretty much whatever the vic was up to. Add a kind of pompous, stick-up-the-ass attitude. Add the subtle change of tone and look in his eyes when he talks about Jolene."

"I did notice that, but not until today."

"I interviewed him; you didn't. He's got a thing for her. She's totally oblivious to it, but he's got one. Look at the replay of the murder again. He's in the wings when Jenkins starts choking, seizing. But he stays where he is. He doesn't run out until after Jolene's gone down. And he goes to her, not the dead guy. He barely gives Jenkins a glance."

"Yeah, I guess I noticed that, too," Peabody said as she played it back in her head. "But there was so much going on, I didn't separate it out. Do you think he did it because he wants Jolene?"

"He won't think so, won't let himself think so. But it's under there. I think he killed him, or so he tells himself, because Jenkins's behavior, and refusal to stop, could have brought down the church, shattered the family. And I think he did it because he tells himself Jenkins wasn't worthy of his position—or that family."

"He made a lot of mistakes. Even without the guilt-stink, it would've come back to him."

"Impulse." Eve powered through a yellow light. "He hears about the dead priest, and he coattailed. He didn't think it through, not like whoever killed Lino. He just jumped."

"Why didn't you push harder? We could get him in to interview, pull it out of him—lawyered or not."

"Guilt's going to do that for us." Eve tipped her wrist to check the time. "He's not going to be able to take it much longer. He'll need to confess. If not, if I'm wrong, we'll be hauling his ass in real soon. Meanwhile, we see if we can track down where he got the cyanide. Impulse, again. It had to be within the last couple of days. And we see how McNab's doing with the many Linos."

"I had an idea about the Lino angle," Peabody told her. "The medal. It was from his mother. Just his mother. It could be his mom just wanted to give him something special, just from her. But maybe she was a single parent at that point. We could cross-reference your list with single parents, or couples who divorced—though I think divorce is still a big deal for Catholics—or with women whose husbands died or took off."

"That's good, Peabody. That's very good. Let's dig into that. Or, better yet, you dig into it. I have to take a meet with Mira."

"I'll get started on it. I'm actually supposed to meet Nadine and Louise about thirteen hundred, if we're not running hot. We're going to finalize plans for the bridal shower-slash-bachelorette party."

"Bachelorette is a stupid, demeaning word."

"Yeah, but it's kinda cute, too." Even the idea of a party had Peabody scooting happily in her seat. "Anyway, we decided, since the wedding's coming up, we'd do the combo. I figured you'd like that, since it means only one event."

"Yeah, yeah."

"And you just mostly have to show up."

"No games." Eve took a hand off the wheel to point. "That's my line in the sand. That and strippers. No games and no strippers."

"Done. See? It's easy."

Maybe too easy, Eve mused, but she tucked it away as she pulled into Central's garage. "Check with McNab," Eve told her, "and get started on that cross-referencing. I'm going to walk over to meet Mira. I should be back within the hour."

"I'll leave whatever I've got for you, in case we miss each other. Oh, and if Billy comes in stinking to confess, I'll tag you."

"Do that." But Eve figured it would take a little longer before he couldn't stand his own stench.

She liked the walk, just striding across New York with its noise, its crowds, its attitude coming at her from all directions. She passed through the greasy smoke of a glide-cart, drew in the smell of grilling soy dogs, fries, veggie hash—and heard the operator snarl at a whiny customer.

"Whaddaya want for five bucks? Freaking filet mignon?"

She passed a couple of cops in soft clothes quick-marching a guy greasier than the dog smoke across the sidewalk and into Central while he proclaimed his innocence in all matters.

"I didn't do nothing. I don't know how that shit got in my pocket. I was just *talking* to the guy. Sweartagod."

She watched a bike messenger—a Day-Glo blur on a shiny jet-bike—gleefully challenge a Rapid Cab for position, and whiz away with lunatic speed, leaving the horn blasts and curses in his dust. An enormous black guy walked a tiny white dog, and stopped to responsibly scoop miniature dog poop.

She crossed the street with a throng of others at the light. Passed a flower vendor who sent perfume madly into the air, a deli that wafted out pickles and onions when a customer walked out. A couple of women walked by speaking what might have been Cantonese.

She crossed again, making the turn north.

And two women flew out of a shop door, screaming, punching, to drop nearly at her feet in a hair-pulling, scratching, teeth-snapping tangle.

"Why?" Eve wondered. "I was having such a nice time."

Pedestrians scattered like pool balls at the break. Others edged closer, calling out encouragement and/or grabbing 'links or cameras to record the bout. Eve barely resisted the urge to just keep going, and instead waded in. She grabbed a hank of hair, pulled hard. When the owner squealed and reared up, Eve nabbed her opponent in a headlock.

"Cut it out!"

Hank of Hair bit her, snapping forward to sink teeth into Eve's shoulder. And got an elbow to the chin in return.

"I'm a cop," Eve stated. "Goddamn it. The next one who bites, scratches, slaps, or squeals is getting hauled over to Central and dropped in the tank."

"She started it."

"Lying bitch. I want to press charges."

"*I* want to press charges."

"I saw it first."

"I—"

"Shut the hell up!" Eve considered just knocking their heads together and calling for a wagon. "I don't give a rat's ass who started what. It's done. Break it up, stand up, step back. Or I'll charge you both with disturbing the peace, creating a public nuisance, and whatever else occurs to me."

They glowered at each other, but said nothing else as they climbed to their feet and stood with Eve between them. A third woman gingerly opened the shop door. "I called the police."

"I am the police," Eve told her.

"Oh, thank goodness." Showing considerable faith, the shopkeeper opened the door wider. "I just didn't know what to do. These ladies were in the shop. We're having a nice sale today. And they both wanted the Betsy Laroche triple roll bag in peony. We only have one. Things got very heated, and before I knew it, they were fighting."

Eve held up a hand. "Let me get this straight. You've got a bloody lip, a ripped shirt, ruined pants, and a black eye coming on between you. Over a bag?"

"A *Laroche,*" the one with the bloody lip lisped. "At ten percent off. And I saw it first. I had my hand—"

"Bull! I saw it first, and you came running across the—"

"Liar."

"Bitch."

And they leaped around Eve and at each other's throats.

"Oh, for Christ's sake."

She broke it up this time by grabbing both by the hair and shoving faces against the wall. "Two things can happen now. You can each go your separate ways, unless this lady here wants to press charges."

"Oh, no." The shopkeeper peered out of what was now a tiny opening. "No. That's okay."

"Your separate ways is option one," Eve continued and noted the black-and-white pulling up to the curb. "And neither of you will come to this establishment for the next month or I'll hear about it. Option two is I'm going to have—I'm on the job," Eve said to the uniforms as they strode across the sidewalk. "Can't get my ID right at the moment.

"Option two is I will have these two officers cuff you both, put you in the back of their vehicle, and take you the few blocks to Central to book you on the variety of annoying charges I will list. Either way, neither of you is getting that stupid bag. Choose."

"I'll leave if she leaves."

"Okay, all right."

"You." Eve tugged the first hank. "Go south. And you." Then the other. "Go north. Don't speak, don't look at each other. Just start walking. Now."

She released them, stood where she was until each combatant limped away. She reached for her ID, winced slightly when the bite on her shoulder objected to the move. "Thanks for the backup," she said. "I think we're clear here."

"Thank you, Officer, thank you so much." The shopkeeper laid a hand on her heart. "Should I take your name and contact information, in case they come back?"

"They won't." With that Eve walked the half a block more to Ernest's.

It was an upscale kind of diner, with service at its stainless counter, or chummy booths. Service was quick, the food simple.

Mira sat at one of the two-top booths, sipping something cold from a clear glass. Her rich brown hair curled at her nape, and in a new flirtatious way, around her serene and pretty face. The look of her, Eve thought, in her spring's-here yellow suit and textured heels in ball-lightning blue, seemed more suited to one of the trendy cafés than the cop diner.

Then again, she supposed the police psychologist and profiler had no more time for fancy lunches than she did herself.

Mira saw her, smiled.

"Sorry I'm late. There was a fight over a Laroche triple roll bag. In peony."

"You had a fight over a purse?"

Eve had to grin at Mira's utter shock. "No, I had to break one up. It's a purse? I figured it had to at least be a suitcase to get that much insanity. Or maybe it was the ten percent off. Anyway—"

"Wait, there's a sale on the Laroche triple? Where?"

"Just down the street. Half a block south. Ah, Encounters, I think it's called."

"I know that shop." Mira pulled out her 'link. "Why don't you decide what you'd like for lunch, and I'll . . . Yes, Mizzie, this is Charlotte Mira. Yes, it's good to talk to you again. You have the Laroche triple, in peony, on sale? Would you put that aside for me? I'm just having lunch at Ernest's, so I'll stop in to pick it up on my way back to work. Yes, thank you. Oh, I'd love to see that, too—if I have time. I'll see you shortly."

With a smug smile, Mira clicked off. "Isn't that my good luck? I've been toying with getting that bag, and talking myself out of it. But, well, a sign's a sign."

"I guess."

"I'm going to have the Greek salad," Mira said when their waiter stopped at the table, "and another iced tea."

"Two salads," Eve said. "Pepsi."

Mira let out a contented sigh. "Gorgeous day, isn't it? It's nice to get out of the office, to score a Laroche, and to see you. You look well, for someone who just broke up a fight."

"One of them bit me."

"Oh." Mira's smile faded into concern. "Is it bad? Do you want me to look at it?"

"No." Eve rolled her shoulder. "I don't get it. Scratch, bite, squeal, slap. Why do women fight like that? They've got fists. It's embarrassing to our entire gender."

"Yes, I can see a fistfight over the triple roll would have been much less embarrassing for all involved."

Eve had to laugh. "Okay, guess not. Anyway, I know you don't have much time. I've got a lock on the Jenkins murder. It's not connected to Flores."

"Unlike the probability?"

"Copycat, impulse. Probably a long, simmering deal that flashed over when the Flores deal hit the media. So, it's loosely connected. But a different killer, and different circumstances."

"A repeat killer or serial was a worry."

"Did you see it that way?"

"It couldn't be ignored. The targeting of figures in religious organizations, the ceremony or 'performance.' But, it also had to be factored in that each of the victims was remarkably different, in the faith base, their public exposure. You have a confession on Jenkins?"

"Not yet. I'm letting him stew in it. If I don't have one within the next few hours, I'll stir it some more. So it's the Flores case I need to kick around."

Mira took one of the table crackers, which looked as unappetizing as what Eve thought of as the Catholic cookie. She broke off a microscopic corner, nibbled on it

"The false priest," Mira said, "killed at the moment of ritual when he stands most emphatically as a servant of God and as his earthly representative. This is *my* blood—that's what's said. If the killer believed him to be Flores, believed him to be a true priest, this would indicate some direct attack on the church and its ritual, on the priesthood. Your investigation hasn't found any evidence of a personal problem with the victim—as Flores. He could, of course, have heard something in confession that the penitent later regretted passing on."

"Which means the killer likely belonged to that church, or is, at least, Catholic."

"I believe whether it was simply a priest—or the individual masquerading as one—who was the target, that the killer has strong ties to the Catholic Church, and to that parish. The method was another kind of ritual, and I don't believe choosing to execute the murder during a funeral mass was happenstance."

"Same page, same line," Eve agreed.

"Poison is a distant kind of weapon. It removes the killer from the victim, but can also afford the killer the advantage of standing back and witnessing the death. The crowd in the church would afford an excellent cover for that. The distance and the intimacy. I would say both were desired. Public execution."

"Why make it public if you can't watch yourself?"

"Yes. But for what crime? The crime had some direct effect on the killer. Exposure wasn't enough. For a person of faith—and the ritual, the method, the time, and the place indicate that to me—the sin, the crime, had to have been deeply and desperately personal."

"It's about the neighborhood, about home, the gang connection. It's in there somewhere."

"Yes, the method, the place mattered. The killer's mature enough to plan, to choose. Involved in this faith enough to know how to use it. Organized, thoughtful, and probably devout. And the intimacy and distance of poison is often a female weapon."

"Yeah, like no fists," Eve commented. "Poison isn't bloody. Takes no force, no physical contact. A hundred-pound woman can take down a two-hundred-pound man without chipping her nail."

Mira sat back as their salads were served. "You believe Jenkins's killer will confess."

"Guilt's going to eat him inside out."

"A man or woman of faith, then?"

"Yeah, I guess. Yeah. He believes."

"Your two cases may not be connected by one killer, but I think they may be connected by the same type. I think he or she is also a person of faith. And if so, he or she will need to confess. Not to you. The Eternal Light doesn't have confession, penance, and absolution by a representative of Christ."

"But Catholics do."

"Yes. The killer will confess to his priest."

12 EVE HEADED BACK TO HOMICIDE WITH THE IDEA of grabbing Peabody and taking on the priests at St. Cristóbal's again. Confession, she thought. She believed Billy Crocker would need to unburden himself. Doing the deed—the impulse, even the restrained passion of it—would have carried him through the murder itself. But the aftermath, all the grief surrounding him would scrape and dig at him. Add in her parting shot, letting him know she recognized him, and yeah, he'd fall under the weight. She'd already seen it in his eyes.

But the Flores killer. That was deeper, felt deeper. More personal, and more tied in with the ritual of faith. Mira put her finger on it, in Eve's opinion. The killer would seek yet another ritual of faith.

Maybe already had.

Hit the priests, and some of the tattoo parlors on her list. But that was long-shot territory. Finding the tat artist who inked her particular Lino after what could be a good twenty years was a crap shoot. But if she couldn't nail it down any other way, it was worth that shot.

She'd started the swing to her division when she remembered

Peabody wouldn't be there. Party planning, for God's sake. Why the hell did people have to have parties all the damn time? Food and drinks and gifts and decorations and agendas, all lined up on lists and talked over incessantly to the last stupid detail.

Another ritual, she thought, slowing her pace. All the trappings, the timing, the words or music, the scheme.

The killer had to be part of that ritual. Had to have been in the church at the moment Lino drank the sacramental wine. Had to watch the death—ritual death. A familial connection of the Ortiz's possibly. But that felt wrong, disrespectful to the old man, unless . . . unless the sin, the crime Lino committed had been in some way connected to Ortiz.

Ran by the Ortiz house every morning, she remembered. Was there a purpose there?

Otherwise, a less intimate connection. Family friend, neighbor, longtime customer, employee.

Turning it over in her mind, she stepped into her bullpen and saw Baxter flirting with Graciela Ortiz. No question about it, she mused, the body language, the eye gleams all said testing sexual interest. Then again, to her way of thinking, Baxter would flirt with a hologram of a woman.

"Officer Ortiz."

"Lieutenant. I stopped by, but the detective told me both you and your partner were out."

"Now I'm in. My office is right through there. Go on in."

"Detective," Graciela said and gave Baxter one last blast with green, liquid eyes.

"Officer." His grin widened, unabashed when he turned it on Eve. And pounded a hand like a happy heartbeat on his chest. "You've got to love a woman in uniform," he said to Dallas.

"No, I really don't. If you've got time to hit on subordinates, Baxter, maybe I need to review your caseload."

"Dallas, sometimes a man's just got to make time."

"Not on my clock. But since you've made all this time, you can use it to do a search on all John Does, deceased, in Nevada, New Mexico, and Arizona, six to seven years ago."

"All? Jesus, you're a hard woman."

"I am. Be grateful I'm adding age between twenty-five and forty."

She turned as he muttered, "Oh, in *that* case," and walked into her office. "Officer."

"I wanted to speak to you in person regarding the interviews with family members and friends. There was nothing I didn't expect— shock, sorrow, even outrage. Father Flores was, as I told you, very popular. Well, when we believed he was Father Flores."

"And now?"

"More shock, sorrow, outrage. In fact, as he married, buried, baptized many of the family over the past five years, you can add a lot of concern. Some of my family is very traditional, very orthodox. There are questions as to whether the marriages are sanctioned in the eyes of God and the Church. Which Father López assures us would be the case. Though he and Father Freeman have offered to renew all the sacraments, for those who wish it. Frankly, Lieutenant, it's a big freaking mess."

She shook her head. "I like to think I'm a progressive sort of person. Practical. But I confessed to that man, and received Communion from him. And I feel . . . violated, and angry. So I understand what many of my family are feeling now."

"His death stopped the violation."

"Well, yes. But it also revealed it. If we'd never known . . ." She shrugged. "We do know, so I guess it's just what we all decide to do about it. My mother thinks we should look on the positive side. Have a mass renewal of vows, of baptisms. And a big party. Maybe she's right."

"There were a lot of people at the funeral who weren't family members."

"Yes. I've spoken to some of them, the ones we're close to, or Poppy was close to. It runs along the same lines. I don't know how helpful any of it is to your investigation."

"You saved me some steps." She considered a moment. "You have several relatives, I imagine, who are about the same age as the victim. Round about thirty-five."

"Sure. We're legion."

"Plenty of them were living in the area when they were kids, teenagers. And plenty of them members of the church."

"Yes."

"Any of them former members of the Soldados?"

Graciela opened her mouth, closed it again. Then blew out a breath. "A few, I suppose."

"I need names. I'm not looking to cause them trouble, not looking to dig at them for what they did in the past. But it may connect."

"I'll talk to my father. He wasn't part of that, but . . . he'll know."

"Would you rather I spoke to him directly?"

"No, he'll be easier speaking to me. I know his cousin was a member and died badly when they were boys. He doesn't have any love for gangs."

"What was the cousin's name?"

"Julio. He was only fifteen when he was killed. My father was eight, and looked up to him. He never forgot it, and often used him as an example, a warning, especially to my brothers and cousins. This is what happens when you go outside family, the law, the church—when you use violence instead of hard work and education to get what you want."

"Your father sounds like a smart man." And the quick math she did in her head told her Julio's death was too early to apply to Lino.

"He is, and a tough one. I'll talk to him tonight."

"Appreciate it. One other thing. I'm told the vic ran regularly in the morning, and the route took him by your grandfather's house."

"Yes, that's true. Poppy mentioned it sometimes. How he joked with the fathers to throw a blessing at the house as they passed. And he might see them when he was out for his morning walk."

"So no friction there?"

"Between Poppy and the priests, or this one who wasn't? No. None. Very much the opposite. The victim often ate in Poppy's restaurant, or even—especially when my grandmother was alive—his home. He came to family parties. He was, we thought, one of us."

"Okay."

Alone, Eve moved back to her board. Rearranged photos, evidence shots. Walked around it, arranged again. Connections. Whose life touched whose, when and how.

She stepped back to her desk, tagged McNab. "Give me something," she demanded.

"Ran down two of the Linos," he told her. "One's living in Mexico, living in a kind of commune deal. Changed his name, which is why he slipped through some cracks. Goes by Lupa Vincenta, all legal and shit. It's a kind of Free-Ager offshoot. Guy's shaved his head and wears this brown robe deal. Raises goats. And is alive and well, if you count wearing an ugly brown robe well, which if you ask me—"

"I didn't."

"Okay. The other's been skimming under the radar, avoiding a couple of ex-wives, who he was married to at the same time. He's in Chile—or was when I tracked him—and the last track was less than three months ago. He weighs in at about two-fifty. Probably skipped by now, as both women have suits pending against him. Apparently, he's got about six legal offspring, and he's dodging the child support thing."

"Prince of a guy. Pass on the info to the proper authorities."

"Already done. You get kids, you take care of them. Working on another one now."

She'd figured as much, as McNab was bopping on the screen. She'd never known an e-geek who could keep still when he worked.

Except Roarke, she corrected.

"I keep losing him," McNab added. "He bounced a lot, switched names, then switched back. What I get is he'd get a little twisted up with some deal under an aka, take off, show up under his real, play it straight, then move on, take another alias."

"What's his real?"

"Lino Salvadore Martinez."

Eve brought it up on her machine. "Right age, right location at birth. Keep looking." Eve clicked off, then refreshed her memory of Martinez's data. Both parents on record, she noted, but whereabouts of the father unknown—and unknown since Martinez hit five years of age. Mother, Teresa, applied and received professional mother status and payments after the birth. Previous employment . . . Eve extended the search, then sat back. "Hector Ortiz—Abuelo's. Interesting. Yeah, that's pretty interesting. Returned to outside work when her son reached the age of fifteen—as a waitress for Ortiz again. Where she worked for six years before remarrying and relocating to Brooklyn. Okay, Teresa."

She noted down the current address. "I think we need to have a little chat."

She pulled out her communicator to contact Peabody. "What's your status," she said when Peabody popped on-screen.

"I'm just walking into Central. We had the best—"

"Meet me in the garage. We're going to Brooklyn."

"Oh. Okay, why—"

But Eve simply cut her off, tucked the communicator away, and started out. She nearly walked straight into Baxter. "No way you finished those searches."

"No way I'll finish those searches in the next twenty man-hours. You've got a couple of visitors. A Luke Goodwin, a Samuel Wright, and a Billy Crocker."

"Quicker than I thought." She stepped back into her office, signaling Baxter to follow. "I need to secure an interview room. Hold on."

She ordered her computer to scan for availability, and book her Interview C. "Okay, tell them I'm going to be a few minutes, escort them to Interview. Make nice, offer refreshments."

"That's going to take time off my current assignment."

"Half of which you've already passed off to your aide. Trueheart can keep it going while you get these guys settled. If I get my confession out of Crocker, have him booked and in a cage within the next ninety minutes." She checked her wrist unit. "From now, I'll take half of what's left of the search off your hands."

"Deal."

When he walked out, Eve tagged Peabody again. "Change of plans, come up, meet me outside Interview C. We've got Crocker and company."

"Jeez. If I was a lesser person, it would piss me off, how often you're right."

"Since I am a lesser person, you'll be good cop in today's performance."

Eve cut Peabody off, then contacted both Whitney's and Mira's offices to relay her prime suspect on the Jenkins homicide was in the house.

"Okay, Billy," she murmured. "Let's see what you have to say for yourself."

She took her time, to give Baxter a chance to settle them in and Peabody a chance to reroute from the garage. She already had her strategy outlined in her mind, and had adjusted that somewhat after her meet with Mira. Due to that, she wasn't surprised that Billy had come in with Luke.

The confessor, she thought.

She slipped into Observation first, studied the setup. Billy sat at the table, flanked by the victim's sons-in-law. The lawyer looked grim, with his gaze cut away from Billy. Luke looked . . . sorrowful, Eve thought. A more sophisticated lay-version of López, to her eye.

And Billy himself? Jittery, scared, and on the edge of weepy.

She stepped back out as Peabody hoofed down the corridor.

"He brought his priest and his lawyer," Eve said.

"Priest?"

"In a manner of speaking. Luke Goodwin. He's already told them everything he intends to tell us and probably more. Yeah, more, because the lawyer may be pissed and shocked, but he's still a lawyer, and he'd advise him how to play it. You're sympathetic, you get why he had to do what he did. You want to help."

Peabody's face went wistful. "Am I ever going to be able to be bad cop?"

"Sure, as soon as you're willing to kick a puppy out of the way to take down a suspect."

"Aww, does it have to be a puppy?"

"Keep that save-the-puppy look on your face. It's perfect." Eve opened the door, nodded to Baxter. "Thank you, Detective. Mr. Goodwin, Mr. Wright, Mr. Crocker."

"My client wishes to make a statement," Samuel began.

"Great. Hold that thought. Record on. Dallas, Lieutenant Eve," she began and ran all the particulars as she took a seat. "Mr. Crocker, you've been read your rights, correct?"

"Yes."

"And have stated, for the record, that you understand your rights and obligations in the matter of the investigation into the death of James Jay Jenkins."

"Yes, I—"

"And have come into this interview of your own volition, and with Samuel Wright as legal counsel?"

Billy cleared his throat. "Yes."

"You would also like Mr. Goodwin to witness this statement, at this time?"

"Yes."

"I am here to bear witness," Luke said, "and to serve as Billy's spiritual adviser. Lieutenant Dallas, this is very difficult, for all of us. I hope you'll take into account that Billy has come in, voluntarily, that the statement he intends to make is sincere and heartfelt."

"I think, of all connected to this matter, all this has been most difficult on Mr. Jenkins, seeing as he's stone dead. As for heartfelt and sincere?" She jerked a shoulder. "I don't much care. I'm interested in the facts. You served up a cyanide shooter for your pal Jimmy Jay, didn't you, Billy?"

"Don't answer that. Lieutenant Dallas," Samuel began in a tight voice, "my client is willing to make a statement, in return for consideration."

"I'm not feeling real considerate."

Something flashed in Samuel's eyes that told Eve he wasn't either. But he did his job. "The media is running with the two recent homicides, and is especially pushing on the death of my father-in-law. The longer it takes to investigate, the more attention will be paid—and much of it to the detriment of this department, and to you."

"You want me to cut your *client* a deal, before he tells me jackshit— and I should do that to spare myself and the NYPSD a little media heat?" She leaned forward. "You know what, *Sam*? I like the heat, and I haven't even broken a sweat yet. I'll have your client tied up and dunked within twenty-four, without his statement. So if that's all—"

She started to rise, and Peabody stepped up. "Lieutenant, maybe we should take a minute."

"Maybe you've got more time to waste than I do."

"Lieutenant, come on. I mean, Mr. Crocker did come in, and if two of the victim's sons-in-law are willing to stand with him, I think we need to hear what he has to say. The circumstances." She sent Billy a sympathetic look. "None of this could be easy, for anyone. I know you and Mr. Jenkins were friends, good friends, for a long, long time. Whatever happened, it has to be rough. It has to be really hard."

"We were friends," Billy managed. "As close as brothers."

"I get that. We can't cut deals here. We don't even know what you're going to tell us. But that doesn't mean we can't, and won't, listen with an open mind."

"You can take Murder One off the table," Samuel argued. "You can contact the prosecutor's office and arrange for that before this goes any further."

"No." Eve spoke flatly.

"The PA wouldn't do it," Peabody continued in that same reasonable, wish-I-could-help tone. "Even if we—"

"*I* won't do it." Eve spared Peabody a glare. "I don't need the statement to close this. Maybe it ties it sooner, and with a bow on it, but I'm not much on the fancy work. Make a statement, or don't. Your choice. And you?" She lifted her chin toward Billy. "You play make a deal with the PA on your own time. This is mine, and you're wasting it."

"Billy," Luke said softly. "You need to do this. Sam—" He simply held up a hand to stop Samuel from arguing. "Not just for man's law. You need to do this to begin to make it right with God. You need to do this for your soul. There can be no salvation without the admission of sin."

Silence fell. It ticked, ticked, ticked. Eve waited it out.

"I believed it was the right thing to do." Billy gulped in a breath. "The only thing. Maybe it was the Devil working through me, but I believed I was acting on the behalf of God."

Billy lifted his hands, a supplicant. "Jimmy Jay had strayed, and was straying farther and farther off the path. The drink, he couldn't see the sin in it, or how his weakness for it corroded his soul. He deceived his wife, his followers, and didn't see it as deception, but a kind of joke. An amusement. He became less cautious, drinking more, and often writing his sermons, even preaching under the influence of drink."

"You killed him because he knocked back too much vodka?" Eve demanded. "Hell, why not just hit any given bar or club on a Friday night and get the group-kill rate?"

"Lieutenant." Peabody murmured it, cocked her head at Billy. "You couldn't convince him to stop?"

"He enjoyed it, and believed every man was entitled, even required to have flaws and weaknesses. To seek perfection was to seek to take the place of God. But . . . he even brought his children into the deception, having Josie—especially Josie—provide the drink. This isn't the loving act of a father, is it? He'd lost his way. The drink corroded him, and made him weak so he fell to the temptations of the flesh."

"And screwed around on his wife."

"That's an unpleasant term." Luke shook his head.

"It's unpleasant behavior," Eve countered. "You knew about his affairs."

"Yes. Five times before he'd committed adultery, broken this commandment. But he repented. He came to me so we could pray together, so he could ask for forgiveness, and the strength to resist temptation."

"You covered for him."

"Yes. For too long, yes, I did. He knew what he risked by falling into such sin. His soul, his wife and family, the church itself. And he fought it."

Tears glimmered in Billy's eyes as he swiped at them with the back of his hand. "He was a good man, a great man, with deep weaknesses, with the pull of good and evil inside him. And this time, this last time, he didn't resist, he didn't repent. He refused to see it as sinful. He'd twisted God's word, you see, to suit his own base needs. He claimed that with this woman, and with the drink, he gained more light, more insight, more truth."

"And still, you covered for him."

"It was becoming more difficult, for my conscience. The weight . . . and knowing I was a party to it, he'd made me a party to it. His betrayal of God, of his good wife. And as with the drink, he became less cautious. It was only a matter of time before his sins were discovered. Sins that could have irreparably damaged all the work that came before. All he'd done, all he'd built, now at risk as he was caught in this cycle of sin."

"So you stopped the cycle."

"There was no choice." His gaze met Eve's, beseeched her to understand that single point. "The church, you must see, the church is bigger than any one of us. And must be protected. I prayed for him, I counseled him, argued with him. He wouldn't see. He was blind to it. We're all just men, Lieutenant. Even Jimmy Jay. He stood as the head of the church, as a representative of the Lord on Earth, but he was only a man. The man had to be stopped to save his soul, and to preserve the work of the Eternal Light."

"You killed him to save him."

"Yes."

"And to save the church."

"To save all he'd built so that it would go on after him, so it would live and thrive, so others could be saved."

"Why here and now?"

"I . . . The papist priest. It seemed a sign. I understood then that if Jimmy Jay was to be saved, if the Eternal Light was to go on without him, his death had to be quick, and public. It would stir others to look inside themselves for the light, to understand death comes to all, and salvation must be earned."

"Where did you get the cyanide?"

"I—" He licked his lips. "I approached a dealer of illegals, in the underground of Times Square."

Eve's eyebrows shot up. "You went into the underground in that sector. That's either brave or stupid."

"I had no *choice*." His hands balled on the table, stayed knotted there. "It had to be done quickly. I paid him to secure it, and paid him twice that when he'd done so."

"Name?"

"We didn't exchange names."

She nodded, unsurprised. Plenty of time to push on that later. "You procured the poison. Then?"

Samuel held up a hand. "Is it really necessary that we—"

"Yes. Then?" Eve repeated.

"I kept it on my person. Such a small amount, really. I had to pray it would be enough. I didn't want him to suffer. I loved him. Please, believe me." Billy looked from Luke to Samuel. "Please believe me."

"Go on, Billy." Luke laid a hand briefly on Billy's shoulder.

"I intended to speak with him again, to try to convince him to acknowledge his sins, repent them. And that same day, he went to the room of his consort. And when I spoke to him afterward, he laughed. Laughed. He'd never been stronger, he told me. Or closer to God. To preach against sin, a man must know sin. He was studying the scriptures, he told me." Billy closed his eyes. "Studying them with a new eye as he had come to believe God meant man to have more than one wife. Each to fill one or more of his needs to clear his mind and heart for God's good work. I knew then it was too late to bring him back, too late to draw him back on the path. That the only way to save him, to save all, was to end his mortal life. To send him to God."

He drew a deep breath when Eve said nothing. "I waited until the stage water was in place. I prayed, and prayed, even as I added the poison to the third bottle. Part of me still hoped that I would see him come back to the light before he reached for that bottle. That there would be another sign. But there was nothing."

"Was anyone else aware of what you planned to do, what you did? Did you take anyone else into your confidence?"

"Only God. I believed I was doing God's work, following His will. But last night, I had terrible dreams. Dreams of hellfire and horrible suffering. Now I think the Devil came into me. I was misled."

"Your defense is you were misled by Satan," Eve concluded. "Not as original an excuse as you might think. And your feelings for Jolene Jenkins didn't play into you spiking her husband's water with poison?"

A dull flush rose into Billy's pale cheeks. "I hoped to spare Jolene from the pain and humiliation of her husband's betrayal."

"With the potential side benefit of stepping into his shoes or marital bed?"

"Lieutenant," Luke interrupted. "He's confessed to his sins, to his crimes. Is there need for more? He's prepared to accept his punishment in this world, and the next."

"And you're satisfied?"

"It isn't for me." Luke reached over, laid his hand over Billy's. "I'll pray for you."

And Billy laid his head down on the table to give in to the tears.

As he wept, Eve rose. "Billy Crocker, you're under arrest for the premeditated murder of one James Jay Jenkins, a human being. The charge is murder in the first degree." She walked around to cuff him, to lift him to his feet. "Peabody."

"Yes, sir, I'll take him. Come with me, Mr. Crocker. You can meet your client after he's booked," she told Samuel.

"Record off," Eve ordered when Peabody took him out. "I appreciate you seeing he came in," Eve said to Luke. "Record's off," she added when he shook his head. "I admire your faith, and your restraint," she said to Samuel. "And your loyalty."

"A good man is dead," Luke said softly. "Another is ruined. Lives are shattered."

"Murder does that. He coveted another man's wife, isn't that how it goes? You know it; I know it. We all know that was part of it, however he justified it."

"Isn't it enough he'll answer to God for that?"

Eve studied Luke. "He'll be answering for plenty in the here and now, so I'll give you the rest. Will you continue to represent him?" she asked Samuel.

"Until more experienced criminal defense counsel can be secured. We want to go home. We want to get the family home as soon as possible."

"I believe I can clear that by tomorrow. If the more experienced defense counsel opts for trial, the circumstances of motive will come out. Something to consider." Eve opened the door. "I'll show you where you can wait."

She went back to her office, wrote and filed the report, requested a media block on the details. No point, she thought, in subjecting Jolene and her daughters to the victim's transgressions. At least not yet.

She looked up as Peabody came in. "He's done," Peabody told her. "I put him on suicide watch. I just had this feeling."

"I don't think he'll take the easy way, but you get a feeling, you go with it."

"You sure had one on this, from the jump. Do you think they'll deal it down?"

"Yeah, I think they'll deal it to Murder Two, and put him in mental defect. Faith as psychosis. He'll spend the next twenty-five repenting."

"That seems mostly right."

"Mostly right's generally enough." She checked the time, saw she had to let Baxter off the hook. "We're coming up to end of shift. I want you to follow up with McNab, keep working on the Lino angle. And since the two of you will kissy-face and eat junk food while doing same, I don't want to see any overtime logged."

"I thought we were going to Brooklyn."

"I'll take that, see if I can hook Roarke into playing backup."

"Will you play kissy-face and eat junk food?"

Eve sent her a withering look. "Unless I contact you to tell you otherwise, meet me at St. Cristóbal's tomorrow morning. Six A.M."

"Ouch? Why so early?"

"We're going to Mass."

Eve picked up her 'link to buzz Roarke.

13 BECAUSE IT GAVE HER TIME TO CONTINUE THE backgrounds she'd begun in her office, Eve asked Roarke to take the wheel for the drive to Brooklyn. As neither of them had finished in their respective offices until after six, traffic was expectedly hideous. Occasionally, she glanced up from her PPC as Roarke maneuvered around, through, and over the horn-blasting, vicious bumper-to-bumper. And wondered why, not for the first or last time, people who worked in Brooklyn didn't *live* in Brooklyn, and people who worked in Manhattan didn't just live the hell there.

"Do they actually like it?" she wondered. "Get off on the rage, consider it a daily challenge? Are they doing some kind of twisted penance?"

"You've been working faith-based cases too long."

"Well, there has to be a point to subjecting yourselves and others to this insanity every day."

"Finances, lack of housing." He flicked a glance in the mirror, then arrowed into the breath of space between a Mini and an all-terrain. "Or the desire to live outside the city in a more neighborhood sort of environment while earning city salaries—while others want the energy and benefits of the city for living, and find work in one of the other boroughs."

In a slick move, he changed lanes again, a dodge and weave that gained them maybe a dozen feet. "Or they're simply going over the bloody overcrowded bridge for some sort of business. Which, I'm forced to point out, we are at this moment. At a shagging crawl."

"We're going to check out a woman who appears to live sensibly, moving across the bloody, overcrowded bridge *and* securing employment where she lives. She has what's probably a ten-minute commute—by foot—to work. Less if she takes the subway. If she turns out to be my Lino's mother, I wonder if he fought his way over to Brooklyn, at a shagging crawl, to visit."

Accepting he was well and truly stuck now—bugger it—Roarke sat back and waited for his chance. "Would you, in his place?"

"Hard to put myself there as what little I remember of my relationship with my mother wasn't cookies and milk. But . . . you come back home, hiding out for five to six years, and your mother—your only living blood relative as far as I can ascertain, excepting the half-sibling she's had since you took off—is living across the bridge—bloody overcrowded or not. It seems you'd be compelled to see her. To check it out."

"Might be it wasn't cookies and milk with his ma either."

"He kept the medal she gave him, so there was something there, some bond. If there's a bond, that something, you'd want to see her, see how she was, what she was doing, who this guy is she'd married, see the half-brother. Something."

"If this is your Lino."

"Yeah, if." She frowned over that, wondering if a hunch was worth the trip to Brooklyn during the inaccurately termed rush hour. "First big one. If we get over that one, and he did make contact, did go see her, then she has to know, with all the media coverage, that her son's dead. How would she handle that? No one's contacted the morgue on

Lino, except for Father López. I checked. No inquiries, no requests for viewing."

Roarke said nothing for a moment. "I considered, spent some time considering actually, not making direct contact with my family in Ireland. Just . . . checking them out, doing a background on my mother's sister, the others. Maybe observing, you could say, from a distance. Not making the connection."

She'd wondered about that. She knew he'd gotten drunk the night before he'd gone to see his aunt. And he wasn't a man to drink himself drunk.

"Why?"

"A dozen reasons. More, a great deal more against it than the single one for making myself knock on that cottage door. I needed to see them, speak to them, hear their voices. Hers, especially. Sinead. My mother's twin. And I would have rather faced torture than knock."

He could remember the moment still, the sweaty panic of it. "It was hideously hard to do. What would they think of me? Would they look at me and see him? And if they did, would I? Would they look at me, see only my sins—which are plentiful—and none of her, the mother I never knew existed? The prodigal son's a hard role to carry."

"But you knocked on the door. That's who you are." She was silent as she considered. "It may not be who he was. Someone who could do what he did, live as someone else, some*thing* else for years. Hard to explain that to Mommy, unless Mommy's the kind who wouldn't give a shit what her baby boy's done. And kills the fat cow anyway."

"That would be fatted, and calf."

"What's the difference?"

"A couple of hundred pounds, I'd say. But, to the point, finding out is why we're going to Brooklyn in this bleeding traffic."

"Partly. But, you know, I could've kept Peabody on the clock. I figured since we're going to check out Teresa at work, and work happens to be her Italian brother-in-law's pizzeria, we could have a nice meal together."

He spared her a glance. "Meaning you can put a check in the column that reads: Went out to dinner with Roarke, and consider that a wifely duty dispensed."

She shifted, started to deny. Didn't bother. "Maybe, but we're still getting all this time together, and what's billed as really mag Brooklyn-style pizza."

"With this traffic, it better be the best shagging pizza in all five boroughs."

"At least I'm not asking you to go to six o'clock Mass with me in the morning."

"Darling Eve, to get me to do that the amount and variety of the sexual favors required are so many and myriad even my imagination boggles."

"I don't think you can exchange sexual favors for Mass attendance. But if I decide to go check it out, and I get the chance, I'll ask the priest."

She went back to her PPC while Roarke battled through the traffic.

By Eve's calculations, it took about as long to travel from downtown Manhattan to Cobble Hill in Brooklyn as it would to take a shuttle from New York to Rome. The pizzeria stood on the corner of a shopping district on the edge of a neighborhood of old row houses with decorated stoops where residents sat to watch their world go by.

"She's on tonight," Eve told Roarke once they'd parked. "But if for some reason she's not at work, she lives a few blocks down, two over."

"Meaning if she's not at work, I'll be whistling for my dinner?"

"I don't know about the whistling, but it might be postponed for the time it takes me to track her down and talk to her."

She stepped into the restaurant and was immediately surrounded by scents that told her if the best pizza in the five boroughs wasn't to be had here, it would be damn close.

Murals of various Italian scenes decorated walls the color of toasted

Italian bread. Booths, two-tops, four-tops cheerfully crowded together under iron ceiling fans that whisked those scents everywhere.

Behind the counter in the open kitchen, a young guy in a stained apron tossed pizza dough high, made the catch, tossed, all to the thrilled giggles of kids wedged into a booth with what she supposed were their parents. The waitstaff wore bright red shirts while they carted trays and weaved and threaded between tables to serve. Music played, and someone sang about "amore" in a rich and liquid baritone.

At a quick scan, Eve saw babies, kids, teens, and right on up to elderly chowing down, chatting, drinking wine, or studying the old-fashioned paper menus.

"That's her." Eve nodded toward the woman setting heaping bowls of pasta on a table. She laughed as she served, a good-looking woman in her early fifties, trim, graceful at her work. Her dark hair, pinned at the nape, framed her face and set off wide, brown eyes.

"Doesn't much look like a woman who recently learned her son had been poisoned," Eve observed.

Another woman hurried up, one older than Teresa, rounder, and with a welcoming smile. "Good evening. Would you like a table for two?"

"We would, yes." Roarke answered the smile. "That section, there"—he gestured to what he'd calculated comprised Teresa's station—"would be perfect."

"It may take a few minutes. If you'd care to wait in the bar, just over there?"

"Thank you."

"I'll come for you when we have a table available."

The bar lay through an arch, and was as lively as the restaurant. Eve took a stool, angled it to keep an eye on the restaurant while Roarke ordered a bottle of Chianti.

"Place does a good business," she commented. "It's been in this spot for nearly forty years. Brother-in-law's second generation to run it. She married the owner's brother about a dozen years ago. Her husband took off—or went missing—when this Lino was about five. He'd be thirty-four now—Lino Martinez. With the records wiped, I can't find out if he had a record."

"Or that he was ever Soldados."

"No. I can confirm he's gone to a lot of trouble over the last half of his life to stay under the radar. Changing locations, identities. If he's not my Lino, he's still wrong."

"Did you look into her finances?" Roarke asked, and tested the wine the bartender poured into his glass. "Very nice," he said.

"As much as I could without legal cause. No bumps or spikes, not on the surface. She lives well within her means, and she works as a waitress, has for a long time."

"For the Ortiz family, you said, when she lived on our side of the bridge."

"Yeah, and that's a connection you want to pick up and look over. Got remarried, moved here. She's got a nine-year-old kid, and went the professional mother route for the first two years of that, then went back to work here. Kid's in public school—no trouble there—and she has a small savings account. Nothing over the top. Husband's an MT with no criminal. They've got a mortgage, a vehicle payment, the usual. Everything runs normal."

The hostess came over. "Your table's ready. If you'll just follow me, we'll bring your wine over. A very nice choice," she added. "I hope you're enjoying it."

Once they were seated, a busboy brought their wine and glasses on a tray. "Teresa will be your waitress tonight. She'll be right with you."

"How's the pizza?" Eve asked him, and he beamed. "You won't get better. My brother's making it tonight."

"Funny," Eve mused when they were alone. "Family restaurants. Another connection. She worked for the Ortiz family in theirs, then comes here to work in another well-established family business."

"It's what she knows, and maybe what she needs. Her first husband deserted her, and you said there were domestic disturbance reports prior to that. She had her first child very young, and he, too, left her. Or left in any case. Now she's part of a family again, a link in that chain. She looks content," he added as Teresa started toward their table.

"Good evening. Would you like something to start? The roasted artichoke is wonderful tonight."

"We'll just head straight for the pizza. Pepperoni." Roarke ordered quickly, knowing if he hesitated, Eve might head straight into interrogation.

"I'll get the order right in for you."

She started for the kitchen, stopping when a diner patted her arm. So she paused long enough to have a quick and lively exchange that told Eve the table was filled with regulars.

Popular, she noted. Well-liked. Efficient.

"Keep that up," Roarke warned, "and half the restaurant will make you for a cop in the next two minutes."

"I am a cop." But she shifted her gaze back to him. "If she's what she looks to be, I bet she keeps up with the Ortiz family. I wonder if she went to the funeral. Her name wasn't on the list I got from Graciela Ortiz."

"Have you checked the floral tributes? Mass cards?"

"Hmm. I did, before. But I wasn't looking for Teresa Franco from Brooklyn. Mira thinks the killer will be compelled to confess—to his priest."

"Sticky."

"Yeah, could be. Billy was easy. He was impulse and lust in addition to faith and righteousness. He knew I knew, and that just tipped it into my lap. If the killer confesses to López or Freeman, it's going to bog down. They'll use the sanctity of confession because they believe it."

"And you don't."

"Hell no. You cop to a crime, the person you cop to has a responsibility to report it to the authorities."

"Black-and-white."

She scowled into her wine. "What am I supposed to see? Purple?

There's a reason we separate church and state. I've never figured how that deal slipped through the cracks in the divide." She snagged one of the bread sticks spearing out of a tall glass.

"I don't like the possibility of depending on a priest to convince a killer to turn himself in. Billy? Weak-spined little sanctimonious hypocrite, he couldn't stomach what he did after the fact. Simple as that."

She bit in, pointed the rest of the bread stick at Roarke. "But Lino's killer? That one thought it through, worked it out, there's some deep motive in there. May be revenge, may be profit, may be protection of self or another—but it's no smoke screen like Billy's 'save the souls' bullshit."

Since it was pointed at him, Roarke stole the bread stick from her. "While I agree, I'm fascinated by the hard line you're drawing over religion."

"It gets used too much, as an excuse, a fall guy, a weapon, a con. A lot of people, maybe most, don't mean it except when it suits them. Not like Luke Goodwin and López. They mean it. They live it. You can see it in them. Maybe that makes the bullshit harder to take. I don't know."

"And the killer? Does he mean it?"

"I'm thinking yeah. That's why he'll be harder to hang than Billy was. He means it, but he's not a fanatic, not crazy. Otherwise there'd have been more, a follow-up, some sort of message to support the act."

She shrugged, realized she should at least give him something more than murder over dinner. "So, anyway, I didn't tell you about the fight I broke up today."

"Successfully, I assume, as I see no visible wounds."

"Bitch bit me." Eve tapped her shoulder. "I got a damn good dental impression. Over a handbag. Not a mugging. A sale on purses. Ah, Laroche?"

"Ah, yes. Highly desired handbags, luggage, shoes."

"I'll say, as these two were ready to fight to the death over something called a triple roll. In peony. What the hell is peony?"

"A flower."

"I know it's a damn flower." Or she probably did. "Is it a shape, smell, a color?"

"I'm going to assume color. And probably pink."

"I told Mira, and she got this gleam in her eye. Called the shop right then and there and bought it."

Roarke sat back and laughed just as Teresa brought their pizza. "I don't have to tell you two to enjoy yourselves, but I hope you enjoy the pizza. Just let me know if I can get you anything else."

Eve watched Teresa move—serving, chatting, picking up orders. "She's got her groove, her routine. Knows her people—staff and customers. Doesn't come off like a woman with a deep, dark secret." Since she gauged the pizza had cooled enough that she could avoid scorching the roof of her mouth, she took a sampling bite. "And okay, damn good pie."

"It is. She also doesn't strike me as a woman who'd fight to the death over a pink designer handbag."

"Huh?"

"Good, serviceable shoes, pretty jewelry, but far from flashy. She wears a wedding ring," he added. "That says traditional. Her nails are short and tended, and unpainted. She has good skin, and wears—at least at work—minimal enhancers. I'll wager she's a woman who takes care of herself, and who likes nice things—things that last—and takes care of what she has as well."

Eve smiled at him over another bite. "You're looking with cop's eyes."

"It's rude to insult me when I'm buying you dinner. I'll also wager her handbag is as good and serviceable as her shoes, and that she'd be as baffled as you are by anyone biting a cop over a pink purse."

"I don't disagree." Eve caught a long string of cheese, folded it back over the slice. "But none of that means she wasn't aware her firstborn was across the bridge, playing a long con."

"But you don't think so."

Taking a moment, Eve toyed with her wine. "I don't think so, but I'm going to find out, one way or the other."

Meanwhile, there was no reason not to enjoy really good pizza while she tracked Teresa's movements through the dining room, the open kitchen.

She waited until Teresa came back to the table. "How was everything?"

"Great."

"Can I interest you in dessert?" she began as she started to clear. "We have homemade tiramisu tonight. It's amazing."

"Have to pass. Is there somewhere private we can talk?"

Eyes suddenly wary, Teresa lowered her order comp. "Is there a problem?"

"I need a few minutes." Eve laid her badge on the table, watched Teresa's gaze shift to it, stall there. "Private's best."

"Um . . . there's a little office off the bar, but—"

"That'll work." Eve slid out, rose, knowing she was crowding Teresa's space.

"I just need to get someone to cover my tables. Ah . . ."

"Fine." Eve glanced at Roarke as Teresa hurried over to another waitress. "Why don't you come with us?" she said to Roarke. "We'll see how close you hit the mark on your evaluation."

They skirted tables, wound through the bar. The office was little, as advertised, and cozily cluttered. Inside, Teresa linked her fingers, twisted them. "Is something wrong? Did I do something? I'm sorry about the flowers, and Spike was very bad. But I—"

"Spike?"

"The puppy. I didn't know he'd dig in the flowers, and I promised to replace them. I told Mrs. Perini, and she said it was all right."

"It's not about the dog, Mrs. Franco. It's about your son."

"David? Is David all right? What—?"

"Not David," Eve said, cutting through the instant maternal alarm.
"Lino."

"Lino." Teresa's hand went to her heart, and her heel pressed there.
"If it's the police, of course, it's Lino." Weariness settled over her like a
thin, worn blanket. "What has he done?"

"When's the last time you had contact with him?"

"Almost seven years now. Not a word in nearly seven years. He told
me he had work. Big prospects. Always big prospects with Lino.
Where is he?"

"Where was he the last time you had contact with him?"

"Out west. Nevada, he said. He'd been in Mexico for a time. He
calls, or sends e-mail. Sometimes he sends money. Every few months.
Sometimes a year goes by. He tells me he'll come home, but he doesn't."
She sat. "I'm relieved that he doesn't, because he carries trouble with
him. Like his father. And I have another son. I have David, and he's a
good boy."

"Mrs. Franco, you're aware Lino belonged to the Soldados?"

"Yes, yes." She sighed. "His *brothers,* he called them. He had their
mark put on him." She rubbed a hand on her forearm. "Nothing I did
stopped him; nothing I said swayed him. He'd make promises, and
break them. Go his own way. There was always police with Lino."

"When was the last time you saw him?"

"He left home when he was seventeen. He's never come back."

"You used to work for Hector Ortiz."

"Years ago. He was good to me. To us. He gave Lino a job, a little
job when he was fifteen. Busing tables, sweeping up. And Lino stole
from him."

Even now, it seemed the memory of it brought an embarrassed flush
to her cheeks. "He stole from that good man, that good family. And
shamed us."

"Did you attend Mr. Ortiz's funeral service?"

"No. I wanted to, but David's parent-teacher conference was that day. Tony, my husband, and I make sure we both attend every one. It's important. I sent flowers." Something flickered in her eyes. "The priest was killed during the Mass. I heard about it. And I heard they're saying—the police are saying—he wasn't a priest at all. Oh God. Oh God."

"Mrs. Franco." Eve crouched until they were eye-to-eye, then drew an evidence pouch out of her field bag. "Is this Lino's?"

Teresa's breath went ragged as she reached for the bag, as her thumb rubbed the front of the medal through the seal. She turned it over, and her eyes blurred with tears as she read the inscription on the back. "I gave him this for his First Holy Communion. He was seven, seven years old. He was still my boy then, most of him was still my little boy. Before he got so angry, before he wanted so much more than I could give. Is he dead? Is Lino dead? Did he kill the priest? Oh God, did he take the life of a priest?"

"I think he may have, Mrs. Franco, in more ways than one. The body of the man who posed as Father Flores had a tattoo removed. From his forearm. The gang symbol of the Soldados. He'd had facial reconstruction. He had this medal hidden in his room."

The color simply leached out of her face. "You think this man, this priest, was Lino."

"Father Flores was traveling out West when he disappeared, nearly seven years ago. We've done some back-checking, and Lino Martinez drops off the grid at about the same time. He moved on and off prior to that. Changing identities, from what we've been able to ascertain. Identity theft has been part of his style, and one of his skills."

"It was always so. He was bright. A bright boy, and smart with electronics. He could have used it for his education, to build a good life, a career. Instead, it was part of his path into the gang. His usefulness in that area. Mother of God." She pressed her fingers to her eyes. "Did it come to this? Is he dead?" She began to rock. "Is he dead? Please, I need my husband. I need my family. I need to see my son. I need to see Lino."

"You haven't seen him in twenty years, and he changed his appearance. Would you recognize him?"

Teresa dropped her hands, and the tears fell with them. "He's still my son."

Eve picked up the evidence bag in Teresa's lap. "I'll make arrangements for you to view the body."

A shudder moved through Teresa. "Please, can it be tomorrow? After my boy is in school. I don't want him to know. . . . Maybe it's a mistake, and he won't ever have to know. If it's not, I want to find the right way to tell him about his brother."

"Tomorrow morning. I can have transportation sent to you."

"Please don't. The neighbors . . ." She choked on a sob, covered her mouth with her hand. "I know how that sounds. It sounds shameful and selfish. But my life is here. My little boy's life is here. We've had no trouble with the police. You can look, you can ask. He's a good boy. My husband, he's a good man. You can—"

"Mrs. Franco, we don't want to bring you any trouble. I can tell you where to come, and meet you there. What time will your son be in school?"

"My boy's in school by eight. We can come to the city, my husband and I. We'll leave as soon as our boy's in school. My husband can—"

"Okay. It's okay. Nine o'clock." Eve pulled out a card, wrote down the particulars. "Go here, ask for me. I'll make the arrangements."

"We'll come. We'll be there, me and Tony, but . . . I need to go home now. Please, I just . . . I need to tell Sophia that I'm not feeling well, and need to go home."

"All right. Mrs. Franco," Eve said as Teresa rose. "Why did Lino leave New York at seventeen?"

The dark eyes that had been so rich and warm were dull now. "To get rich, to be important. 'When I come back,' he said to me, 'I'll be a rich man, and we'll live in a big house. A big house like Mr. Ortiz. I'll be somebody.'"

"One more thing. Can you give me the names of friends he was closest to? Other gang members?"

"Steve Chávez was his closest friend, and the worst of them. He and Steve left together." Teresa pressed her fingers to her eyes, rubbed hard. "Joe Inez, Penny Soto. Penny was his girlfriend. Others, there were others. Some are dead or gone. I'll think, and write them down for you. But please, I need to go home."

"I'll meet you tomorrow."

Eve stepped out of the office behind Teresa, watched her hurry to the woman who'd seated them. "I guess we should leave her a big tip," Eve observed. "But either way, I pretty much ruined her night."

**14** EVE RAN THE THREE NAMES TERESA HAD GIVEN
her as Roarke drove home. "Chávez, Steven, has him-
self a long, crowded sheet, in various states. Assault,
assault with deadly, couple of illegals pop, sexual assault— acquitted—
grand theft auto, fraud, robbery. Crossing lots of state lines, and grac-
ing many state facilities to do his penance."

"A traveling badass," Roarke commented.

"Arrested numerous times and/or questioned and released. A bit
over seven years ago he got popped for possessing stolen goods,
made bail and walked away. That was in Arizona." She glanced over
at Roarke.

"And the last time Teresa had contact with Lino was seven years
ago, in Nevada. A neighbor of Arizona."

"What do you bet he and Lino hooked up and had some old times'
sake over a brew?"

"Only a sucker would bet against it. Where is he now?"

"Dropped off the grid, just about the same time Lino did. Inez and
Soto are still in New York. Inez is a maintenance mechanic at an apartment complex in the old neighborhood. Did some time for robbery in

his late teens. A slap for drunk and disorderly after his release. Scans clean since, more than a decade of clean since. Soto has hits on illegals—sale and possession, sexual solicitation without a license, assault. She's recently off parole—and, isn't this handy, is employed at the bodega next door to St. Cristóbal's. I'm really enjoying the coincidences."

"Who could blame you? Which one are we going to see?"

It was a pretty lucky cop, Eve thought, who hooked a guy that easy about the work and the hours. "I could catch them both in the morning, but . . . since Inez lives in the building where he works, he's a pretty sure bet." She reeled off the address. "Thanks."

"You'll owe me, as this sort of cop work is fairly tedious. All this talking, and no one's trying to kill us."

"Well, it can't be fun all the time. But maybe Joe will pull a sticker and try to take us out."

"Don't placate me, Eve."

She laughed, stretched out her legs. "You want to talk deadly? Peabody had a meet today with Nadine and Louise, about planning this prewedding girl party. I'm hosting it, apparently, but they've relieved me of any actual duties."

"That doesn't sound deadly. In fact, it sounds quite sane and safe."

"I guess. I drew the line at games and strippers. Figured I can handle anything else. Which means probably sitting around drinking girly drinks and eating cake." At least the cake part was a good deal, Eve thought. "I probably have to buy Louise a present."

She slid a look in his direction.

"No," he said definitely. "I won't be taking on that little chore for you as I have no more idea than you what would be the appropriate gift for a wedding shower."

As that small hope dissolved, her shoulders slumped. "There are entirely too many presents attached to too many things. And after this, we'll have to buy them a wedding present, right? What the hell do you buy for two adults who both already have everything they want—or can buy it themselves—anyway?"

"They're outfitting an entire house," he reminded her. "I spoke with Peabody's mother about making them a tea set. Pot, cups, saucers, and so on. She's an excellent and creative potter."

"Huh. That was a good idea. Why didn't I think of that idea for the Louise present?" She brooded over it for a short time. "Inez is the only one of the group Teresa named who ever married."

"And how we wind around," Roarke commented.

"It just made me think—you know, showers, weddings. He's the only one who got married, had kids."

"And the only one who, at least, appears to have rehabilitated himself."

"I don't know if one has to do with the other, but it's interesting. Then there's Teresa herself. The way it reads, she got knocked up, married a wrong guy. Got kicked around, did what she could, or did what she thought she had to. Guy takes off, and she raises the kid on her own. Supports them, but she can't keep the kid out of trouble. Then the kid takes off. She gets married again, to a decent guy, and has another kid. Makes a decent life, and this kid stays out of trouble."

"Is it nature or nurture?"

"It's both. It's always both, and more, it's about making choices. Still, Lino spent the first few years of his life watching his mother get knocked around, watching the father abuse her. So he hears about the Solas bastard beating on his wife, sticking it to his daughter, he breaks out of the priest mold long enough to kick some ass. His weak spot. He carried that medal—didn't see his mother, didn't come home to her, but he carried the medal she gave him."

"And sent her money occasionally."

"Yeah. Going to come home a rich man—important. Nothing like that bastard who knocked his mother up. That'll be an underlying factor in his pathology. If we give a rat's ass."

"Why do you?"

She said nothing for a few moments. "She knew he was lost. Teresa. She knew there was something in him that she could never pull out, get rid of. Something that made him take the course he did. She's got her good life now, and still, she's going to grieve for him. Hell, she already is."

"Yes. She is."

"And when I can clear it and give it to her, she'll keep that medal for the rest of her life. Her reminder of her little boy. I've interviewed people who knew him these past few years, worked closely with him, and they liked him. Respected him, enjoyed him. I think he was a stone-cold killer, or at least someone who killed or did whatever he wanted when it was expedient. But there was something there, something buried under the hard case. Sometimes you wonder why, that's all. Why it gets buried."

"He wanted more," Roarke said. "Wanted what he couldn't have, or didn't want to earn. That kind of desire can overtake all the rest."

She paused a moment. "You were going to be a rich man. Important. That was the goal."

"It was."

"But you never buried who you were under that goal."

"You see the parallels, and wonder. For me, the legal lines were . . . options. More, they were challenges. And I had Summerset, as a kind of compass at a time when I might have taken a much darker path."

"You wouldn't have taken it. Too much pride."

His brow winged up. "Is that so?"

"You always knew it wasn't just the money. Money's security, and it's a symbol. But it's not the thing. It's knowing what to do with it. Lots of people have money. They make it or they take it. But not everybody builds something with it. He wouldn't have. Lino. If he'd gotten the rich, he'd still never have gotten the important. And, for a short time, he stole the important."

"The priest's collar."

"In the world he came back to, that made him important. I bet he liked the taste of it, the power of it. It's why he could stick it out so long."

"A little too long, obviously."

"Yeah." How much longer had he needed to go? she wondered. How much longer before he'd have collected on those riches and that honor? "Teresa may not be able to confirm the ID—actually, I can't figure how she could. But it's Lino Martinez in that steel drawer downtown. Now I just have to figure out who wanted him dead, and why."

Maybe Joe Inez would have some of the answers. Eve studied the twelve-story apartment building, a tidy, quiet block of concrete and steel with an auto-secured entrance and riot bars on the windows of the first two levels.

She bypassed security with her master and took a scan of the small lobby. It smelled faintly of citrus cleaner and boasted a fake fichus tree in a colorful pot and two chairs arranged together on a speckled white floor.

"He's 2A." She eschewed the two skinny elevators and took the stairs with Roarke. Muted sounds leaked from apartments into the corridor—shows on entertainment screens, crying babies, salsa music. But the walls and doors were clean, as the lobby had been. The ceiling lights all gleaming.

From a glance, Inez did his job.

She knocked on 2A. The door opened almost immediately. A boy of around ten with a wedge of hair flopping over his forehead in the current style of airboard fanatics stood slurping on a sports drink. "Yo," he said.

"Yo," Eve said. "I'd like to speak to Joe Inez." She held up her badge.

The badge had him lowering the drink, and his eyes going wide with a combination of surprise and excitement. "Yeah? How come?"

"Because."

"You got a warrant or anything?" The kid leaned on the open door, took another slurp of his bright orange drink. As if, Eve thought, they were hanging out at the game. "They always ask that on the screen and stuff."

"Your father do anything illegal?" Eve countered, and the boy *phffted* out a breath.

"As if. Dad! Hey, Dad, cops are at the door."

"Mitch, quit screwing around and get back to your homework. Your mom's gonna . . ." The man who walked in from another room, wiping his hands on his pants, stopped short. Eve saw the cop awareness come into his eyes. "Sorry. Mitch, go finish getting the twins settled in."

"Aw, come *on*."

"Now," Inez said, and jerked his thumb.

The boy muttered under his breath, hunched his shoulders, but headed in the direction his father indicated.

"Can I help you with something?" Inez asked.

"Joe Inez?"

"That's right."

Eve looked, deliberately, at the tattoo on his left forearm. "Soldados."

"Once upon a time. What's this about?"

"Lino Martinez."

"Lino?" The surprise came into his eyes as quickly as it had his son's, but with none of the excitement. What Eve saw in them was dread. "Is he back?"

"We'd like to come in."

Inez raked both hands through his hair, then stepped back. "I got kid duty. It's my wife's girls' night. I don't know how long Mitch can keep the twins in line."

"Then we'll get right to it. When did you last have contact with Lino Martinez?"

"Jesus. Must be fifteen years ago. Couple more maybe. He took off when we were still kids. About sixteen, seventeen."

"You've had no contact with him in all this time?"

"We had some hard words before he left."

"About?"

Something shuttered over his eyes. "Hell, who remembers?"

"You were both members of a gang known for its violence, and its blood ties."

"Yeah. I got this to remind me, and to make damn sure my kids don't make the same mistakes. I did some time, you know that already. I drank, and I kicked it. I've been clean for almost thirteen years now. When's it going to be long enough?"

"Why did Lino take off?"

"He wanted out, I guess. He and Steve—Steve Chávez—said they were heading to Mexico. Maybe they did. I only know they took off together, and I haven't seen or heard from either of them since."

"Do you go to church?"

"What's it to you?" At Eve's steady stare, he sighed. "I try to make it most Sundays."

"You attend St. Cristóbal's?"

"Sure, that's . . . This is about that priest." Relief bloomed on his face. "About the one who died at the funeral. Old Mr. Ortiz's funeral. I couldn't make it, had a plumbing problem up on the fifth floor. Are you talking to everyone in the parish, or just former gang members?"

"Did you know Flores?"

"No, not really. I mean, I saw him around now and then. Most Sundays we'd go to the nine o'clock Mass. My wife liked to hear Father López's sermons, and that was fine by me as he usually keeps them short."

"Your boys don't go to the youth center."

"Mitch, he's wild for airboarding. Doesn't give a shit about team sports, at this stage anyway. The twins are only five and—" Whoops and shouts burst from the back of the apartment. Inez smiled grimly. "Right now, we're keeping them on a short leash."

"What about Penny Soto?"

His eyes shifted, went cold. "She's around the neighborhood, sure.

We've got different lives now. I've got a family, a good job here. I stopped looking for trouble a long time ago."

"What kind of trouble was Lino Martinez in when he took off?"

It was in his eyes again, a knowledge, a fear, a regret. "I can't help you with that. Lino was always in trouble. Listen, I can't leave those three back there by themselves. I don't know anything about Flores, and as for Lino? This is the only thing we've had in common for a real long time." He tapped the tattoo. "I gotta ask you to leave so I can keep my boys from beating on each other."

Something there," Eve said when they were outside. "Something went down, and the something is why Lino went rabbit all those years back."

"But you don't think he knew Lino was back."

"No, didn't buzz for me. He wants to be done with all that, gets pissed off when he's not. Can't blame him, really. He's got a parallel going with Teresa. He built a new life, and he wants to keep it. But there's Lino."

She got in the car, sat back. "There's Lino," she repeated when Roarke slid behind the wheel. "An obstacle, a reminder, a weight, whatever you want to term it. And Lino is that element of the past, of the mistakes, of the trouble, of the hardship that shadows the new life. And his being dead, for these two? It doesn't change that."

He pulled out, headed toward home. "If whatever went down to send Lino running from New York was big enough, we can find it. Media search of that time would turn it up."

"Maybe. But you know, the mother didn't get that look in her eyes. That 'oh shit, here it comes again' look Inez got. Why didn't she know? Her take was he left to get rich and important, not because he was running. Maybe I'm reading too much into it." She scrubbed at her face. "I'm getting conflicting vibes on this case. Everyone I talk to has a different pop for me. I need to sort it out."

"You're learning who he was now."

"Need the official ID to make that, well, official. But yeah, I'm getting a picture. Gonna have to skip church tomorrow," she decided, and sent a text to Peabody's mail with the change.

"I don't suppose it counts against you as you'll be skipping church to interview Soto, and identify your victim."

"Hmm. Still want to hook López. Hit him at the rectory after Soto. Girlfriend," she mused. "Childhood connections. I don't really have any. You do. How far does the loyalty go?"

"That's much too vague and open-ended a question for a definitive answer."

"A friend from back in the old days did something, or didn't do something, that caused a rift between you—something that you argued about, disagreed about. He takes off. Do you continue to protect him? Do you keep it zipped for all time because you were once, let's say, part of the same team?"

"And now too black-and-white, Lieutenant. Some would depend on what he'd done, or hadn't, and how—or if—it affects me and mine. Would unzipping it change what had happened, or balance some scale if I felt it needed to be balanced?"

"You'd keep it zipped," she muttered. "It's that pride again, as much as loyalty. I can get it out of Inez if I need to."

"No doubt. He didn't have the kill mark on his tattoo," Roarke added.

"No, he didn't. Unlike Lino and Chávez. His sheet had his identifying marks. But how do I find out who Lino killed when a bunch of snivelers crying 'Oh, the poor misunderstood children'—who are killing, maiming, wreaking havoc—'need a clean slate,' wiped the records? If there was a record," she added.

"Given a bit of time and the unregistered, I could get you that information—if Lino was charged, or arrested. Even questioned."

She slanted him a look. She'd thought of that possibility already. "How much is a bit of time?"

"I can't say until I get my hands in it."

She blew out a breath. "I can't make it work. As far as I know, there's nobody's life on the line, no imminent threat. It's just the easy way to get around a block."

"What's that I hear?" He tapped his ear. "Ah yes, that would be *your* pride talking."

"Shut up. It's not pride, it's procedure. I'm not going around the law just to shortcut procedure and satisfy my curiosity. And so what if it is pride?"

As they drove through the gates, he picked up her hand, tugged it over, and kissed her knuckles. "Here we are, two prideful people. That would be one of the seven deadlies. Want to explore any of the others? Lust would be my first choice."

"Lust is always your first choice. And your second, and right down to your last choice."

"Sometimes I like to combine it with greed." Even before he stopped the car, he pressed the release for her seat belt, then gripped her shirt, pulled her over.

"Hey."

"Maybe it's all that talk about the old days, and youth." Smooth and clever, he had his seat back and her straddling him. "Brings back fond memories of getting the girl naked in whatever vehicle I could . . . acquire at the time."

"You had time for sex after grand theft auto?"

"Darling, there's always time for sex."

"Only on your clock. Jesus, how many hands do you have?" She batted them away, but not before he'd managed to unbutton her shirt and stir her up. "Listen, if you need a bounce, there's a perfectly good bed, probably about two dozen of them, in the house."

"It's not about the bounce, or not altogether." He skimmed a finger down her throat. "It's about the moment, and recapturing for that brief time, the foolishness of youth."

"Speak for yourself. I didn't have time for foolishness." She started to reach for the door, with the intention of opening it and wiggling out, but he locked his arms around her, laughed.

"You never had sex in a car."

"Yes, I have. You get ideas at least half the time whenever we're in the back of one of your limos."

"Not the same at all. That's a grown-up venue, a limo is. It's sophisticated sex. And here we are, crammed together in the front seat of a police issue, and the lieutenant is both aroused and mildly embarrassed."

"I am not. Either." But her pulse jumped, and her breath hitched when his thumbs brushed over the thin cotton covering her breasts. "This is ridiculous. We're adults, we're married. The steering wheel is jammed into the base of my spine."

"The first two are irrelevant, the last is part of the buzz. Music on, program five. Skyroof open."

She narrowed her eyes at him. "It's not going to work. It's uncomfortable and it's stupid. And I have to work in this vehicle."

"I can make you come in ten seconds."

She actually smirked at him. "Ten," she said, "nine, eight, seven, six, five . . . oh shit." She'd underestimated his quick hands, his skilled fingers. He had her trousers unhooked, had her wet and throbbing. And over.

"Go again," he murmured, and yanking down her tank, took her breast in his mouth.

He drove her, hands and mouth, while the cool air washed over her face, while her cry of release echoed into the night.

Her hands flailed out for purchase as she heard the cotton rip. That cool night air flowed over her bare skin now, a thrilling counterpoint to the heat.

She let go, he could see it, feel it. Let go of the day, the work, the worry—and more, deliciously more—that odd and appealing line she carried inside her between the should and the shouldn't.

Once she'd had no time for foolishness. Was it any wonder he was compelled to give that to her? And all the love that wound through it and made it real?

His wife, his lover, his sweetheart groping with him in the front seat of a car while the music played and the night shimmered.

His hand bumped her weapon, and he laughed. Wasn't that part of it, too? His dangerous and dedicated cop, yielding to him, lost in her own needs. Demanding he give and he take.

Her mouth was like fury on his, burning away at his control until he was as desperate as she. Until there was only one need, one thought. To mate.

"I can't—how do we . . ." Her breath tangled, her body ached as she struggled to shift, to angle, to somehow defeat the confines so that he could fill her.

"Just move . . . let me—bloody hell." He rapped his knuckles on the wheel fighting to shift her hips, banged his knees on the dash and was fairly certain she cursed because her head struck the edge of the open skyroof.

Well, they'd get over it.

She was laughing like a mad thing when they finally managed to insert tab B into slot A.

"Oh, thank Christ," he whispered, and held her, just held her as her body rocked with laughter. "Well, when you've finished your laughfest, get to work. I'm pinned here and can't get things started without a bit of help."

"Really?" She could barely get her breath between the laughter and the . . . why was this ridiculous situation so damn sexy? she wondered. "You're stuck?"

"Shagging poor design on your police issue."

"More like poor design for shagging." Watching him, she rocked—just a little. Lifted her hips—a fraction. Lowered again. "How's that?"

"You're killing me."

"You started it." She rocked again, a little more, torturing him, torturing herself. Then more, and more still, letting her need set the pace, thrilling to the control until the control was an illusion.

She felt his body tense, coil, shudder on his release, saw those amazing eyes go dark, go blind as she took him. And she rode him, chasing that peak of pleasure until she streaked over it.

She collapsed on him, as much as she was able. Her breath chugged in and out of her laboring lungs; her body quivered, trembled, then stilled. "I better not have any cause to strip tomorrow," she told him. "Because I'm going to have steering wheel bruises on my ass."

"You seem obsessed recently with the possibility of stripping on the job. Is there something I should know?"

"You just can't be too careful."

"Speaking of, how's your head?"

"Glancing blow." She rubbed it absently. "How do we uncouple? Or are we stuck like this until somebody finds us in the morning?"

"Give us a minute." He nudged her back. "That was worlds better, and entirely more challenging, than any previous experience in vehicle sex."

Look at him, she thought, his hair all messed up from her hands, buttons popped off his shirt, and his eyes all sleepy and smug. "Did you really steal rides so you could have sex in them?"

"There were all manner of reasons to steal rides. For fun, for business, and for somewhere semiprivate to bag the girl." He leaned up to give her a quick, friendly kiss. "If you like, I'll steal something so you can have that experience as well."

"Pass on that." She glanced down at herself. "You ripped my underwear."

"I did." He grinned. "It was expedient. Here now, let's see if we can pry ourselves out of this." He slid her up until she could scoot over toward her seat, and bring her leg over him. Once they'd buttoned, fastened, and hooked, he coasted the few feet to the house, parked.

"You know, Summerset knew when we drove through the gate. And even with the narrowness of his mind, he knows what we just did out here."

"Yes, I believe Summerset's fully aware we have sex."

Eve rolled her eyes as she got out. "Now he knows how long and what kind of sex."

Shaking his head, Roarke walked with her to the door. "You're the most fascinating prude."

She only muttered to herself as they went inside. And if being hugely relieved Summerset wasn't hovering in the foyer made her a prude, so be it.

Still, she made a beeline upstairs, and for the bedroom. "I'm going to go ahead and run that search, one looking for media-worthy crime or events here at the time Lino left New York."

"Do you want help?"

"I can run a search."

"Good. I want a shower, and an hour or two for some work of my own."

She narrowed her eyes. She wanted a shower, too—but the man was sneaky. "Hands off in the jets," she ordered.

He held his up, then started to undress. He was down to trousers when he frowned and crossed to her.

"Hands off out here, too," she began.

"Quiet. You weren't kidding about the bite on your shoulder."

She tipped her chin down, turned her head. Grimaced at the marks and bruising. "Bitch had a jaw like a rottweiler."

"It needs to be cleaned and treated, and a cold patch would help."

"It's fine, Nurse Nancy," she began, then yelped when he poked his finger on the mark.

"It will be, unless you insist on acting like a baby. Shower, disinfectant, medication, cold patch."

She might have rolled her eyes again, but she didn't trust him not to make his point a second time. And now the damn shoulder ached.

She let him deal with it, even to the point of adding a chaste kiss. And was forced to admit, at least to herself, that it felt better for the care.

In cotton pants and a T-shirt, she sat at her desk, coffee at her elbow, and ordered the search. While the computer worked, she leaned back to juggle the various players in her mind.

Steve Chávez. He and Lino left New York together—according to Teresa—and that was corroborated by Inez. Chávez does time here and there; Lino bobs and weaves. No convictions on record. But comparing McNab's search with Chávez's sheet, she noted that there were a number of times both men had been in the same area.

Old friends, hanging out?

And to the best of her knowledge, they dropped off the grid at about the same time in September of '53. No way she'd buy coincidence.

Had Chávez come back to New York with Lino? Had he, too, assumed a new identity? Could he be somewhere else, waiting for whatever Lino had waited for? Had he eliminated Lino—and if so, why? Or was he—as she believed Flores was—dead and buried?

Penny Soto. No love lost between her and her former gang partner, Inez. She'd seen that on his face. She'd warrant an interview. She'd had more trouble with the law than Inez, but had no family to protect. And a little digging would probably turn up something Eve could use as a lever to pry information out of her.

She'd go see Soto before she headed downtown to meet Teresa at the morgue.

And maybe she'd missed a step with Teresa. She believed the woman had told her all she was capable of telling her at the time. But another round there might jiggle something else loose.

When her computer announced its task complete, Eve scanned the media reports for the weeks surrounding the time of Lino's departure.

Murders, rapes, burglaries, robberies, assaults, one kidnapping, assorted muggings, illegals busts, suspicious deaths, and two explosions.

None of the names listed in the reports crossed her list, but she'd run them as a matter of course. Still, it was the explosions that caught her interest. They'd occurred exactly a week apart, each in rival gang territory and both had cost lives. The first, on Soldado turf, at a school auditorium during a dance, had killed one, injured twenty-three minors, two adults—names listed—and caused several thousand in damages.

The second, on Skull turf, at a sandwich joint known as a hangout, a homemade boomer—on timer as the first, but more powerful—had killed four minors, one adult, and injured six.

The police suspected retaliation for that explosion, blah blah, Eve read. Known members of Soldados were being sought for questioning.

She used her authorization to request the case files on both explosions. And hit a block. Files sealed.

"Screw that," she muttered, and without thinking contacted her commander at home. The blocked video and rusty voice had her glancing at her wrist unit. And wincing.

"I apologize, sir. I didn't check the time."

"I did. What is it, Lieutenant?"

"I'm following a lead, and it involves a pair of explosions in East Harlem seventeen years ago. I believe the as-yet-unofficially identified victim may have been involved. Those files have been sealed. It would be helpful to know if any on my list were questioned or suspected of involvement."

He let out a long sigh. "Is this a matter of urgency?"

"No, sir. But—"

"Send the request to my home and office units. I'll have you cleared in the morning. It's nearly midnight, Lieutenant. Go to bed."

He clicked off.

She sulked for a few seconds. Stared thoughtfully at the doorway connecting her office and Roarke's for a few seconds more. Roarke could get into the sealed files in minutes, she had no doubt. And if she'd thought of that *before* she'd tagged Whitney, she might've been able to justify asking Roarke to do just that.

Now she'd started the tape rolling, and had to wait for it to unwind.

She sent the formal request, added the evening's interviews and notes to her own case file. She pinned more names and photos to her board. Teresa, Chávez, Joe Inez, Penny Soto.

Then she crossed to the doorway. "I'm done. I'm going to bed."

Roarke glanced up. "I'll be done shortly."

"Okay. Ah, could you make a boomer, on timer? I don't mean now, because, duh, I mean back when you were a kid?"

"Yes. And did. Why?"

"Could you because you're handy with electronics or with explosives?"

"Both."

She nodded, decided it would give her something to chew on until morning. "Okay. 'Night."

"Who or what did Lino blow up?"

"I'm not sure. Yet. But I'll let you know."

15 A MORNING STORM RUMBLED OUTSIDE THE WIN-
dows. The thunder, a bit dim and distant, sounded like
the sky clearing its throat. Rain slid down the windows
like an endless fall of gray tears.

As much for comfort as light, Roarke ordered the bedroom fire on
low while he scanned the morning stock reports on-screen.

But he couldn't concentrate. When he switched to the morning
news, he found that didn't hold his interest either. Restless, unsettled,
he glanced over as Eve grabbed a shirt out of her closet. He noticed
she'd removed the cold patch.

"How's the shoulder?"

She rolled it. "It's good. I sent a text to Peabody last night to have her
meet me here this morning. I'm going to go down and head her off before she comes up and tries to cage breakfast. What?" she added when
he rose and walked to the closet.

He took the jacket she'd pulled out, scanned the other choices
briefly, and chose another. "This one."

"I bet everyone I badge today is going to take special note of my
jacket."

"They would if you'd worn the other with those pants." He kissed the top of her head. "And the faux pas would, very possibly, undermine your authority."

She snorted, but went with his selection. When he didn't move, but stood in her way, she frowned and said, "What?" again.

This time he cupped her face in his hands, and kissed her mouth, very gently. "I love you."

Her heart went gooey, instantly. "I got that."

He turned, crossed to the AutoChef, and got more coffee for both of them.

"What's wrong?" she asked him.

"Nothing. Not really. Miserable morning out there." But that wasn't it, he thought as he stood, staring out through the dreary curtain of rain. That wasn't it at all. "I had a dream."

She changed her plans, and instead of going downstairs walked over to the sofa, sat. "Bad?"

"No. Well, disturbing and odd, I suppose. Very lucid, which is more your style than mine."

He turned, saw that she'd sat down, that she waited. And that was more comforting than any fire in the hearth. He went to her, handed off her coffee. And sitting beside her, rubbed a hand gently on her leg in a gesture that was both gratitude and connection.

"It might be all the talk about the old days, childhood friends, and so on kicked my subconscious."

"It bothered you. Why didn't you wake me up?"

"When I woke it was over, wasn't it, and I didn't see the point. And then, just now . . . Well, in any case, I was back in Dublin, a boy again, running the streets, picking pockets. That part, at least, wasn't disturbing. It was rather entertaining."

"Good times."

He laughed a little. "Some of them were. I could smell it—the crowds on Grafton Street. Good pickings there, if you were quick enough. And the buskers playing the old tunes to draw the tourists in.

There were those among them, if you gave them a cut, they'd keep the crowd pulled in for you. We'd work a snatch, pass, drop on Grafton. I'd lift the wallet or purse, pass it on to Jenny, and she to Mick, and Brian would drop it at our hidey-hole in an alley.

"Couldn't work there often, no more than a couple hits a month, lest the locals caught wind to it. But when we did, we'd pull in hundreds in the day. If I was careful enough with my share, even with what the old man kicked out of me, I'd eat well for a month—with some to spare for my investment fund."

"Investment fund? Even then?"

"Oh aye, I didn't intend to live a street rat the whole of my life." His eyes kindled, but unlike the mellow fire in the hearth, dark and danger flashed there. "He suspected, of course, but he never found my cache. I'd sooner he beat me to death than give it over."

"You dreamed about him? Your father?"

"No. It wasn't him at all. A bright summer day, so clear I could hear the voices, the music, smell the fat frying for the chips we always treated ourselves to. A day on Grafton Street was prime, you see. Full pockets and full bellies. But in dreaming it, it went wrong."

"How?"

"Jenny'd wear her best dress on Grafton day, and her hair would be shining with a ribbon in it. Who'd look at a pretty young girl like that and see a thief, was the thought behind it. I passed to her, clean and smooth, and moved on. You have to keep moving. I set my next mark, and the fiddler was playing 'Finnegan's Wake.' I heard it clear, each note, lively, quick. I had the wallet—and the mark never flinched. But Jenny . . . she wasn't there for the pass. Couldn't take the pass because she was hanging by her hair ribbon. Hanging and dead, as she'd been the last I saw her. When I was too late to save her."

"I was too late."

Roarke shook his head. "She died because she was mine, part of my past. And I ran to try to get her down, across Grafton, with the buskers playing, still lively and quick, while she hung there. But there was

Mick. Blood spreading over his shirt. The kill blood. He was mine, too. He took the knife for me. The fiddler kept playing, all the while. I could see Brian, far off. Too far to reach, so I was there with dead friends. Still children in the dream, you know? Still so young. Even in the dream I thought, wondered, if they were, in some way, dead even that long ago. And me and Bri, all that's left of us.

"Then I walked away. I walked away from Grafton Street, and from the friends who were same as family to me. And I stood on the bridge over the River Liffey, a grown man now. I saw my mother's face under the water. And that was all."

"I could tell you that what happened to them wasn't your fault. Part of you knows that. But another part will always feel responsible. Because you loved them."

"I did. Aye, I did." He picked up his neglected coffee, drank. "They're part of me. Pieces that make me. But just now, standing with you, I realized I can stand all that, stand the loss of all those parts of me. Because I have you."

She took his hand, pressed it to her cheek. "What can I do?"

"You just did it." He leaned over, kissed her again.

"I can reschedule some stuff, if you want me to—"

He looked at her, just looked, and the heaviest of the grief that had woken with him eased. "Thanks for that, but I'm better just for having it out." He skimmed a finger down her chin. "Go to work, Lieutenant."

She wrapped her arms around him first, hugged hard. And holding her, he drew in her scent—hair and skin—knowing it would come with him through the day.

She drew back, stood. "See you tonight."

"Eve? You asked me before if I thought your victim, your Lino, would tell someone who he really was. I think, if they stood as family for him, if he considered them part of him—any of the pieces that made him—he had to. He didn't go to his mother, but there had to be someone. A man can't stand on a bridge alone, not at home, not for five years. Even the hardest needs someone to know him."

She managed to cut Peabody off, but barely. Eve jogged down the steps just as Summerset opened the door to her partner. Eve kept going. "Peabody, with me."

"But I was just . . ."

"We're moving," Eve said and pointed toward their vehicle. "Get in. One minute." Eve turned to Summerset while Peabody sulked her Danish-deprived way to the passenger side. "Roarke could use a call from his aunt."

"He wants me to contact his aunt in Ireland?"

"I said he could use a call from her. He's fine," Eve said, anticipating him. "He could just use the connection."

"I'll take care of it."

Knowing he would, Eve climbed behind the wheel, and put her mind back on the job.

"Are we running hot or something?" Peabody demanded. "So a person can't take a minute to have a cup of coffee and maybe a small bite to eat, especially when the person got off a full subway stop early to work off the anticipated bite to eat."

"If you're finished whining about it, I'll fill you in."

"A real partner would have brought me a coffee to go so I could drink it while being filled in."

"How many coffee shops did you pass on your endless and arduous hike from the subway?"

"It's not the same," Peabody muttered. "And it's not my fault I'm coffee spoiled. You're the one who brought the real stuff made from real beans into my life. You addicted me." She pointed an accusing finger at Eve. "And now you're withholding the juice."

"Yes, that was my plan all along. And if you ever want real again in this lifetime, suck it up and do my bidding."

Peabody stared. "You're like Master Manipulator. An evil coffee puppeteer."

"Yes, yes, I am. Do you have any interest, Detective, in where we're going, who we're going to see, and why?"

"I'd be more interested if I had coffee." At the utter silence, Peabody sighed. "Okay. Where are we going, Lieutenant, who are we going to see, and why?"

"We're going to the bodega beside St. Cristóbal, and I can actually *hear* you thinking 'breakfast burrito.'"

"Psychic Master Manipulator! What, besides breakfast burritos, is of interest at the bodega?"

Eve went through it, taking Peabody through the interviews, the search results, and the agenda.

"You woke Whitney up?"

She would hone in on that single point, Eve thought. "Apparently. We need the access. Two explosions, one likely in retaliation for the first, both with fatalities. Gang turf. And that's when Lino Martinez and friend skipped town. Lino was upper rung in the Soldados, he had skills with electronics. No way this went down without his participation."

"And this Penny Soto may know."

"Inez knows something, and the something caused a rift. It's worth feeling Penny out."

"Do you think he made contact with the old girlfriend, gang friend, and didn't make contact with his mother?"

"I think he didn't make contact with his mother. I think she played it straight with me. I don't think he connected with Inez because the guy was too wigged out to be lying about it. Maybe he burrowed in for five years, but he probably passed the bodega most every day, saw this woman—his girlfriend—nearly every day."

She thought of Roarke, and his lost Jenny.

"It would take a hell of a lot of willpower not to connect, not to have somebody to talk about the old days with."

Peabody nodded. "Besides, why come back here, specifically, if you didn't want to connect?"

"There you go. And if you want to connect, isn't it going to be with someone you're comfortable with, who you trust? Mom loves him, sure, but she didn't like where he was heading, tried to rein him in— and she's got a new life. New husband, new son. How can he cozy up and tell her he's pretending to be a priest?"

Eve hunted up parking. "If he connected, if he trusted," she continued as she squeezed into a spot at the curb, "he might have shared his secrets."

Even from the sidewalk, Eve could hear the jingle of the bell as people went in and out of the bodega. She spotted Marc Tuluz from the youth center stepping out with a large, steaming go-cup.

"Mr. Tuluz."

"Oh. Lieutenant . . ."

She could see him searching mental files for her last name. "Dallas."

"Right. Morning hit," he said, lifting the go-cup. "I can't fire all cylinders without a jumbo *sucre negro*. Are you here about Miguel?" He paused, looked flustered. "I don't know what else to call him. Do you have any news?"

"There may be, later today. So, you hit this place daily?"

"Sometimes twice a day. This stuff's probably corroded all my pipes, but hey." He lifted the cup like a toast. "Who wants to live forever?"

"Did you run into Flores here?"

"Sure, now and again. Or if we were both up at the center, and one of us got the jones, he might spring for a couple of hits. Killer burritos, too, best in the neighborhood. One of us usually picked up lunch here at least once a week when we had meetings at the center. I still can't be-lieve . . . Is there anything you can tell me, Lieutenant? Anything I can pass on to Magda? She's having a rough time of it over this."

"We're working on it."

"Yeah. Well. I'd better let you get back to that, and get myself to the center."

"Came in most every day," Eve stated when Marc walked away. "Just how much temptation can a fake priest handle?"

She went inside, to the jingle of the bell. It was colorful, in looks and scents, with the counter of breakfast choices doing steady business. Others jammed at the coffee kiosk or did morning shopping, filling red handbaskets with items off shelves.

Two women worked the breakfast counter, and Penny was one of them. She had improbably large breasts on a bony build—man-made breasts, Eve concluded. Junk-made build. Ink-black hair streaked with magenta coiled inside a net designed to keep customers from finding stray hairs in the *huevos, torrijas,* and frittatas. Her mouth, dyed a hard red, clamped in a line of boredom as she scooped, piled, and served.

Eve stepped to the end of the line. The few minutes it would take to reach the counter would give her more time to observe. Gold hoops, wide enough to slide a burrito through, swung at Penny's ears, while a platoon of bracelets jangled on her wrist. Her nails were painted as dark as her mouth, with the half-moons etched out in black.

On her forearm rode the symbol of the Soldados, with the kill mark.

"Go ahead and order," Eve told Peabody.

"There is a God." When she reached the counter, Peabody ordered the hash and egg (substitute) burrito and a *café con leche.*

"How's it going, Penny?" Eve said while the other woman filled Peabody's order.

Penny shifted her gaze up, over, fixed it on Eve. The dark, bored mouth turned sour. "Thought I smelled cop. Got nothing to say."

"That's fine, then we'll go down to Central, see if you change your mind."

Penny sniffed, sneered. "I don't have to go anywhere, you don't have a warrant and cause."

"You know, you look suspiciously like the suspect who rolled a guy a couple blocks from here last night. Detective, arrange for Ms. Soto to be taken downtown for a lineup."

"That's bullshit."

"While you smell cop, I smell several hours of detention and paper-work. Maybe you should call a lawyer."

"I don't need a stinking lawyer. What are you hassling me for? I got a job here. I'm doing my job."

"Hey, me, too. Do you want to talk here or downtown?"

"Shit." Penny jerked back from the counter. "Back the alley," she snapped, then swaggered off.

Eve signaled Peabody to go around by the front, then followed Penny into the cramped back room, and out the alley door.

"Lemme see ID," Penny demanded.

Eve pulled out her badge. "You've had some trouble along the way, Penny."

"I got gainful employment. My rent's paid. So screw you."

"Actually, I think you might be the one getting screwed in all this. Miguel Flores."

Penny jerked one pointed shoulder, shot out one bony hip. "Dead priest. Everybody knows. So what? I haven't been inside a church in years. That's bullshit, too. I figured it out when I was ten."

"You knew him."

A gleam lit her eyes, accenting the sneer. "Everybody knew him. Everybody knows all the priests. They're all over the neighborhood like lice."

Eve acknowledged Peabody with a glance as her partner turned into the alley. "You knew him," Eve repeated.

"You hearing defective or what? I just said I did."

"Lino Martinez."

The anger wavered for an instant before Penny aimed an unconcerned look a few inches over Eve's right shoulder. "I don't know anybody by that name."

"Oh now, you don't want to lie about something that stupid. It just tips me you're going to lie about more. Lino Martinez," Eve said again, and gripped Penny's forearm. "You should cover this up if you don't want to admit to old allegiances."

"So what? I haven't seen Lino since I was sixteen. He took off. Ask anybody who was around back then, they'll tell you the same. Shit, ask his whiny, sainted mother. She's slinging pasta over in Brooklyn somewheres. Got herself a nice house, a dipshit husband, and snot-nosed kid."

"How do you know that?"

A flash of annoyance darkened Penny's eyes. "I hear things."

"Did Lino tell you?"

"I just said I haven't seen him since—"

"You know, you can have these removed," Eve interrupted, giving Penny's forearm a light squeeze. "So you can hardly tell anything was ever there. Except when you're meat on the slab, under microgoggles and all that nasty autopsy equipment, pop."

"So—"

"—what," Eve finished. "The thing is we know Lino Martinez was masquerading as a priest, right next door. We know he came in to see you nearly every day. For over five years. We know how far back you go with him, with Chávez, with the Soldados. And gee, Penny, you're the only one here. Tag, you're it."

"That's bullshit."

"I hear things, too," Eve said cheerfully. "Like you and Lino used to tango. How he came into the bodega where you work every day."

"That doesn't mean shit. I didn't do a damn thing. You can't prove I knew Lino was back. You've got nothing."

"Give me time. I'm taking you into custody."

"For what?"

"Material witness."

"*Screw* that!"

Eve made a deliberate move to take Penny's arm again, and smiled as Penny slapped her hand away. "Uh-oh, did you see that, Detective Peabody?"

"I did, Lieutenant. I believe this woman just assaulted a police officer."

"Screw that shit." Temper burning her face, Penny shoved Eve aside, swung toward the door.

"Oops, *another* assault. And now resisting arrest." Eve made the grab, twisting Penny's wrist as the woman dug for her pocket. "Goodness, what do we have here?" she said as she pushed Penny's face against the wall.

"Why, Lieutenant, it looks like a knife."

"It really does." Eve tossed it, hilt first, to Peabody. "This is just turning into a mess, isn't it?"

"Puta!" Penny whipped her head around, spat in Eve's face.

"Okay, now I'm no longer entertained." Eve cuffed Penny's hands behind her back. "Call for a wagon, Peabody, to take our prisoner downtown. Book her on assaulting an officer, armed, and resisting."

"Bullshit charges. I'll be out in twenty minutes."

Eve took the napkin Peabody passed her, wiped the spit off her face. Then leaned close to Penny's ear, and whispered, "Wanna bet?"

We won't be able to hold her very long," Peabody commented after they'd turned Penny over to a pair of uniforms.

"Sure we will." Eve took out her 'link, called Homicide. "Jenkinson," she said when one of her detectives came on-screen. "I'm having a female prisoner transported down. Soto, Penelope. Charged with assaulting an officer and resisting. I'm going to be a couple hours. Jam it up."

"Got that."

Eve clicked off, checked her wrist unit. "No time to talk to López or Freeman. Let's head down and take care of making Lino official."

"You really just pissed her off."

"Yeah." Smiling a little, Eve got behind the wheel. "That was the good part."

"Maybe pissed her off too much to talk to you, especially if she lawyers up."

"Oh, she'll lawyer. I'm counting on it. And that's why she'll talk to me about Lino. The lawyer will so advise."

Baffled, Peabody scratched her head, and at last, long last, bit into her now stone-cold burrito. "Hmcum?"

"How come? Because admitting she knew Lino was posing as a priest, had contact, was friendly with him, should bump her down the list of murder suspects."

Peabody swallowed. "Are we liking her for it?"

"Not particularly. Not yet. As we've just witnessed, she's hotheaded. It's hard to see her sneaking into church—where she'd stick out like, well, a whore in church, and poisoning the wine. That's cunning, and it's symbolic. She'd just cut his throat and leave him in the alley." Eve thought about it for a minute. "I almost like that about her."

Teresa Franco and her husband were already waiting at the morgue when Eve arrived. Tony Franco kept his arm around his wife's shoulders, his right hand rubbing, rubbing gently up and down her biceps as they stood, listening to Eve.

"I'm sorry I kept you waiting. I checked on the way in, and they're ready whenever you are."

Shadows haunted Teresa's eyes. "Will you tell me what to do, please?"

"We're going to look at a monitor, a small screen. If you're able to identify the body, you just tell me."

"He never sent pictures. And if he called, always blocked video. In my head—my heart—he's still a boy." She looked up at her husband. "But a mother should know her son. She should know him, no matter what."

"It's not your fault, Terri. You did everything you could. You still are."

"If you'd just come with us." Peabody touched her arm, led the way.

In the small room with its single chair, little table, boxy wall screen, Eve moved to a com unit. "This is Dallas," she said into it. "We're in Viewing Room One." She paused. "Are you ready, Mrs. Franco?"

"Yes." The hand gripped with her husband's went white at the knuckles. "Yes, I'm ready."

"We're go," Eve said, and turned to the screen.

A white sheet covered the body from armpits to toes. Someone, Morris she imagined, had removed the tag for the viewing. Death didn't look like sleep—not to Eve—but she imagined it might to some. To some who'd never seen death.

Teresa sucked in a breath, leaned into her husband. "He . . . he doesn't look like Lino. His face is sharper, his nose longer. I have a picture. See, I have a picture." She drew one out of her bag, pushed it toward Eve.

The boy was early in his teens, handsome, smirky, with dark, sleepy eyes.

"We've established he had facial reconstruction," Eve began. But the shape of the eyes, she noted, was the same. The color nearly so. The dark hair, the line of the throat, the set of the head on the shoulders. The same. "There's a resemblance."

"Yes. I know, but . . ." Teresa pressed her lips together. "I don't want it to be Lino. Can I—is it possible for me to see? To go in, where he is, and see?"

She'd hoped the screen viewing would be enough. Eve realized she'd set it up that way for the same reason Morris had removed the toe tag. To spare the mother. "Is that what you want?"

"No, no, it's not. But it's what I need."

Eve moved back to the com. "I'm bringing Mrs. Franco in."

Eve led the way out, down the corridor, and through double doors. Morris came in from the back. He wore a suit, the color of polished bronze, without any protective cape.

"Mrs. Franco, I'm Dr. Morris. Is there anything I can do to help you?"

"I don't know." Clinging to her husband's hand, Teresa stepped closer to the body. "So tall," she murmured. "His father was tall. Lino, he had big feet as a boy. I used to tell him he'd grow into them, like a puppy does. And he did. He was nearly six feet when he left. And very thin. No matter what he ate, so thin. He was like a whip, and when he played ball, fast as one."

Eve glanced at Peabody. "Basketball."

"Yes. His favorite." She reached out a hand, drew it back. "Can I, or can you . . . the sheet. If I could see."

"Let me do that." Morris stepped forward. "There's an incision," he began.

"I know. Yes, I know about that. It's all right."

Gently, Morris lowered the sheet to the victim's waist.

Teresa took another step. This time when she reached out, she touched fingertips to the body's left side, high on the ribs. And the sound she made was caught between sob and sigh.

"When he was a little boy, and would still let me, I would tickle him here. This way." She traced her finger in a quick Z pattern. "The freckles, you see. Four little freckles, and you can make a Z."

Eve studied the pattern—so faint, so light, so vague. Something, she supposed, only a mother would notice.

"See how long his eyelashes are? So long and thick, like a girl's. It embarrassed him when he was little. Then he was proud and vain about them, when he noticed the girls noticed."

"Do you know your son's blood type, Mrs. Franco?" Morris asked.

"A-negative. He broke his arm when he was ten. His right arm. He slipped while he tried to sneak out the window. Only ten, and already sneaking out. You can tell if his arm had been broken when he was a boy?"

"Yes." Morris touched a hand to hers. "Yes."

"This is my son. This is Lino." Leaning down she pressed her lips to his cheek. *"Siento tanto, mi bebé."*

"Let me take you out, Mrs. Franco." Peabody put an arm around Teresa's waist. "Let me take you out now."

Eve watched her go, Peabody on one side, her husband on the other.

"It's a hard thing," Morris said quietly. "A hard thing for a mother. No matter how many years between."

"Yeah. Very hard for her." She turned back to the body. "He had someone who loved him, all the way, every day. And still, it looks like every choice he made brought him here."

"People are messed up."

"Yeah." It lightened her mood, just enough, made her smile into Morris's understanding face. "They really are."

16

TO GIVE TERESA A LITTLE TIME TO COMPOSE
herself, and Penny more time to stew, Eve asked Tony
Franco to bring his wife to Central. She booked the
smallest conference room.

"I'll handle the mother," Eve told Peabody. "I started a run on a partial list of John Does, in the area and at the time of Flores's disappearance. Start following up. If I'm not done in thirty, check on Spitting
Penny. She'll be crying lawyer by then. Let her contact one."

"Check. What about the case file access?"

"I'm hitting that between the mother and the bitch. Tag Baxter, see
if he got anywhere with his part of the John Doe list you're on. And
check my incoming. I'm expecting lists of names from Officer Ortiz
and from López on former members of the Soldados still in the neighborhood. Soto's the key," Eve added, "but we'll cover the bases."

"On that. It's coming together. It feels like it's coming together."

"Parts of it." Eve peeled off, set up her conference room. At her go,
one of her men brought in the Francos.

Teresa's eyes were swollen and red, but she appeared to have the
weeping under control.

"I want to thank you for your help. I know that wasn't easy."

"It was never easy with Lino. I made mistakes. I can't unmake them. Now I'll bury my son. You'll let me do that."

"As soon as I'm able. I need to ask you questions now."

"All right. I feel like I'm between worlds. The one that was, the one we have." She took her husband's hand. "And that I won't ever be all the way in either again."

"Why was he here?" Tony asked Eve. "Do you know? I think it would help to know."

"Yes." Teresa steadied herself. "It would help to know. Why was he pretending to be this priest? I raised him to have respect for the Church. I know he went wild. I know he went bad. But I raised him to have respect for the Church."

"I think he was hiding, and I think he was waiting. I don't know why yet. But I think some of the answers go back to when he was with the gang. Do you know what the Clemency Order was?"

"Yes, they told me. I didn't know where Lino was, but he contacted me after it passed. I begged him to come home. He could start fresh. But he said he wasn't coming back until he drove back in a big, fancy car with the keys to a big, fancy house."

"Due to the Clemency Order, even though it was later repealed, all of Lino's police records from when he was a minor were deleted. What can you tell me about the trouble he'd been in?"

"He stole. Shoplifting, that was first. Little things, foolish things . . . at first. If I found out, I made him go back to the store with me, take back what he stole. Or I'd pay for it. He broke into places after they'd closed, and into cars on the street."

She sighed, then reached for the water Eve had on the table. "He broke windows, tagged buildings, started fights. The police would come, take him, question him. He went to detention, but it didn't help. It was worse after. He got into more fights, worse fights. He'd come home bloody, and we'd argue. They said he cut a boy, and put him in the hospital, but the other boy said no. He lied, I know, but the boy said he didn't see who cut him. He killed, my Lino. He took a life."

"Whose life?"

"I don't know. They never came for him, never arrested him, not for that. It was always smaller things. But I knew he'd killed. I knew what it meant the night he came home with the mark under the tattoo on his arm. We fought—terrible, terrible fight. I called him a killer. I called my son a murderer."

She broke then, tears rolling. Pulling out a tissue, she mopped at her ravaged face. "He told me I didn't understand, that he did what he had to do, and he was *proud*. Proud, and now the others, they knew he was a man. Now, he had respect. He was fifteen years old. Fifteen years old when he came home with the kill mark still raw on his arm."

She stopped, struggled. "I wanted to get him out of the city. If I could get him away from the streets, the gangs. But when I told him what I planned to do, that I was buying two bus tickets to El Paso . . . My godmother lived there, and said she'd let us come, help me find work."

"Your godmother?"

"A friend of my mother's, from their childhood. My mother was dead. My father beat her to death when I was sixteen. I ran away, and he beat her to death. So I married the same kind of man. I know it's typical, it's a cycle. It's a sickness. But my godmother had a house and work, and she said to come. I told Lino, and he refused. I threatened, argued, and he went out, slammed out. He was gone a week."

She stopped, sipped water.

"Terri, it's enough." Tony stroked her arm. "It's enough now."

"No, I'll finish. I'll finish it. I went to the police, afraid then he was dead. But a boy like Lino, he knew how to hide. He came back when he wanted. And he told me I could go, but he wouldn't. Go, he said, he didn't need me. But if I thought I could make him go, he'd just run again. He wouldn't leave his family. He wouldn't leave the

Soldados. So I stayed. He defeated me. He lived as he chose, and I allowed it."

Eve let her get it out. "He kept the medal, Mrs. Franco."

Teresa looked at her, eyes blurry with tears and gratitude.

"Mrs. Franco, you said he'd left before, for days, even a week. But this last time he told you he was leaving—leaving New York, when he'd objected and refused to leave New York before, when you had somewhere to go."

"Yes, yes, that's true. I didn't believe him, even when he packed his things. I didn't really believe he was leaving, and part of me hoped he was. That's a terrible thing to feel, but I did. Still, I thought he was just angry, in a mood. I know he'd fought with Joe—Joe Inez—about something, and Lino was so mad at him. I wondered since it was just Lino and the Chávez boy planning to leave, if Lino had fought with Penny."

"What were they fighting about? Lino and Joe Inez?"

"I don't know. He never told me his business, the gang business. Lino didn't talk to me about that kind of thing. But I know they were all mad, all upset about the bombing at the school. The neighborhood was in an uproar. A girl died. A young girl. Other kids had been hurt. Lino had cuts and burns. One of his friends—one of the other Soldados—was very badly hurt, in the hospital. They thought he might die. We held a prayer service at St. Cristóbal's for him. He got better, but it took a long time. It took months and several operations, I think."

"There was another explosion, and there were several fatalities, only days later."

"Yes, it was horrible. They thought it was retaliation—the other gang members said, and people were scared there'd be more violence. The police came to talk to Lino, to question him, but he was gone."

"He left New York after the second explosion."

"No, before. Two days before. I remember thanking God he'd gone, that he didn't have a part in that, in taking those lives."

"How did he leave New York?"

"By bus. I think. It was all so fast, so quick. I came home and he was packing. He said he'd come back one day, rich, he'd be somebody. He'd be the most important man in El Barrio. More than Mr. Ortiz, Mr. Ortega, others who were rich and had position. Big car, big house. Big dreams." She closed her eyes. "A couple weeks later, when I went to pay the rent, I found out he'd taken the money out of my account. He'd gotten into my bank account by the computer, he was clever that way. He stole from me before he left, and I had to ask Mr. Ortiz for a loan, an advance to pay the rent. Lino, he'd send money now and then, as if that made it all right that he'd stolen from me so I had to beg for money to pay the rent.

"He was my child," she finished, "but he was his father's son."

"I appreciate all you've done, Mrs. Franco, and I'm sorry for all you've lost. As soon as I'm able, I'll notify you so you can make arrangements for your son."

After she'd led them out, she went to her office. At her desk, she checked access for the case files she wanted, found Whitney had come through.

She got coffee, sat, and as she read made notes of the names of the investigating officers, the witnesses, the victims, the fatalities.

She stopped on Lino's name, saw the notation that the subject could not be located, and the statement from Teresa about him leaving town two days prior. A statement corroborated by others. Including Penny Soto.

Joe Inez had been questioned and released, alibied up tight. And he, too, had corroborated Teresa's statement regarding Lino. The investigators had canvassed the neighborhoods, hit all of Lino's and Chávez's known haunts, followed up at transpo stations. Lino had gone into the wind—and reading between the lines of the detective's report, he hadn't believed Lino had blown prior to the incident.

"Hey, me either," Eve concurred. She took what she had and headed out to take a swing at Penny.

The lawyer wore a chunk of gold the size of home plate on the middle finger of his right hand, and a suit the color of radioactive limes. There was enough oil in his hair to fry a small army of chickens, and his teeth were a blinding white gleam.

Eve thought: *Do you actually want to be a cliché?*

He got out of his chair when she entered and rose to his full five feet, five inches. And an inch of that came from the heels of his snake-patterned boots.

"My client's waited over two hours," he began, "and nearly all of that without benefit of legal counsel."

"Uh-huh." Eve sat down, opened her file. "Your legal counsel, which I assume is this." Eve glanced up at the lawyer. "Should be aware that two hours is well within the reasonable time frame, and that you haven't been questioned since you requested counsel. Therefore, he should sit down so we don't waste any more time. Record on." She read off the salients, cocked her brow at the lawyer. "Ms. Soto is represented by?"

"Carlos Montoya."

"Who is present. Mr. Montoya, did you present your identification and license to practice for scan?"

"I did."

"Good. Ms. Soto, you've been read your rights, and have stated you understand them, and your obligations in this matter."

"It's all shit."

"But you understand all the shit?"

Penny shrugged. "I understand fine, just like I understand me and my lawyer are going to sue your ass for false arrest."

"Won't that be fun? You're charged with assaulting an officer, which includes assault with a weapon and resisting arrest."

"I never touched you."

"As the touchee, I beg to differ. However, I'd be willing to negotiate those charges if you find yourself now willing and able to answer questions regarding Lino Martinez, and events pertaining to him."

"I told you already, I haven't seen Lino since I was fifteen."

"You lied."

"My client—"

"Is a liar, but you probably get that a lot. Me, too. The body of Lino Martinez has been officially identified. We are aware he posed as one Father Miguel Flores for a period of more than five years, and frequented the bodega where you work. We are aware of your previous relationship. You want to keep insisting you didn't know, then we'll stick with the assault and resisting, and given your record, you'll be doing a little time in a cage."

Eve closed the file, started to rise.

"I'm not doing time for knocking your hand away when you went to grab me."

"Oh yeah, you are, and for pulling a knife, for spitting in my face, and resisting. And since you don't know me, let me point out to you—and your counsel—that if you had even one private conversation with Lino Martinez, met him anywhere, any time outside the bodega, I'm going to find out. Then I'm going to knock you back for making a false statement—and I'm going to start wondering if you got your hands on some cyanide, then—"

"This is bullshit."

Eve only smiled, turned for the door.

"Wait a damn minute. I want to talk to my lawyer before I say another thing."

"Pause record. I'll just step out so you two can chat."

Eve left them, considered risking Vending for a tube of Pepsi, but decided it wasn't going to take that long. Inside three minutes, Montoya came to the door.

"My client may be willing to amend her statement."

"Okeydokey." Eve stepped back in, sat, smiled, folded her hands. "Resume record." Waited.

"If my client addresses your questions regarding Lino Martinez, you will drop the charges currently against her."

"If she answers truthfully, to my satisfaction, she gets a pass on the charges."

"Go ahead, Penny."

"Maybe I kinda had this feeling, this vibe, you know, when he started coming in. He didn't look like Lino, or not a lot. But there was something. And after a while, maybe we flirted some. Weird, him being a priest, and I don't like the holier-than-thou types. But Lino and I, we always had something. We made it a lot back in the day, and I kept getting this buzz from him."

"Did you start banging before or after you knew who he was?"

Penny smirked. "Before. I think he got off on it. Maybe I did, too. Back room of the bodega, after closing. Man, he *hammered* me. Pent up, you know? Had to figure it was all that celibacy song. Couple times after, we'd meet at this flop a friend of mine has. She works nights. Or we'd use a rent-by-the-hour. Then this one time, after we'd made it, he tells me. We had a big laugh."

"Did he tell you what happened to Father Flores?"

"What did I care? How'm I supposed to know there ever was one?"

"Why was he masquerading as a priest?"

"He wanted to come back, lay low. He liked people looking at him like he was a big deal, he liked the respect."

"Five years, Penny. Don't string me. What was the angle?"

"He liked the secrets, too, the sins. He used them when he could, when he wanted."

"Blackmail?"

"He had some ready, sure. More than a priest earns. When he was in the mood, he'd get us a room at a fancy hotel, and we'd order room service and shit. Paid cash."

"Did he buy you things?"

"Sure." She flipped her finger at one of her earrings. "Lino wasn't stingy."

"He trusted you a lot."

"Lino and I went back, all the way back. We needed each other. That's what this is about." She slapped her palm on her tattoo. "This is family, and it's protection. My mother was useless, more interested in her next fix than me. More interested in that than stopping my old man from moving on me. Barely twelve years old the first time he raped me. Slapped me around good, too, and he tells me I'll keep my mouth shut about it, and he won't slap me around next time. Kept it shut for two years before I couldn't take it anymore. I joined the Soldados, and I got family."

"Your data states that your father was killed when you were fourteen. Stabbed. Cut to pieces."

"No loss."

"Did you kill him?"

"My client's not going to answer that. Don't answer that, Penny."

Penny only smiled, rubbed a fingertip on her kill mark.

"You and Lino," Eve concluded. "Makes a hell of a bond. And two years later, he's smoke. Gone."

"Nothing lasts forever."

"Were you in on the planning of the Skull bombing?"

"My—"

Penny held up a finger to stop her lawyer. "Questioned and released, a long time ago. Nobody ever proved that was Soldado work."

"People died."

"Happens every day."

"Lino planned it. He was one of the leaders, and he had the skills."

"I guess you'll never know, seeing as he's dead."

"Yeah, he's dead. You're not. And your legal counsel will tell you there's no statute of limitations on murder."

"You can't hang it on me now any more than they could then."

"What was Lino waiting for? When was payday, Penny?"

"I don't know what you're talking about." Her eyes skittered away. "He's dead, so I guess we can't ask him."

"Where's Steve Chávez?"

"Don't know. Can't say." She yawned. "We done?"

"Lino was marking time, picking up some grease along the way so he could show off, live high, then duck back under the collar. A man doesn't do that for five years so he can bang an old girlfriend."

"He loved me. We used to talk about taking off, making a big score, and coming back riding high. Never worked out, but he came back."

"Do you have an alibi for the day of his death?"

"I opened the bodega at six A.M., along with Rosita. We did the prep, and worked the breakfast counter for three hours straight. Around ten, Pep and I—stock boy—took our break together in the back room, then I was back on the counter when the first cops came in asking questions. And I heard he was dead."

"What did you do then?"

"Worked my shift, went home. What was I supposed to do?"

"All right. You're free to go."

"About damn time."

Eve waited until they'd left the room. She sat alone, in silence another full minute. "Record off," she said.

When she was back in her office, standing, staring out the tiny window, Peabody came in.

"Any luck with Penny?"

"Yeah. A twisted mix of lies and truth. More lies than, but enough truth to get a picture. She claims she doesn't know what happened to the real Flores—lie. That she doesn't know what Lino was waiting for here—lie. She admits no knowledge of the bombing. Not a lie, more a 'Prove it, bitch.' Same with Chávez's whereabouts. She said Lino loved her. I think that's truth, or she believes it to be. She never said she loved him. If she had, it would've been a lie. But she had been banging him for the past few years."

"If they've been having it on for that long, he told her what he was up to."

"Yeah. I think he may have helped her kill the first time, earn her mark—maybe they earned them together as the timing jibes with Teresa's statement. Her father. He'd been sexually abusing her. She had enough. They cut him up."

"She admitted—"

"No. She admitted the abuse, and that was truth. She admitted she'd joined the gang at fourteen to escape it, to make family, for protection. Her father was found hacked to pieces in an abandoned building when she was fourteen. He was a known dealer, and the cops put it down to an illegals deal gone bad. Probably didn't work it very hard. Why bother? She and Lino would've been covered for it anyway. Others in the gang would've alibied them, or threatened someone else into it."

She heard Peabody close the office door, turned.

"Are you doing okay?" Peabody asked.

"Yes." Eve walked to the AutoChef, programmed coffee. "Let's keep going. We're going to want to dig back into that case file. I've got the case files for the bombings, and we'll need to reach out to the investigators. I need to put some pressure on Penny. More pressure than a couple months in over slapping at a cop."

"Do you think she killed Lino?"

"We'll check her alibi, but I bet it's nice and tight. She had it ready for me, and on a platter. No, she's the hothead. I don't think she did the kill. But I think she's connected. At the very least she knows who did."

"Maybe they had a fight. Lovers' tangle."

"Maybe. I can't see her going five years without getting pissed off at a lover. Or being exclusive," she said slowly, and handed one of the coffee mugs to Peabody. "Let's find out if she was banging anybody else besides Lino. Lino used his confessional privileges to blackmail when it suited him. Can't see him hitting up for nickels. So we see who'd use the church who had enough to make paying for sin worthwhile. And we need full information on the victims and fatalities of the restaurant bombing."

"You know how I said I thought it was starting to fall into place? Now it feels like it's spreading out all over."

"Just more pieces. They're going to fall somewhere. Let's start with the bombings, work forward. The primary investigator's still on the job. Contact Detective Stuben, out of the Four-six. See if he and/or his old partner have time for a sit-down."

"Okay. Dallas." She wanted to say more, it was all over her face. The need to comfort or reassure.

"Right now let's just work the case, Peabody. That's it."

With a nod, Peabody stepped out, and Eve turned back to the window. Time enough, Eve thought, time enough later to feel it, to let herself feel any empathy or connection to another young girl who'd killed to escape the brutality of her father.

She finished off her coffee, then requested the case files for the Soto murder. And was grateful that Peabody buzzed through with an affirmative from Stuben before she had the chance to dig into them.

Stuben wanted to meet at a deli by his own cop shop. He was already packing into a mystery sandwich and a side of slaw when Eve and Peabody arrived. "Detective Stuben, Lieutenant Dallas. My partner, Detective Peabody." Eve offered a hand. "Thanks for taking the time."

"Not a problem." His voice was tough-edged Bronx. "Getting my lunch in. Food's good here, if you want to eat and meet."

"Wouldn't mind." Eve settled on a steamed dog and some sort of pasta curls, and noted Peabody was offsetting her morning burrito with a melon plate.

"Kohn, my old partner's off on a fishing trip. Testing retirement out, see if it suits him before he takes the jump," Stuben began. "If you want to talk to him, he's due back tomorrow."

Stuben dabbed at his mouth with a paper napkin. "I used to take that file out every couple months, the first year or two after the bombings. I guess longer." He shook his head, bit into his sandwich. "Take it out again, review, maybe do more follow-ups once or twice a year for another stretch. Dack, too—my partner. We'd sit down like this, over a meal or a brew, and go through it again. Ten, twelve years down, I'd still get it out. Some of them don't leave you alone."

"No, they don't."

"That area, it was going through a bad time then. Couldn't bring itself back after the Urbans. We didn't have enough street cops, not enough on the gang patrols. And the gangs shoved it up our ass, if you don't mind me saying."

"Did you know Lino Martinez?"

"I knew the little bastard, and the rest of them. I worked those streets when I was in uniform. He was a badass by the time he was eight. Stealing, tagging stores, busting things up just to bust them. His mother, she tried. I'd see her dragging him to school, to church. I caught him with a pocketful of Jazz when he was about ten. I let him off, 'cause of the mother."

"Did you know Nick Soto?"

"Dealer, street tough, liked to rough up women. Slippery bastard. Then someone slipped a knife in him. Fifty, sixty times. I didn't work that one, but I knew him some."

"Did anyone talk to the daughter or Lino on that one?"

He paused, rubbed a finger over his cheek. "Had to. Lino and the Soto kid were tight. The fact is, I think she was worse than he was, worse than Lino. He stole something, it was for money. He beat the shit out of somebody, there was a reason. Kid had a purpose. Her? Carried hate around in her. She stole, it was to take it from somebody else. She beat the shit out of someone, it was for the hell of it. You're sniffing at them for that case?"

"I had Penny Soto in on something today. She claims her father raped her, regularly. That didn't come out."

"Like I said, I didn't work it. But I knew some of the particulars." He shook his head. "That had come out, I'd know."

"You looked for Lino after the bombing."

"He'd taken over the Soldados by then, him and Chávez served as captains. The site wasn't strict Skull territory. It was in the disputed turf, but plenty of them hung there. It was retaliation. I know it was Soldados, and the Soldados didn't breathe without Lino telling them to. Mrs. Martinez said Lino took off, two days before the bombing."

He shook his head. "I had to believe her, or I had to believe *she* believed it. She let us go through the place. No sign of him, and we checked with neighbors, and not all of them had any love for the son of a bitch. Got the same story. He lit out before the incident. We put the heat on the Soldados, and turned it up. We couldn't get one of them to refute that. Not one. But they did it, Lieutenant, they set it up, Martinez and Chávez. I know it in my guts."

"My guts say the same."

"Have you got a line on them? Either of them?"

"I've got Lino Martinez in the morgue."

Stuben scooped up noodles. "Best place for him."

"How about any of the alternate gangs? Would any of them take a hit at Lino after all this time?"

"Skulls, Bloods. Most of them are dead, gone, or locked up. Always a few around, both sides of that. But that fire's been out a long while. How'd he buy it?"

"You've heard about the murder at St. Cristóbal's? The one posing as a priest."

"Martinez?"

"Yeah. How's that play for you, him going under like that for five years—in plain sight?"

Stuben sat back, gave it some thought over his tube of cream soda. "He was wily. He had brains and could stay frosty. It was hard, even when he was a kid, to pin anything on him. Knew how to cover his tracks, or get someone to do it for him. He fought his way up to the top level of the Soldados by the time he was sixteen. Had to be something in it for him, some game. Something big to keep him under. You had the Soto girl in on this?"

"Today."

"She'd have known, no question in my mind. He came back, he'd go to Penny Soto. Lino had a weak spot, she was it. He made her a lieutenant, and she's not fifteen, for Christ's sake. Word was, there was some dissention in the ranks about that. Lino took out the dissenter with a pipe, and let her kick the shit out of him. 'Course, the dissenter claimed, from his hospital bed with his jaw wired, that he fell down some stairs. Back then? You couldn't work one of them against the other. They'd take a knife to the heart first."

"Times change."

Stuben nodded. "They do. You might try Joe Inez."

"I ran it by him once. Weak link?" she asked, but for courtesy as she already knew.

"That'd be the one. Joe, he didn't have the kill switch in him. Didn't have the hardness for it."

"Is there anyone else I should talk to? Any other former members? I've got a couple people working on getting me names, but you'd know better."

"I can tell you anybody who was top rungs back that time, they're gone. Dead, in a cage, or in the wind. Some are still around, but they'd've been rank and file. Martinez and Chávez were in charge. And Soto. She took it over when they lit out."

"I appreciate it, Detective."

"You get anything leads to closing the bombing, we're square."

She got to her feet, paused. "One more thing. The families of the victims. Are you in touch?"

"Now and then."

"If I need to, can I tap you again on this?"

"You know where to find me."

**17** EVE FOLLOWED HER NOSE TO ST. CRISTÓBAL'S. Rosa, her hair bundled over a face prettily flushed, answered the door. She wore an apron over a colorful top and slim black pants.

"Hello. How can I help you?"

"A couple of questions for you, and for Fathers López and Freeman."

"The fathers aren't here right at the moment, but . . . Would you mind coming back to the kitchen? I'm making bread, and you caught me right in the middle."

"Sure. Making it?" Eve added as she and Peabody followed Rosa through the rectory. "Like from flour?"

"Yes." Rosa tossed a smile over her shoulder. "And other things. Father López is especially fond of my rosemary bread. I was just about to shape the dough, and don't want it to over-rise."

In the little kitchen, a work counter held a large bowl, a stone board, a bin of flour.

"My mother bakes bread," Peabody commented. "And her mother, my sister. My dad gets his hands in sometimes."

"It's a nice skill, and a relaxing chore. Do you bake?"

"Not much, and not really in a while."

"It takes time." Rosa punched a fist into the bowl of dough, and had Eve frowning. "Therapeutic." Rosa laughed, then turned the dough onto the board, and began to pat and pull. "Now, how can I help you?"

"You lived in the neighborhood," Eve said, "in the spring of 2043. There were two bombings."

"Oh." Rosa's eyes clouded. "A terrible time. So much loss, pain, fear. My kids were just little guys. I kept them close, took them out of school for a month because I was afraid of what might happen next."

"There were never any arrests."

"No."

"Did you know Lino Martinez?"

"If you lived in the neighborhood during that time, you knew Lino. He ran the Soldados, him and that gorilla Steve Chávez. To *protect* the neighborhood, he'd say. To keep what was ours. His poor mother. She worked so hard. She worked for my uncle, at the restaurant."

"The investigators suspected Lino for the bombing, but were never able to talk to him."

"I always thought he had his hand in it. The gang was his religion, and he was, at that age, a fanatic. Violence was his answer. But he was gone before it happened—the second bombing, I mean. Most thought he'd planned it, set it in motion, then ran off to avoid arrest."

She formed three long, narrow rolls of dough, and to Eve's reluctant fascination, began to braid them like a woman braided hair. "He was supposed to be at that dance, when the first bomb went off," Rosa continued. "He liked to dance. But he didn't go. None of his inner circle, except Joe Inez, were there when it happened. Lupe Edwards's daughter, Ronni, died in that bombing. She was barely sixteen."

Eve cocked her head. "And neither Lino nor Chávez were there? That would've been unusual?"

"Yes. As I said, he liked to dance, and he liked to swagger and show off. I heard they were on their way there when the bomb went off. So, maybe that was true. In any case, Ronni was killed. A lot of kids were hurt, some seriously, and the rumor was Lino was the target. When he left, so soon after, a lot of people said it was because he knew the Skulls would try again. They said, some said, he left to prevent innocent people from being hurt." Her lips twisted. "Like he was a hero."

Eve studied Rosa's face. "That's not what you said."

"No. I think he left because he was a coward. I think he ordered the second bombing and made sure he was far away when it happened."

"There were no arrests on that bombing either."

"No, but everyone knew it was the Soldados. Who else?"

Eve debated with herself a moment. "Did you ever have any trouble with Lino, you specifically?"

"No." As she spoke, she turned the braided dough into a circle, set it on a baking sheet, then began to form three more strips. "I was older than he was, of course, and my kids too young to interest him as recruits. Plus, his mother worked for my family. He left me and mine alone. I know he tried to recruit some of the older kids, but my grandfather had a talk with him."

"Hector Ortiz?"

"Yes. Lino respected my Poppy, I think, because of what he'd built, and my Poppy's pride in the neighborhood. Lino left us alone."

She stopped braiding the second batch to look at Eve. "I don't understand. Lino's been gone for years and years. Do you think he's involved with Father Flores—well, whoever he was—with his death?"

"The man posing as Flores was Lino Martinez."

Rosa's hands jerked away from the dough as she took a stumbling step back. "But no. No, that can't be. I _knew_ him. I would have known. I cooked for him, and cleaned, and . . ."

"You knew him at seventeen, stayed out of his way, and he left you alone."

"Yes. Yes. But still, he would come into the restaurant, or I'd see him on the street. How could I not know him? Penny Soto! At the bodega next to the church. She was . . . they were—"

"We know."

Rosa went back to her dough, but now her eyes were hard. "Why would he come back like this? Pretend all this time. And I can promise you, she knew—the one at the bodega. And they would have gone to bed. They would have had sex while he wore the collar. It would've excited her. Bitch. *Puta.*"

She rolled her eyes, paused to cross herself. "I try not to swear in the rectory, but there are exceptions. And I can tell you this," she continued, wound up. "If he was here like this, it wasn't for good. However much he pretended, however much time he gave to the center, to the church, his reasons wouldn't be for the good."

"He had friends here, old friends. But old enemies, too."

"Most he warred with are gone. I don't know, and I'd tell you if I did, who would kill him if they'd known. Whatever he'd done, whatever he was doing or hoped to do, killing isn't the answer. So I'd tell you."

"If you have any thoughts on it, I hope you'll tell me that, too."

"I will." She sighed, slowly turned the braid into a circle. "His mother, Teresa, she sent flowers to the funeral. I talk to her now and then, not as often as I should. Does she know?"

"Yes."

"Is it all right if I talk to her? If I give her my condolences? He was her son. Nothing changes that."

"I imagine she'd like to hear from you. Can you tell us where we'd find either Father López or Father Freeman?"

"Father Freeman is doing home visits. He'll probably be back in an hour or so. Father López went to the youth center."

"Thanks. We'll get out of your way. One last thing. Penny Soto, who does she run with? Sleep with?"

"If she has friends, I don't know them. And she has a reputation for sleeping with many. Her mother was a junkie, and her father was a dealer. He was killed when she was still a child, and her mother OD'd years ago."

Shaking her head, Rosa placed the second braided circle on the baking sheet, began to brush both with some sort of oil. "It was a hard life, hard beginnings, but she refused help from the Church, from the neighborhood, from everyone. She chose the gang instead. She chose her life."

Impressions?" Eve asked as she and Peabody started toward the youth center.

"She's a straight arrow, and one who's kicking herself for not clueing in on Lino while she kept house for him. She's going to think about all this, and think hard. If she comes up with anything, she'll contact us."

"That's how I read her, too. Now try this. Lino and company routinely attend the dance deal where the bombing took place. But they're not there when it gets hit. Just Joe's there, in what you could call the line of fire. And days later, right before Lino takes off, he and Joe argue. No arrests. The cops look hard at members of the Skulls, but they can't tie them. Maybe because there was no tie."

"You think Lino was behind both? Wait a minute." When they got out at the center, Peabody leaned on the vehicle, stared off into middle distance. "You want war, you want to be a hero—important. Retaliation's sexier than unprovoked offense. The bombings kicked the level up from street fights. Bomb your own turf—school dance, plenty of innocents. Even people who don't look kindly on you, on gangs, they're worked up."

"Spread the word that you were the target. They came after you. Now you hit back, hit harder."

"Okay, but why leave?"

"You leave important, your name on people's lips. You make sure word goes that you've left so no more innocent people are killed when the Skulls try for you again. And you leave a body count behind."

Like Peabody, Eve leaned on the car. Across the street a woman swept her stoop, and beside it flowers made a colorful waterfall down a glossy white pot. The early morning rain still glittered on petals and leaves.

"The cops can't hassle you," Eve continued, "not only because you aren't there, but because evidence says you weren't. He's patient, the son of a bitch was patient. You're going to come back one day, come back rolling in it. Could be he didn't plan for it to take so long. You're seventeen, and full of yourself. You think, I'll score, big score, in a few months, go back, live like a king."

"Doesn't work that way," Peabody mused. "Plus, you're seventeen, and you're out of the box for the first time in your life. There's a big world out there. You're whoever you are, whenever you want to be. I like it."

"So do I. Might be half bullshit, but some of it's got to play in."

They went into the center. Magda stood behind the counter making a 'link call. A couple of boys sat on bright yellow chairs, with expressions that indicated to Eve they were planning nefarious deeds. Another woman stood nearby, keeping an eagle eye on them.

Magda held up a hand, two fingers indicating two minutes. "I know, Kippy, but this is the third fight in two weeks. That's an automatic suspension. Both Wyatt and Luis need to be picked up as soon as possible. I've already contacted Luis's dad. Yes, that's fine. I'm really sorry. Oh, I know." Magda rolled her gaze toward the two boys. "I absolutely know."

She clicked off. "Okay, sorry about that. One more second. Nita? Wyatt's mother and Luis's father are coming in. It's going to take Kippy about an hour to arrange it. Can you hold them until then?"

Nita, a sturdy-looking woman with her back to the desk, nodded. "I'll stay here. Do you need me to man the desk?"

"No, I— This won't take long, will it?" she asked Eve, then angled back toward Nita. "Nita's in charge of our six- to ten-year-olds, and our nurse. We'd be lost without her. Nita, this is Lieutenant Dallas and Detective Peabody." Magda gave the boys a meaningful look. "In case anybody around here needs to be arrested."

Nita turned slightly, a cold look in her eye. Eve started to speak, but the boys needed only that split second. They fell on each other like wolves.

Even as Eve started forward, Nita waded in. Eve had to admire the way the woman grabbed both kids by the shirt collars and yanked them apart.

"You there. You there." She hauled them to chairs. "You think punching each other makes you strong? It makes you stupid. Fighting's for those not smart enough to use their words."

Eve might have disagreed—she liked a good fight—but the lecture had the kids staring at the floor.

"My partner and I can take them downtown," Eve said casually. "Looks like a couple of assaults, disturbing the peace, and being general dumb-asses to me. Couple hours in a cage . . ." She let it trail off.

Both boys stared at her, jaws on the toes of their skids, which had been the intention. Nita, however, stared holes through her, with no trace of humor, for an icy moment before turning her back again. "It's for their parents to deal with."

"Sure. So . . ." She turned back to Magda. "I'm looking for Father López."

"Yes, he's in the gym. Marc told me he ran into you this morning, that you said you had some leads."

"We're working it. Gym?"

"Through that door, straight down to the end of the corridor, turn left."

"Thanks. And, ah . . ." She jerked her head toward the boys. "Good luck."

"It'll be fine."

"Nita doesn't like cops," Eve commented as she headed down the corridor with Peabody.

"Either that or she took you seriously. If I didn't know you, I'd have taken you seriously."

"I thought scaring kids out of being little assholes was SOP."

"Well . . . It's a method."

"Did you see the kid on the right. Little bastard can take a punch."

And so, Eve noted when they went through the gym doors, could López. What looked like a portable sparring ring stood behind the center court line. A scatter of kids practiced on equipment on the other half, under the supervision of a couple of women in gym shorts. López—red boxing gloves, black face guard, black baggy shorts, and a white tee—sparred with Marc.

And Marc snuck one in.

Other kids grouped around the ring, called out encouragement. The gym rang with voices, the slap of feet, and the whop of padded gloves finding meat.

Both men had worked up a sweat, and despite the age difference appeared evenly matched to the casual onlooker. But Eve saw López was quicker, and carried that innate boxer's grace.

An out-fighter, she noted, making his opponent come to him.

He weaved, jabbed, danced right, hooked. Disciplined poetry in motion.

Why, exactly, was fighting the answer of the weak and brainless? Eve wondered.

She watched until the timer rang, and both men stepped back. She'd counted two hits for Marc, six for López. And the way Marc bent at the waist to catch his breath told her he was done.

She walked forward. "Nice round."

Puffing, still bent over, Marc turned his head. "The guy kills me."

"You drop your right before you jab."

"So he tells me," Marc said bitterly. "You want a shot at him?"

Eve glanced up at López. "Wouldn't mind, but I'll rain-check. Have you got a few minutes now?" she asked López. "We have some questions."

"Of course."

"Outside maybe? We'll wait for you on the blacktop."

"He's built," Peabody said when they walked out of the gym. "Who knew that under all the priest gear he was Father Seriously Ripped."

"Keeps in shape. And something's up. Father Seriously Ripped had his sad eyes on, but there was more. There was dread."

"Really? I guess I wasn't looking at his eyes. He could have heard about Lino by now. Word like that starts traveling fast. Since he's the man in charge, he's going to have to explain, I guess, why he didn't realize a man like that was working under him. Everybody needs a fall guy, right? Maybe the church brass is aiming at him."

Since the blacktop was swarming with kids, Eve stayed at the side of the building. "Why aren't these people in school?"

"School's out for the day, Dallas. On the technical end of things, it's nearly end of shift."

"Oh. Maybe he's worried about his career. Do priests have careers? But that wasn't it. I know the look that says, 'I don't want to talk to the cops.' That's what he had in his eyes."

"You think he's hiding something? He didn't know Lino—as Lino. He's only been in the parish for a few months."

"He's been a priest a hell of a lot longer." She thought of what Mira had predicted, and decided not to dance and jab, but to try for the knockout as soon as López came out.

His hair was damp, and the sweat had his T-shirt clinging to his chest. Yeah, Eve mused, he kept in shape.

She didn't wait a beat. "The victim's been officially identified as Lino Martinez. You know who killed him. You know," Eve said, "because whoever did told you."

He closed his eyes briefly. "What I know was told to me within the sanctity of the confessional."

"You're protecting a murderer, and one who is indirectly responsible for a second death in Jimmy Jay Jenkins."

"I can't break my vows, Lieutenant. I can't betray my faith, or the laws of the Church."

"Render unto Caesar," Peabody said, and had López shaking his head.

"I can't give to man's law with one hand, and take from God's with the other. Please, can we sit? The benches over there, away from the building. This needs to be very private."

Resentment bubbling, Eve walked over to where benches, their legs set into concrete, were facing the court. López sat, rested his hands on his knees.

"I've prayed on this. I've prayed since I heard this confession. I can't tell you what was told to me. It was told not to me, but to God through me. I received this confession as a minister to God."

"I'll take the hearsay."

"I don't expect you to understand, either of you." He lifted his hands from his knees, palms up. Lowered them again. "You're women of the world. Of the law. This person came to me to unburden their soul, their heart, their conscience, of this mortal sin."

"And you absolved them? Good deal for them."

"No, I did not. Cannot absolve them. I can't unburden them, Lieutenant. I counseled, I instructed, I urged this person to go to you, to confess to you. Until this is done, there can be no forgiveness, no absolution. They will live with this sin, and die with it unless they repent it. I can't do anything for you, for them. I can't do anything."

"Did this individual know Lino Martinez?"

"I can't answer you."

"Is this person a member of your church?"

"I can't answer you." He pressed his fingers to his eyes. "It makes me ill, but I can't answer."

"I could put you in a cage. You'd get out. Your church will campaign, send their lawyers, but you'd do time first while we're fighting it out."

"And still, I can't answer. If I tell you, I'll have broken my vows, betrayed them. I'll be excommunicated. There are all kinds of cages, Lieutenant Dallas. Do you think I want this?" he demanded, with the first hint of heat. "To block your justice? I believe in your justice. I believe in the order of it as much as you. Do you think I want to stand by, knowing I can't reach a wounded, angry soul? That my counsel may have turned it away instead of bringing it to God?"

"They may come after you. You know who they are, what they did. I can take you into protective custody."

"They know I won't break my vows. If you took me away, I'd have no chance to reach them, to try, to keep trying to persuade them to do true penance for the sin, to accept man's law and God's. Let me try."

She could all but feel herself beating her fists against the solid, the impenetrable wall of his faith. "Did you tell anyone? Father Freeman, your superiors?"

"I can't tell anyone what was said or who came to me. As long as they live with it, so do I."

"If this person kills again . . ." Peabody began.

"They won't. There's no reason."

"It goes back to the bombings in 2043."

"I can't tell you."

"What do you know about them?"

"Everyone in the parish knows of them. There's a perpetual novena for the victims and their families. Every month a Mass is dedicated to them. To all of them, Lieutenant, not just the victim from El Barrio."

"Did you know that Lino selectively blackmailed some who came to him in confession?"

López jerked as if struck with sudden, shocking pain. Rather than sorrow, it was fury that flashed into his eyes. "No. No, I didn't know. Why didn't any of them come to me for help?"

"I doubt seriously they knew who was blackmailing them, or where the blackmailer got the information. And now I know whoever killed him wasn't one of them."

Eve pushed to her feet. "I can't force you to tell me what you know. I can't make you tell me who used your church, your faith, your ritual, your vows to murder. I could squeeze you, and sweat you, but you still wouldn't tell me and then both of us would be pissed off. But I'll tell you this: I'm going to find out who it was. Whatever kind of slime Lino was, I'm going to do my job, the same as you."

"I pray you will find them, and I pray that before you do, they come to you. I pray that God gives me the wisdom and the strength to show them the way."

"I guess we'll see which one of us gets there first."

Eve left him sitting on the bench.

"I get he's doing what he thinks he has to," Peabody said. "But I think we should be taking him in. You could break him in Interview."

"Not sure I could. He's got titanium for faith. And even if . . . isn't that going to make him one more victim? I break him, make him slip enough, and he'd never be the same. He wouldn't be a priest anymore."

She remembered what she'd felt like when they'd taken her badge. How she'd felt empty, helpless. Like nothing, like no one.

"I'm not doing that to him. Have I even got a right to do that to an innocent man? One who's taken an oath pretty much the same as ours?"

"Protect and serve."

"We do people, he does souls. I'm not going to sacrifice him to make my job easier. But I'll tell you what we are going to do." She got into the vehicle, switched on the engine. "We're putting him under surveillance. We're getting a warrant to monitor his communication devices. I'd put eyes and ears in the damn church if they'd clear it, but that's not going to happen. We're going to know where he goes, when, who he sees."

"Do you think the killer will go for him?"

"He's got that titanium faith, so he thinks not. Me? I've got faith that people mostly look out for their own ass. So we cover him—we protect—and we leave him out here as bait, hoping the sinner needs another shot at redemption. Put it in play, my authorization."

As Peabody started that ball, Eve glanced at the time. Thought, *Shit.* "One more stop. We'll see if we can jangle anything out of Inez."

A woman answered this time, a looker with warm brown hair pulled back in a jaunty tail from a rose-and-cream face. Behind her, two little boys rammed miniature trucks together and made violent crashing noises.

"Pipe down," the woman ordered, and they did, instantly. The crashing noises continued, but at whispers.

"Mrs. Inez?"

"Yes?"

"We'd like to speak to your husband."

"So would I, but he's stuck in New Jersey, there's a jam at the tunnel. He'll be lucky to get home in under two hours. What is it?"

Eve took out her badge.

"Oh, Joe said the police were here last night. Something about one of the tenants being a witness in a hit-and-run."

"Is that what your son told you?"

"Actually, Joe filled me in." Awareness came into her eyes. "And that wasn't entirely accurate. What is this about?"

"We're investigating an old connection of your husband's. Do you know Lino Martinez?"

"No, but I know the name. I know Joe was in the Soldados, and I know he did time. I know he had trouble, and he pulled himself out of it." She gripped the doorknob, eased the door closed a few more inches, as if to shield the children behind her. "He hasn't had anything to do with any of that business for years. He's a good man. A family man with a decent job. He works hard. Lino Martinez and the Soldados were another life."

"Tell him we were here, Mrs. Inez, and that we've located Lino Martinez. We're going to need to follow up with your husband."

"I'll tell him, but I'm telling you he doesn't know anything about Lino Martinez, not anymore."

She closed the door, and Eve heard the locks snick impatiently.

"She's pissed he lied to her," Peabody commented.

"Yeah. Stupid move on his part. It tells me he's hiding something from his wife. Something from now, something from then? Either way, something. I'm going to drop you at the subway and work from home. Keep on those John Does. I think I'll comb through those old case files, see if something swims up from the deep."

"I know what you said back there to López is right. We've got to do the job no matter what a creep Lino was. But when you know some of the shit he pulled, and the shit we think he pulled, it's hard to get worked up because somebody ended him."

"Maybe if somebody had gotten worked up a long time ago, he wouldn't have been able to pull so much shit, his mother wouldn't be crying tonight, and somebody who strikes me as an especially good man wouldn't be honor-bound, or faith-bound, to protect a murderer."

Peabody sighed. "You've got a point. But I like it better when the bad guys are just the bad guys."

"There's always plenty of them to go around."

18 SHE NEEDED THINKING TIME. CLOSED IN WITH the case time where she could put the pieces of everything she knew, didn't know, everything that had been said, left unsaid together with people, events, evidence, and speculation, and see what kinds of pictures formed.

She needed to take a good hard look at the victims in the two bombings, and their families, their connections. She needed to consider the blackmail angle, which she already knew would be a deep and sticky well. If López wouldn't tell her the name of a murderer, he sure as hell wasn't going to share the names of people who'd confessed blackmailable transgressions to him.

She didn't buy murder for blackmail in Lino's case, but she couldn't discount it as possible. Or connected.

How had Lino collected the money? she wondered as she drove home. Where had he kept the funds, or had he just pissed it away as it came in? Expensive hotel rooms and lavish meals, gaudy jewelry for his bed partner.

Not enough, she thought. A few thousand here and there? What was the point in risking exposure for a fancy suite and a bottle of champagne?

Showing off to the old girlfriend? Stuben said Penny Soto had been his weak spot. So . . . It could be that simple. Wanting to be rich, important, and having his woman see him as both.

Or as simple as needing the rush, of knowing you were pulling a fast one. Reminding yourself who you were while you were pretending to be another. Like a hobby.

Something else to think about.

She drove through the gates, then slowed down. There were flowers where she was damn sure there hadn't been flowers that morning. Tulips—she was pretty sure—and daffodils. She liked daffodils because they were so bright and silly. Now there were rivers of both where there hadn't been so much as a drop ten hours earlier.

How did that happen?

In any case it was . . . well, it was pretty, and added a splash to the hazy green of the trees.

She continued on, stopped and parked. And there were three enormous red pots literally engorged with petunias. White petunias—her wedding flower. Sentimental slob, she thought even as she went gooey herself. Simple pleasure warred against the ugly tension she'd been fighting to ignore since her interview with Penny Soto.

She walked in to see Galahad perched like a pudgy gargoyle on the newel post—new spot for him—and Summerset hovering, as usual, in the foyer.

"I assume the city has been cleared of all crime as you're only an hour late and appear to be unbloodied."

"Yeah, we're renaming it Utopia." She gave Galahad a quick rub as she started upstairs. "Next stage is to get rid of all the assholes. You should get a head start and pack your bags." She paused briefly. "Did Roarke talk to Sinead?"

"Yes."

"Good."

She went directly to the bedroom. Roarke was probably home, she thought—Summerset would've said if he wasn't. And he was probably in his office, so she should've gone there, connected with him.

But she wasn't ready, just not ready for the connection. That war continued, beefing up now that she'd made it home. Where she knew she was safe, where she knew she could let go, just a little. Home, where she could acknowledge her belly was raw, the back of her neck tight knots of stress.

She laid back, closed her eyes. When she felt the thump beside her, Eve reached out, let her arm curl around the cat.

Stupid, she thought, it was stupid to feel sick, to have to fight against being sick. To feel *anything* but suspicion and disgust for a woman like Penny Soto.

She didn't realize Roarke had come into the room until his hand brushed her cheek. He moved so quietly, she thought, barely stirred the air if he didn't choose. No wonder he'd been such a successful thief.

"What hurts?" he asked her.

"Nothing. Nothing really." But she turned to him, turned into him when he lay beside her. And pressed her face into his shoulder. "I needed to be home. I needed to be home first. I was right about that. But I thought I needed to be alone, just be alone until I got level. I was wrong. Can we just stay here awhile?"

"My favorite place."

"Tell me stuff. Stuff you did today. I don't care if I don't understand it."

"I had a 'link conference here shortly after you left this morning regarding some R&D at Euroco, one of my arms in Europe that deals primarily with transportation. We have a very interesting sea-road-air personal sports vehicle coming out early next year. I had meetings in midtown, but Sinead called from Ireland before I left. It was nice to hear from her. They've acquired a new puppy and named it Mac, who she claims is more trouble than triplet toddlers. She sounds madly in love with him."

She listened to his voice, more than the words. Something about a meeting with team leaders on a project called Optimum, and a holo-conference dealing with his Olympus Resort, a lunch session with key members of one of his interests in Bejing. A merger, an acquisition, conceptual drawings.

How did he keep it all straight?

"You did all that, and still had time to get petunias?"

His hand trailed up and down her back, up and down. "Did you like them?"

"Yeah. Yeah, I liked them."

"It's been nearly two years since we were married." He kissed the top of her head, then turned his to rest his cheek there. "And with Louise and Charles about to have their wedding here, it made me think of the petunias. How the simple—a flower, a few minutes to talk to a relation—makes the complicated worthwhile."

"Is that why we have tulips and daffodils? They are tulips, right?"

"They are. It's good to be reminded that things come around again, fresh and new. And some things remain, steady and solid. The call from Sinead brought both back to me. Are you ready to tell me what's the matter?"

"Sometimes things come around again that are old and hard." She sat up, shoved at her hair. "I brought Penny Soto in for questioning to-day. Actually, I baited her into taking a pop at me so I could charge her with assault and resisting."

He took her chin, tracing his thumb in its dent as he turned her face right and left. "You don't appear to be popped."

"The assault was mostly technical. She was Lino's main lay when they were teenagers. Works in the bodega right next to the church, the bodega he frequented, pretty much daily."

"So they reconnected."

"She was the one who knew him," she said, remembering Roarke's words from the morning. "The one he needed to tell. Yeah, they re-connected, and in the biblical sense—according to her. I buy that. You'd have to buy that. So she knew who he was, and some of what he was up to—maybe all, but I couldn't get that out of her. Yet.

"She claims he blackmailed some of the people who came in to con-fess. Plays, but I can't quite figure it all."

"Hobby. More," Roarke continued, "habit. The masquerade didn't change who and what he was under it, and what was under it would need the hit. The buzz."

"Yeah, I circled around that. It doesn't feel like motive. I know, tried and true," she said before he could disagree, "I'll get to why I don't think it's going to weigh in, or not much."

First she wanted to get the rest out, get it off her chest. "The thing is . . . Once I get Soto in the box, putting some pressure on, pissing her off, it comes out of her that her father . . ."

"Ah." He didn't need the rest, didn't need it for his stomach to tighten.

"She's snapping and snarling it at me, how her old man started on her when she was about twelve, how her useless mother was a junkie, how he beat her and molested her for two years before she joined the Soldados. They were her way out, the escape hatch. And there's a part of me that gets it, that feels for her, that's trying not to look at her and see me. To see . . ."

She pressed a hand to her belly, used the pressure to finish it. "Be-cause when she was fourteen, after she'd joined the Soldados, her fa-ther was stabbed to death—hacked to bloody death. It went down as a bad illegals deal, since that was his business. But I know, I know when I'm looking at her, and seeing myself, that she had the knife in her hand. That she rammed it in him, again and again. Probably her and Lino together—first kill, lovers' bond. And no matter what I know, part of me's saying you did the same as she did. How can you blame her? You did the same."

"No, you didn't. No, Eve," he said before she could speak, "you didn't do the same. I don't have to hear the rest to know it. To know that while fourteen is still a child, it's six years and a world beyond what you were. And you were in prison, not able to get out as she was, and as she did. No escape hatch for you, no friends, no family, not of any kind. She did it for revenge, not for survival."

She rose to go to the bag she'd dropped on the way to the bed, and took out a photo. She laid it on the bed. "I see him when I look at that. I see my father and what I did."

He picked it up, studied the harsh crime scene still of the man sprawled on a filthy, littered floor, swimming in his own blood. "No child did this," Roarke said. "Even a terrified, desperate child couldn't, not in self-defense, not alone."

She let out a breath. It probably wasn't the time to mention he'd make a good cop. "No, there were two attackers. They established that as the wounds were from two different knives. Different blade types and sizes, different force, different angles. I expect one of them lured him there, and the other laid in wait. They came at him from the front and from behind. The sexual mutilation was post-mortem. She probably did that. But—"

"It amazes me," he said quietly. "It astounds me that you can look at this kind of thing, every day. You can look every day and continue to care, every day. Don't stand there and tell me you did the same. Don't stand there and tell me you see yourself in her."

He let the photo fall to the bed as he rose. "She wears the tattoo?"

"Yeah."

"With a kill mark."

"Yeah."

"She's proud of it, proud she's killed. Tell me, Eve, can you tell me you have pride in any of the lives you've had to take?"

She shook her head. "It made me sick—no, made me want to be sick. And I couldn't be. Wouldn't be. I couldn't think about it, not really think about it, until I got home. I could think about it here, in case I fell apart. I know we're not the same. I know it. But there's a parallel."

"As there is between me and your victim." He laid his hands on her shoulders. "And yet here we are, you and me. Here we are because somewhere along the line, those parallels verged, and took markedly different paths."

She turned, picked up the photo to put it back in her bag. She'd look again. She would look again. "Two years ago—a little more—I wouldn't have had anyone to say these things to. Even if I'd remembered what happened when I was eight, and before. Nobody, not even Mavis, and I can tell her anything. But I couldn't show her a photo like that, I couldn't ask her to look at that, and see what I see. I don't know how long I could've kept looking, kept caring, if I didn't have someone to come home to who'd look with me when I needed it."

She sat on the bed again, sighed. "Jesus, it's been a day. Penny knows more than she's saying, and she's hard. She's got layers and layers of hard on her, slapped right over mean and possibly psychotic. I have to find the way through."

"Do you think she killed him? Martinez?"

"No, but I think she made sure she was alibied tight because she knew it was going down. I think the asshole loved her, and she loves no one. Maybe she used that against him. I need to think. I saw López, and Mira hit the target there. Lino's killer confessed to his priest, and there's nothing I can do. I look at this guy, Roarke, at López and I see another victim."

"Do you think the killer will go after him?"

"I don't know. I put him under surveillance. I could bring him in, legally, I could bring him in and wind him up for a few days, until the lawyers cut through it. But I need to leave him out, need to hope the killer will go back to him. And I look at him and I see he's sick in his heart. I know he's got this fist pounding on his conscience. There's nothing I can do," she repeated. "Just like there's nothing López can do. We're stuck, both of us, stuck with our duty."

She flopped back on the bed. "I need to clear my head, come at it again. It winds all over hell and back. Flores—why him, and where did his path cross with Lino? Where the hell is Chávez? Dead? Hiding? What was Lino waiting for? Was he killed for that, or does it go back to the past? The bombings? He did both of them, I'm damn well sure, so—"

"You're losing me."

She pushed up again. "Sorry. I need to lay it out, reorganize, look at the time lines, change up my board. I need to do runs on a whole shit-load of people and look at all that from various angles."

"Then we'd best get started." He took her hand, pulled her to her feet.

"Thanks."

"Well, I owe you one for the call from Sinead."

"Huh?"

"What do you take me for?" he asked, looping his arm around her waist. "My aunt just happens to get in touch the same morning I'm a bit off thinking about my connections in Ireland, and what—who—I've lost there? It's nice to be looked after."

"So that would be looking after as opposed to poking in and interfering? It's hard to tell the difference."

"It is, isn't it? But we'll muddle through it."

As they passed, one of the house screens came on. "Your guests are coming through the gate," Summerset announced.

"What guests?" Eve demanded

"Ah . . ." Roarke raked his fingers through his hair. "Yes. A moment." He dismissed Summerset. "I'm sorry, it slipped my mind. I can go down, take care of it. I'll simply tell them you're still at work, which you will be."

"Who? Damn it, why can't people stay home? Why do they always want to be in somebody else's?"

"It's Ariel Greenfeld, Eve, and Erik Pastor."

"Ariel." She had a flash of the pretty brunette who'd been held and tortured by a madman for days. And stayed sane, strong and smart.

"She got in touch today, and asked if they could come by this evening. I can take it, move them along."

"No." Reaching down, she took Roarke's hand. "It's like the call from your aunt. It's good to remember what matters. Ariel matters. So," she continued as they moved toward the steps, "she and Erik the neighbor are making it work."

"Engaged, getting married in the fall."

"Jesus, it's like a virus, this marriage thing. I could've met her at Central—or elsewhere," she added. "Probably should have. You can't have victims and wits and all manner of God knows dropping in here."

"I think this would be a clear exception. She did work for me, af-ter all."

"Yeah, but . . . did? She quit? Goddamn that sick-ass Lowell. Did he take that away from her? She loved to bake, and your place down-town had to be a great gig."

"She's baking. And you'll see for yourself she's in a good place. She's happy and doing very well."

Eve's eyebrows drew together. "You seem to know a lot about it."

"I know a lot about so many things." He gave her hand a squeeze. As they started down the steps, Eve heard the voices from the parlor. She heard Ariel laugh.

She'd cut her hair. It was the first thing Eve noticed. Robert Lowell had liked his victims with long hair, long brown hair. So Ariel had cut hers into a short, sleek cap and punched red into it. It looked good on her, Eve thought—though it probably helped that the woman wasn't pale, bleeding, and battling pain.

Her eyes were bright as they met Eve's, and the smile exploded onto her face.

"Hi!" Then tears popped out as she rushed across the room and clamped her arms around Eve. "Not crying, not really crying. And I'll stop in a minute."

"Okay."

"I kept wanting to come see you. I just wanted to get myself together before I did."

"That's okay, too."

"Well." Ariel stepped back, grinned. "So how've you been?"

"Not bad. How about you?"

"Pretty damn terrific, considering." She held out a hand for Erik's. "We're getting married."

"So I hear. Hey, Erik."

"It's really good to see you. Nice to see you again, too," he said to Roarke, and had Eve sliding Roarke a look.

"Again?"

"I've been giving Ari a hand setting up the new shop." He grinned at Roarke, all spiky black-and-bronze hair and happiness. "It rocks."

"My own little bakery boutique. I'm going to make you a lot of money. I wasn't sure I could do it, or much of anything when I first got out of the hospital. But you were so sure I could," she said to Roarke. "You and Erik. Now I am."

"I had it on good authority that you could handle anything that came at you. We should have a drink to celebrate."

"Your . . . I don't know exactly what he is," Ariel admitted. "The tall, skinny guy?"

"No one knows exactly what he is," Eve put in, and made Ariel laugh.

"He said he'd bring in something that would suit. I hope that's okay. Um, I don't know if you remember, but when you saved my life and all that, I promised I'd bake you a cake. So . . ."

She stepped to the side and gestured. Following the direction, Eve walked forward.

One of the tables had been cleared off, probably by Summerset. There, on its glossy, pampered surface stood an enormous cake.

More like art, Eve thought.

An edible New York spread out, with its streets, its buildings, its rivers and parks, the tunnels, the bridges. Rapid cabs, maxibuses, jet-bikes, scooters, delivery vans, and other vehicles crammed those streets. People jammed sidewalks and glides. Shop windows held tiny, glittery displays, and glide-cart vendors served soy dogs and veggie hash.

She actually expected, for just a moment, to see it move, to *hear* it. "Holy shit."

"That's a good holy shit, right?" Ariel asked.

"That's a kick-my-ass-and-call-me-Sally holy shit. There's an illegals deal going down off Jane Street," Eve murmured, "and this guy's getting mugged in Central Park."

"Well, it happens."

Stunned, Eve crouched down to stare at the image of herself Ariel had created. She stood on a slim tower, over the city. She wore her long, black coat, caught in mid-billow and boots even she could see were scuffed at the toe. In one hand she held her badge—right down to her rank and badge number, and in the other her weapon.

"Wow. Just . . . wow. It's insanely iced. Do you see this?" she said to Roarke.

"I do. And I believe I've made an excellent investment. It's spectacular, Ariel."

"She spent weeks on the design," Erik told them, pride riding in every word. "Kept changing it. The good part is I got to sample the rejects."

"It's by far the frostiest thing I've ever seen. I'm going to be the cop who ate Manhattan." Laughing, Eve straightened. "Listen, I've got these friends getting married pretty soon. She's really going to want to talk to you."

"Louise and Charles? We're going over the final cake design tomorrow."

Eve nodded to Roarke. "Always one step ahead, aren't you, ace?"

"I hate to lag behind. Ah, champagne," he said as Summerset came in with a tray. "I'd say that's very suitable."

"I can get with that. I think I'm going to have a slice of the Upper East Side since . . ." Eve trailed off, narrowed her eyes. And crouched again.

"Is something wrong?" Ariel began and gnawed her lip as she leaned over.

"No. This sector here? Are the streets, the buildings to scale—or close? Or did you just make what worked best?"

"Are you kidding?" Erik interrupted. "She used maps and holos, did freaking math. Ari was obsessed."

"It's different from a map. Different even from being there, being in it. This . . . it's kind of like a God's-eye view."

She rose, circled, squatted down. "Boundaries change, depending on the people. Who comes in, who goes out. Back fifteen, twenty years ago, the Soldado turf ran from East 96th up to 120th. Solid fourteen blocks from the East River over to Fifth. And the Skulls held 122nd up to 128th, with some territory west of Fifth where they disputed borders with the Bloods. But this area right here, this eastern slice between 118th and 124th, that was the hot zone of the battleground, that was where each wanted more territory. That was where the bombings took place."

"Bombings?" Ariel's eyes widened as she edged closer to the cake to study it. "I didn't hear about any bombings."

"They happened seventeen years ago," Roarke told her.

"Oh."

"Here's the church, and the rectory behind it," Eve continued. "Deep in Soldado territory. The youth center—northwest of the church, but still in boundaries. Now, up here . . . What's happened here, just a few blocks north of where the youth center was built? In that one-time hot zone."

"What?" Ariel bent closer.

"Gentrification. Homes and properties, just hitting the edge of St. Cristóbal's parish. A few were there before, the ones that held on during and after the Urbans. And in the last ten, twelve years, there's more. Successful business owners and so on, settling here, cleaning it up, increasing its value. He'd see this every day. Somebody who lived here, crossed up and over to the center, visited parishioners—and bonded with the Ortiz family—would see this neighborhood, the houses, town homes, condos every day. He'd have seen them twenty years ago. He'd have seen that section every day. He wanted to keep it. He wanted more."

"Seven Deadly Sins again," Roarke commented.

"Huh?"

"Envy. In your face, day after day? You covet."

"Yeah. Yeah. We're hitting a lot of them. Got your lust, greed, pride, and now envy. Interesting."

"I'm completely lost," Ariel said, and brought Eve back to the moment.

"Sorry. Something just hit me, made me think about a case." She straightened, but kept her gaze on the Upper East Side. "I think maybe we'll take that slice out of the Lower West. SoHo looks good enough to eat."

She ate cake, she drank champagne, and spent the better part of an hour doing her duty—and trying to keep at least part of her mind on the conversation. The minute their guests were out the door, Eve went back to the cake.

"Okay, so I need to hack this sector off and take it up to the office. It's a good visual for—"

"Eve, for God's sake, it's cake. I can program you a holo-model of that sector in about twenty minutes. Probably less."

Her brow furrowed. "You can? Oh. That would probably be better."

"And involve less calories. But before I do . . ." He crooked his finger, then started toward the steps. "What's the point?"

"I'm not sure, exactly. It was just looking down at it that way, different perspective. You can see, clearly, how the borders between gang turf ran, how they blended, putting certain areas in contention. And how the neighborhood's changed. Where everything is. Church, rectory, youth center, the Ortiz home, the restaurant. Then there's Lino's former apartment building. And I'm thinking about what Lino said to his mother, to Penny. He'd come back with a big car, have a big house. You can get a car anywhere, but the house—"

"Would have to be in the neighborhood. He can't show it off unless it's in the neighborhood. But, if he had a big house in the neighborhood, why was he living in the rectory?"

"I don't know if he actually had it, or if he was just coveting it. But he was waiting for something. Years of waiting, deliberately on his home turf. If he sticks that long, and under those circumstances, doesn't it follow he may have planned to stick for good?"

"The big house, the wealth, the importance, and the girl." With a nod, Roarke strode down the hall with her. "And the ground you've always considered yours."

"When he got what he was waiting for—and it has to be money, or something that leads to money—why leave again? He wasn't here for shits and smiles. He had a purpose. I haven't looked for it here, because I was going on the assumption he came here to hide. Maybe so, probably so."

She pushed at her hair as they turned into her office. "Maybe so. But there could have been something here he was waiting for. Something he got to see every day, and feel smug about. That kept him going, kept him playing the part that had to squeeze at him."

She paced around the murder board, thinking it through, working it out. "How much do you own on Grafton Street?"

She threw him for a moment, then he nodded slowly. "A bit of this, a bit of that. Yes, I wanted to have what I could only envy as a boy."

"Rosa knew him, but made it clear he left them be—mostly. He liked old Mr. Ortiz, respected him. Envied, maybe, if we go back to the Deadlies, maybe." She hooked her thumbs in her pockets, circling it in her mind as she'd circled the board.

"The Ortiz group is a big, tight family. Like a gang? They look out for each other, hold their territory. He gets close to them as Flores, marries them, buries them, visits them in their nice homes. The big house. He wants what they have. How does he get it?"

"Are you thinking he killed Hector Ortiz?"

"No, no, natural causes. I checked that through and through. And he respected Hector Ortiz. He, in his way, admired him. But the Ortizes, they aren't the only ones with nice houses, with a big house, with ties to the church. I need to run some of the properties, just see, just play this line out and see. I could use that holo."

"Then I'd better get to work." He held up the figure of Eve from the cake. "And this is my payment for the time and skill."

Amused, she cocked her head. "You're going to eat me?"

"Too many obvious and crude rejoinders on that one. But no, I'm going to keep you."

He leaned down, kissed the woman. "What are you looking for with those properties?"

"I hope I know when I find it."

19

IT WOULD TAKE A WHILE, EVE KNEW—LIKELY longer than Roarke and his magic hologram—to do the search and run on properties and owners thereof. She opted to start with a basic triangulation between church, youth center, and the Ortiz home.

Probably a waste of time, she told herself. Just some wild hair, wild goose, wild whatever.

But it had always been a con, hadn't it? At the core, she thought as her computer worked the task, Lino Martinez had run a long con. A long con meant planning, dedication, research, and the goal of a fat payoff.

Considering, she went to her 'link, checked with a good friend who knew the grift.

Mavis Freestone, her hair currently a sunburst the color of spring leaves, filled the screen with cheer.

"Hey! Good catch. Baby's down and Leonardo just split to go get some ice cream. I had a yen for Mondo-Mucho-Mocha, and we didn't have it on tap."

"Sounds good. I wanted . . . Yen?" Eve felt the blood drain out of her head. "You're not pregnant again."

"Pregs? That's a negativo on being knocked up." Mavis's eyes twinkled, the same improbable green as her hair. "Just got the yums for the triple M."

"Okay." *Whew.* "Quick question. What's the longest con you ever ran?"

"Ah, gee, trip in the way-back. I'm getting all nostalgic. Let's see. There was this time I ran a Carlotta, named it after an old friend. I think she's on Vegas II now. Anyway, to run a Carlotta you've got to—"

"No details. Just the length."

"Oh." Mavis pursed her lips. "Maybe four months. Carlottas take a lot of foundation and seeding."

"Do you know anyone that ran one for years? Not months. Into the years."

"I know plenty who ran the same game, into years. But different marks, you know. Same game, same mark?"

"Yeah, that's the idea."

"There was this guy, frigging genius. Slats. He ran a Crosstown Bob for three years. Then poofed. Just poofed for five more. Came back around, I heard. He'd moved to Paris, France, changed his name and all that shit. Buzz was Slats lived high on the take from the Crosstown Bob. Kept his hand in though, over there, 'cause you can't help it."

"Why did he come back?"

"Hey, once a New Yorker, you know?"

"Yeah. Yeah. That's the deal. What about religious cons?"

"Those are the cheesecake. Sweet and creamy, go down smooth. There's Hail Mary, Praise the Lord, Kosher, Redemption—"

"Okay. Ever hear of a grifter named Lino? Lino Martinez?"

"Doesn't ring. But I've been out of the game awhile now. I'm a mommy."

"Right." And, Eve realized, she hadn't asked about the baby. "So how's Bella doing?"

"She's the maggest of the mag, the ultest of the ults. In snoozeland now or I'd put her on. Nobody goos like my Bellarina goos."

"Yeah. Well. Give her a goo back from me. Thanks for the info."

"No prob. I'll see you at the girl bash if not sooner. We're revved top-less over it."

"Great. Wear a top anyway. Thanks, Mavis."

She turned, and walked straight through a scale model of St. Cristó-bal's. And said, "Jesus."

"I've heard he visits there often."

"How did you do that? That wasn't twenty minutes."

"I'm often even better than I think I am."

"Nobody's better than you think you are."

He'd scaled the holo down, but constructed it considerably larger than Ariel's cake. The simple cross atop the church came to Eve's knee. She stepped out of church and surveyed. "This is pretty much iced."

"I can take it to the holo-room if you want larger scale."

"No, this is good. Church, bodega, rectory," she began, moving into the holo. "Youth center, Hector Ortiz's house. Site of first bombing." She moved south and east. "It's still a school. Site of second. Now west and north. It was a sandwich shop–type hangout, now a 24/7."

Roarke studied the holo himself. "I could, in about the same amount of time, program one from '43, or any given year."

"You just want to play," she countered. "This is what he saw in the now, every day. Whatever was in the . . . way-back," she decided, using Mavis's term, "is in the now. Changed a little maybe. But something he wanted then he wanted now."

"I actually understand that," Roarke commented.

"Peabody and I are going to locate and interview survivors, family members. Five dead in the second bombing." She frowned down at the bright red and yellow of the 24/7. "It's not part of St. Cristóbal's parish. It's outside, and was clearly in disputed territory, but leaning toward Skulls, when it was hit. Close to the boundaries, of both. Lino liked to run, ran with the other priest, Freeman, when they could hook that up. Their typical route took them from the rectory, east, then turning north before heading west again, taking them through this part of

Spanish Harlem—past these middle- and upper-middle-class properties, past Hector Ortiz, on, turning south, then hitting the youth center.
He grew up here, but he bypassed the street where his old apartment is.
Still is. Not interested in that, doesn't need to see that. Likes to look at
the snappier properties."

Roarke started to speak, then decided to stand back and watch her
work. While she did, he poured himself a brandy to add to his enjoy-
ment.

"Habits get formed for a reason," she muttered. "You do something,
keep doing it, form a routine for a reason. Maybe this was his habitual
route because it just worked out that way, and he fell into the habit. But
he could've gotten the same time and distance in by mixing it up, and
most people who run habitually like to mix it up. Stay fresher. He
could've done that going west out the door, heading south, then doing
the loop, but Freeman said he never varied. So what does he see when
he does his route? And who sees him? Habitually."

She crouched, ran her hand through buildings that wavered and
shimmered at the contact. "All through here, all these homes, apartments. Part of the parish, and also part of the school district. Anybody
living here then would have known Lino. Big bad dude. Sure, there's
been turnover. People move out, people move in, people die and get
born. But there are plenty, like the Ortiz family, who're rooted deep
here. Every day, every day," she murmured. "Hey, Father. Good morning, Father. How's it going, Father. I bet he juiced on that. Father.

"It's a patrol, isn't it? A kind of daily patrol. His turf, his territory.
Like a dog marking his territory." She poked her finger at the Ortiz
house. "How much is it worth, today's market? A private home like
this, this sector?"

"Depends. If you're looking at it as a residential property—"

"Don't nitty-gritty it. Just basic. Single-family home, pre-Urban
construction. Well-maintained."

"Square footage? Materials? It does depend," he insisted when she curled her lip at him. "But if you want a very general ballpark . . ." He crouched as she did, studied the house, and named a figure that had her eyes bulging.

"You're shitting me."

"No indeed. That's a bit of low-balling actually because I haven't really studied the property. And that estimate will likely increase as the neighborhood gentrification continues to spread. Now if it's a straight home-owner to home-owner sale you're thinking, that would fluctuate somewhat due to the interior. Is the kitchen, are the baths, high-end, how much of the original materials remain, and all manner of things."

"That's a lot of tacos."

"New York tacos, darling Eve. The same house in a different location. Let's say . . . Baltimore or Albuquerque? About a third to a half of that market price."

"Geography." She shook her head. "Once a New Yorker," she added, thinking of Mavis's remark. "So he runs by this, and the rest every day. Patrols this area, every day. And whoever killed him knew him, whoever killed him goes to St. Cristóbal's, whoever killed him lived in this sector when Lino lived here as Lino. Knows Penny Soto, because that bitch, she's in this. She's in all of it. Whoever killed him was smart enough to wait for a big ceremony like the Ortiz funeral, or got lucky enough to hit. I think smart. I just think smart.

"Cyanide. Doesn't come cheap. We're not pulling anything from black market sources, but hell, I didn't expect to ring the bell there."

"There are buttons I could push there."

"Yeah, I bet there are. If it comes to it, maybe, but either way, it costs. Whoever killed him's Catholic enough to be compelled to confess to his priest. I don't know, I don't know, that says older to me. That says it's not some kid, but someone mature. Yeah, Mira said mature," she said half to herself. "Mature enough to pull this off, mature enough to feel guilt over it. Not for gain, not for gain, that angle's bullshit. If the killer was looking for gain, knife the bastard."

She tapped her fingers on her knee as she ran it through, imagined it. "If it's just gain, even the most simple kind of revenge or survival instinct, you'd work with Penny and lure him, hack him up like he and Penny hacked up her father. Make it look like a mugging—you're smart enough to do that."

"But you don't," Roarke put in, "because it's not simple."

"It goes too deep for that. Penny, she's in this for gain. That's all she's in it for. But you? It's not about that. It's about payment and penance. An eye for an eye. Who'd he kill or harm? One of yours. But you don't confront him, you don't report him, you don't point the finger."

She slowly straightened. "Because it didn't work before. He got away before. No payment, no penance. It has to be done, and it has to be done in God's house. You've held on to your faith all these years. You've been faithful, even though you lost something so vital. And here he is, back again, blaspheming, defiling the church, running free, every day. In your goddamn face. Doing it for five years, and you had no way of knowing. Not until Penny told you."

She frowned down at the holo, could almost hear the conspiratory whispers. "Why, why, what's the angle there? Gotta get back to that. Because that has to be it. Penny ratted him out to you, and you had to act. You had to balance the scales."

She stepped back. "Damn it. There's this, and this and that. And I can see it. I can see each point, but how do they come together?"

"Keep going. If it's an eye for an eye, who did Martinez kill?"

"Soto. Nick Soto because of what he'd done and was doing to Penny. And thinking of her, of what it was like for her, he beat the crap out of Solas. But nobody gave a shit about Soto, nobody looked at a couple of kids, fourteen, fifteen years old to rip a man to pieces like that. Probably a lot of people had several small, private celebrations when he was offed. It may have been his first kill—Lino's first kill. Made his mark with it. The timing's about right, and the cop I talked to from back then remembers him as a troublemaker, as a badass, but they never hauled him in for questioning on murder—not for Soto, not before. After . . ."

She went back to check her notes. "Gang-related violence, questioned numerous times regarding the deaths or disappearances of several known members of rival gangs. No evidence, alibied."

"Members of the parish?"

"No. But there's those blurred boundary lines." She moved back to the holo. "Could be friends, family along that blur, connections who were in the parish, were members of the church. But . . . Catholic question."

"I don't know why in hell you'd ask me."

"Because. Could it be eye for an eye—payment, penance—if the past vic was a known gang member—out there doing pretty much what Lino was doing? If he was killed or harmed during a gang altercation?"

"If it was a loved one I don't see why it would matter. Love doesn't qualify."

"From the Catholic angle," Eve insisted.

He sighed, sipped brandy, and tried to put his head into it. "It seems, if we follow your way of thinking through this, that to justify murder— as it bloody well was—the act should have been in reciprocation for the death of an innocent. Or at least someone who was minding his own at the time, and hadn't done murder himself. But—"

"That's what I'm thinking. I get the but," she added, waving a hand in the air. "Murder isn't logical, it doesn't follow nice clean lines. Those who set out to kill make their own rules. However, butting your but—"

"Christ, no wonder I love you."

"This *was* logical, and it does follow lines. Kill priest in church with God's blood. Well, technically wine because Lino wasn't ordained and all so he couldn't actually do the transubstantiation."

"And you have the nerve to ask me Catholic questions when you can spout off transubstantiation."

"I studied up. The point is the motive's going to fit the method. I think—"

She broke off when her computer announced, Task complete.

"I think," she continued, "that the killer is a core member of the church. One of those who never misses Sunday Mass, and goes to confession . . . How often are you supposed to go to confession?"

Scowling, he jammed his hands into his pockets. "How the bloody, buggering hell should I know?"

She smiled at him, very sweetly. "What is it about asking you Catholic questions that gets you all jumpy?"

"You'd be jumpy, too, if I asked you things that make you feel the hot breath of hell at your back."

"You're not going to hell."

"Oh, and have you got some inside intel on that?"

"You married a cop. You married me. I'm your goddamn salvation. Computer, display primary data, screen one. These are the owners and/or tenants of the properties along Lino's jogging route."

"My salvation, are you?" He caught her around the waist, yanked her in. "And what would I be to you then?"

"I guess you're mine, pal. And if I'm wrong? Hey, we'll go down in flames together. Now, try for some more redemption and check out this data with me."

He kissed her first, long and lingering. "I can't figure out something about hell."

"What's that?"

"Would there be plenty of sex, because all the tenants are sinners, or none at all, with celibacy as the eternal punishment?"

"If I get around to it, I'll ask López. Data."

He obliged her by turning her around to face the screen, then drawing her back against him, and studying it over the top of her head. "And what do these names tell us?"

"I've got more data—runs on the owners, the tenants, including how long at current address, previous address. Ortega . . . Rosa O'Donnell mentioned that name. Computer, display secondary data, screen two."

"So, following your hunch, we're looking for longevity in that neighborhood. Someone, or a family, who's lived there since Lino was Soldado captain."

"Yeah, that's one point. Another is the jogging route. What there could be along it that connected to Lino, or interested him. Gain. He was gain and ego. First point is revenge. A lot of people stick," she observed. "Look at that. Ortega. Third generation in that property. And this one. Sixty years ago it's a piecework factory—probably gray market and a hive of illegal workers. Now it's lofts and condos, owned by the same guy. Huh. Who also owns the house next to Ortiz. Computer, complete run on Ortega, José."

Working . . .

"I know that name," Roarke said quietly. "Something about that name. Ah . . . Another building, East Side, middle Nineties. Retail space street level, studio space on the second. Living—I believe—living space on third and fourth. I looked into buying it a few years ago."

"Looked into?"

"I can't recall all the details, but I know I didn't buy it. Some legal tangle with Ortega."

Task complete . . .

"Let's see. Computer, split screen two, display new data. José Ortega's listed as thirty-five years of age—the vic's age. How the hell did he own that property sixty years ago?"

"Ancestor of the same name, I'd say. I remember José Ortega died several years ago. Yes, I remember now, the legal tangle was with his estate. This must be the grandson, and heir."

She ordered the computer to check, then shook her head at the data hiccup. "Okay, José Ortega, died 2052, age of ninety-eight. One son, Niko, died 2036, along with his wife and his mother in a hotel fire in Mexico City. The old man survived as did his then eleven-year-old grandson."

"The old man raised him. Yes, I'm remembering bits and pieces now. And the grandson, naturally, inherited when the old man passed. Word was—when I was interested in the property—and a bit of poking confirmed, that the younger Ortega didn't have his grandfather's business sense. And some of the property amassed declined somewhat. I liked the building on the East Side, and made an offer."

"He said no?"

"He couldn't be located when I was putting out feelers. And I found something I liked better."

"Couldn't be located. It lists the place on East 120th as his current address."

"That may be, but four—or it may have been five—years ago, when I wanted the building, Ortega wasn't in New York. We had to work through a lawyer, who was—if my memory serves—considerably frustrated by his client's disappearance."

"Computer, search for Missing Persons reports on Ortega, José, with this last known address."

"I didn't say he was missing so much as incommunicado," Roarke began, then his eyebrows lifted when he saw the reports come onscreen. "Aren't you the clever girl?"

"Reported missing by Ken Aldo, his spouse, in September of 2053 in Las Vegas, Nevada. Computer, display data and ID photo, Aldo, Ken." She waited, then felt it fall into place. "Well, hello, Lino."

"Your victim."

"Yeah, that's Lino. He changed the hair, added the beard, dicked with the eye color, but that's Lino Martinez."

"Who entered into marriage with Ortega shortly before the old man's death, according to this."

"Which is bullshit. Just another con. I've got nothing that points at Lino being gay or bi. Straight hetero. Liked women. He'd have known Ortega. Had to. They grew up in the same area. Computer, full data on Ortega, José, DOB 2025. Same age, same school. I guess the old man supported public education. And look here, got some slaps for illegals use and possession. Stints in rehab."

She went with the gut. "Computer, list any tattoos on current subject."

Acknowledged. Working . . . Current subject bears tattoo on left forearm. Describe or display?

"Display."

"There it is," Eve said, when the cross with its center heart pierced by the blade came on-screen. "Ortega was Soldado. He was one of Lino's. Not his spouse, never his fucking spouse. That's bogus. His captain."

"The marriage records could have been faked, and post-recorded. Easy enough for someone with the skill to fake the Flores ID as he did."

"Yeah. Easy enough. Who's the lawyer?" Eve demanded. "Who's the lawyer you dealt with on the Ortega thing?"

"I'll get that for you."

"I'll put money that Ken Aldo sought legal counsel, that he made inquiries about declaring his spouse legally dead. Seven years. It takes seven years. He'd gotten through six of them, and was rounding for home. Long patience," she said. "Just a few more months to go, and if he'd lined up his ducks correctly, he'd inherit—the promise. Big house, businesses, buildings. Millions. Many, many millions."

"And with that much riding," Roarke put in, "you'd want to keep your eye on it—I would. Yes, you'd want to have a look at it, make sure it was being tended to."

"Flores has been missing about the same amount of time. Add the time from when Flores was last reported seen, and when Lino, as Flores, requested the assignment at St. Cristóbal's."

"Time between to have the face work." Roarke nodded in agreement. "To study, plan, have the tat removed, alter records. A few months for that," he calculated. "More than enough if you focused."

"What better way to keep an eye on things without anyone making any connection between you and who you are, or who you intend to be when the time's right?"

"That residential is listed as Ortega's last address, but there's a tenant listed." Roarke gestured to the screen. "Or tenants. Hugh and Sara Gregg. At that location for nearly five years."

Eve called for their data. "They look straight. Two kids. Both of them doctors. We'll have to chat at some point. I need coffee."

She strode to the kitchen to program it, lined up her thoughts.

"Ortega and Lino knew each other as kids, grew up in the same area, went to the same school. Ortega joins the Soldado, which aligns him with Lino. Not high up, as his name hasn't come up from any of my sources. Foot soldier maybe, or with his grandfather's money, a kind of treasure chest. They connect again, or may have kept in touch. But after Ortega's grandfather died and leaves him pretty stinking rich, Lino's wheels start turning."

She drank coffee, then pinned Ortega's ID shot to her board. "Lino gets Ortega out West. Let's hang. Gamble, screw around. Gets rid of Ortega, pulls out the fake documentation, and reports him missing. Nice and legal. I'll need the reports on that."

"Then Martinez would contact the lawyer," Roarke added. "He has to have the documentation. Surprise, I'm Ken, José's same-sex spouse, and he's missing. I've told the police. He'd probably cover, ask if the lawyer would contact him if he hears from José, or gets any information. He's very worried, after all."

"As legal spouse, you'd have some access to some funds, could petition for more. But he's not worried about that. He has a plan. He's got to be patient. Seven years' patient. But then? Jackpot. Problem is, he can't keep his hands off Penny, or his mouth from running to her. He actually loves her. He wants to share all this good fortune with her. He's back—or will be back—and riding high."

"As Ken Aldo?"

"No, no, that would take the shine off. He'd want the shine. He'd have to come back as himself at the end of it. He'd have that worked. How would you do that?" she asked Roarke.

"Transfer properties—on paper. I imagine as Ken Aldo he'd have a forged will from Ortega, with him as full beneficiary. Once that's in his hand, some bogus sale of the properties. Aldo to Martinez."

"Yeah, yeah, it's all paper. It's all just follow the dots. Lino gets his face back and comes home a rich man, with some bullshit about making a killing out West. Seven years on the down-low, and he'll have everything he ever wanted."

She turned to study the holo again. "His father took off when he was a kid. Eventually his mother had him declared legally dead so she could get on with her life. Lino wouldn't have forgotten that. And seven years. Why would the cops out West sniff around Ken Aldo when there's no body, no sign of foul play? Instead you've got a screwup, with an illegals record, taking off."

"Still they'd have looked at this Aldo, wouldn't they?" Roarke took her coffee to have some himself. "Isn't that what you do? Suspect the spouse first?"

"Rule of thumb. They'd have run him, asked questions. He was smart, it was smart to pick Vegas for it. Gambling, sex, make sure they're seen together. Maybe talk Ortega into some high stakes. He wins, he loses, it doesn't matter. Money, loss or gain, it's always a motive for taking off. He'd have played that right with them," she considered. "Admit maybe they weren't getting along perfectly well, having a few marital problems, but they loved each other. He's just so worried. He just wants to know José is all right. He had to lay some groundwork for it. If the cops weren't complete idiots, they'd check with people who knew the MP, who knew the person who reported him missing."

"It just takes knowing the right people, and how much they cost."

"Yeah, there's a point. It's earlier there, right, in Vegas. The stupid time zone crap actually works for me this time. I can get those investigators' reports tonight."

"And your killer's killer?"

"Working on it. I've got more pressure to put on Penny now. She knew all of this. He'd have told her the details of it. And if she had a part in his murder—and she damn well did—she had a line to the Ortega money. No way she'd have given up millions just to ditch Lino. She helped kill him so she could have it all. I'm going to need the name of that lawyer."

"I'll get it now." He turned toward his office, glanced back. "That's quite a bit from one cake, Lieutenant."

She grinned fiercely as she went to her 'link. "It was one hell of a cake."

In short order, she read over the initial report, the statements, the interviews. It didn't come as much of a surprise to read one of those statements came from one Steven Jorge Chávez, identified as a longtime friend of the MP who'd come to Vegas to meet up at the MP's request.

"Chávez, Lino's co-captain in the Soldados, backed him on Ortega," Eve told Roarke. "As Ken Aldo's data stated he'd been born in Baja, and had spent his childhood in California and New Mexico, there was no reason to look for a connection between him and Chávez. He told the cops Ortega had confided in him one night that he was feeling closed in, pressured—by his marriage and his responsibilities back East. That he wished he could just 'disappear.'"

"Laying it on a bit thick," Roarke commented.

"Yeah, but they bought it. Had no reason not to. And the high stakes played through. Ortega rolled in a couple hundred thousand at the blackjack tables two days before he was reported missing."

"Lucky streak, good or bad, depending on your point of view."

"Yeah, could have been the springboard for getting rid of him."

"In any case"—Roarke studied her board, crowded now with all the players—"it's enough to buy a new face."

"The rest of the finances wouldn't zip straight to the spouse as, until they had a body, the MP would be considered alive and well. At least for seven years."

He looked over at Eve. She was revving now, he noted. Juiced. Between the adrenaline and the coffee, she'd run half the night. "And Chávez goes in the wind shortly after the statement."

"Both he and Flores. Check this. In the investigators' notes, they mention that Aldo was so distraught, he asked if there was a priest or a chaplain he could talk to."

"And Flores was there."

"I think Flores was in the wrong place at the wrong time on his sabbatical. I think when Lino worked a con, he went into it deep. When he came back to check with the police the next day, he had Flores with him. The report says he identified himself as Miguel Flores, and Aldo referred to him as Father. The cop did the job, checked Flores out, ran him, and got the background, verified. He came in twice more, with Flores, then stated that he intended to return home, to Taos, and left his contact information with the investigators. He checked in weekly for three months, and every month for a full year. Then he dropped it."

She sat back. "I think we narrow our search for Flores, for his remains to Nevada. A lot of desert around Vegas. A lot of places to bury a body. Or two. We'll focus that on the area from Vegas to Taos, figuring if he convinced Flores to travel with him at all, he'd have stuck to the route he gave the cops."

"You won't be able to close this, not in your mind, until you find Flores. Or what remains of him."

She sat back. She didn't need the board, the photos to see Flores. She had his face in her head. "Peabody said that cases like this make her wish bad guys would just be bad guys. There are plenty of those, that's what I said. Somebody like Flores, he never did anyone any harm. He got a big cosmic slap when bad guys took his family, but he doesn't do any harm. Tries, in fact, to live a life that does the opposite."

"It's more often than not innocents, isn't it, who get caught in the cross fire."

"Yeah, and this one wanted to examine his life. His faith, I guess. That's what I get from it. They took that life because he tried to help someone he thought was in need." No, she didn't need the board, didn't need the photo. "I've got to find who killed Lino Martinez. That's my job. But Flores deserves somebody to stand for him. He deserves that. Anyway." She glanced at the memo cube Roarke had put on her desk. "Is that the lawyer?"

"It is, yes."

She turned to her 'link with the memo.

"Eve, you're in the same time zone now, and it's closing on midnight."

She only smiled. "Yeah, there's this small, petty satisfaction I'm getting at the idea of waking up a lawyer. It's wrong, but it's there."

20

THE LAWYER DIDN'T APPRECIATE THE MIDNIGHT call, but she snagged his interest.

"Mr. Aldo and I are in contact regularly, and have been since Mr. Ortega's disappearance."

"You've met Mr. Aldo."

"Not in a personal sense. We correspond via e-mail most usually. He lives in New Mexico, and has a secondary residence in Cancún. He travels extensively."

"I bet. Mr. Ortega owns a number of properties in New York, businesses, his residence, rental properties. How are those finances handled?"

"I really don't see how that's relevant, or how it warrants being disturbed at this time of night."

"The investigation into Mr. Ortega's disappearance may be cold, but it's still open. As his spouse and only beneficiary on record, Mr. Aldo stands to inherit a big, fat bundle if and when Mr. Ortega is declared legally dead. You ever wonder about that, Mr. Feinburg?"

It was hard for a guy with a sleep crease across his cheek to look snooty, but Feinburg gave it his best shot. "Mr. Aldo has handled every aspect of this matter by means both legal and aboveboard."

"I have evidence that Ken Aldo is an alias for one Lino Martinez, a violent criminal who I suspect duped and disposed of your former client. I can and will get a warrant, within the hour, to access the financials on the Ortega properties, or you can answer the question and get back to sleep a lot sooner."

"You can't possibly expect me to believe—"

"And as Lino Martinez is currently cooling it down at the morgue, I don't believe you have a client left alive in this matter. Do you want me to wake up a judge, Feinburg?"

Feinburg blinked like an owl blasted with sudden sunlight. "I'd require verification before—"

"Let me ask you this," Eve said, and played another hunch. "Did Aldo contact you recently? Say in the last few weeks, to inform you that he had a beneficiary? A female. He'd want her listed as his legal partner, with full power of attorney."

There was a long silence. "Why would you ask that?"

"Because I believe the con got himself conned. Your client's dead, Feinburg, and his killer will continue to correspond with you under his name, and whatever name she's opted to use. Answer yes or no: The profits from the Ortega properties go into some kind of escrow or trust, and will—once Ortega is declared legally dead at the end of another year—become Aldo's assets."

"That would be the usual procedure, yes."

"When did you last hear from Aldo?"

"About six weeks ago. I did, however, hear from his . . . new partner only yesterday. It's my understanding that Mr. Aldo plans to travel for several months."

"I can pretty much guarantee he's doing his traveling in hell."

"Lieutenant." Feinburg shifted, tugged on the robe she assumed he'd pulled on before unblocking video. "What you're outlining is very disturbing."

"You think?"

"But at this time, I'm bound by client-attorney confidentiality. I can't give you information."

"We'll work around that. You can do this. Do not correspond or contact your clients until I clear it. If the woman claiming to be Aldo's partner contacts you, don't respond. Contact me. I don't think she will, not yet, but—and trust me on this—I will find a way to tangle you up in obstruction and accessory after the fact if you give my suspect the smallest clue she's on my screen. Understood?"

Unable to pull off snooty again, Feinburg just looked aggrieved. "I'm a property and tax lawyer, for God's sake. I've done nothing to earn threats from the police."

"Good. Keep it that way. I'll be in touch."

She ended transmission, then frowned at the bowl Roarke set in front of her. "What's this?"

"Food. We had cake for dinner, if you recall. And since you show no signs of winding down for the night, we're going to eat."

She sniffed at the soup. She'd bet a month's pay there were vegetables lurking around under the surface, but it smelled good. "Okay. Thanks. You don't have to stick."

"You couldn't peel me off with dermalaser." He sat across from her, sampled his own soup. "Do you think Lino opened himself to all this by making Penny his legal partner and heir?"

Eve ate. She'd been right about the vegetables. "Do you?"

"You said he loved her. Love blinds and binds and often makes bloody gits out of us. So, yes. She likely nudged him along that route, using sex or withholding it—as sex makes bloody gits of us even more often than love. He'd have told her all of it, every detail. A bit at a time maybe, but over these five years? He'd have laid it all out for her. How smart is she?"

"Not very, I'd say. More hotheaded. But he was, yeah, I think Lino was pretty smart. And all she had to do was springboard off the game he'd already laid out. He'd have gotten away with it," she added. "Another few months, the properties and trust transfer to Aldo—all legal-schmegal. Aldo sells out to Martinez. Martinez gets his face back, and comes home rich and important. Yeah, he was smart enough, but Penny Soto was his athlete's heel."

"Achilles'." Roarke paused, studied her face. "Do you do that on purpose? The misnomers?"

"Maybe. Sometimes. Anyway, she'll know what happened to Flores."

Roarke smiled at her. "How much will you bargain with her for the information?"

"I won't. Can't. But I'll get it." She scooped up soup. The vegetables weren't such a bad deal when they were disguised in noodles and a thick, zingy broth. "Yeah, he told her all of it. Pillow talk, bragging, puffing himself up. And she has to figure, what does she need him for? She can have it all if she works it right. She's waited almost as long as he has, right? Why does she have to share it with this loser?"

"Left her once, didn't he?" Roarke pointed out. "What's to stop him from tossing her aside once he's riding the money train. So she tosses him first. Permanently."

"Plays the right tune for me. She gets him to hook her up first. If you loved me, you'd respect me. If you loved me, we'd be partners. If you loved me, you'd make sure I had security. Don't you trust me, Lino, don't you love me—all while probably giving him a blow job." Eve wagged her spoon at Roarke. "Men are dicks so often because they have one."

"I can use mine without thinking with it."

Eve grinned over another spoonful of soup. "If I went down on you right now, you'd give me anything I asked for."

"Try me."

Now she laughed. "You're just trying for a bj, and I'm working."

Saying nothing, he took out his memo book, keyed something in. Then smiled when she cocked her head in question. "I'm just making a note that you owe me a blow job to prove your theory."

Amused, she finished off the soup. "Okay then, if you're going to stick, the next step is to check out the families and close ties to the fatalities and injured at the two bombings back in '43. I'm working on the theory that Lino was behind both. I'm starting with the second, because of the eye-for-an-eye thing."

"Because most, if not all, would have no reason to think Martinez set the boomer, on his own turf."

"But the second," Eve agreed. "People knew, or strongly suspected he had something to do with it. He made sure that buzz got around. Plus, the single fatality in the school bombing has no close friends or relatives left in the area. Her family moved to Barcelona three years after her death."

"So you study the fatalities on the second, as death has more weight."

"Your kid, brother, father, best pal, whatever, gets hurt seventeen years ago and you have a chance for payback, you find a way to hurt them back. Exposure, a good ass-whooping. But death? It's final. Payback needs to be final, too."

"Yes. And the law is often transitory."

She knew he thought of Marlena again, what had been done, what he had done. His eyes came to hers.

"If I'd stepped away, if I'd never exacted payment from those who tortured, raped, murdered an innocent girl, Jenny would be alive. It ripples, and you can never know how or where they'll spread."

"Sometimes the law is transitory, and sometimes, even with it, those ripples spread out too far or in the wrong direction. But without the law, well, eventually, we'd all drown."

"Some of us are excellent swimmers. I'm more inclined to believe in the face of the law, since I look at it every day, than I ever did before I saw it." He reached in his pocket, took out the gray button that had fallen off her suit the first time they'd met. When she'd viewed him as a murder suspect. "And I have my talisman to remind me."

It never failed to baffle her—and on a deeper level delight her—that he carried it with him, always. "What ever happened to that suit anyway?"

Humor flickered in his eyes. "It was hideous, and met the fate it deserved. This"—he held up the button—"was the best part of it."

He was probably right. "Well. Break's over," she announced. "Computer, list fatalities in East 119th Street incident from Detective Stuben's case file."

Acknowledged. Working . . .

"There would have been others," Roarke commented. "Other fatalities, on both sides of the war, while your victim was a captain. And therefore in charge."

"Yeah, got that covered. Stuben's going to get me the data by tomorrow. I don't hit here, I'll start looking there."

Task complete.

"Display, screen one. Five fatalities," Eve said. "There's another whose injuries were severe enough I'll need to look at. Guy lost an arm. Three of the fatalities were members of the Skulls. Of the other two, one was the manager and one was a part-time counter guy. All fatalities were minors, except the manager."

"Four children dead."

"Yeah. Well, two of the gang members, according to Stuben's file, had done time in juvie, had been arrested for assault with deadly—and released when the wits failed to identify—and had been suspects in the bludgeoning death of a Soldado."

"Boys will be boys."

"And scum will be scum. The manager . . . Computer, display data for adult victim. Kobie Smith, some bumps in his teens and early twenties. No time inside. Employed there for three years, manager for six months. Left a wife of eighteen months and a kid. Kid was two at the time of his father's death, making him about twenty now. Too young to fit Mira's profile, or my gut, but we look." She ordered the data.

"Well, well," Roarke commented as he read. "It seems he's attend-ing the Police Academy in Orlando, Florida. In the land of speculation, his father is killed in what is believed to be gang violence, and the son sets a goal to become a cop. To serve and protect."

Eve frowned thoughtfully at the data on-screen. "No criminal. Two half-sibs. Mother married again. Huh. Married a cop after relocating to Florida, three years after husband's death. Can't see Penny tracking her down, getting her hyped enough to come back and poison Lino. But the vic had parents, too, and a brother."

She ran their data, studying it, considering it. Parents divorced, she noted. Mother residing in Philadelphia, father in the Bronx, as was one brother. The second brother in Trenton. "None of them stayed in the neighborhood. It's going to be someone in the neighborhood."

"That's most likely, I agree, but it's very possible your bad Penny—"

"Ha-ha."

"That she went out of the neighborhood to add more distance be-tween her and the murder. I would have."

"She's not as smart as you."

"Well now, billions aren't, but it's good strategy, and she had plenty of time to work on that strategy."

"Yeah. Damn. I see hikes to the Bronx and Trenton in my future. Possibly Philadelphia because it's poison, and poison skews most often as a female weapon. And look at that, the mother's never remarried, works as a medical assistant in a rehab facility. Medicals can access poi-sons easier than the rest of us."

"She lost not only a son, but a grandson, as the mother took him to Orlando, remarried. Of course, it may be there's been effort to main-tain a relationship on all sides."

"And it may not be," Eve finished and blew out a breath. "Okay, top of the list goes Emmelee Smith. I may be able to work a warrant for checking her communications and travel over the past few weeks." She yawned. "I need coffee."

"You need bed."

She shook her head, rose. "I just want to run through the others. I can start looking into the ones that give me the buzz tomorrow."

She hit the kitchen and the AutoChef for both of them.

"I called up the data on the counter boy," Roarke told her when she returned. "He was barely sixteen."

"Quinto Turner. Quinto. That sounds like a Spanish name. Mother Juanita Rodrigez Turner. Hmmm. Father Joseph Turner. He was mixed race, Mexican and black, straddling a line between gangs, racially and geographically. No sibs. Father deceased. Look at that. Self-terminated by hanging, on the one-year anniversary of his son's death."

"So the woman lost two."

"Computer, all data on Juanita Rodrigez Turner, on-screen."

"She lives three blocks from the church," Roarke began.

"Wait. Wait. I've seen her. Computer, enlarge ID photo, twenty-five percent. I've seen her," Eve repeated. "Where was it? It was quick, it was just a . . . Goddamn, goddamn, the youth center. She works at the youth center. Day-care manager, on-site medical. She wasn't pissed and irritated, she was nervous. That's why she kept her back to me. Magda didn't call her Juanita, but that's her. Nita," Eve remembered. "She called her Nita.

"She'd have seen him every day, nearly every day for those five years. She probably worked with him, joked with him, helped him counsel kids. She confessed her sins to him, and all the while, all the while, he killed her son, and that death had driven her husband to suicide. Every day for five years she gave him respect, because of his calling. And then she finds out who he is, what he is."

"What's that I hear?" Roarke wondered. "Ah, yes, it's buzzing."

"Put those trips to Trenton and beyond on hold," she said. "She'd pass the bodega where Penny works any time she went to church, and she's been going to that church—I'll lay odds—for most of her life. One of the faithful," she murmured. "But for Penny, just a mark, just a means to an end. Now I have to bring this woman in, I have to put her in the box and make her confess to me. And when she does, I have to put her in a cage."

"Sometimes the law is transitory," Roarke repeated. "And sometimes it turns its back on real justice."

Eve shook her head. "She took a life, Roarke. Maybe it was a bad life, but it wasn't her right." She turned to him. "The cops did nothing about what happened to Marlena. They were wrong cops at a wrong time. But this woman could have come forward with what she'd been told, or what she knew. Detective Stuben? He'd have done what had to be done. He cared. He cares. Part of him's never stopped working the case, and none of him has ever forgotten the victims of the bombing, or their families."

"How many are there like him?"

"Never enough. She has to answer for Lino Martinez, whatever he was. She won't answer for Jimmy Jay Jenkins, but her act of revenge led to his death, too. It planted the seed. Or . . . tossed in the pebble. Ripples," she reminded him. "We can't be sure where they'll spread. Somebody's got to try to stop them."

"He was barely sixteen." He brought the ID photo back on-screen of the young, fresh-faced, clear-eyed boy. "The line's less defined on my side than it could ever be on yours. What now?"

"Now, I contact Peabody and have her meet me here, so I can brief her in the morning before we go pick up Juanita Turner for questioning. Contact her voice mail," Eve said when she caught his look.

"And then?"

"We go to bed." She glanced back toward the screen. "She's not going anywhere."

She slept poorly, dogged by dreams, images of a boy she'd never met who'd died simply because he'd been in the wrong place. The young, fresh face was torn and ruined, the clear eyes dull and dead.

She heard his mother weeping over his body. Mindless, keening sobs that echoed into forever.

As she watched, Marlena—bloodied, battered, broken as she'd been in the holo Roarke had once shown her—walked up to the mangled body of the dead boy.

"We were both so young," Marlena said. "We'd barely begun to live. So young to be used as a tool. Used, destroyed, discarded."

She held out a hand for Quinto Turner, and he took it. Even as his blood poured over the floor of the church, he took it and got to his feet.

"I'll take him now," Marlena said to Eve. "There's a special place for the innocents. I'll take him there. What was she to do?" She gestured to the grieving mother, covered with her son's blood. "Can you stop it? Can you stop it all? You couldn't stop what happened to you."

"I can't stop it all. But murder isn't an end. Murder isn't a solution."

"She was his mother. It was her solution."

"Murder doesn't resolve murder. It perpetuates it."

"What of us, then? What of us? No one stood for me. No one but Roarke."

"And still it wasn't an end. He lives with it."

"And so do you. Now you'll perpetuate her loss, her grief, for justice. You'll live with that, too." With her hand holding Quinto's, Marlena led him away.

Eve stared at the pools of blood, the ripples in them.

And watched them spread.

She woke edgy, and with none of the energy the imminent closing of a case usually brought her. She knew the answers, or most of them, saw the pattern clearly, and understood, accepted, what she had to do.

But the acceptance and the restless few hours of sleep left her with a dull headache.

"Take a blocker," Roarke ordered. "I can see the damn headache beating at your skull."

"So, you've got X-ray vision now, Super-Roarke?"

"No point in taking slaps at me." He rose, walked toward the bathroom. "I won't slap back. You've got enough weighing on you."

"I don't want a damn blocker."

He came back with one, walked up to her as she yanked on her weapon harness. "Take it, or I'll make you take it."

"Look, step back or—"

He cupped his hand on the back of her neck. She braced for him to try to force the pill down her throat. In fact, she welcomed the attempt and the battle. Instead, his mouth came down on hers.

The hands she'd lifted to fight dropped to her sides as lips simply defeated her with tenderness.

"Damn it," she said when his lips left hers to brush her cheek.

"You hardly slept."

"I'm okay. I just want to close it down, get it done."

"Take the blocker."

"Nag, nag, nag." But she took it, swallowed it. "I can't leave it open. I can't pretend I don't know. I can't just let her do murder and turn away."

"No. You can't, no."

"And even if I could, even if I could find some way to live with it, if I let her go, I let Penny Soto go. How can I?"

"Eve." He rubbed at the knots of tension in her shoulders. "You don't have to explain yourself, not to me. Not to anyone, but especially not to me. I could turn away. I could do that. I could do that and find some way outside the law to make sure the other paid. You never could. There's that shifting line between us. I don't know if it makes either of us right, either of us wrong. It just makes us who we are."

"I went outside the law. Asked you to go outside it with Robert Lowell. I did that to make sure he paid for the women he'd tortured and killed. I did that because I'd given Ariel my word he'd pay."

"It's not the same, and you know it."

"I crossed the line."

"The line shifts." Now he gave those shoulders a quick, impatient shake. "If the law, if justice has no compassion, no fluidity, no humanity, how is it justice?"

"I couldn't live with it. I couldn't live with letting him take the easy way out, letting the law give him the easy way. So I shifted the line."

"Was it justice, Eve?"

"It felt like it."

"Then go." He lifted her hands, kissed them. "Do your job."

"Yeah." She started toward the door, stopped, and turned back. "I dreamed about Marlena. I dreamed about her and Quinto Turner. They were both the way they were after they'd been killed."

"Eve."

"But . . . she said she'd take him, and she did. She said there was a special place for the innocents, and she'd take him there. Do you think there is? A place for innocents."

"I do, actually. Yes."

"I hope you're right."

She left him, went to her office to prepare for what had to be done.

When Peabody and McNab came in, she simply gestured toward the kitchen. There were twin hoots of joy as they scrambled for the treasure trove of her AutoChef. She stuck with coffee. The blocker had done the job—and maybe the conversation with Roarke had smoothed the rest, at least a little.

She cocked her eyebrows when Peabody and McNab came back in with heaping plates and steaming mugs.

"Do you think you've got enough to hold you off from starvation during the briefing?"

"Belgian waffles, with seasonal berries." Peabody sat down, prepared to plow in. "This may hold me forever."

"As long as your ears stay as open as your mouths."

She began with Ortega, took them through her premise.

"At the end of the seven years, he'd stand to inherit, by spousal right, upward of six hundred and eighty-five million—not including personal property, and the profits from the real property and businesses over the seven."

"That's a lot of waffles," McNab commented.

"Set for life," Peabody agreed. "Well, if he'd lived."

"His bed buddy didn't want to split. She wanted it all. We're going to prove that, nail her for accessory after the fact on Ortega and Flores, fraud, conspiracy to murder on Lino, and being a basic skank bitch. We'll meet with the lawyer later today, and set up a little sting."

"We lay down on her," Peabody added, "and get her to flip on her co-conspirator."

"Don't need it. Screen on," she ordered, and Juanita's data flashed on. "Juanita Turner. Her son was a victim in the second bombing."

"How did you . . ." Peabody paused, narrowed her eyes at the image. "She looks a little familiar. Did we interview her? Was she at the Ortiz funeral?"

"If she was, and I think it's likely, she slipped in and out before the scene was secured. We saw her at the youth center. The medical."

"That's it! I didn't get much of a look at her there. Her son?"

"And her husband, a year later—to the day—by self-termination." Eve ran through it, flatly. "Penny needed a weapon," Eve concluded. "And Juanita fit the bill."

"Man, man, it had to be horrible for her to realize this guy she'd thought was . . . that he was the one responsible for her son's death."

"Yeah. It's rough." But it couldn't influence the work. "I've contacted Reo," Eve said, referring to the APA she preferred working with. "We've got enough, in her opinion, to get the communications. Which is where e-boy here comes in. I want you to dig in, dig out," she told McNab as he gorged on waffles. "Anything that so much as sniffs like it's connected. We're picking up Juanita. While we have her in the box, you find us a communication with Penny. Find a memo, a journal, a receipt for the cyanide. Find something hard, and find it fast."

Peabody swallowed waffles and berries. "We're picking her up before Penny?"

"Penny orchestrated it. Juanita executed it. I've contacted Baxter. He and Trueheart are keeping a tail on Penny. Now, if you've finished stuffing yourselves, let's get to work."

Peabody said nothing as they walked downstairs. She got into the passenger seat, finally turned to Eve. "Maybe we get Penny on conspiracy, but it's a stretch. It's more likely we get accessory after the fact there. And that's a maybe. She can claim she let it slip out about Lino, or felt guilty and spilled it to Juanita Turner."

Peabody put a hand on her heart, widened her eyes. "I swear, your honor and members of the jury, I didn't know she'd do murder. How could I know?" Dropping her hand, she shook her head. "Juanita's going to get hit with first degree, no way around it unless Reo wants to deal it down, but Penny? She's likely to slither out of it."

"That's not up to us."

"It just seems wrong. Juanita loses her son, her husband. And now, all these years later, she gets used. And she's the one who's going to go down the hardest."

"You play, you pay. She killed a guy, Peabody," McNab said from the back. "If Dallas has this right, and it sure fits nice and tight, she did the premeditated—cold-blooded killed his ass."

"I *know* that. But she was set up to do it. Jesus, you ought to see the crime scene photos from that bombing. There wasn't much left of her kid."

"Vic was a downtown bastard, that's coming crystal. And I give you she took the hardest of the hard knocks. But, come on, that gives her the go to poison him?"

"I didn't say that, you ass, I'm just saying—"

"Shut up and stop arguing," Eve ordered.

"I'm just pointing out," Peabody said in the gooey tones of reason that told any detractors they were stupid, "that Juanita took some really mean hits, and Penny—who probably was in on them—used that. And—"

"*I'm* just pointing out, hello, murderer."

Peabody swung around to glare at McNab. "You're such a jerk."

"Bleeding heart."

"Shut *up*!" Eve's snapped order had them both zipping it. "You're both right. So stop bickering like a couple of idiots. I got rid of one headache this morning. If you bring one back, I'm booting both of you to the curb and finishing this myself."

Peabody folded her arms, stuck her nose in the air. McNab slumped in the backseat. It was, in Eve's mind, a sulkfest all the way over to the East Side.

EVE DOUBLE-PARKED IN FRONT OF THE YOUTH center, flipped on her On Duty light. The same group of kids shot hoops on the court, while adults hustled, dragged, and carried smaller ones into the building.

The daily life of kids was a strange one, she thought. You got hauled to various locations, dumped there, hauled out again at the end of the day. During the dump time, you formed your own little societies that might have little or nothing to do with your pecking order in your home life. So weren't you constantly adjusting, readjusting, dealing with new rules, new authorities, more power, less?

No wonder kids were so weird.

"You wait for the warrant," she told McNab. "Once we confirm Juanita's here, or confirm her location, Peabody will relay that information. You can make your way to her apartment."

"I don't see how I can relay information when I'm supposed to shut up—and if I wasn't supposed to, I still wouldn't be speaking to him."

"Do you really want to experience the thrill of having my boot so far up your ass it bruises your tonsils? Don't even think about it," Eve

snapped at McNab when he snickered. "Detective Jerk, stand by. Detective Bleeding Heart, with me."

She strode off. In seconds, Peabody clipped along beside her, insult
in every step. "Be pissed later," Eve advised. "There's nothing about
this that's going to be pleasant or satisfying. So do the job now, and be
pissed later."

"I just think I ought to be able to express an opinion without being—"

Eve stopped, whirled. Fire kindled and flashed in her eyes as she
scorched Peabody with them. "Do you think I'm looking forward to
hauling in a woman who had to bury the torn and bloody pieces of her
son that could be scraped up off the floor? That I'm rubbing my hands
with glee at the prospect of putting her in the box and sweating a confession out of her for killing the man who I believe was responsible
for that?"

"No." Peabody's shoulders drooped. "No, I don't."

The fire shut down, and Eve's eyes went cop flat. "Personal opinion,
feelings, sympathy—none have any place in this. This is the job, and
we're going to do it."

Eve pulled open the door and stepped inside to the morning chaos.
Crying babies, harassed parents, squealing kids milled around—
including one who appeared to be making a break for it, at surprising
speed on all fours.

Peabody scooped it up before it could make it to the door, then
passed it to the man rushing after it.

Eve wound her way through, caught Magda's attention. "Juanita
Turner."

"Oh, Nita's riding herd on the earlies in the activity room. That
way." Magda signaled. "Through the double doors, up the stairs one
level. Second door, left. It's open."

When Peabody started to pull out her communicator, Eve shook
her head. "Not until we see her. In all this insanity, she could have
walked out."

Eve followed the direction, and the noise. The activities room held tables, chairs, shelves full of what she supposed were activities. Sunlight blasted through the windows to wash a space done in aggressively bright primary colors. Six kids sat at tables, drawing, doing puzzles, and talking at the top of their lungs at the same time.

Juanita walked among them, looking over shoulders, patting heads. The easy smile she wore dropped away when she saw Eve. If guilt had a face, Eve thought, Juanita Turner wore it.

Eve gestured, stepped just outside the doorway. "Tag McNab," she mumbled to Peabody. "Step off aways."

She waited until Juanita walked to the doorway. "Is there something I can help you with?"

"You're going to need to have someone cover for you, Mrs. Turner."

"Why would I do that?"

"You know why. You have to come with us now. We can do it quietly." Eve glanced beyond Juanita to the half a dozen kids. "It would be better for you, for the kids, if we do this quietly."

"I'm not leaving the children. I'm not—"

"Do you want those kids to see me take you out of here in restraints?" Eve waited two beats, watched it sink in. "You're going to get someone to cover for you, Mrs. Turner, and I'm going to arrange for you to be taken down to Central. You're going to wait there until I come to question you."

The thin skin of outrage couldn't cover the bones of fear. They poked through, raw and sharp. "I don't see why I should go with you when I don't know what this is about."

"I'm going to have Penny Soto in custody by the end of the day, Mrs. Turner." Eve nodded at the jolt of awareness. "You understand exactly what this is about. Now choose how you want it to go down."

Juanita walked across the hall, spoke briefly to the young man inside. He looked puzzled, and mildly irritated, but crossed over into the activities room.

"I don't have to say anything." Juanita's lips trembled on the words.

"No, you don't." Eve took her arm, led her down the stairs, led her out of the building. And waited until they were on the sidewalk, away from the kids still shooting hoops, before she read Juanita her rights.

At Central, she had Juanita taken to an interview room and split off to her own office. She had some arrangements to make. As she turned toward the bullpen, she spotted Joe Inez and his wife on the waiting bench. Joe rose.

"Ah, the guy said you were on your way, so . . ."

"Okay. You want to talk to me, Joe?"

"Yeah, I . . ." He glanced toward his wife who nodded, a kind of support gesture. "We need to talk about before. It's about before, about what happened. The 2043 bombings."

Eve held up a hand. "Why did you come in? Why are you here, on your own?"

"We talked." His wife laid a hand on Joe's arm. "After you came by, we talked, and Joe told me about it. We're here to do what's right. Me and Joe. Together."

"You answer this one question." Eve stepped closer so that her face was close to Joe's. She kept her voice low, her eyes hard on his. "I haven't read you your rights. You know what that means?"

"Yeah. But—"

"I want an answer to this before we go forward, before anything you tell me is on the record. Did you kill anyone, or have part in killing anyone?"

"No, Jesus, no, that's—"

"Don't say anything else. Don't tell me anything. I'm going to have you taken to an interview room. You're going to wait there until I make some arrangements." She poked her head into the bullpen, snagged a uniform. "Take Mr. and Mrs. Inez to Interview B. Sit with them." Eve turned back to them. "You've got nothing to say until I tell you to say it."

She went straight to her office, contacted APA Cher Reo. "You need to get down here, but before you do, I need you to approve immunity for a witness."

"Oh sure." The pretty blonde waved a graceful hand. "Just let me get my special magic immunity wand."

"I've got a wit, one who just came in voluntarily that may close out two cases that've been open for seventeen years and involved six deaths. The wit may give information that leads to an arrest in those matters."

"What—"

Eve plowed right over her. "In addition, I'm about to close the St. Cristóbal's homicide with two arrests. The wit was a minor at the time of the earlier incident, and would likely fall under the idiotic Clemency Order, or it could so be argued if there were charges brought. You do deals with scum to get bigger scum every day of the goddamn week, Reo. I'm talking family man here, one who comes off as doing a one-eighty on where his life was going. You authorize immunity, or I'm cutting him loose."

"I can't just—"

"Don't tell me what you can't. Make it work. Get back to me." Eve clicked off, contacted Mira's office. "I don't care what she's doing," Eve began when the ferocious admin answered. "I need to speak with her now. Put me through, or I'm coming down there."

The screen went to hot, waiting blue.

Moments later, Mira came on. "Eve?"

"I need you in Observation," Eve began, and explained. "Maybe I'm wrong," she added. "You'll know if I'm wrong."

"I can be there in about twenty minutes."

"I'll wait for you."

She made the last call to Feinburg, and set in motion the last of her plan. When Reo tagged her back, Eve grabbed the 'link.

"I'm on my way. Immunity isn't out of the question, but I need more information."

"The wit was approximately seventeen years old, and a member of the Soldados when the bombings in 2043 occurred."

"Jesus, Dallas, if he was part of that—"

"I believe his part, if any, was minor, and after the fact. And that he can give us information on the major players. Later today, I'm going to be picking up the only one of them I believe is still alive, as part of the St. Cristóbal's arrest. They could skate on this anyway, Reo, but what he gives me would be another nail for you to hammer."

"The Clemency Order's a murky area as it was revoked. If a suspect wasn't arrested and charged during the time it was in place, and information after its repeal—"

"Don't lawyer me, Reo. You're going to give my wit immunity." No, she couldn't stop them all, Eve thought. She couldn't save them all. But she could save some. "I'm not taking this guy down for it."

"What's the wit's name?"

"It's going to be Mr. X until you give me the damn immunity."

"Goddamn it, what is he, your brother? All right, conditional immunity. If he did murder, Dallas, I'm not giving him a wash."

"Good enough."

"I'll be there in five minutes."

"Interview B. You may want to clear your slate for the rest of the day. It's going to be a long one."

She swung out, met up with Peabody, and went in to talk to Joe Inez.

"Record on. Dallas, Lieutenant Eve, and Peabody, Detective Delia, in interview with Inez, Joe, and Inez, Consuela. I'm going to read you your rights at this time." Once she had, she sat at the table across from them. "Do you both understand your rights and obligations in this matter?"

"Yeah, I do, but Connie isn't involved."

"This is for her protection. Mr. Inez, have you come in to interview of your own volition?"

"Yeah."

"Why?"

"Why?"

"I'd like you to tell me, for the record, why you chose to come in and make a statement today."

"I . . . I did a lot of things I'm not proud of, in the past. But I got a family. I've got three kids, three boys. If I don't do what's right, how am I supposed to tell them they have to do what's right?"

"Okay. Do you want something to drink?"

"I—no." Obviously flustered, he cleared his throat. "I'm good."

"Mrs. Inez?"

"No, thank you. We just want to get this over with."

"Tell me what happened, Joe. What happened back in the spring of 2043?"

"Ah, most of us, even if we didn't go to the school, went to the dances. Maybe to dance, or pick fights, do some dealing, look for recruits."

"Who are we?"

"Oh. The Soldados. Lino and Steve were co-captains then. Well, Lino mostly ran the gang. Steve was more muscle. Lino wanted more recruits, and he figured you got more recruits when you had trouble. When you had, like, a common enemy. He talked like that," Joe added. "But I didn't know, I swear to God, I didn't know, until later."

"Didn't know what?"

"The bomb. I didn't know. I'd been a member for about a year, year and a half, and Lino liked that I was good with my hands. That I could fix stuff. That I could boost cars." He let out a breath. "He used to say I'd be somebody. He'd make me somebody. But I had to make my mark."

"Your mark."

"The kill mark. I couldn't be upper level until I did a kill, until I'd made my mark."

"You still wear the Soldado tattoo," Eve pointed out. "It doesn't in-clude the kill mark, the X below the cross."

"No, I never made my mark. I didn't have it in me. I didn't mind a fight, hell, I liked fighting. Get out there, get a little bloody. Blow off steam. But I didn't want to kill anybody."

"And still, you and Lino were friends," Eve prompted.

"Yeah, or I thought we were. Lino used to razz me about it, but . . . just like guys razz each other about shit. I guess that's why I didn't know what he had going, what he set up."

"He didn't tell you about the bomb."

"He never said anything to me. He said how he'd meet up with me there, at the dance. The bomb at the dance, when it went off, I was right there. Right there. Ronni Edwards got killed. She went up ten feet away from me. I knew her."

He stopped, and rubbed his hands over his face. When he dropped them again, Connie took one in hers.

"I knew her," Joe repeated. "Since we were in kindergarten I knew her, and she blew apart in front of me. I never . . ." He lowered his head, fought for composure. "Sorry."

"Take your time," Eve told him.

"It went—it went to hell in seconds. Music's playing, kids are danc- ing or hanging. Then it went to hell. The noise, the fire. More kids got hurt, and then they're running around, crazy scared, and more get hurt in the trample. Lino and Chávez and Penny, they're hauling kids out like heroes, and saying how it was the Skulls, the motherfriggin' Skulls."

He wiped his mouth with the back of his hand. "But they weren't there, not when it went down."

"Lino, Steve, and Penny weren't there," Eve qualified.

"Yeah. I mean no, no they weren't there when the place exploded. I'd been looking for Lino. I had a couple guys who wanted in—wanted in the gang, so I was looking for Lino. Nobody'd seen him. Just min- utes before it blew, nobody'd seen him or Penny or Steve. He never missed a dance. I figured, well, he was just late getting there. And probably lucky for him, I thought that after. Lucky for him because we figured he was the target. It was later when I realized he was the one making the noises about being the target."

"Were you hurt in the first bombing?"

"Got some burns, cut up some from the stuff that was flying around. Not real bad. If I'd been standing where Ronni was . . . I thought about that. Thought about that and how Ronni had just blown. It got me up, got me thinking, yeah, those Skulls needed some killing. So I'm up, think I'm up to get my mark because of that, and I hear Lino and Penny talking."

"Where were you when you heard them?"

"We had a place we used, like a headquarters. This basement in a building on Second Avenue, right off 101st. Big basement, the place was like a maze. Rattrap," he said with a sour smile. "They fixed it up about ten years back. It's apartments now. Nice apartments."

"Just for my curiosity, do you know who owned it?"

"Sure." He looked puzzled by the question. "José Ortega—the old guy—kind of a big deal in the neighborhood. José was one of us. Soldado—I mean the old guy's grandson was one of us. But the fact was, Lino said it was our place."

Ripples, Eve thought. "Okay. So you heard Lino and Penny talking when you went into the basement, into the headquarters."

"Yeah, like I said, it was a big place, lots of rooms, and corridors. I was heading for the war room. I was up, and I wanted in on the retaliation. Hell, I wanted to lead the charge. But I passed one of the flop rooms, and I heard them talking about how it worked. How planting the boomer at the dance got the community—that's how Lino put it—the community involved. How they'd hit the Skulls now, and everyone would cheer. The Soldados would be heroes because everybody thought the Skulls attacked, the Skulls brought blood to neutral territory. And Penny said they should've used a bigger bomb."

He looked down at his hands, then lifted his gaze back to Eve's. Tears glazed it. "She said that. Said how Lino should've built a bigger boomer so there'd be more dead instead of just that little bitch Ronni. How a bunch of bodies would've gotten people really juiced. And he laughed. He laughed and said, 'Wait a few days.'"

He reached for his wife's hand. "Can I get some water? I think I could use some water."

Peabody rose, walked over to fill a paper cup. "Take your time, Mr. Inez," she told him.

"I couldn't believe it, couldn't believe they'd do that. To our own. Chaz Polaro was in the hospital, and they didn't know if he was going to make it. And they're in there, laughing. They're the ones who did it, and they're laughing.

"It could've been me that night, dead or maybe dying. It could have been any of us, and he'd done it. They'd done it. I went in, so pissed off. They were on this old mattress we had down there, and she was mostly naked. I said, 'What the fuck, Lino.' I'm sorry, Connie, that's what I said."

Joe began to talk quickly now, pushing the words out, pushing the memories. "I said, 'You fucking bastard, you set that boomer on us.' He started telling me to chill, frost it up. How it was strategy, for the good of the gang, and all this *bullshit*. I told him to get fucked, and I walked out. He came after me. We had a lot of words—and Connie's going to get steamed if I say them all. Upshot was he told me he was captain, and I'd follow orders, I'd keep my mouth shut or he'd set Chávez on me. He said we were going to hit the Skulls and hard, that he'd already made the boomer for the hit. If I didn't want him to shove it down my throat and hit the remote, I'd keep my mouth shut. I guess he wasn't sure I got the point because I got jumped a few hours later, got the shit kicked out of me.

"I kept my mouth shut. I kept it shut and the next day Lino and Chávez took off. I kept it shut when Penny hunted me up and told me to remember it might be Lino's boomer, but her finger was on the trigger now, and if I didn't follow orders they'd do to me what she and Lino had done to her old man."

"Hold it there a second," Eve told him. "Did Penny Soto tell you what she and Lino had done to her father?"

"Hell, they bragged on it all the time. How they'd diced up Nick Soto. How they made their mark together."

"Okay. Keep going."

"I guess there's not much more. A couple days after Lino left, the bomb hit the diner. And I kept it shut. I didn't say anything to anybody, and five people died."

"You knew about the second bomb beforehand?"

"Yeah, I knew." He crushed the water cup in his hand. "I didn't know the when and where, but I knew they were going to do it. I knew people would die, because Penny wanted bodies, and Lino liked to get Penny what she wanted. I didn't do anything about it. I went and got drunk, and stayed drunk for a long time."

"When did you last see Lino Martinez?"

"The day we had it out. I kept waiting for him to come back, but he never did. Chávez neither. Penny ran the Soldados for a while after, but it all fell apart. I got busted for robbing a 24/7, did some time. She looked me up when I got out to remind me worse things could happen than a beating if I ever thought about running my mouth."

"Okay, Joe, let's go over some of the finer points again."

Eve worked him through it, then punched details. When she thought she'd run him dry, she nodded. "I want to thank you for coming in today. You've been a big help."

He stared up at her when she rose. "That's all?"

"Unless you have something to add."

"No, but . . . am I under arrest?"

"For what?"

"For, I don't know, withholding evidence or . . . accessory or something."

"No, Joe, you're clear. You may be called on to testify in court as to the statements you've made today. If so, will you testify in court as to the facts?"

"We've got three kids. I have to show them how to do the right thing."

"That's all I need for now. Go home."

Eve stepped out, wound her way to Observation and Reo.

"He's clear," Reo said, "but if you think we can make and win a case against Penny Soto on the word and the memory of a former gang member, ex-con—"

"Don't worry about that. I'll get you more. I'll get you plenty. The next on our lineup is Juanita Turner, the mother of one of the bodies Penny wanted, and the woman who poisoned Lino Martinez. She's in A. I might as well tell you, I've got Mira coming to observe the interview, and believe she'll conclude diminished capacity."

"Today you're a cop, lawyer, and shrink." Sarcasm coated each word. "How do you do it?"

"You're going to put her away, Reo, but if after the interview you want to put her away for first, I'll send you on an all-expense paid vacation to Portafino."

"I've always wanted to go there."

Eve fueled up with a coffee, then turned to Peabody. "Ready?"

"Yeah."

"Take the lead."

"What? What?" Peabody jogged after Eve. "Did you say I should take the lead?"

For an answer, Eve stepped into the interview room. She sat, said nothing.

"Ah, record on," Peabody began and recited the salients. "Mrs. Turner, have you been read your rights?"

"Yes."

"And do you understand those rights and obligations?"

"Yes, yes."

"Mrs. Turner, are you a member of St. Cristóbal's Catholic Church?"

"Yes."

"And were you acquainted with Father Miguel Flores?"

"No." Juanita lifted her head now, and her dark eyes smoldered. "Because Father Flores never came to St. Cristóbal's. A liar and a murderer came with his face. He's probably dead, this Father Flores. Probably murdered. What do you think about that? What are you doing about that?"

Peabody kept her voice clipped, cool—and whatever her thought might have been, they were boxed outside the room. "Do you know the identity of the man who posed as Father Flores?"

"Lino Martinez. A murderer."

"How did you come to be aware of his identity?"

"I figured it out." She shrugged, looked away.

First lie, Eve thought.

"How?" Eve demanded. "Just how did you figure it out?"

"Things he said, how he acted, certain looks. What does it matter?"

"You worked with him at the youth center for over five years," Eve added. "Went to the church. How long had you known who he really was?"

"I knew what I knew." She folded her arms, stared hard at the wall. But the gestures of defiance lost impact with the quick, light shudders that worked through her. "It doesn't matter how long."

"Mrs. Turner, isn't it true you were told his identity?" Peabody drew Juanita's attention back to her. "You didn't figure it out. You were told." Peabody's voice softened, into that confide-in-me tone Eve considered one of her partner's finest tools. "Has Penny Soto threatened you, Mrs. Turner?"

"Why would she?"

"To ensure your silence. To make sure you take the fall for Lino Martinez's murder alone. You did kill Lino Martinez, didn't you?"

"I don't have to tell you anything."

"Bullshit." Eve stood so abruptly, her chair flew back. "You want to play, Juanita, let's play. Penny Soto told you Martinez was conning you, conning everyone. Lino Martinez, the man responsible for your son's death, was right under your nose, playing priest. You could see it then, you could see right through him then, once she told you. Once she told you all about how he'd planted that bomb that ripped your son to pieces."

Eve slammed her hands on the table, leaned down close. The gesture and the words had Juanita jolting, had tears sheening over the defiance in her eyes.

"And she helped you plan it, every step of your vengeance. She walked you right through it, didn't she?"

"Where were you?" Juanita demanded. "Where were you when he killed my baby? When my husband grieved so he took his life. Took his own life and will never see God, never see God or our boy again. This is what that bastard did. Where were you?"

"You had to exact payment." Eve rapped a fist on the table. "You had to make him pay for Quinto. The police didn't so you had to."

"He was my only child, our only child. I told him, I taught him never to look at skin—the color of skin is nothing. We're all God's children. He was a good boy. I told him, he had to work, that all of us must earn our way. So he took the work there, there where they killed him. Because I told him to."

Tears spilled down her cheeks, streaming out of misery. "Do you think it matters what you say, what you do? I sent my boy to the place where they killed him. Do you think it matters if you take my life from me now, if you put me away for the rest of it? I can't see God, just like my husband. There's no salvation without redemption. I can't ask for true forgiveness. I killed the one who killed my son. And I *don't* repent. I hope he's burning in hell."

"Mrs. Turner. Mrs. Turner." Peabody's voice soothed, calmed. "You were Quinto's mother. He was only sixteen. It must have been devastating, the loss. It must've been devastating all over again when Penny told you that the man you believed to be Father Flores was Lino Martinez."

"I didn't believe her. At first I didn't believe her." When Juanita lowered her head into her hands, Eve gave Peabody a small nod of approval. "Why would she tell me this? She'd been his whore once. How could I believe it, believe her? I worked with him, took Communion from him, confessed to him. But . . ."

"She convinced you," Peabody prompted.

"Little things. The way he walked, the swagger of it. The basketball, so much pride. He had so much pride in his skill with a ball and a net. His eyes. If you really looked, if you really looked he was there. Inside the priest's eyes."

"Still she could've been lying," Eve insisted. "You killed a man on her *word*? The word of Lino Martinez's whore?"

"No. No. She had a recording, she'd recorded him, talking to her. Talking about how he was fooling everyone. How he could play the priest and be the sinner. She asked him to say his real name, and he laughed. Lino Martinez, he said. And even his mother didn't know it. But how everyone would know him again, respect him, envy him. In just a little more time."

"She made the recording for you."

"She said she made it because I'd need proof. That she was ashamed of what he'd made her do. What he made her do still. She had loved him as a girl, and she'd fallen back when he'd come to her. But then he told her what he'd done. The bomb, and she couldn't live with that."

She wiped at her eyes. "Who could live with that? Only evil can live with that. She couldn't. She'd found God, found strength, and came to me."

"And helped you," Peabody said, very gently. "She understood how shattered you were, and offered to help."

"He wouldn't pay for Quinto. He would never pay, unless I made him pay. Unless I stopped him. I could get the poison. I could get in the church, the rectory, the tabernacle. Still, I waited. I waited, because to take a life, even in justice, is a terrible thing. Then she showed me another recording, where he'd talked of the bombing, bragged about it. How he'd pretended to leave days before, but how he'd watched the store blow up. Blow up, with my boy inside. How he'd watched that, and then drove away. His work done."

The memory straightened her spine. Defiance cut through again as she stared at Eve. "Would God want him to go unpunished?"

"Take us through it, Juanita," Eve said. "How did you do it."

"Old Mr. Ortiz died. He was such a good man, so well loved. I took it as a sign. I knew the church would be full, and this murderer on the altar. I went to the rectory before Rosa got there, when Father López and that one were at morning Mass. I got the keys for the tabernacle. I waited until Father López left from morning Mass, and I went in, put the poison in the wine."

Juanita's whole body trembled. "Only wine, and never to be the blood of God. I'd be God's hand, she said."

"Penny said?"

"Yes, she said I would be God's hand and strike him down. So I sat in church and watched him do his false prayers over that good man, and I watched him drink the wine. Watched him die. And as he had, with my baby, I walked away."

"You confessed to Father López," Eve said. "No, he didn't tell me. He wouldn't. But you confessed to him. Why?"

"I hoped somehow, I could be forgiven. But Father said I must tell the police, I must be repentant in my heart. I'm not. How can I be? If I join Lino in hell, that's God's will. I know my boy is in heaven."

"Why didn't you go to the police, or to Father López with what Penny told you?"

Anger pushed color into her face. "She'd been to the police. They didn't believe her. And she said he'd kill her. He'd told her he would kill her if she ever betrayed him. She showed me the bruises, where he'd beaten her. I wouldn't have her life on my hands."

"She played you." Eve said it flatly, then rose to pour herself a cup of water. "She played Lino, played you, and you both did exactly what she wanted. Did he make the bomb that killed your son? Yeah, we can be pretty sure of that. Did he plan the bombing? Same thing. But what

Penny left out in her 'I've found God' routine was that she's the one who told him to up the explosives to multiple-kill level, and she's the one who pushed the button. She killed your son, Mrs. Turner. And used you to kill Lino."

All the angry color ran out of her face, but she shook her head. "I don't believe you."

"You don't have to. I'm going to prove it. The point is, Mrs. Turner, you didn't do God's will, you did Penny Soto's. You weren't God's hand, you were Penny Soto's. The person every bit as responsible as Lino Martinez for your son's death. For your husband's suicide."

"You're lying."

"It was for money." Eve sat back, let the idea spin out. "Didn't you ever ask her, ask yourself why he'd come back, why he'd played priest for over five years?"

"I . . ."

"You didn't. You didn't because all you could think about, all you could see was your son. Ask yourself now. Why would a man like that live the way he'd been living? Money, Juanita, a lot of money. Money he had to wait for, money he planned to share with the only person he really loved. Penny Soto. Thanks to you, she doesn't have to share."

"That's not true. That can't be true. She was afraid he'd kill her. He beat her, and made her do things, and said he'd kill her."

"Lies. Lies. Lies. If any of that were true, why didn't she leave? She's got no ties here. No family, no real friends, and the kind of work she could do anywhere. Why not just get on a bus and go? Did you ever ask her?"

"He said he watched the bomb, he laughed. He said his name."

"And he did all of this, freely? He said all this to a woman he had to threaten, he had to beat, he had to force? *Think*!"

Her breath began to hitch and heave. "She . . . she . . ."

"Yeah, that's right. She. But this time, I'll be the hand of God."

She left Juanita with Peabody, closed the door on the woman's weeping. And just leaned back against it for a moment. When she walked into Observation, she found Reo, Mira, and Father López.

"May I see Juanita, Lieutenant," López asked. "To counsel her?"

"Not yet, but if you'd wait outside, I'll arrange it shortly."

"Thank you. Thank you for allowing me to come." He turned to Reo. "I hope you can temper the law with compassion."

Eve waited until López left. "What's the charge?" she asked Reo.

"Second degree." She glanced at Mira. "With special circumstances. I'll ask for ten to fifteen, on-planet, minimum security. And she'll have a full psych eval."

Eve nodded. "She won't do the full dime. This isn't about rehabilitation. It's about salvation."

"She needs to pay, Eve." Mira studied the weeping woman through the glass. "Not only for the law, but for herself. She can't live with what she's done unless she does penance. She can't find that salvation unless she finds forgiveness."

"I get that. We'll book her."

"I'm pretty bummed to be giving up that all-expense paid vacation." Reo sighed. "I know a decent defense lawyer who'll take her pro bono. Let me tug that line. Meanwhile, get me that bitch Soto, and sew it up tight."

"Got that cooking."

"Keep in touch. Dr. Mira, I'll see you at Louise's party."

"Thanks for coming down," Eve said to Mira, "for giving Reo your take."

"I think she'd have come to it on her own. You ran that very well, devastating her at the end, with the knowledge Penny had orchestrated it all. She'll reach out to her priest now. She'll reach out for that salvation."

"That's up to her. I ran it so she'd give me what I needed on Penny."

"That, and the other."

Eve lifted a shoulder. Maybe.

22 McNAB SASHAYED INTO THE HOMICIDE BULLPEN, and gave Peabody a big, eyebrow-wiggling leer. She stared holes through him. Undeterred, he continued his sashay over to her desk, where he plopped his butt down.

"Move that sorry excuse for an ass. I'm working."

"You love my sorry excuse for an ass. It's still got your finger dents in it from last night."

She sniffed, angled away. "This has nothing to do with sex."

"Let's take five."

"I said I had work." She swiveled back to him. "Maybe you've got all the time in the world to screw around, but I don't. You'll be happy to know I'm typing up the report on our interview with Juanita Turner, and the streets of New York are now safe from a grieving mother some greedy, heartless bitch used as a murder weapon."

His fingers danced over his knee as he studied her furious face. "Okay. Let's take that five and hash this through."

"Your head's as bony as your ass. I just said I'm busy."

"Right." McNab glanced over at the next desk. "Hey, Carmichael, you want to watch while Peabody and I fight, then play kiss and make up?"

"Sure." Carmichael gestured with one hand while peering at data on the comp screen. "Take off your clothes first."

"Perv," Peabody muttered, but she pushed up from her desk and strode out.

McNab shot Carmichael a grin, and followed.

"Hey! Does this mean you're not stripping off?" Carmichael called after them.

"You probably thought that was funny," Peabody began—and found her back against the wall next to Vending, and her mouth very busy. Heat flashed straight up from her belly and out the top of her head. She managed to catch her breath just as two uniforms passing by stopped to applaud.

"Jeez! Cut it out. What's wrong with you?"

"I can't help it. Your lips were right there, and I missed them."

"God, you're such an idiot." She grabbed his hand, pulled him down the corridor. She poked her head into a conference room, then dragged him in after her. "Listen."

This time her back hit the door, and while her mouth was busy, so were his hands. She forgot herself long enough to grab his sorry excuse for an ass, and squeeze. Then she remembered herself and shoved. "Stop it. You're such a dick."

"I might also have dent marks on my dick." He cocked his head. "But you didn't mean this wasn't about sex, you meant you didn't want it to be about sex. Okay."

He stepped back and slipped his hands—to her partial and secret regret—into two of his many pockets.

"You're still in the steam room about this morning, so let me ask you: Do you want me to agree with you about everything?"

"No, but . . . Maybe. You want me to agree with *you* about everything."

"Not so much. I like when you do because then we're all smug and snuggled up together, which could lead to the sex this isn't about—or just a good feeling of, you know, solidarity. But I kind of like it when you don't because then you're all pissy and hot, and I'm pissy and horny, which again could lead to the sex this isn't about. But mostly, when you don't run on my line, it makes me think. And even after, I think if I don't switch my line to run on yours, it's okay. Because what you think makes you who you are. And that's my girl."

"Well, damn," she said after a moment. "Damn. You have to go and be all lucid and smart." No matter how she tried, it seemed it just wasn't the day for keeping the wind in her sails. "And right. I guess, see I felt sorry for her, for Juanita, and you coming down on the hard line made me feel like maybe I wasn't a straight enough cop."

"It's not what it means." He gave her a light, affectionate poke in the shoulder. "Bogus, Peabody."

"Some days I can't believe I made it here. New York, Cop Central, Dallas, a detective's shield. And you know somebody's going to take a good look and say, what the hell, send her back to the farm."

"You start heading there, think about all the bad guys you've helped put away."

"Yeah." She took a breath. "Yeah. But . . . Juanita's not a bad guy. Not the kind you can just lock up and say, 'Real good job, have a brew.' It's hard to shake, feeling that and knowing that's just what we have to do."

He gave her another poke, and a good, straight look in the eye. "Did you make the case?"

"Yeah."

"That's all there is. You can't take on the PA's job, the judge, the jury. You just make the case."

"I know. I know. But this one . . . Dallas worked some stuff. She had Reo and Mira, even the priest. Juanita's got to go down for it, but not as hard as it could've been."

"The other one's going down harder. That's what you and Dallas are aiming for, right? And I've got a little something that's going to help."

"What?"

"I was on my way to tell Dallas, when I saw you. I got distracted by the She-Body."

"Let's go."

"Hey, maybe we could just take five more to—"

"No." But she laughed, and gave his ass another squeeze. "Absolutely no. But tonight? Your dents are going to have dents."

"Hot damn."

In her office, Eve studied the map on her comp screen. Calculated. There were ways, she thought, and ways to run a con. The problem— and she could work around it if need be—was that every one of the Ortega properties was currently occupied. If she ran an op in any of them, even anything as simple and basic as the sting she had in mind, she would have to move them out.

If anything went wrong, if a civilian got hurt, it would be on her.

But there were ways, she thought, and ways. She turned to the 'link and contacted Roarke's office. Knowing the routine, she did the obligatory chitchat with Roarke's admin, Caro.

"He's in a meeting," Caro told her, "but I can put you through if it's important."

"No." Could be. "Can you give me an idea when he'll be done?"

"He has another appointment scheduled in thirty minutes. So I'd say no longer than that."

"Thirty would be fine for him to get back to me. If it's longer, I may hit you up for that interruption. Appreciate it."

"Happy to help, Lieutenant."

Eve programmed coffee, went back to studying the map. "If you don't have something for me," she said when Peabody and McNab came in, "go away."

"How about a toss-away 'link Juanita Turner didn't toss away?"

Eve's head came up, and her gaze burned into McNab. "If you've got Penny Soto on there, talking about murder, I'll ignore the next time the two of you play grab-ass on duty. And may, in fact, grab your ass myself."

"My ass is sure getting a lot of play today." McNab pulled the 'link he'd sealed, and a disc, out of one of his pockets. "I copied the transes onto disc. The caller blocked video on her end, but there's plenty for voice match. Which, anticipating, I went ahead and ran against the interview you did with Penny Soto. Bull's-eye."

Eve snatched the disc, shoved it into her comp slot.

"The last one should do it," McNab said.

"Computer, run last transmission on current disc."

Acknowledged . . . Transmission is voice only. Running . . .
Hello. Pen—
No names, remember? And don't forget. It's really important for you to toss the 'link in a recycler when this is over. Don't forget.

Eve's smile spread, went fierce.

I won't forget, but—
I just thought you might need someone to talk to, just to know you've got a friend, someone who understands what you're doing tomorrow. Who understands why you have to.
I've been praying, all day, all day, asking God to help me. To help me find the strength to do the right thing. To see the right thing. I'm not sure—
He raped me again tonight.
No, oh, no.
I got through it. With prayer, and by knowing it wouldn't happen again. It would never happen again because you were going to stop him. I think, I'm afraid, if I didn't know that, I couldn't get through. I think, I'm afraid I might take my own life to escape the hell he's brought me in this one.

No! Pen—no, you must never, never think that. Must never take the
most precious gift. A life. A life. And that's what I'm asking myself, asking
God. Even after everything, do I have the right to take his?
He killed your son, your husband. He's killed so many, and no one stops
him. Now he's laughing at God. And . . . tonight, after he raped me, he
said he's getting bored. He may leave—make me go with him. But
before he does, he's going to put a bomb in church. He wants to blow it
up. Some Sunday, he said, when we'd never know, when the church
was full of people, he'd set it off.
No. No. My God, no.
You're our only hope. God's put this in your hands. You're the only one.
You are God's hand now. Tomorrow. Tell me you'll stop him tomorrow, or
I don't know if I can get through the night. Tell me, promise me you'll end
this, so he'll finally know God's punishment.
Yes. Yes. Tomorrow.
Promise me. Swear it on your son. On your murdered son.
I swear it. I swear it on my Quinto.
Destroy the 'link. Don't forget. As soon as it's done, destroy the 'link.
God bless you.

"Voice print match, sender Penny Soto, receiver Juanita Turner.
Absolutely, positively," McNab said. "Smells like conspiracy to murder
to me."

"Yeah, we'll get that. And we're going to pile it on from there."

"My ass is now available for grabs," McNab announced, and was ignored by both women.

"I guess Juanita forgot to toss the 'link," Peabody commented.

"No. She didn't forget. She needed it, needed to play it back before
she did him, after she'd done him. She needed to hear what Penny fed
her, to help ease her conscience. We'll get Soto on this count, and we've
got some weight toward the bombings. But we haven't got a lock there."

Need to turn the key a little more, Eve thought. Just a little more.

"Then there's the accessory after the fact on Flores and Ortega, the fraud," she continued. "The fraud's going to help lock down the accessory. If we do this right, she's never going to see the light of day again. So we're damn well going to do it right."

Her 'link beeped. A glance at the incoming display told her Roarke was tagging her back. "Get me a conference room. I want Baxter and Trueheart."

"They're on Penny."

"Relieve them, bring them in. Briefing in thirty. Now," she added, "and take your ass with you." She answered the 'link. "Dallas."

"What can I do for you, Lieutenant?"

"Have you got a property—commercial or residential—preferably on the Upper East Side that's not tenanted?"

"I imagine I do. Why?"

"I need it for a few hours."

"Are we having a party?"

"Sort of. In El Barrio or close would be the icing."

"How about a nice four-story duplex on East 95th, currently being rehabbed?"

"Did you just pull that out of your ass?"

"No. I looked it up." He sent her a quick, cocky smile. "Is that what you had in mind?"

"Pretty much nailed it. I need the exact address, a legal description, current market value, all that kind of crap. If I could get it, and the pass codes for the locks, by . . ." She checked the time. ". . . by sixteen hundred, it would hammer that nail."

"I thought we were icing a cake. In any case, I'll get back to you."

Eve studied the map again. It could work. It would work. She contacted Feinburg again. "You're going to need to come down to Central."

"Lieutenant, as I tried to explain before, I have clients scheduled all day."

"You're going to have to reschedule anything you've got cooking for the rest of today. I need you here, Homicide Division, within the hour.

You don't want it getting out, to those clients, that you've been strung along on a major fraud scam, which included multiple murders, for the last six years. Right?"

"I'll be there as soon as I can."

"Damn right you will," Eve mumbled after she'd cut transmission.

She gathered what she needed, checked to see which conference room Peabody had booked, then contacted the commander to update him while she was on the move.

"The voiceprints along with Turner's statement are enough to bring her in on the St. Cristóbal's case."

"Yes, sir."

"We want that closed down, Lieutenant. There's going to be a lot of sympathy for Turner, a lot of media attention. Having Soto locked to it will defuse some of that."

"I intend to lock her to it, and to a lot more. This op will do it. She'll bite. It's greed that had her set Juanita up to kill Lino. It's greed that'll have her walking right into this. She won't be able to help herself. And once she does, she's locked for the fraud, and the fraud locks her to Flores and Ortega, possibly Chávez. Three additional murders."

"Suspected."

"Yes, sir. I can use some of that, will use some of that to grease the rails and get the confession for the bombings."

"You've got the day, you've got the op. Anything starts to slip or slide, you nail up the St. Cristóbal's case. Nail it tight."

"Yes, sir." She clicked off, stepped into the conference room.

"Relief is heading uptown, Lieutenant," Peabody began. "Baxter and Trueheart will head back as soon. It's going to be more than thirty."

"Okay. Contact Detective Stuben at the Four-six, ask if he and his former partner want any piece of this."

"Can I tell him piece of what?"

"Of closing their cases. Are you still here?" she asked McNab.

"You said briefing, and didn't tell me to go away."

"Actually, I can use you. I've got the lawyer this skank's been using coming in. I need you to set him up at a D&C so it transmits like it's from his own. She may know how to check that, Lino could have shown her how to verify transmissions. And I want it right here. I want any incomings traced and copied—and whatever you e-geeks do to ID them to a specific unit and location and account."

"Can do."

"Then do." Eve slapped a photo of Penny Soto to the center of a board. "Because she goes down today."

Within the hour she had the room set, with McNab refining the details of an e-station. On the board, surrounding Penny's photo were photos of every victim who could be associated with her.

When Feeney came in, she glanced over in surprise. "Hey."

"Hey. When you steal one of my boys for an op, I like knowing why."

"Sorry." She scooped her hair back. "I should've tagged you. I got caught."

"I'm hearing." He wandered to the e-station, examined McNab's work. His hands stayed in the baggy pockets of his baggy pants. "So I figured I'd sit in."

"I'd appreciate it. Baxter, Trueheart," she said when they walked in. "We have a couple of detectives coming in from the Four-six. I'll wait for them before I start the briefing. We'll need to—" She broke off, frowned as Roarke strolled into the room. She moved to intercept him.

"I just needed the data."

"My data, my property." He smiled at her. "I want to play." He handed her a disc, then wandered over to examine the e-work with Feeney.

With the arrival of Stuben and his partner, Kohn, she made brief introductions, followed with a short overview of Penny Soto.

"We're keeping the arrest of Juanita Turner quiet for the moment. I'd like to surprise Penny with that, once we pull her in. I've got the lawyer on tap. If McNab's done his job, we'll be able to track the transmission from here to her location and unit, and track the transmission back from her. Another lock in. We lure her here."

She brought up the info on Roarke's disc, scrolled through to an image of the building. "Untenanted residential unit—no civilian factor. The lawyer contacts her, relays that this property—alludes that her partner knew of it—is now added to the inheritance due to the recent death of old Mr. Ortega's cousin. Just need some lawyer bullshit, she's not going to question it too deep. As José Ortega is named heir, and so on, so on, she'll be counting the profits. He'll do his legal dance about escrow, trusts, market values, taxes, whatever. And he'll say he's hesitant to transmit the passcodes.

"She'll want them, she'll demand them. And she'll go there as soon as she can to take a look. She'll use them. And when she does, we've got her. We keep the tail on her." She brought up the map, called for zoom and enhancement of 95th Street. "Baxter and Trueheart, stationed here and here. Soft-clothes. Detectives Stuben, Kohn, will you take this half of the duplex?"

"Happy to."

"Peabody and I here. E-team and vehicle, here. Lure her in, scoop her up. Keep it tight in case she gets frisky. Bring her in, and lock it up all the way back to 2043. Questions?"

It took another twenty before she brought the lawyer in.

"This is what you're going to say." Eve handed him a printout. "You can use your own words, legal it up, but this is what gets across. Understand?"

"Not entirely. If there had been property in probate, I certainly would have informed Mr. Aldo—or, well, the person I believed to be Mr. Aldo."

"How does she know you didn't? Be as vague about that as you want. Lawyers are good at being vague and incomprehensible. I want her to believe she's going to be getting this property. This duplex at this address, with a fair market value of eight point three mil. I want her to be compelled to respond, to demand more info. That's all you have to do."

"Well, yes, but . . ."

"I could go around you, Feinburg, but I don't want her smelling even a whiff of the game. She'll believe it's from you, because it is from you. And she'll believe the contents because, hey, eight point three mil. Get it done."

"Do you do mail by keyboard or voice?" McNab asked him.

"Ah, voice."

"Okay. Just do what you do, but don't authorize the send. I'll take care of it. Anytime," McNab added.

"All right." Feinburg sat, blew out a breath. He recited the recipient's name, account name, then began the text.

Eve nodded as he spoke. Yeah, he lawyered it up, she thought, used ten words when one would do. She knew exactly what he was saying and still barely understood half of it.

She signaled McNab to send.

"What now?" Feinburg asked.

"We move the station to portable. She doesn't have the address or the codes. She'll want them. We'll be in place when she gets them. Let's move it out, set it up, take it down."

At the duplex, Roarke let Eve and Peabody in the westernmost door. He glanced over as the two detectives entered the second. "You're banking on her coming to this side first."

"I want to give them a shot at taking her. But yeah, I figure she'll come to this one first. Aren't you assigned to the e-machine?"

"I'd sooner hang with you and Peabody." He glanced around the short foyer, down the hall, into the room on the left. "It needs a bit of polish yet, but should be quite nice."

"The trim's original, isn't it? And wow. My brother would pee his pants."

"Gee, Peabody," Eve began, "if you'd like a tour, why—" She broke off, pulled out her communicator. "Dallas."

"She bit," Feeney told her. "McNab's ready to work the lawyer through the response."

"Wait twenty. Let her sweat. Then give it to her. Give it all." She contacted the other members of the team. "Now we wait," she said. "And it won't be long."

The streetlights blinked on. Eve could see their glow against the dim when Baxter beeped her an hour later. "Suspect is approaching from the west, on 95th. On foot. Red shirt, black pants, black handbag. Moving fast. Your location within one minute."

"Copy that. Maintain position. Nobody moves in until she's inside the building. Come on in," Eve coaxed. "Come on in."

"Dallas, she's at the door. You're a go."

"Hold positions." Come on, bitch, she thought. She saw, from her position, the security light blink from red to green as the locks opened. She waited, holding, as Penny came in, closed the door quickly behind her.

Penny looked toward the stairs as a wild grin spread on her face. And Eve hit the lights.

"Surprise."

"What the fuck is this?" Penny edged back toward the door.

"It's a little party I call You're Under Arrest—for fraud, for falsifying official documents, for utilizing forged identification, and practicing said fraud over the Internet. For accessory to murder. Multiple charges on that. And we're just getting started."

"This is bullshit. You're bullshit."

"If you try to go out that door, you'd be resisting."

"You tried that shit before, didn't you? Got squat." Penny turned, whipped open the door. As Eve moved forward, she whirled back, hacked out with a knife.

It caught Eve's sleeve, and the tip broke skin. She hacked again, and Eve merely stepped back to evade. "You tried *that* shit before," Eve reminded Penny.

Behind her, Roarke put a hand on Peabody's shoulder. "No," he told her when Peabody reached for her weapon. "She'll want this one on her own."

"Jesus, you really are that stupid." Eve drew her own weapon. "Knife. Full-power stunner. You be the judge. Drop it, or I drop you. And I'd love to."

"I don't need a goddamn knife to take you down, bitch." Penny tossed it aside where it skidded across the floor. "Bitch like you needs a stunner."

"Is that a challenge? I love a challenge. And what the hell. Roarke." Barely glancing over, Eve tossed him her weapon. "Try me," she invited.

Hate and excitement merged on her face as Penny charged. Eve felt the blood rush to her heart, her head. The sting of the wound in her arm focused her. She deflected Penny's fist, but gave the woman credit for what had been behind it. She took a kick—a glancing blow on the hip—and felt the quick heat of fingernails as they swiped at her jaw.

Eve maneuvered, evaded, took a blow here, another there. And saw the violent light of pleasure in Penny's eyes.

"You can't fight worth shit," Penny yelled out. "Pussy cop."

"Oh. We were fighting? I didn't realize we'd started. Okay then."

And she moved in. A shorthand jab knocked Penny's head back like a ball on a string. A roundhouse kick doubled her over when it plowed into her gut. An uppercut brought her up again. And a right cross took her down.

"That last one?" Eve bent over her as Penny lay unconscious at her feet. "That was for Quinto Turner. Get a wagon," Eve ordered, then gave Roarke the come-ahead sign for her weapon.

"Your nose is bleeding, Lieutenant."

"Yeah. Peabody, do you take note that my nose is bleeding?"

"Yes, sir, and your arm."

"And these injuries were incurred as the suspect attempted to escape arrest and resisted same, thereby assaulting an officer, assaulting said officer with a deadly with intent?"

"All the above."

"Good. Thanks," she added when Roarke handed her a handkerchief.

He reached over, covered her lapel recorder with his hand. "You wanted her to go for you. You played with her, let her get a few in so you'll have the cuts and bruises to prove it. So you could whale in."

"Maybe." She grinned as she stanched her bloody nose. "But that's going to be really hard to prove. I've got to take her in, get her in the box."

"I'll be coming with you. Might as well see it through. And see that arm's tended to."

Penny called in the same lawyer, screamed police brutality, false imprisonment. Montoya made lawyer noises about suing, even when Eve came in with the wound on her arm raw and fresh, her face bruised, and claw marks at her jaw.

"Let's have a look at this first, just to get it out of the way. Record playback." While the scene inside the duplex ran, with Penny spinning at the door, striking with a knife, Eve spoke. "As we expected to make an arrest, record was on throughout, and record clearly shows the subject attacking me with a knife concealed on her person. Which, in fact, she had done on a previous occasion."

Which, Eve thought, was why I counted on her repeating the performance.

She shut the recording off. "The charges there are assault with a deadly and with intent to kill a police officer. That's fifty years."

"That's bullshit."

"Oh, tired tune, Penny. Got it on record, got witnesses, got MTS report, got it all. Also, got you cold on the fraud. Our e-trace—duly authorized—nailed your pocket PCC for the receiving of Feinburg's transmission, and the sending to same."

"That's nothing."

"Penny," the lawyer began.

"Nothing!" She elbowed Montoya aside. "That was Lino's deal. He set that up. I just followed it through. Why the hell not? I just went to the damn house to see it. No crime in walking into a house when a freaking lawyer gave me the pass codes."

"You'd be wrong. You perpetuated fraud. But I might be willing to deal on that, and on the charges stemming from your attack on me, if you can tell me the whereabouts of Miguel Flores, José Ortega, and Steven Chávez. We want to close it up."

Eve rose, and made sure Penny saw the irritation cross her face. "My bosses want to close it up, so there's a deal on the big hit for coming at me with a knife, and a deal on the fraud."

"What kind of deal?"

"Let the fraud go down to falsifying documents. Deal the intent to kill a police officer down to simple resisting. Couple of years against oh, maybe seventy."

"That's on record."

"Yeah, that's a deal on record. I hope you don't take it. I hope you don't."

"One moment." Montoya leaned in close, whispered in Penny's ear. She jerked that bony shoulder.

"Maybe Lino told me some shit."

Eve dropped back down in the chair as if annoyed, and disappointed. "You've got the goddamn deal of a lifetime, thanks to my superiors, Penny. But some shit has to lead to results, or no deal."

"Okay. I've got plenty, so eat this." She sneered across the table. "Lino and Steve hooked up with Ortega, figured they'd skin him for some of what the old man left him. Played him awhile, scammed him for a couple hundred thousand. Chávez got him hooked again, so they played him some more. Lino said how he figured they'd just about tapped it, and he's working on getting the deed for our old headquarters out of Ortega. That's the prize—or was—then the idiot ODs. They got a dead guy on their hands, and Lino is pissed."

She leaned back in her chair and laughed. "'Til he thinks how to work it. They take him out to the desert, and they bury him. And Lino does his thing with ID. He's got the skills, and he's got a nice, fat pile from the scam, and Ortega's winning in Vegas. He invests, gets a marriage license on record for him and Ortega. Ortega always was a queer anyway, and they've been sharing this big, flashy house out there for close to three months."

Idly, Penny examined her red and black nails. "Backdates the license, pays some guys he knows back in Taos or some shit, back here and all that to say how they knew this Aldo guy, and Ortega. Happily married couple."

She tipped back up, snorted out a laugh. "That Lino, he covered his ass. Mostly. So, he reports Ortega missing. Now he's sitting pretty. Real pretty, 'cause Ortega's got millions back here in property and shit."

"But he has to sit for seven years."

"Got that. He figures he'll sit as this Ken Aldo guy, except he can't come back here with that one—it's just a beard, some hair changes. Anybody who knew him would see it. Then the priest just falls into their lap. Lino said he wasn't going to kill the guy. It just gave him the idea, you know? He was going to make up another ID, work that, maybe come back here as an indie priest or some shit. But Chávez got mouthy, and the priest started clueing in, and Chávez killed him. Hacked him up bad, Lino said. Lino, he had some religion, you know? Didn't like the idea of killing a priest like that. Bad luck, wrath of God, or whatever."

"Yeah, I bet he felt bad."

"Bad enough so he killed Chávez. He said he tried to stop Steve from slicing and dicing the priest, and hey, it just happened. Besides, he'd enough of the screwups. He buried them out where he'd buried Ortega."

"Where?"

"You want the where?" Penny's eyes went sly. "I can give you the where but, the charges go away—all the way."

"My client has valuable information," Montoya put in. "She's cooperating. I believe if you want further information, further cooperation, the charges must be dropped. I'm sure the families of these men want closure."

Eve didn't have to fake the disgusted look. "You tell me where, and the bodies of Miguel Flores, José Ortega, and Steven Chávez are recovered, the falsifying docs and resisting go away."

"He said he buried them, all of them about fifty miles south of Vegas, in this place the native guys call Devil's Church because there's this rock formation thing with what looks like a cross on top. He put them in right at the base. He always had that religion thing in him, see? He liked burying them under the cross."

Penny sneered, tipped back in the chair again. "Nice doing business with you, pussy cop."

Eve studied her face. That was the truth, as Penny knew it. "We've got more business. Now we go back, Penny, we come home and go back. The bombings in 2043."

"That was Lino's deal. And with no charges on record, I'm free to go. Bitch."

"No, bitch, you're not. You had prior knowledge regarding the bombings. You knew he intended to set both those bombs, blaming the first on the Skulls. It's called accessory."

"I was, like, fifteen, what the hell did I know?"

"Enough, according to my witness, to be a part of the planning and execution of the first, and to help plan the second. And push the button yourself."

"You can't prove that."

"I've got a witness, willing and able to testify. That wraps you up in six murder charges."

"Bullshit. Bullshit." She slapped at Montoya when he started to speak. "I know how to handle myself here, asshole. I was a minor. So what if I pushed the button, so the fuck what? If there'd been twice as many assholes blown to hell when I did, it doesn't mean dick. Clemency Order covers me."

"You'd think, but the PA's just chomping to challenge that, and given the fact you were neither arrested nor charged for that crime before or during the Clemency period, you're fair game."

"What kind of shit is this? It's bull." She looked to her lawyer. "It's bull. I was a minor."

"Just don't say anything. Lieutenant," Montoya began, in a tone of outrage, "my client—"

"Not done yet. You'll also find on the menu conspiracy to murder Lino Martinez. She didn't toss the 'link, Penny. And now that she knows your finger was on the button, she's cooperating fully."

"That bitch Juanita killed Lino." Penny shoved to her feet, stabbing a finger in the air. "I never touched him. I was never in that goddamn church. Juanita Turner did Lino, and she can't pin it on me."

"I never said who *she* was," Eve commented.

"I don't give a shit what you said. Juanita poisoned Lino, over her kid. You can't pin that on me. I wasn't fucking *there*."

"That's why it's called conspiracy to murder."

"I want a deal. I want a deal and I'll tell you just how she did it. Shut the fuck *up*!" she screamed at Montoya when he tried to silence her. "Listen, just listen." She sat back down. "The bitch went psycho when she found out Lino was back, that he'd been back, using the priest cover."

"How'd she find that out?"

"Look, so I let it slip one day, that's all. I let it slip. It's not a crime. She's the one who did it. She used Old Man Ortiz's funeral for cover, got the keys out of the rectory. She poisoned the wine. She did it because her son got blown to hell, and her old man offed himself."

"Thanks for confirming it, on record—which is, again, why it's called conspiracy to murder. There's also accessory after the fact in the matter of the murders of Miguel Flores and José Ortega and Steven Chávez."

"What the fuck! What the fuck! Why don't you say something?" she demanded of the lawyer.

"I think he's struck dumb."

"We had a deal. On record—"

"For the fraud, for the assault with intent on a police officer. No deal on the rest." Now it was Eve who tipped back in her chair. "I could afford to let those slide, seeing as you'll be in for, oh, a couple lifetimes. Off-planet, concrete cage, no possibility of parole. And even though those words sing to me, that's not everything you deserve. Detectives."

At her word, Stuben and Kohn came in. "The charges are murder in the first," Stuben began, "in the deaths of . . ."

He spoke all the names, all the dead from 2043. When Penny leaped up, Eve simply wrenched her arms behind her back and cuffed her.

"I thought you'd like to take her down, book her," she said to the detectives. "On all the charges."

"It'd be a nice cap on it. Thanks, Lieutenant. Thanks."

She listened to Penny scream obscenities as they hauled her out. "Record off. This is probably a lot more than you bargained for," she said, casually to the lawyer. "If I were you? I'd run."

She turned, walked out. Roarke stepped out of observation.

"Would we be leaving for Nevada tonight?" he asked.

Hardly a wonder she was raving nuts about the man. "Yeah, that'd be best. I'm going to want to take someone along, if that's okay with you."

EPILOGUE

THE ROCK CROSS CAST A SHADOW ON SAND STRUCK GOLD BY A vicious sun. That sun bleached the sky white, and forced a breathless heat into the air.

Eve stood under it, under the shadow and the sun.

The gauges found the bodies quickly, and the diggers unearthed them, the remains of what had once been men. And in one burning grave, with the bones, lay a silver cross, and a silver medal. Santa Anna, in honor of a dead priest's mother.

It was enough.

Still, they verified with DNA, with dental.

She stood and remembered what the local cop, the detective who'd run the missing persons on Ortega had said.

"You know how you smell something, but you can't figure out where it's coming from? I smelled something on this one. But the guy—the ID, the records, wits—it all checked out."

"No reason for you not to think he wasn't who he said he was."

"Except that smell. We checked out the house they'd rented. Sweet place, let me tell you. Fancy. No signs of foul play. We looked good, too. I like to think we looked good. We didn't find a damn thing. MP's clothes, or most of them, gone and this guy Aldo—Martinez—leaking like a bad faucet. I get the background on the MP, see he's got some illegals trouble. You figure he took off, went on a binge. And the other, he asks for a priest, a counselor. Jesus, I watched that priest walk off with him. Just let them go."

Wrong place, Eve thought. Wrong time. Like young Quinto Turner.

Death was a mean bastard.

So she'd come back, to the shadow of the cross, to the graves dug in the sand under the violent sun. Because the priest had asked her to.

She knew he was praying over those now empty graves. And suspected he prayed for all three with equal devotion. It made her feel odd, so she stayed back with Roarke.

López turned, and aimed those sad, serious eyes on her. "Thank you. For all you've done."

"I did my job."

"We all have them. Thank you both. I've kept you out in the sun long enough."

They walked to the small, sleek plane waiting on the plate of the sand.

"A drink, Father?" Roarke asked when they took their seats.

"I should ask for water, but I wonder, would you have any tequila?"

"I would, yes." Roarke fetched the bottle and glasses himself.

"Lieutenant," López began. "May I call you your name?"

"Mostly people call me Dallas."

"Your name's Eve. The first woman God created."

"Yeah, she doesn't have a real good rep."

A smile ghosted around his mouth, around those sad eyes. "She shoulders blame, I think, not entirely her own. Eve, I've put in a request to hold Father Flores's funeral mass at St. Cristóbal's, and to bury him in the place our priests are buried. If I'm allowed to do this, would you attend?"

"I can try."

"You found him. Not everyone would have looked. It wasn't your job to find him."

"Yes, it was."

He smiled, sipped the first of his tequila.

"I've got a question," Eve said. "I'm not Catholic or anything—he sort of is."

Roarke shifted, drank. "Not precisely."

"What I mean is I'm not, so it's not like I'll—how is it put—take it as gospel, but I'd like an opinion from, you know, a rep of the church."

"What's the question?"

"It's something Juanita Turner said in the box, in interview. It bugs me. Do you believe that someone who self-terminates can't go to heaven, on the supposition there is one?"

López sipped again. "The Church has a firm policy regarding suicide, even as suicide has become legal in most places, most parts of the world, with proper authorization."

"So that's a yes."

"The Church ruling is very clear. And rules often ignore the human and the individual factor. I think God ignores nothing. I think His compassion for His children is infinite. I can't believe, in my heart, God closes his door to those in pain, to those in desperation. Does that answer your question?"

"Yeah. You don't always follow the rules." She glanced at Roarke. "I know somebody else like that."

Roarke slid a hand over hers, laced fingers. "And I know someone who thinks about them entirely too much. Lines can blur, wouldn't you agree, Father?"

"Chale. And yes, lines can, and sometimes should, blur."

She smiled, listened to two men she found fascinating and intriguing debate, discuss over glasses of tequila.

And she watched out the window as the dry gold of the desert receded. As the plane banked east, to take them home.